Magic A[wakening]
The Five Kingdoms Book Two

Toby Neighbors

Published by Mythic Adventure Publishing
2483 Partridge Loop, Post Falls, ID, 83854 USA

Magic Awakening
Copyright © 2011, Toby Neighbors

ISBN-13: 978-1497303072
ISBN-10: 1497303079

Copy-editing by Alexandra Charles
http://aacharles.elance.com

Cover design by Camille Denae

Find out more about Toby Neighbors and join the mailing list to receive an email whenever new titles become available at
www.tobyneighbors.com

Other Books By Toby Neighbors
Third Prince
Royal Destiny
The Other Side
Wizard Rising
Hidden Fire
Crying Havoc
Fierce Loyalty
Evil Tide
Wizard Falling
Lorik
Lorik The Protector
The New World

Dedication:
To Jim and Carolyn Johnson,
With your support and encouragement we are living our dreams.
Thank you for being such great friends.

And to the love of my life
Camille.
Your love and strength make every story possible.
I love you.

Prologue

The beast felt the shock of power, although it was deep in its hibernating sleep. Hundreds of years had passed since it last opened its scaly eyelids. The fat that kept it warm through the years was gone now, but the lair, deep in the earth, was well above freezing, despite the fact that it was high in the mountains. The thick rock maintained a constant temperature, and the dragon's body shed heat like a bonfire. Still, it shivered and the beast's pale, outer skin sloughed off.

The pulse of magical power echoed in his mind as a growl rumbled through his thick chest. Dark smoke rose from his nostrils. His stomach burned with hunger, but he wasn't ready to wake yet. Without opening his eyes, he unhinged his jaw and let flames jet into the darkness. The light flared through his thin, scaly eyelids, but the heat from the fire that was bouncing off the walls and igniting the skin he had shed, felt blissful. He stretched his legs, his wings, his long neck and tail, then settled back down into the smooth depression where he slept. The temperature in the cave had risen dramatically, and the rock walls of the dragon's lair began to weep.

The beast, whose newly shed hide was burned completely to ash, lay gleaming in the darkness. The ashes glowed red and cast the only light in the cave, which reflected off the condensation that now covered the rocky walls and winked off the dragon's shinning scales as it breathed deeply, sliding slowly back into slumber.

Remember, it thought as it lingered between waking and sleep. *Remember the magic.* The dragon could sense the magic, as bright as the flames that he had just spewed through the darkness

9

of his lair. It was powerful and enticing, like the smell of roasting meat. He wanted that magic, that bright pulse of power that quickened his blood and sent dreams of conquest once more through his mind as he drifted off to sleep again.

***

Black smoke rose from the mouth of the cave where the sudden blast of heat had blown through the snow that covered the dragon's lair. The smoke was dark and carried a sulfurous stench, had anyone been close enough to smell it. Against the bright snow, where the sun was reflecting off the high mountains, the smoke stood out in contrast. It would have been an ominous sign, had there been anyone around to see it, but the dragon had made his home high in the treacherous mountain peaks where the only way to access the entrance was to climb the vertical cliff faces for hundreds of feet. Unless, of course, you could fly, but even the eagles who kept their nests high among the mountain peaks stayed far away from this area. Most predators have an instinctive knowledge of danger, and so the mountains around the dragon's lair were abandoned, except for one lone climber. He didn't see the smoke, his focus was entirely on the ledge where he had managed to find a slight perch and rest his weary arms and legs after the tedious climb. He was a young man, an adventurer from the valley, who spent most of his time in the mountains.

When the super heated smoke blew out the entrance to the cave, chunks of ice and snow rained down the mountainside. The man braced himself, pushing his body as close to the cliff face as possible. He thought the snow and ice was an avalanche, and he shut his eyes and held his breath instinctively, but after the initial drop of snow, everything settled back down. Before long the climber was ascending the mountain once more.

It took him two more hours to reach the cave, although he had no idea he was even approaching it. When his thickly gloved hand reached the hole in the side of the mountain, he expected it to be another perch were he might stop and rest. He was hungry, and the thought of finding a suitable place to rest was welcome.

Even though he was covered from head to toe in thick wool and waterproof venison hide, he could feel the warmth from the cave as he scrambled into the opening. He was surprised by the cave; although there were many caves in the mountains, he couldn't remember finding one this high up. There was plenty of daylight left, but he didn't expect to be able to find a more suitable place to camp for the night. Here he could rest, even warm up a little, then push on to the summit in the morning, he reasoned. It seemed like a good idea and, after unslinging his pack and eating some of the dried rations and sipping the water in his canteen, he decided to explore the cave a little.

He had a small torch in his pack, which he lit with flint and a thick steel knife. He knew it was foolish, but he kept the knife out. Just having the weapon in his hand bolstered his confidence as he entered the pitch darkness of the cave. Outside the sun was bright and reflected off the snowy mountains until a person was forced to squint in the dazzling light. A few steps into the cave and the darkness swallowed every bit of sunlight. The torch seemed weak and inadequate, the flickering, yellow light casting shadows all around the climber.

The cave sloped down into the mountain, and the air grew warmer as the man navigated the twisting tunnel. The sides of the cave were rough, but not overly jagged. It didn't seem like a crack in the mountain, as many caves were, nor did it seem to have been formed by water. It was probably a vent that released superheated gases from deep in the earth, the man decided. He was about to turn back when he came around a corner into a larger cavern. The floor was level here and smooth. Along the sides of the cave, the torch light now reflected back at him. Where the stone had seemed to absorb the light in the cave tunnel, in the cavern it was bright from just the single torch. The man inspected the wall closest to him and found that the wall was smooth, yellow gold. He couldn't really believe what he was seeing. He had seen a gold vein before; it was usually mixed with quartz, which was white, and the vein was jagged like a lightning bolt captured in stone.

The man rubbed a gloved hand over the wall, amazed. He was about to return to the surface for his climbing hammer when he remembered the knife in his hand. He pressed the thick blade into the wall, which gave way under the pressure. He angled the blade down and, with a little effort, shaved a sliver of gold from the wall. He pulled off his thick glove and turned the metal over and over in his hand. It was pure and heavy. He couldn't believe it.

There was a rasp from deeper into the cavern, beyond the glow from his torch. It sounded like a tree with rough bark being dragged along the ground. The man froze, his blood turning icy in his veins. He felt the hair on the back of his neck stand up, and his legs felt weak. He turned and looked into the darkness as he slowly backed toward the entrance to the cave. He had forgotten about the gold, and the knife. He clutched his ungloved hand to his chest and held the torch out toward the rear of the cavern, at arm's length.

The rasp came again and then out of the darkness came a pale, snake like appendage. It whipped forward and knocked the man's legs out from under him. The torch fell to the floor but didn't go out. The man screamed in agony, his leg broken from the blow. He pushed himself along the smooth floor, noticing for the first time that the cavern floor was also smooth, yellow gold, not stone. He scrambled forward, despite the wrenching pain, desperate to escape whatever lived in the cave.

He couldn't believe how stupid he had been. His father had warned him that nothing good lived in the mountains; that his "thirst for adventure," as his father called it, would lead to his death. He should have stayed on the farm. He could have married and lived in peace. He didn't want to be in the mountains anymore. It was stupid to have come, he cursed himself. What had he been thinking? He didn't want to die here. How was he going to climb down the mountain with a broken leg?

Then he heard the rasp again, as the dragon's tail slid across the floor toward him. He screamed at the sight of the pale, milky scales. The tail coiled around the ankle of his unbroken leg. The man tried to kick it, but his broken leg was useless; the pain at his attempt to move it hit him so hard he went limp. As the dragon's tail pulled him further into the cavern, the man's broken leg bent double at mid-thigh, the jagged bone digging painfully into the big muscles along his leg, the tendons stretching then snapping. The man screamed, but his mind had already shut down the pain receptors that would have registered the agony of his broken leg. Fear gripped the man even more tightly than the dragon's tail, and his heart began to flutter in his chest.

The area where the dragon lay was gold, too, but here the floor and walls were wet with condensation, the air heavy with a musky, reptilian scent and the smell of sulfur. It was warm beside the beast, which lay still in the darkness. The tail had shifted around the man as it drew him near, so that it began pushing him forward rather than pulling him. For several minutes the man lay in the dark, fear squeezing his heart so hard it was difficult to breathe. Finally, when nothing happened, the man calmed down slightly. The drop in his adrenaline allowed his brain to receive the pain signals from his mangled leg, and he moaned in agony.

The dragon was relishing his unexpected treat. The man reeked of fear, sweat, and blood. He could hear the ragged breathing and the man's strong heart beating quickly in his chest. The dragon, whose eyes were still closed, could imagine the taste of warm blood flooding into his mouth. It made his mouth water, and his forked tongue flicked out into the air in anticipation. It had been a long time since the dragon had tasted flesh, and human flesh was a special treat. Humans were the only species that posed a danger to the dragon, and he often found it necessary to roast them with his fiery breath before eating them. This one he wanted to savor.

The pain was so overwhelming that it took a minute for the man's other senses to come back. He could feel the heat from a large creature beside him. Even though the cavern was shrouded in darkness, he could sense the looming body coiled beside him, hear its deep, even breathing. On the smooth floor he felt a thick layer of ash, although he mistook it for dirt. He couldn't keep the moans of agony in check as they washed over him again and again. He knew he was dead, even if the creature beside him didn't kill him, his leg was ruined and he would never be able to climb back down the mountain. As rational thought fought through the fog of pain, he realized that he had a choice. He could die quickly, or die slowly, racked in agony from his broken leg, which would only become worse over time as the wound festered and he suffered from dehydration.

He still had the small knife. He had forgotten about it, but he hadn't dropped it, not even when the beast's scaly tail had snapped his leg like a twig underfoot. Now he would use it to end his suffering. He laid the blade on his good thigh and fumbled with his heavy cloak, which was fastened with leather thongs he kept tied tightly so that his garment didn't impede his climbing. It took several moments for his trembling fingers to untie the laces, the effort made his head swim and sweat poured from his head and stung his eyes. Finally he could reach inside the cloak to his neck and chest. He picked up the knife; it was only about as long as his hand from palm to fingertips. The grip was simple wood and the blade a dark grey, but it held an edge well. He stroked the blade with his thumb and felt the skin part with a flash of pain.

The dragon smelled more blood as he felt the man struggle beside him. He had been enjoying the panting and groaning noises, now he sensed something else. The man had cut himself, the dragon realized. Normally he wouldn't allow his prey to rob him of the joy of the kill, but his heavy sense of slumber still lay on him, and the man would still be delicious and nurturing if he were dead. When a dragon hibernated, the world changed. Now the beast was curious to see what type of courage this man had. Would he strike at the dragon in a futile attempt to slay him? It was laughable, but it would be telling to realize that the courage and strength of the human race had grown while he slept.

The man had planned to slice his own throat, but the small cut on his thumb was aching and throbbing with every beat of his heart. He wasn't sure he could kill himself. It might be easier to stab the creature and let the vile thing do the killing. It appealed to him, to strike a blow in his defense, even if it were a futile effort. But the beast might not kill him quickly, either; it might merely strike him with that awful tail—at least, he thought the snaky appendage seemed like a tail. He lay undecided, fear of more pain battling with his fear of death. There was no easy choice, but finally he decided to take his own life. It was the surest way to end the suffering, he thought to himself.

The blade trembled in his hand. He laid it on his throat and, despite his body's response to the overwhelming pain from his broken leg, he could feel the menace of the cold steel. His throat felt weak and soft under the blade, and he could feel the pulse of blood through the thick veins there. Just a sudden slash, he told himself, and he could fade away. But his arm felt frozen, heavy, and immovable. He shuddered as his body struggled with his injuries and fear. Do it, he told himself, just end it, now!

The dragon slowly opened one eye. The cavern was too dark to see in. Most dragons can see well enough at night, but their eyes become accustomed to the bright flare of their fiery breath, and with age they lose their night vision. The dragon turned its head sideways and blew a thin gout of blue flame toward the ceiling. The fire turned red, then orange, and finally yellow as it danced and flowed around the roof of the cave before winking out. The light danced across the golden surface of the cavern, and the dragon could see the man lying beside him, his leg folded at an unnatural angle. The man had a small knife to his throat, his hand was shaking, his eyes opened wide at the sight of the dragon.

The creature's body was pale white, with traces of darker designs across its skin that shinned in the strange light of the dragon fire. Its head moved closer to look at him, the eyes barely open but full of malicious intent. Its tongue flicked out and brushed the man's face. The beast's tongue had a rough, sandy surface that was abrasive, and the man threw his hands up to cover his head while squeezing his eyes tightly shut.

"Well?" came a deep voice, an inhuman voice that rattled deep in the beast's thick chest. "Do it!"

The man screamed, his bladder failing him, and he tried to scoot away from the dragon.

"Pathetic," said the dragon. His mouth opened wide and snapped off the man's head, allowing the hot blood to pulse into his mouth. Then he chewed, the skull snapping and splintering between the massive jaws. "But..." the dragon said out loud to himself, "delicious."

Chapter 1

"Dig deeper, Zollin," Kelvich urged. "You have to find that reservoir of power that's inside you."

"I told you that I won't."

"Don't be foolish," the sorcerer chided.

"It's evil, I don't need it."

"It's not evil. Magic isn't good or evil, I've told you that. The wizard may be evil, but not the magic."

"You also said that magic is alive."

"No," Kelvich corrected, his shaggy white hair fluttering in the cold winter air. "I said that it has a mind of its own. There's a difference."

"I felt it," Zollin said. "It was intoxicating, but evil. I wanted to destroy the town and everyone in it."

"That was just your emotions. Your father had almost been killed. Trollic was threatening everyone you cared about."

"I know what you're saying, and it makes sense," the young wizard explained. "But it was more than that. It was hateful and cruel. I know it."

"But how can that be?" Kelvich asked. "You are not hateful and cruel, so why would your magic be?"

"I don't know, but it was."

Zollin was trying to move the heavy timber beams into position for the bridge that would replace the one his father had burned when the Skellmarian's had approached the town of Brighton's Gate. It had been part of their defensive strategy, one that had saved the town after Zollin used his power to break the ice along the river that separated the valley from the northern mountains. But that power had exhausted Zollin, and it wasn't until his desperation to save his father, who had fallen into the icy river, had taken over that he had been able to tap into the well of magic that was inside of him. Kelvich had been right; he had been operating on the overflow of that magic, what felt like a hot wind inside him. But when he tapped into the magical core, he felt as if had stepped into dancing flames of magic. It was amazing, by far the most powerful thing Zollin had ever experienced, but it was also frightening. He knew, as he plumbed the depths of that hidden reservoir of magic with his inner eye, that he could do whatever he wanted. The stone buildings felt like dry, autumn leaves he could crunch under foot, the people were like smoldering candles that he could extinguish with a breath. It had been exhilarating, but then the dark thoughts had come, lust for death and destruction that seemed almost irresistible. He had pulled back from that power, and the desire to destroy had subsided. Now he knew he could tap into that well of magic at will, but he was afraid to.

"I don't know how to help you, Zollin."

"Perhaps I don't need help," he said. He had been fighting depression since the battle with the Skellmarians. "I just need to finish this job and then..." he let the thought trail off.

"Leaving won't help," his mentor said.

"How do you know?"

"These people would be dead or enslaved if you hadn't saved them."

"You don't know that."

"Don't I? You didn't bring the barbarians down from the mountains, Trollic and his miners did that. Brighton's Gate was a ripe plum with no defenses. They would have been overrun in a matter of minutes. The miners wouldn't have helped. I couldn't help them. It was your father's strategic plan and his willingness to work with these people that made the difference, and your power. Why must you fear it?"

"I can't explain it to you, I just know."

"Alright, son," came Quinn's gruff voice. "Can you drive that post through the ice?"

Quinn had worked for days with one hand; his left arm had been crippled in his duel with the Skellmarian chieftain. Once Zollin had regained his strength, he'd healed it in less than an hour. Since then, Quinn had been planning to rebuild the bridge he'd burned. He had designed a system so that the townspeople could raise and lower the new bridge as the need arose. It wouldn't be as wide as the original, whose stone pilings were being used to support the new bridge, but it would aid the town in its defense from the Skellmarians.

Quinn was convinced that the raiders who had attacked the village were merely a foraging party and that a large group would be coming. It had been difficult to convince the town elders that the threat was still imminent, but he had finally done it. After celebrating their victory, of which the town really had no part, they got back to work fortifying their defenses.

Zollin was raising two large pine trees that had been cut and trimmed to serve as the supports for the pulley system that Quinn had designed to raise the drawbridge. He would not only need to lift the pine posts, but drive them down through the thick ice and then into the soft mud so far that the posts would be secure enough to bear the weight of the bridge. Quinn was planning to install support ropes as well, but the key was Zollin's ability to position the heavy posts.

Zollin had his staff in one hand; his willow belt had been destroyed and he wasn't sure he had the strength to do what his father was hoping for without delving into the power he now feared. Kelvich, the sorcerer who had become Zollin's mentor, stood looking on, as did several of the townspeople. Mansel was there as well, his sword hanging from his hip as it always was now. He had been lauded as a hero by the citizens of Brighton's Gate for defeating Trollic's assassin. Zollin, on the other hand, hadn't been shunned, but was certainly feared. People refused to look him in the eye and would even leave the room when he entered. He had begun spending more and more time with Kelvich in the little cabin in the woods. His only regret was that he didn't get to see Brianna as often as he wanted to. She had been working hard, too, and while she wasn't rude, she seemed preoccupied. Zollin had suspected that she and Mansel were lovers, but he had no real proof. She didn't seem anymore attentive to Mansel than to Zollin.

He pushed the thoughts of Brianna from his mind. Dwelling on his feelings for her would not help him lift the log pole. He concentrated on the long post until he could feel every fiber of wood. He willed it to rise into the air and immediately felt the weight of the big pole. It was easily twice as tall as the inn he'd helped his father build in Tranaugh Shire, his hometown. The pressure of the weight felt like tight bands circling around his chest and squeezing his head. He opened his eyes and saw that the pole was rising up from its prone position, but the pointed end, which Mansel and Quinn had shaped using heavy axes, was still on the ground. Electric, blue energy crackled and popped up and down Zollin's staff. He could feel his inner magic churning and longing to connect with the power of his staff.

"Can you lift it?" Kelvich asked.

"Don't know," Zollin said through clenched teeth.

"That's it, nice and slow," Quinn said, reminding Zollin of his apprentice days, working for his father to learn carpentry. He had been a hopeless student, woefully unskilled with his hands. When he had discovered his power, it had been the most exciting thing in his young life.

He grunted under the strain of the heavy pole and could feel the weight pressing the pole down into the frozen ground. He hoped that if he could lift it over the ice and then let it fall in the right spot, the pole's massive weight would do a lot of the work for him.

"Okay, move it over the riverbank," Quinn ordered.

Zollin tried to lift the pole, but it was too heavy. It was taking all his strength just to keep it from falling over.

"I can't do it," he said through clenched teeth.

"Don't let that pole fall," his father called out. "We can't afford to waste good timber."

It was the mantra he'd heard all his life. He hated it, but he hated the thought of letting his father down even more. As he grew up, they had rarely seen eye to eye, but over the last several weeks, he'd seen all his father had sacrificed for his sake. Quinn had risked his life more than once to protect his son, and Zollin was determined not to let him down.

He could feel the magic inside of him, yearning for release. He finally gave in, and the flames of power billowed up like smoke from a bonfire. The tree was still heavy, but it was manageable. He raised it several feet off the ground and moved it quickly over to the spot his father had marked on the frozen surface of the riverbed. He let the post fall while maintaining his control around the timber. It was like letting his staff slide through his hands. The post punched through the ice with a crash and lodged in the soft mud below. Even though the sheer weight of the pole had driven the post several feet into the riverbed, Zollin knew he needed to drive it down further. He pushed with his mind, willing the post to force its way deeper and deeper. Sweat poured out of every pore, but within minutes the post was firmly planted beside the new bridge.

"That's good," Quinn called out. "Great job, son."

He and Mansel went to work untying the thick ropes that had been wrapped around the post to help support the towering beam.

Zollin stood in the flames of magic power, reveling in the feeling of strength. The world seemed to fall away from him, and he could feel the distant sparks of the other wizards. Two were in the west and another was far to the south, all three seemed stationary. Two more were moving north, slowly approaching. They were much too far away to identify, but there was something about them that made Zollin uneasy. He knew instinctively they were searching for him. It seemed like everyone was.

"Alright, let's move the other pole," Quinn said.

"He may need a break," Kelvich explained.

"No, I'm okay," Zollin said.

He lifted the other tree, this time the work was much easier. He rammed it down into its place in one swift motion, wrapping the tree up in his power to keep it from splintering under the impact. The job done, he released his hold on the magic.

"That was amazing," Kelvich said, his face flushed as if he was drunk.

Zollin didn't answer; the effort to control his power had left him exhausted. He sat down on the snowy ground and hung his head between his knees. Kelvich handed him a bottle of wine.

The rich liquid burned its way down Zollin's throat to his empty stomach, and he felt the heat of it roll out through his whole body. The magic had felt like powerful flames, but the wine felt like a warm bath. He savored the feeling until Kelvich supplied a cold chicken leg left over from their supper the night before. Zollin bit off a large hunk of the flavorful meat and swallowed it half chewed. Then he washed it down with more wine.

"Does it always feel like that?" the sorcerer said quietly.

Zollin thought about the question as he chewed another bite of food. He knew that his mentor had the power to control other magic users, but sorcerers had no power of their own. Kelvich could feel Zollin's magic, and the temptation to take control of Zollin and dominate his power must have been almost irresistible.

"It was only my second time," Zollin said.

"Well, I didn't feel any evil or malice," Kelvich continued.

"But you felt the power."

"Yes, as vast as the ocean."

"I wouldn't know, but right now I feel like I could eat every fish in the sea. I'm starving. Do you have any more chicken?"

"No, you're eating me out of house and home. We better eat at the inn tonight," Kelvich explained.

"We're ready if you are," Mansel said.

"What, you're done working and there's still daylight?" Zollin teased his father.

"We've done enough for today," Quinn said stoically. "Let's head back."

They walked through the snowy path that led to the Valley Inn. It was a long, low building with smoke pouring from its stone chimneys. It reminded Zollin more of an animal's den than a structure built by men. Still, it had been their home since they had arrived at Brighton's Gate. The other inn had been damaged in a fire, and Quinn had earned their keep by working on the repairs.

"I've been thinking," Quinn said as they walked along the path. "Perhaps we should take a ship down the coast, perhaps even spend some time in Toogah."

"Why?" Zollin asked.

"It'll get you away from the Torr, for one thing. I've heard it's an amazing place."

"It's primitive," Kelvich said. "But very beautiful, especially along the coast."

"Brianna would probably like it," Mansel said.

Zollin bristled but did his best to hide his feelings. He hated the fact that Mansel and Brianna were getting along so well, but he wanted the girl to be happy. She hadn't had a chance to be happy with Todrek. Zollin thought back to their wedding. He had stood as Todrek's second when his best friend had married Brianna. The next day, the wizards from the Torr had shown up with their mercenaries, and Todrek had been slain. The merest thought of that horrible day made Zollin's eyes sting, but he was learning to deal with the guilt. He no longer thought of Brianna only as Todrek's widow, but he still wished that things had turned out differently.

"I hope Ollie has something good prepared to eat," Quinn said. "I'm starving."

"Well, we know there'll be plenty of ale," Mansel said, smiling.

"The drunkard returns to ale like a dog returns to its vomit," said Kelvich in a cheerful voice.

"I'm not a drunkard, old man," Mansel said angrily.

"Never dreamed that you were, my boy," Kelvich said, throwing a wink to Zollin.

"You two go ahead," Quinn said. "I need to speak to Zollin for a moment."

Mansel and Kelvich went inside the inn. It was growing colder as the sun sank behind the mountains. Zollin shivered in his cloak. It was still damp from the sweat his exertion had produced.

"You know when we left home, I really didn't have time to get much," Quinn said. "But I did get two things. One was your mother's silk scarf. She gave it to me before we were married and then after she died..." his voice broke. "It reminds me of her."

"Dad, are you okay?" Zollin asked.

"Yes, but there is one other thing. It's not much, and your seventeenth birthday is special, unfortunately this is all I have left," he said, holding out a small leather pouch.

Zollin had completely forgotten his birthday. It seemed so ordinary, and nothing was ordinary in his life anymore. The small bundle was light, but the item inside the pouch was hard.

"What is it?" he asked.

"My father gave it to me when I was your age. I don't know how he knew I was leaving home, but somehow he did. I don't want you to leave, but this is all we have left. It's the last thing that is part of our family. Whatever the future holds for us, I want you to have it. Perhaps someday you'll have a son to share it with."

Zollin felt his eyes stinging again. His dad had remembered his birthday. It was one of those moments when he felt loved and accepted. There had been so few of them in his life that each one was sweet. He looked at his father, who was nodding at him. He opened the little pouch, the cold completely forgotten even though the light was fading.

"It's a pathfinder," said Quinn. "The little needle always points north, no matter where you are. It's a simple tool, but one I've always cherished."

"It's amazing," said Zollin. "Thank you."

"You're welcome, son, I'm very proud of you."

They hugged for a moment before Quinn pulled back and looked at Zollin.

"I know that you're experiencing a lot of change right now, but you're up to the challenge. I have faith in you."

"I hope you're right," Zollin admitted.

"I know I am," Quinn said, smiling. "Now, let's go celebrate!"

Chapter 2

The two assassins had survived the voyage up the icy coast to Whistle Bay. They had a specific mission and were now traveling across the snowy landscape in search of a wizard. Neither cared about the cold that was their constant tormentor. They wore the finest seal skins, but there were no fires to warm themselves by, not even a horse to increase their body heat. The thick snows rarely melted in the valley, so they were forced to use dogs to pull sleds across the frozen land. It was an efficient way to travel, but cold. At night they burrowed down into the snow just like the dogs, and while they never got warm, they didn't freeze to death, either. They ate cold rations and drank melted snow.

The dogs were friendly, but they shied away from the assassins, somehow sensing that the men were devoid of any feelings of compassion or companionship. They were like arrows fired from an archer's bow, intent only on their target and oblivious to anyone who inadvertently got in their way. They talked only when necessary to plan their movements, or to discuss what they had learned spying on the people of the small villages they passed through along the Great Valley. They were heading east and both expected to reach Brighton's Gate shortly after dark. Even in the frozen valley, word had spread of the Skellmarian attack and how a group of outsiders had saved the town. The other villages looked forward to spring, when they might learn more, but the assassins had heard enough. They had caught scent of their quarry, and now they were focused on only one goal, to find and kill the wizard in Brighton's Gate.

* * *

It had taken the pigeon the better part of three days to return to Isos City. Branock had taken up with the pale leader of the Mezzlyn. Branock feared no man other than his master, but the leader of the Mezzlyn, Owant, as his unsavory companions called him, was enough to set the wizard's nerves on edge. Of all the Mezzlyn assassins, Owant alone seemed to have the capacity to enjoy anything. The others, the ones trained to kill without hesitation or feeling, were like empty shells. They were alive, but they had no personality, no emotion what-so-ever. Owant, on the other hand, was petty and cruel. He mistreated everyone, and only his ranks of soulless killers kept Branock from putting the man in his place. They were settled into a nice inn, although Branock had no idea where the Mezzlyn assassins actually stayed. He had a notion that they slept out in the stables, or perhaps were strategically positioned throughout the town. Their leader, however, preferred the finest food, wine, and entertainment. Women did not seem to interest him, but he ate and drank in a way that defied his skeletally thin frame. He also insisted that singers and storytellers perform nightly. Throughout the day, he saw to his pigeons, although how the filthy birds found their way to the man from all across the Five Kingdoms was a mystery to Branock. Still, he was glad that his suspicions had been confirmed when the bird arrived bearing the name of the town Brighton's Gate. Branock has suspected that Zollin would settle in the town. It was a good strategy, in a way. The snows had blocked their pursuers and given them time to plan their next move. Unfortunately, it also gave them a false sense of security. The assassins had learned that

Zollin was at Brighton's Gate and would continue on in hopes of killing him there.

Branock was not happy about the situation, but he knew there was nothing he could do about it. There was no way to warn Zollin, and the army that Prince Simmeron had promised him wouldn't arrive until the spring thaws. Then he could set his own plan in motion, dispatch his rival, and take control of the boy. He had spent his days refining his plans and, unfortunately, had spent his nights keeping the despicable Owant company. He envied Whytlethane with his solitude. The elder wizard was also waiting to travel with Branock into the valley to claim their prize, although they had no reason to believe the task would be that simple. They had been shocked by the young wizard's attack at his village. Branock had been gravely wounded in a battle with the boy, a battle that still troubled him. He had been confident that he was winning until his blast of fire rebounded onto him so quickly that it had burned much of his left side. He had repaired the damage, mostly, but his scalp was now bald, his beard had been burned away and no longer grew. His face was still scared somewhat, and his left eye was now milky white and sightless. His appearance intimidated many, but Owant didn't seem to mind, although his own pale skin, colorless hair, and yellow teeth were shocking as well.

So Branock waited, knowing the attack would come soon. He reached out with his power to feel the spark of the young wizard. Zollin was still alive, but for how much longer Branock did not know. But if the assassins were successful in killing the boy, Branock would have to face the wrath of his master. His plans would certainly be revealed, and his treason would be dealt with in a most painful death. It was not something he cared to dwell on, so he waited, fully expecting to feel the flash of power that would come from Zollin as he battled the assassins.

* * *

Zollin opened the door to the inn and was met by a wave of warm air. The common room was full of people, all eating and drinking. It was a common sight, although none seemed to notice Zollin or pay him any attention at all. Quinn stepped in behind his son, and they made their way over to where Mansel and Kelvich sat, cups in hand. They settled onto the benches just as Ollie arrived with steaming cups of mulled wine.

"This should warm you up," she said merrily. "I hear we have a birthday to celebrate."

Zollin felt his face grow warm with embarrassment. He wasn't fond of attention and hoped that his father wasn't going to make a spectacle of him. He nodded politely to the inn keeper's wife, and she returned the smile. Buck and his wife and daughter were among the small circle of people who didn't seem to hold his powers against him. They did their best to treat him well, the only exception being that their daughter Ellie no longer lavished him with her affections. He wasn't sure if that was a decision that had been made by her parents, or if the girl had simply realized that falling in love with a wizard was a bad idea, but either way it was one less thing for Zollin to worry about.

"Where's Brianna?" Zollin asked.

"She'll be along soon enough," Mansel said.

"So how does it feel to be a year older?" Kelvich asked.

"It feels like a lifetime has passed since we left home," Zollin admitted. "It's kind of hard to believe it has only been a couple of months."

"Time flies when you're having fun," Mansel said.

"I wouldn't call running for our lives fun," Quinn said, but there was twinkle in his eye.

"I say this calls for a toast," Kelvich said. "To the promise of a bright future," he said holding his cup in the air.

"And a happy life," Quinn added.

"With plenty of excitement," Mansel said, smiling.

"And love," Brianna said. She had come up quietly from behind them.

"Here, here!" Quinn and Kelvich said loudly.

They all took long drinks from their wine cups, except for Zollin. He had turned around to find Brianna in a long dress of pale yellow. The neck line stretched around her upper arms leaving her shoulders bare. Her long, dark hair glistened in the light of the fire. Her eyes seemed to sparkle, and she was holding a package tied with a brightly colored ribbon. Zollin was frozen by her beauty. He had hoped to see her and had been pleasantly surprised when he heard her voice, but he hadn't been expecting to see her looking so incredibly beautiful. She had followed him from Tranaugh Shire wearing a plain wool dress and thick winter hose. She had begun wearing soft leather pants instead of a skirt, and she almost always had a cloak around her shoulders.

"Have a seat here," Mansel said, sliding over so that Brianna could sit down beside him.

"You look very lovely," Quinn said.

"Thank you," Brianna said. Then she turned to Zollin. "Happy birthday."

Zollin was having trouble finding his voice, but at last he managed to say thank you.

"It's not much, just something I made for you," she said hastily. "I hope you like it."

33

Zollin pulled the ribbon, which he recognized as one of Brianna's, and folded it neatly. He knew everyone was watching him, and he lifted up the shirt that Brianna had made. It was a dark brown color and there was a black leather vest as well. The shirt was made from soft wool, and he held it up in front of his chest.

"That's very nice," Kelvich commented.

"Much better than your old clothes," Quinn added.

"I think it brings out the color in his eyes," Brianna said.

"I love it," he told her, and they held one another's gaze for a moment, until Mansel started shouting.

"More wine, we need more wine over here!"

Someone across the room took up the chant.

"No, we need wine over here. Serve us first," came shouts from around the room.

People were laughing and shouting, some had already been served their supper and were talking about the events of the day. Quinn was telling Brianna about their work, but Zollin was staring at the ribbon she had tied his gift with. He tucked it quietly into a pocket.

The night wore on, with stories and laughter that grew louder the more drink the inn's patrons consumed. Zollin wanted desperately to talk to Brianna, and so he waited for her to retire to her room. When she finally did, he followed her down the long hallway that led to the guest rooms. There were lanterns on the walls, but Zollin had never seen them lit. Guests carried candles from the common room to light their way and to light the lamp in their room. Brianna carried one and its soft glow was like a bubble of light around her. Zollin was hurrying to catch up and was just about to call her name when he saw a shadow rise up from the gloom beyond the glow of her candle.

Brianna caught sight of the assassin just as Zollin called out to her.

"Brianna, get down!" he shouted as he ran forward.

He didn't have his staff, but he threw up a magical shield to ward off the attack he knew was coming. He had expected an arrow or a knife, but it was only a small dart that hit his defenses. Brianna had dropped her candle and was crouching down by her door as Zollin rushed forward, the magic inside of him churning wildly. He raced past Brianna, but he could see nothing in the darkness.

"Flame," he said loudly, holding out his hand palm up. A bright flame sprang to life just above his hand, casting a strong, yellow light down the hallway, but there was no one in sight. "Where did he go?" Zollin asked.

"I don't know," Brianna said.

"You saw him, right? A shadowy figure."

"Yes, I saw something."

"How could anyone disappear like that?"

"It was dark," Brianna said. The light she was carrying had gone out when she dropped the candle on the floor. "He could have gone into any of those rooms."

Zollin bent over and picked up the dart that had hit his shield. It was nothing more than a needle with a puff of dark feather on the end.

"Well," he said. "Here is our proof. Let's see if anyone knows about this."

They walked back to the common room together. Zollin was scanning the crowd for any face he didn't recognize. The fireplace in the common room was large and cast the room in a dancing light that faded gradually toward the kitchens. Buck, the inn keeper, was hurrying out of the brightly lit rooms where the ale and wine were kept as Zollin scanned the dark corners of the room. The light from the storeroom was just enough for Zollin to see the man in dark clothes standing as stiff as a pole in the farthest corner. Zollin snatched up his staff and was spinning back around to confront the man, but the shadowy figure was already slipping away. He had bolted for the storerooms and slipped through the swinging door.

"There!" Zollin shouted as he sprinted after the man.

"Zollin, wait," Quinn called, but Zollin wasn't listening.

The room had gone quiet as he ran past the tables and patrons, who where nursing their cups of wine and ale. He knew racing blindly into the maze of store rooms and work rooms the inn keeper used was dangerous, but he didn't care. All of his pent up frustration and uncertainty were driving him forward and the release felt right. He ran into the hallway and caught a glimpse of the man in dark clothing rounding the corner. With a thought, Zollin sent a wave of magic that knocked the assassin's feet out from under him. The man had already turned the corner, but Zollin heard him stumble and fall with a crash. He was still hurrying forward, intent on capturing the man. As he rounded the corner, the assassin had just gotten back to his feet. Zollin was still taking in the scene when the man attacked. He was fast, his dagger swiping at Zollin's throat as the man spun around. The young wizard stumbled back but managed to cast a bolt of energy from his staff at the assassin, who dove to the floor to avoid it.

"Don't kill him!" Quinn shouted as he rushed down the hallway toward his son.

The assassin was coiling like a snake when Zollin pinned the man to the floor with his magic. It was like trying to hold a fish on the riverbank, the man was kicking and thrashing on the floor, but Zollin didn't budge, he held the man firmly. Quinn had drawn his knife, which was big and heavy. He took hold of the blade and swung the handle down on the man's head. The assassin's body stiffened for a moment, then lay still.

"Tie him up, quickly," Quinn said to Mansel. Then he turned to Zollin and asked, "Are there more?"

"We saw one in the hallway," said Zollin, panting.

"We better check the whole inn," said Quinn angrily. He stormed back toward the common room and Zollin followed him.

Chapter 3

"What's going on?" the slump shoulder elder named Henrik asked.

"Assassins," said Quinn without further explanation.

"Assassins," cried the man in alarm. "What are you talking about?"

"I'm talking about people here to do us harm," said Quinn angrily. "You saw the man yourself."

"I saw someone running from your son, but I'd run from him if he chased me."

"He wasn't alone," Zollin explained. "There was one hiding in the hallway, and he shot this at me."

He held up the little dart and the crowd leaned in to see it in the firelight.

"That looks more like a fishing lure," said someone in the crowd, earning a chuckle for his wit.

"You say he shot that at you?" said another man. "How could you shoot something that small?"

"It's a blow dart," said an elderly man. "I've seen 'em used by tribes in Toogah."

"So there's an assassin from Toogah in the inn?" asked Henrik, sarcasm dripping from his voice.

"Look, the man we caught is still alive," Quinn said. "Question him. I'm going to make sure there aren't any more surprises waiting for us tonight."

The crowd murmured as Quinn moved away. Zollin followed him as he lit a lantern and held it high, causing the shadows of the long hallway to scatter. He walked slowly down the hall toward their rooms.

"We'll check these one at a time," said Quinn. "I've never seen a dart like the one you showed back there, so be careful. I'm not sure what we're dealing with here."

"I understand," said Zollin.

They opened the door to his room first, but it was empty. After checking the tiny room thoroughly, they moved on to the room Quinn shared with Brianna. It was empty as well.

"What now?" Zollin asked.

"If he was in the hallway, he should still be in the inn. Perhaps in one of the other rooms."

The checked the other doors. None were locked, the doors swinging open easily and the light revealing nothing.

"Is it possible that the man escaped while we were chasing his companion?" Quinn wondered aloud.

"That wouldn't explain how he disappeared after he attacked me," Zollin said.

"He could have slipped into a room and waited for the distraction," Brianna said. Once again she had come up behind them so suddenly that neither of them noticed her.

"I guess that's possible," said Zollin. "But wouldn't someone have noticed him in the common room?"

"Let's go find out," Quinn said.

They walked back into the common room and found the crowd gathered around one of the tables. They were just pushing through the murmuring crowd when Mansel saw them.

"He's dead, Quinn. He must have swallowed something when he came to. I didn't see anything."

The assassin lay dead on the table, his bowels had released and he smelled awful. Zollin saw Brianna cover her nose and he started to the do the same, but didn't want to appear weak in front of her. He pushed his infatuation away and looked down at the man. He was small, thin, and wiry, much like Quinn. He was dressed all in black, and the skin on his face was chapped. There was a white, foamy residue on his lips. The site of the dead assassin made Zollin think of Todrek. He'd watched his best friend die on the day he'd been attacked by the wizards of the Torr in Tranaugh Shire. Todrek had been cut down by a mercenary's blade, and the sight of his friend's blood arching through the air after the soldier's killing stroke was burned forever in his memory, as were his friend's pleading eyes as Zollin had tried to help him. He knew now that his lack of knowledge had been what kept him from healing the wound, although Todrek had bled so fast it was doubtful that Zollin could have saved him even if he had known what to do.

"This is insanity," Henrik cried. "I've lived at the Gate my whole life, and I've never heard of assassins anywhere in the Great Valley."

"Well your eyes don't lie," said Mansel. "How do you explain who this stranger is?"

"How do we know you didn't kill him?" Henrik argued. "Or your brother there, the sorcerer, might have cursed him."

Zollin saw Kelvich flinch, but he didn't say anything. Instead, it was Brianna who spoke up.

"Zollin's no killer, he saved your village, remember?"

"That's right," said Quinn. "We've done nothing but help since we've been here, Henrik. There's no need to blame Zollin."

"It seems danger follows you four like a bad smell. We've heard the rumors from Tranaugh Shire. We aren't daft, you know."

"Well then stop acting like it," said Quinn angrily. "You've heard rumors, but you haven't asked us what happened. You'd rather believe the lies and gossip you hear than find the truth."

"What are you saying, carpenter?" spat Henrik. "I'm a town elder; I've earned the right to be suspicious."

"Fine, be suspicious, but be reasonable, too. There's a stranger here, does anyone recognize him?" Quinn asked. No one spoke so he continued. "Alright, so did anyone see him come in?" Still no one spoke.

"How did he get inside with no one seeing him?" Zollin asked. "Are there any other ways into the building other than the main door and the one leading to the stables?"

"No," Buck answered. "Not even windows to crawl through."

"I was sitting by the door," said a man with a lazy eye. "I didn't see 'im come in that way."

"I guess it's possible that he came in through the back door," Buck said. "But I would have thought we'd have noticed. I've been back and forth all night long."

"Well, he was fleeing that way. It makes sense that he might have been trying to escape the same way he came in."

"He was standing in that corner when I saw him," said Zollin.

"It would have been much easier to go out the main door," Ollie added.

"So why go toward the kitchens?" Quinn wondered.

"Maybe he was trying to distract us," Brianna said.

"Distract us from what?" Henrik asked.

"I think the other man used the distraction to get away," she said.

"What other man?" Henrik cried.

"The one who attacked us in the hallway," Zollin said, the magic inside him churning as he struggled to control his emotions. "This one would have gotten away if I hadn't been able to trip him with magic."

The crowd was busy mulling over this latest information when one of the older men on the edge of the group toppled over. The townsfolk cried out in alarm, surrounding him to see what was wrong. The man lay convulsing on the floor, and a woman screamed in fright.

"Don't panic," Kelvich called out as he tried to hold the man's head still.

"What's happening to Bolliver?" Henrik shouted.

The older man gave one hard spasm, and there was a loud crack. The man died suddenly, his back broken from the power of the spasms.

"What in God's name is going on here?" Henrik said.

Kelvich was searching the man's body. He was wearing thick, homespun wool breeches and a simple shirt. There were no marks on his body, no blood. Then Kelvich checked his hand. There was a tiny drop of blood where something had pricked his finger.

"The dart," Kelvich said. "Where's the dart? I think it's poisoned."

The crowd gasped and everyone moved back quickly, as if the dart could suddenly come to life and slay them all. Quinn held his lantern high and cast its light around Bolliver's corpse. The dart was nearby, lying innocently on the rough, wooden floor. Zollin picked it up carefully by the feathers.

"Throw it in the fire," Kelvich told him.

Zollin complied quickly, tossing the tiny, but deadly, instrument into the flames.

"This is serious," Quinn said fiercely. "Poisoned darts are outside my experience."

"Not mine," said Kelvich. "It's the Mezzlyn."

The sorcerer had been talking to Quinn, but the crowd in the inn was hanging on every word and they gasped at the mention of the Mezzlyn.

"First wizards and now Mezzlyn," said Henrik. "Good God, what is happening here?"

"Don't," Quinn warned him. "You're a town elder. Show a little leadership before you throw everyone into a panic."

"I thought the Mezzlyn were just a myth," said Brianna.

"Sort of like wizards and magic," Mansel said sullenly.

"Well, they're a secret cult," said Kelvich. "They don't advertise their existence, but I've heard of them using poisoned darts and killing themselves if they're captured. It makes sense, if the rumors are true."

"If this guy really was a Mezzlyn assassin, what can we do?" Buck asked.

"I say we give them what they want," said Henrik.

"They want my son," Quinn said angrily.

"Better him than one more innocent life like Bolliver."

"Bolliver's death was an accident," Kelvich said loudly. "Anyone of us could have been killed by the poison. It's not Zollin's fault."

"He led them here," argued Henrik. "They're here because of him, and they'll keep coming until he's gone. I say the sooner the better."

"Sure, now that he's done the work on the bridge for you," Mansel said. "I guess we're all expendable, as long as you're safe and sound."

The crowd was getting rowdy, and no one noticed the kitchen door as it opened slightly. The first assassin had come back and was now in the room with them. He stayed in the shadows, his dark clothing blending with his surroundings. He had a short, hollow tube, just long enough for the silent killer to wrap both of his hands around it. He raised the blowgun to his lips and filled his lungs with air. He had a perfect shot at the wizard, who was still holding his staff but had his back to the kitchens. The shot made a small sound that no one seemed to notice. The man was moving toward the exit just as the projectile hit its target.

"Ouch!" Zollin called out, spinning around. The dart felt like a bee sting, but the burning sensation of the poison soon overshadowed the puncture wound.

The cold night wind swirled into the room as the assassin made his escape. And Zollin's dire predicament was lost in the fear and shouting of the townspeople. Brianna was the first to notice that something was wrong. Zollin was sitting hunched on a bench, his eyes closed.

"What's wrong?" she said to him over the noise of the crowd.

"Dart...in...my...back," Zollin said. His voice could barely be heard in the noisy room. "Can't reach it," he gasped. "The poison is moving fast."

"Quinn!" Brianna shouted, and suddenly Quinn and Kelvich were at Zollin's side.

Kelvich pulled the dart out and flung it into the fire.

"Oh, my god," Quinn said, the fear evident in his voice. "It's going to be okay, Zollin."

"We've got to get him outside," Kelvich said. "He's fighting the poison, but the cold will help slow it down."

They each grabbed an arm and dragged Zollin out into the snow.

"Stay focused, Zollin," Kelvich was saying. "You can do this. Quick, cover him with snow."

Mansel and Brianna helped pack the snow around Zollin until only his face showed in the lantern light. The townsfolk were watching from the doorway of the inn, but none had come outside to help.

"Is he going to be okay?" Brianna asked.

Kelvich only shrugged his shoulders, and Quinn looked at her with fear in his eyes. He couldn't imagine losing his son. When his wife had passed away, it had been the most horrific time in his life. He had wished he would die so many times, but he had Zollin to look after. The townsfolk pitched and helped with the baby, but Quinn fought down the pain and grief to be a father. Zollin became the center of Quinn's world. Nothing else mattered. Images of his son as a toddler and then as a curious young boy flashed through Quinn's mind. The dread of losing his son rose up and threatened to crush him.

Zollin felt the poison spreading quickly through the muscle the dart had lodged in. It started as a hot, searing pain, but then the muscle cramped so hard he felt the ligaments pull and crack. He withdrew inside himself, unleashing the powerful magic that he tried so desperately to contain most of the time. He was making progress, but the poison seemed to branch out almost faster than he could find it. His mind was racing through each cell of his body, but the poison was simply moving too fast. When they dropped him in the snow, he barely felt the cold. He was too focused on saving his own life. His back was starting to spasm, and he knew that if he didn't do something soon, his spine could snap just as the villager's had.

The cold seeped into his body and even though he was near panic, his heart rate slowed. The poison, dependent on blood flow to spread through the body, was also slowed. It took several long minutes, but Zollin finally pushed all the poison back toward its point of origin.

"Cut my back," he said through chattering teeth. "Cut me where the dart went in," he managed to explain.

Quinn and Zollin reacted instantly, heaving Zollin out of the snow and onto his stomach. Quinn's knife slid under his collar and cut the fabric in one long line down Zollin's spine. The skin was bright red from the cold, and the wound was small, but the skin around the tiny hole was swollen, effectively blocking the wound, and there was no blood. Quinn, his hands shaking slightly, cut a small gash in Zollin's back. It was very shallow, but blood spilled out. Brianna gasped and took hold of Kelvich's arm.

"Deeper!" Kelvich ordered. "You need to cut down into the muscle."

Quinn looked at the older man with disbelief, but his hesitation only lasted a second, then he bent back over his son and pressed the razor sharp blade into the wound. Zollin groaned, but the blood spilled out, black and steaming in the cold night air.

"Brianna, get blankets," Kelvich ordered. "He'll need several. Mansel, stoke the fire."

Brianna and Mansel pushed their way through the crowd at the door of the inn, each rushing to the task they were assigned.

46

"Is he going to make it?" Quinn asked in a shaky voice.

"I don't know," Kelvich said. "Only Zollin knows that."

Kelvich was a sorcerer, which meant he could control magic in others, but he had no real power himself. He had been tempted to take over for Zollin. He was certain he could save the boy, but he held himself back for good reason. The first was that he had made a promise that he would never usurp Zollin's magic again. It was a promise he intended to keep, especially since the temptation to delve into Zollin's amazingly deep well of magical power was so intoxicating. He was afraid that if he tasted that power for himself, he wouldn't be able to let it go. Kelvich understood a great deal about magic. He had lived three times as long as most men, traveling the world and learning as much as he could. At last he had decided that taking people's power was wrong. When he tapped into that source of magic, the victims, as he had finally admitted they were, lost all control. They became like puppets, totally under his control. He was determined never to do it again, but Zollin's power was almost more than he could resist.

Zollin began to shake from the cold. His body temperature had risen as he fought off the poison, and the snow had melted into his clothes. He could feel that the last of the poison was almost out of his body, but he had to be sure. He pushed the blood out of the wound.

"Okay," he said through chattering teeth. "I got it."

Kelvich grabbed a handful of snow and scrubbed his back.

"It's probably not a good idea to leave the poison on his skin," he said.

Quinn nodded and waited while the older man did his best to clean the tainted blood off of Zollin. Then they carried him back inside. He was shuttering violently from the cold. The townspeople all backed away as if they were afraid the poison might somehow infect them. Mansel had thrown several logs on the fire and it was roaring in the fireplace. Brianna had gathered an armful of woolen blankets and met them at the fireplace.

"We need to get these wet clothes off of him," Kelvich said, and he began tugging at Zollin's boots.

Brianna felt her face growing red as they struggled with Zollin's pants. She handed the blankets to Mansel and turned away. She was shocked to see the townspeople staring at Zollin. She stepped in front of Zollin to obscure their view. His pants came off next, and he curled into a ball in front of the fire. Kelvich and Quinn wrapped him in the blankets, rubbing his body to restore his circulation. It took several minutes before his shaking finally stopped. His back burned from the deep cut his father had been forced to make. Zollin concentrated and healed the wound. Finally he opened his eyes.

"I'm alright," he said. "But hungry."

Quinn dropped onto a bench, the relief on his face all too evident. He looked more exhausted than Zollin had ever seen him. It was if he had aged ten years.

"Good thing Brianna made you a new shirt," Mansel said. "This one's ruined."

Brianna turned back around and there were tears in her eyes.

"What about the assassin?" she asked. "He's still out there somewhere."

"Not for long," Zollin said. "Mansel, fetch me some clothes. We're going hunting."

Chapter 4

Ellie hurried forward with half a loaf of crusty bread and some warm broth.

"You aren't really going out there?" said one of the town elders.

Zollin only nodded as he tore off a chunk of the bread and soaked it in the broth. Buck, the inn keeper, brought out a tray with clean cups and a bottle of wine. He poured some for Zollin, then Quinn and Kelvich.

"It's dark out there," Henrik said. "What do you expect to find in the dark?"

"What do you suggest we do?" Zollin said. "Sit here and wait for the assassin to return? I'm sick to death of your whining, old man. You are never pleased. Either come up with a solution or keep your mouth shut."

"Zollin," Quinn said, surprised at his son's manner.

Henrik was stammering, unsure what to say. Zollin's power was like a living flame. It felt good to let it burn, he thought to himself. He was tired of feigning humility. He had the power to crush everyone in the village and wasn't going to let them dictate his future anymore.

He crammed his mouth full of food again. It was bland, the broth only lukewarm, but it was food, and he could feel his strength returning. In fact, he was feeling stronger than ever. The power was somehow enhancing his physical attributes. He couldn't keep from smiling. Nor could he remember why he had kept himself cut off from his own power for so long. His staff had been dropped on the floor when his father and Mansel carried him outside. It had been a faithful companion on his journey, but he saw it now for what it was: merely a crutch. Its power seemed dim in the flames of his own magic.

"Perhaps we should consider our options," Kelvich suggested. He had a strange look on his face, Zollin thought.

"Why? It's just one man," Zollin said.

"We don't know that."

"We know that someone is trying to kill me. I'll sleep better knowing they're dead and I'm alive."

"He's right son," Quinn said. "Going out alone might be just what they want you to do."

"I won't be alone," Zollin said. "Mansel's going with me." He took a long drink of the wine.

He normally didn't care for strong drink, but, at that moment, he thought he had never tasted better. He sopped up the last of the broth with a bite of bread and finished his hasty meal. He would need more later, he thought, but he was anxious to find his assailant.

"Zollin, I think perhaps you were right about your power. Why don't you pull back a bit?" Kelvich urged. "It seems to be affecting you."

"Yes," Zollin said, "it is. In a good way."

"Son, think about what you're doing. Let's calm down and form a plan."

"Calm down?" Zollin said angrily. "That bastard just tried to kill me. More than once. I'll calm down when he's dead."

He was on the verge of shouting when Brianna laid her hand on his.

"Zollin," she said softly. "This isn't you. Come back to us."

The young wizard was about to snap at her, but there was something in her eyes that made him pause. He felt a stirring in his heart—not magic, but something equally strong. He didn't want to disappoint her. She was looking at him as if she could see his soul. He had to fight off the urge to shake her hand off his and charge out into the night, blasting everything in his path until he found the killer who had hunted him down across the snowy, highland valley. Instead, he took a deep breath and pulled the magic back into his inner reservoir.

A wave of fatigue washed over him, and he felt his eyelids droop a little. He smiled at Brianna weakly and was thrilled by the twinkle in her eye as she looked at him. Then Todrek's ghostly image appeared to Zollin's eyes, and he looked away.

"Okay," he said quietly.

There was an audible sigh of relief from Quinn, and the tension in the room seemed to ease a bit. Mansel came back into the room with a change of clothes for Zollin. He stood up on shaky legs, the blankets still wrapped around him, and took the clothes. Kelvich helped him leave the common room to change.

"So, what's the plan?" Mansel asked.

"I think the best thing to do is to bar the doors and take turns standing watch," Quinn said, his voice raised to carry to the townspeople and not just Mansel. "I don't think it's a good idea for any of you to try and go home tonight. In the morning, we can search the village for this assassin."

There was murmuring, but no one seemed to disagree. Ollie and Buck served more wine and ale, while Mansel and Quinn secured the doors. When Zollin came back to the common room, he asked for more food. Ollie served him a plate of broiled mutton with potatoes and stewed vegetables. He ate slowly, watching the room. He had retrieved his staff, and he sat near the fire. He was still cold despite the warm clothes he was wearing. Kelvich joined some of the other locals to discuss their situation, and Brianna took a seat beside Zollin.

"Thanks again for the clothes," Zollin said. "I really appreciate them."

"You'll look handsome in them," she said teasingly.

"Only because they are so finely made," he added.

They settled into a comfortable silence. It was the first time since they had left Tranaugh Shire that Zollin had been comfortable with Brianna. Her beauty overwhelmed him. His guilt at having feelings for his best friend's widow made him feel terrible, but just being close to Brianna made him feel wonderful. The contrasting emotions warred inside him, but he tried not to let it show. Brianna had been distant, but perhaps it was just because she had been working on his birthday present.

"So, how is Mansel?" Zollin asked.

"Fine, why?" she asked.

"I just know he's..." Zollin wasn't sure how to finish his thoughts.

"He's what?"

"Well, I don't want to interfere or anything."

"Interfere with what?" she asked with a puzzled look.

"I know," he said, staring at the floor.

He was silently kicking himself for bringing Mansel up at all, but he didn't want to do anything stupid that would make her feel uncomfortable. He was convinced that she and Mansel were seeing each other, although they seemed to be hiding it. He couldn't blame her, Mansel was stronger and older. He was a much better match than a fledgling wizard.

"You know what?"

"I know you're together," he said in a quiet voice.

When the group had first come to Brighton's Gate, they had pretended to be a family. Zollin doubted that anyone still thought that they were, but they hadn't openly denied it either. He didn't want to be overheard by the townsfolk and give them something else to gossip about.

"We are not," she said. "I don't know why you would even think it," she said defensively.

"I was... I mean, I didn't mean to upset you," he stammered.

"Look, Zollin, I don't know what you think or why you think it. Every time you look at me, you get a strange look on your face like you've done something wrong. You avoid me at every turn. And whenever things seem good between us, you say something stupid, like you *know* about me and Mansel."

"I wasn't trying to be rude," he said.

"It isn't rude, it's just..." she thought for a second. "It's just unnecessary."

"I don't know what you mean," he said.

"Why can't you just tell me how you feel about me?"

"How I feel?" he asked, suddenly very uncomfortable.

"Yes...?" she said, drawing out the word into a question.

"I feel good about you," he said. "I'm glad you're here."

"But why can't you look at me?" she asked.

"I can look at you," he said, staring at her hands in her lap.

"No, you can't. You feel guilty because you blame me for Todrek's death," she said quietly.

"No, I don't," he said rather loudly. "Why would you say that?"

"Because I dragged him after you," she said simply.

"He died because of me," Zollin said. "I should have protected him. He was my best friend."

"There was nothing you could do," she said softly, laying her hand on his.

He felt an electric tingle run up his arm; it was intoxicating. Her hand was soft and warm. He looked at her, this time he pushed back the image of his friend.

"I don't blame you for anything," he said.

"And I don't blame you," she replied.

They sat there for a long moment, and then Quinn came trudging up.

"We're going to take turns standing watch," he said. "We'll look for the intruder in the morning. This way we keep the people here safe and stand the best chance of finding this assassin."

"He could be miles away by morning," Zollin argued.

"He's here for a kill, he won't leave until he's gotten it."

"He probably thinks he did," Brianna said. "There's no way Zollin should have survived the poison dart."

"She's right. We could lose him," Zollin said, suddenly feeling pressure to find the assassin. He had been content to sit with Brianna a moment before, but that peaceful moment was gone forever.

"That might not be so bad," Kelvich said as he joined their conversation. "What if we pretend that you are dead? The assassins won't come back, we may even be able to sneak out of the valley come spring, before anyone realizes Zollin is still alive."

"For that to work, the people here would have to believe he was really dead," Quinn said. "That's the only way to get the rumor mill going."

"So we stage his death," Kelvich said. "He spends the rest of the winter at my cabin. It buys you some time and perhaps even some good will with the people here."

"I don't think-" Brianna began, but Quinn cut her off.

"No, it's a good idea. We came here to have some time to plan our next move. If everyone thinks Zollin is dead, we won't have to be looking over our shoulders all the time. We might even be able to settle into one of the other valley towns."

"The Torr will know I'm alive, Dad," Zollin said. "I felt the wizard die on the road. They'll know."

"Well, at least we'll have a little more time," Quinn said with a pained expression on his face.

The group was silent for a moment while they considered their next move. Zollin knew that Quinn wanted nothing more than to return to a quiet life. He felt a wave of remorse that he had driven his father from the home and life he'd worked so hard to build in Tranaugh Shire. It seemed like Quinn had been making sacrifices for the people he loved all his life, but Zollin couldn't focus on that now. He would give his father the life he wanted, if that were possible, but it wasn't. Still, he could encourage his father to settle here. He didn't have to endure the danger that Zollin constantly found himself in.

"Let's do it," Zollin said. "If the people here think that I'm dead, they might not push so hard for you to leave."

"But we won't be able to see you," Brianna said, and Zollin thought he heard a note of desperation in her voice.

"It's only for another month or two," Zollin said. "When the snows melt, we can decide what to do next."

"I think it's the smartest thing," Quinn said.

55

"I have some gypsum flower in my kit," Kelvich said. "It'll put you into a deep sleep.   When you're found in the morning, everyone will assume the poison killed you in the night. Then I'll offer to keep the body at my cabin until the ground is soft enough to bury you. No one will argue with that. If they don't see you as the source of all their problems, they will soon. This way, you'll be out of sight and out of mind."

"Okay," Zollin said. "That sounds reasonable enough."

"I'll prepare it," Kelvich said, then he left the little group.

"Mansel is guarding the back door," Quinn said.   "I'll be watching the common room. Brianna, you stay with Zollin. When you wake up in the morning, make a show of not being able to wake Zollin up. Work up some tears if you can."

Brianna swallowed then nodded, just as Kelvich came back to their table.

"Here you are," he said loudly enough for everyone to hear. "Drink up, you'll feel better soon. It's a miracle that poison didn't kill you."

Zollin nodded. His voice was too dry to speak. He knew that going along with the plan to fake his death was the best option. But he had hoped to be able to spend more time with Brianna. He had no idea how fast the Gypsum Flower would work, or even for how long, but he could sense the herb's potency. He took a drink of the wine but couldn't taste anything different.

"Are you okay?" Brianna asked him.

"Yeah, I'm fine," he said.

"I'll miss you," she said quietly.

He smiled at her, his eyes drinking in her beauty. Her face was perfect, he thought. Her eyes held his even as his eyelids began to droop.

"Finish your drink," Kelvich said, smiling, but the authority of the suggestion wasn't lost on Zollin.

He turned up the wooden cup and finished the wine. His head swam and the room seemed to spin around him as he lowered the cup. He yawned but couldn't help but notice Brianna's disappointed look.

"Is it supposed to work that fast?" she whispered to Kelvich.

"It's fairly fast acting, especially if the person is tired already," the sorcerer said.

"I think I'm going to lie down," Zollin said, his words running together.

He stumbled over to the fireplace and stretched out on the floor. This was common during the heavy snows that often fell in the Northern Highlands; in fact, everyone in the inn would eventually find a place to rest in the common room. Brianna sighed and took a sip of her own wine. She felt frustrated that something always seemed to come between her and Zollin.

"You better get some rest soon, too," Kelvich said. "I'd prefer for you to wake up early."

"Won't the people here grumble about that?" she asked.

"Yes, I'm counting on it. Hopefully they'll be too hung-over to pay too much attention to what is going on. By the time they regain all their senses, we'll be gone and all of this will seem like a bad dream."

"It feels like one to me now," Brianna said.

Kelvich smiled at her. He felt bad for the girl and understood her feelings, but also knew how important it was that they do everything in their power to keep Zollin safe. Too much depended on the boy for them to take unnecessary chances. He could feel the world waking up, and Zollin was the key. He needed to be ready by the spring, and Kelvich had a very short amount of time to prepare him for that.

Chapter 5

The next morning, Brianna woke stiff and cold on the floor of the common room. Unlike the majority of townsfolk, she hadn't consumed enough ale to have passed out on the rough wooden floor. Instead, she had tossed and turned all night, barely doing more than dozing. Just before dawn, the fire had died and the cold night air had invaded the inn. She shivered as she sat up, rolling her head on her shoulders to work out the kinks. She found Kelvich and nudged him awake with her foot. To be honest, she didn't like the sorcerer's plan. She was jealous that Zollin would be kept hidden in the old man's cabin, especially after she had worked so hard over the past few weeks to make him the clothes for his birthday. Now she would have to spend the rest of winter trapped in the inn with no friends other than Mansel, who seemed to have no time for her now that the local girls thought he was a hero.

She longed to be on the road again. Their trip from Tranaugh Shire had been difficult and full of dangers, but she had loved every minute of it. In fact, she had already begun to make herself a new set of clothes. A pair of thick, leather breeches lined with soft wool would be warm and hopefully give her a little protection from saddle sores. That had been the hardest part of the trip for her. She could ride well enough, but she had never had reason to go on prolonged rides. The old mare, Lilly, was a gentle animal, but Brianna had been sore and she knew she would be again when they set out in the spring. Still, she also knew she would adjust and get over the soreness, just like before.

She sat looking at Zollin. He looked so peaceful, lying wrapped in one of the blankets she had brought to him last night.

He didn't look dead, only sleeping, although his breathing was so shallow that she had to watch intently to see it. She needed to work up some tears to give a convincing performance, not that many of the people sleeping off their night of excess drink would be aroused enough by the commotion she was about to make to see it. Still, it was part of the plan and, although she resented it, she could see the wisdom of it.

More than anything, she wanted Zollin alive and well. When the assassins had shown up the night before, her fear for Zollin had been like an icy dagger in her heart. She hadn't felt afraid for herself, although she guessed she should have been, but she couldn't stop thinking about Zollin. When he'd been hit with the dart, she'd almost broken down in tears. Her hands had shaken uncontrollably. It had been the worst time in her life, even if it was only a few minutes. She had never been more frightened.

"Let's get this show on the road," Kelvich whispered to her.

She nodded and stood up, looking over to where Quinn was guarding the front door. He looked tired, but he nodded to her and she bent over Zollin.

"Wake up," she said loudly. "Zollin, wake up. Zollin? Wake up, Zollin! This isn't funny. Zollin? Oh, my God, he's dead!"

The townspeople began to stir, and Kelvich hurried to her side.

"What?" he asked in surprise. "He was fine last night."

"He isn't breathing," Brianna said.

"No," cried Quinn, who came running to them.

People were sitting up now and looking around in bleary-eyed wonder at the early morning commotion.

"Zollin!" Quinn shouted. "Zollin, wake up, son! Wake up right now." He shook Zollin, but he didn't stir or make a sound. "You can't die," Quinn said, hugging his son's limp body to his chest.

Brianna felt tears stinging her eyes. Mansel came into the common room from the kitchens and joined the inn keeper and a few of the townspeople who were just starting to gather around Zollin.

"It must have been the poison," one of them said.

"I can't believe it, he seemed fine last night."

"Poison's tricky that way," someone else said.

Kelvich put his hand on Quinn's shoulder. "He's gone, Quinn."

"No," Quinn howled.

Brianna couldn't stop the tears now. She knew that Zollin wasn't really dead, but she couldn't help but imagine that he was as she watched Quinn grieve. She covered her face, and before she knew it, Mansel had his arm around her.

"What happened?" he asked.

"Zollin's dead," she said through her tears

"It must have been the poison," Kelvich said. "He must not have gotten it all out."

For several minutes the scene grew as more people started to wake up and come over to see what was happening. Finally, Kelvich offered to keep Zollin's body at his cabin.

"I've got a shed out back, and there's room for him. He won't be disturbed and, come spring, we can bury him properly."

Quinn nodded. He and Mansel lifted the body. The townsfolk were frightened at the thought of the poison and none offered to help. They carried Zollin out to the shed. Buck the Inn Keeper followed them.

"I've got a sleigh you can use," he offered. "We don't use it much, but your horse can pull it on the snow. It's over there, on the other side of those empty wine barrels."

"Thank you," said Kelvich.

Quinn was pretending to be too distraught to talk. Mansel and Kelvich hitched one of their horses to the sleigh. Brianna laid out a blanket on the sleigh, and Quinn laid Zollin down tenderly. Then they climbed onto the sleigh on either side of Zollin. There was enough room on the bench seat for Kelvich and Mansel to sit side by side. The sleigh was obviously intended to haul firewood or hay. It was completely utilitarian. There weren't even springs under the driver's seat. Mansel led the horse out of the stable and into the bright sunlight before climbing up to sit next to Kelvich.

"It seems too beautiful a day to be doing this," Quinn said.

Brianna looked down at Zollin, whose only signs of life were the goose bumps on his neck from the cold wind. She wanted to cover him up, but there would be no need if he were really a corpse. The inn keeper had stayed with them until they left the stable, and no one talked as they maneuvered the sleigh through the little town. They saw no one, but they could feel the eyes of people watching. Silently they all hoped that the assassin would see them and move on.

Once they were far enough outside of Brighton's Gate, Quinn began talking.

"We should sweep the town for the assassin," he said to Mansel. "Once we get Zollin settled, we'll come back and see what we can find."

"We're far enough from town," Mansel suggested. "We could hop down and double back."

"No, I'm afraid there were too many people watching us. We've got enough time in the day to play the grieving family. When we come back to town we can pretend to be the vengeful family."

They made the rest of the trip in silence. Kelvich stopped the sleigh at the back of his little cabin. They carried Zollin's body inside while the sorcerer built a fire in the hearth. Soon the frigid, little cabin was warm and cozy. Brianna helped Kelvich prepare breakfast. He had plenty of eggs and some old biscuits. It wasn't as good as the food they were accustomed to at the inn, but it was suitable.

"When will Zollin wake up?" Brianna said. She knew the herb had put Zollin into a deep sleep but seeing Quinn grieve for his son, even if he was just pretending, made her uneasy. She wanted to see him wake up and reassure her that he was okay.

"It generally lasts a full day and night," Kelvich explained. "He'll probably wake up this evening, shortly after dark."

"Oh, I was hoping to see him come around before we left," she said sadly.

"Well, you'll get to see him soon enough," said Kelvich. "I suppose we could say that you decided to stay and help settle the body."

"You'll need to come back to the inn with us," said Quinn. "Then you can gather some of his things and return with your own horse."

"That's a good idea. Zollin has some of my things," Kelvich said. "He'll need them here. If anyone asks, you can show them those and explain you are returning them to me.

Although, from the looks on everyone's faces at the inn, I doubt anyone will care. They all seemed a bit relieved to be rid of their Wizard.

"Cowards," Brianna said bitterly. "He saved their lives, and they can't even thank him?"

"People always fear what they don't understand. Magic has been asleep in the Five Kingdoms for a long time. Zollin is going to change that, and there are some powerful people who don't want that to happen. Our job now is to get him ready for whatever he'll have to face in the spring."

"Why is everyone so intent on killing him?" Mansel asked.

"That's a good question," Kelvich said as he sipped the hot tea he'd made after they finished their breakfast. "I suppose there are different reasons. Most people are simply afraid of magic. They've heard stories but never experienced it for themselves. They say sorcerers are all evil demon worshipers who steal children, but I've never done any of those things. Then there are the people who do know about magic, yet can't explain what it is exactly or where it comes from. There's no logical reason why one person is born with magical power and another isn't. In ancient times, it was believed that in every generation a great wizard was born. It was nature's way of keeping the world in balance. But the Torr began enslaving or killing any person with magical power about the same time that the Five Kingdoms formed their confederacy. They were given sanction by the leaders of each realm to consolidate all the magical power in one place, so that the leaders of each realm could be reasonably sure that their neighbors wouldn't use magic to invade their lands. In a way it worked out well, there's been no full scale war in the Five Kingdoms for over three centuries."

"How do you know so much?" Mansel asked.

"Oh, an old sorcerer like me has his ways," he said, smiling. "Knowledge is the key to magic, and those of us with the gift are wise to learn as much as we can."

"So if the Torr was a good thing," Brianna asked, "why don't we want Zollin to join them?"

"Well, I said that it worked out in a way. The truth is the Five Kingdoms are in essence ruled by the Torr. The wizards of the Torr were successful in consolidating all the magical power in the Five Kingdoms, but their means were cruel. Anyone who did not bow their knee to the wizards was killed. Bands of mercenaries were dispatched with one or two wizards to roam through the Five Kingdoms. There was no way to check their power, and they began to rob and plunder the innocent as well as the magical. The people began to resent anyone with magical abilities, and soon there were so few people with magical gifts left that the thing that made our land so wondrous eventually faded away. For hundreds of years now magic has been asleep because of the Torr's dominating control."

"But there are still magic users," said Quinn. "Yourself for instance."

"True, but we all either joined the Torr or fled for our lives. I've been living in secret for most of my life."

"What's so wondrous about magic?" Mansel asked. "I mean, I've seen Zollin do amazing things, but I'd call it more scary than wondrous."

"That's because you're experiencing those things in a land where to be gifted means to be hunted. You saw what Zollin was able to do with those posts for the drawbridge. Imagine what the world could be like if dozens of wizards pooled their power to build monuments and cities. And it's not just about wizards; magic has been instrumental in all of mankind's greatest discoveries. Apothecaries could have the freedom to expand their knowledge of the healing arts. Alchemists could delve into their lore and create new things no one's dreamed of. Imagine the lushness of the forests tended by dryads, and the dwarves returning from their hidden lairs to craft weapons and jewelry and tools so fine you've never seen anything like them. Imagine the wonder of seeing a magical creature like a unicorn or an angel fairy. That's the potential that Zollin holds, to rouse the magic of the world wherever he goes. It's not just about his power, but what he represents.

"The wizards of the Torr don't want that. They covet power so much that they are constantly striving for more. Their leader now is a cruel man named Offendorl, who helped his mentor slay the wizards who founded the Torr and then murdered his mentor so that he alone could be the master of all the others. It's Zollin's destiny to break their strangle hold on the Five Kingdoms and revive the true nature of the world. It's already happening, I can feel it. That's why he is so important, and why so many people want him dead."

"Then we have to protect him," Brianna said fiercely.

"Yes," Kelvich agreed, "protect him and prepare him."

Chapter 6

Quinn and Mansel set off to search for the assassin after they returned to the Valley Inn. Both were fully armed. Quinn had donned his chain mail and collected his short sword and throwing knives. Mansel preferred a longer sword, which he had now strapped to his back. He had a thick, leather vest over his shirt and a wide, leather belt where he kept a wide dagger. He also carried his hunting bow and a small quiver of arrows. They started by looking for any tracks outside of the shoveled paths that were used by the townspeople. They searched every shed, lean-to, and out building in town with no success. The one place they didn't search was the Gateway Inn, where they had been working for weeks to rebuild the fire damaged building. If they had, they would have come upon the assassin, who had been waiting to see the reaction to his kill.

He had seen Quinn and the others leaving the inn shortly after dawn with Zollin laid out in the back of the sleigh. He was confident of his kill now, but he had decided to wait until after dark to head back to the sleds he and his companion had arrived on. They had left their cross country sleds several miles from the town so that no one would see or hear the dogs. They had made their way to the town of Brighton's Gate on foot using snow shoes which were made of light birch wood, woven into a grid and strapped to their feet. It spread their body weight across the snow so that their feet didn't sink more than a couple of inches and allowed them to move much more quickly. They had watched the village for most of the day, had seen the wizard working on the drawbridge at the edge of town. They saw him return to the inn, and they made a plan.

Now he needed to get back to his sled and release the last pigeon with a note relating his success. He had already written the tiny note and was just waiting for the cover of darkness to make good his escape. He'd been awake for 36 hours, but he knew that sleep was not a good idea. He'd seen Quinn and Mansel searching for him. It was like so many other kills before. And while he didn't fear dying, he had been trained not to throw his life away needlessly. The Mezzlyn spent years training their assassins from the time they were very young. And their ruthless efficiency was ample evidence of the success of their system.

Quinn was frustrated, although he hadn't expected to find evidence of the assassins easily. Still, he was anxious to find out who had sent the silent killers to harm his son. He had just about gotten used to his son's extraordinary powers, but he still struggled with the fact that people who didn't know him or his son wanted to kill Zollin. It made him angry, but he had learned long ago that his anger did not help him deal with violent problems, so he pushed the anger down and focused on finding out as much as possible.

"There's no sign of them," Mansel said in frustration.

"Keep that anger in check. Odds are he's still here."

"What makes you say that?"

"Because," Quinn said, scanning the snowy horizon, "he'll want to confirm his kill."

"Alright, so where would be the best place to do that?"

"That's an excellent question," Quinn said. "Ideally, they would need to be able to see both exits of the inn."

"The only place to do that is the Gateway, from the second story."

"You're right, so let's check it out. But we don't want to kill him, not right away."

"You want to question him?"

"Yes, but even more importantly, we need him to report that he was successful. If they think that Zollin survived, they'll send more assassins."

They approached the Gateway Inn and laid down their weapons. They tried to look as natural as possible. They went inside and began talking about the restoration work. Quinn pretended to send Mansel for supplies. Then he trudged up the stairs and began to inspect the long hallway. The Gateway was a tall building, with guest rooms on the second story. The fire had been contained on the first floor, causing a lot of damage to the lower level, but not the second. Quinn and Mansel had already replaced all the support beams, and there was very little for them to do on the second floor, but Quinn was guessing the assassin didn't know that. He made some noise in one of the rooms near the stairs. He needed to give Mansel enough time to get into position to follow the assassin, if the man managed to get past Quinn.

It was a delicate operation. Quinn didn't want the man to escape, but he did want the man to report back that Zollin was dead. He needed to capture and question the man, then let him escape, but first he needed to find the man and survive the encounter. Assassins, Quinn knew, were trained killers, not necessarily trained fighters. The assassin would have no qualms about killing Quinn, and he certainly wouldn't fight fair. Quinn needed to take him out quickly, preferably knocking the man unconscious so that he couldn't use poison like the first assassin had to escape interrogation.

Quinn moved noisily back down the stairs and then retraced his steps as silently as possible. He had his shield held in front of him in case the assassin shot one of the poison darts at him. He also had a short, wooden club. He began to quietly check the rooms. There was no sign of anyone, but Quinn had a feeling the man would be hiding in the last room down the long hallway, which gave the best view of the Valley Inn. When he finally reached the room, he pushed the door open slowly with the club. The attack happened so fast that Quinn had no time to react. The assassin's dagger should have stabbed through Quinn's neck, killing him instantly. Instead, the blade struck the chain mail which Quinn had pulled back off of his head and bunched just under the collar. The assassin had been waiting just beside the door, and when Quinn stepped into the room, he struck. The force of the blow staggered Quinn and sent a lancing pain down his back and into his left leg. Without thinking, Quinn swung the club in a backhanded blow that the assassin just managed to duck under. He stabbed out with his dagger again, this time the point broke through one of the metal rings and stabbed into Quinn's side. The blade didn't penetrate more than the width of Quinn's pinky, but the force of the blow cracked his rib and knocked the breath out of him. He staggered back, but he was still in the doorway, blocking the assassin's escape. The man didn't wait or try to attack Quinn again. He'd been foiled twice, and he knew his chances of surviving against an armed and armored adversary were slim. He ran across the room, instead, and dove out the window, shattering the glass and the wooden window frame.

Quinn was in agony with each step, but his adrenaline was still coursing through his veins, allowing him to ignore the pain. He hurried over to the window and saw that the assassin had landed in a snow bank which padded his fall. By the time Quinn arrived, the man, now dressed in all white garments, was climbing out of the thick, powdery snow. Quinn turned to head back down the stairs. He was moving much too slowly to keep up with the intruder. He only hoped that Mansel would leave an indication as to which way he had gone after the assassin.

In the far corner of the room was a small pack; Quinn made a mental note to retrieve it as soon as possible. But first, they needed to catch the assassin. Mansel had heard the window shatter, and he saw the assassin flip in midair before landing on his back in the snow. It was an impressive acrobatic feat, but Mansel was more concerned about Quinn. He glanced up at the window and saw Quinn. He immediately focused all his attention on the assassin. He was satisfied that his mentor was still alive.

The assassin moved quickly, ducking out of sight on the back side of the inn. Mansel waited a moment before crossing the street to follow the man. He knew the snow was thick behind the inn; no one had even tried to deal with the thick snow where it wasn't necessary to. It would be at least waist deep, and Mansel knew he could follow the assassin's trail easily enough. In fact, he would be able to move much more quickly through the snow than the man fighting to make the trail. Mansel peaked around the edge of the building and saw the man struggling through the snow. He decided to wait on Quinn before going after the man. He wasn't afraid to face an opponent on open ground, but in the snow, the assassin would have the advantage. Besides, his instructions had been to keep an eye on the man, not confront him.

Mansel heard Quinn grunting with each step as he rounded the corner of the building. Quinn saw Mansel, who was standing with his back to the far corner of the inn. He hurried to where Mansel stood waiting, but each step was like being stabbed all over again. He could only take shallow breaths, and he was wheezing by the time he reached Mansel.

"He's that way," Mansel, said pointing around the building.

"You'll need to go after him, but stay a long bowshot behind him. The bastard broke my rib; I won't be able to keep up."

"How am I supposed to capture him?" Mansel asked.

"Don't, just tail him. See if he has any companions waiting for him. Then come back here."

"Yes, sir," Mansel said, nodding. He pulled his bow off his shoulder and nocked an arrow. He wasn't taking any chances. The man had escaped Zollin and broken Quinn's rib. He didn't plan to give the assassin any more opportunities to do them harm.

The trail was easy to follow, but the man making it was so well camouflaged that Mansel had trouble keeping him in sight. He moved slowly, trying not to draw attention to himself. He kept his eyes focused on the trail, expecting to find booby traps along the way, but the assassin obviously thought that his best chance of success lay in outdistancing his pursuers.

The sun was beginning to set, and Mansel had been on the assassin's trail for almost an hour. He was probably two miles from Brighton's Gate, but it was hard to tell since cutting through the snow was so difficult. Not far from the village, the assassin's trail had merged with an earlier trail and, although the snow was easier to traverse, Mansel had trouble keeping up with the other man. In the fading light, Mansel was able to see that the assassin was heading for what looked like two long, narrow sleds. There were dogs sitting in their ganglines. The man reached the first and was busy doing something Mansel could not see. He was sure the assassin knew he was there, but the man seemed to have no interest in stopping Mansel. Then he saw a bird of some kind, flying up and away from the sled. Mansel guessed correctly that the bird was carrying a message, hopefully one that said their mission had been successful. Mansel drew his bow and took aim. He wanted to kill the assassin, but he couldn't be sure what the message said, or if it was even a message at all. He fired the arrow, but intentionally aimed to the left so that the arrow hit the sled, not the man. The assassin wasted no more time, he shouted a command at the dogs, which leapt ahead, running nimbly over the snow and pulling the sled with the assassin standing at the rear of it. The other dogs, still attached by their gangline to the second sled, barked and shuffled nervously as they watched their companions race away.

Mansel moved quickly to the second sled; it was lightly equipped, but there was still a lot of useful gear packed on it. It looked like a strange chair, with a long, narrow seat mounted on thin rails. The back came straight up, and there were handles that curved back away from the sled. The thin rails that the sled rode on extended back, past the awkward seat, where the equipment was tied down. There was a snowhook anchoring the sled and the team of dogs. Mansel pulled it free and tossed it onto the sled. Then, having seen the assassin standing behind the strange looking seat, he stepped onto the rails and took hold of the handles. There were no reins, and he wasn't sure how to steer the sled. He noticed a long, thin whip. He pulled it from the pack and steadied his grip on the sled. It was pointed away from the village, and Mansel wasn't sure how to steer the animals or even how to get them moving.

He cracked the whip, which made the dogs jump, but they did not pull the sled. He thought for a moment and remembered that he had heard the assassin shout at his dogs.

"Go!" he shouted, but again the dogs didn't move.

"Haw!" he shouted and suddenly the dogs were moving.

"Turn!" he shouted, but the dogs kept running straight. "Left!" he cried, and the dogs began to turn.

It was a long, looping turn, but it finally got them going in the right direction. The dogs ran hard, and it was only a few minutes before the village was in sight. Mansel could see lights in the small homes, and the dogs seemed to be drawn toward them. They ran straight down the main street, with Mansel hanging on for dear life. They raced past Quinn, who was waving one arm, but Mansel wasn't sure how to make the dogs stop.

"Stop!" he shouted, but they continued to run. "Whoa!" he cried, which seemed to have an effect. The dogs didn't stop running, but they slowed down. The sled, moving on its own momentum, slid past the Valley Inn and several surprised townsfolk, before finally coming to a stop.

Quinn was walking slowly toward him, Mansel saw. He was carrying a pack of some sort and limping slightly. Mansel got off the sled just as a young boy came running up to him.

"Where did you get the dog sled?" the boy asked.

Mansel wasn't sure what to say.

"Xanadan, it isn't polite to ask questions," said an older man.

"Sorry," said the boy.

Mansel recognized the man from the inn, where he'd seen him eating and drinking with some of the other townsfolk. He nodded and smiled at the boy.

"No, that's okay," he said. "No offense taken. I found it."

"It looks like it's from up the valley," said the man. "I'm Alphon. Someone's probably missing it tonight," he chided gently.

"No, the assassins used them to get here," Mansel said, trying to keep his anger out of his voice. "I chased the other one away on one just like this."

"Mansel!" Quinn said loudly from up the street, his face flushed. He was breathing heavily and holding his side.

"I need to get back," Mansel said to the man.

"Well," said Alphon, "I can help with the dogs. I'll see to them and feed them for a small fee. Or I'll buy them from you."

"If you take them, Quinn and I will work something out tomorrow," Mansel said.

"Fair enough," Alphon said. "Come on, Xanadan, let's get these dogs settled and fed."

"Yes, sir!" said the boy excitedly. They began to unhook the gangline as Quinn finally hobbled up.

"Where did you get this?" he asked.

"The assassins used them," Mansel explained. "The one I was following escaped on one just like this, but not before he released a bird of some kind."

"He released a bird? He didn't just scare it away?"

"I couldn't see for sure, but it looked like he threw it up into the air," Mansel said. "There were no other birds around, and I can't believe they would venture so close to the dogs."

"Speaking of dogs, where are they taking them?"

"Alphon offered to take care of them for a fee or buy them from us. I told him we would settle up tomorrow."

"Good idea, let's get this gear back to the inn. The assassin left it in the room when he jumped out the window. I want to go through it all, tonight. There's got to be a clue about who sent those assassins after Zollin."

Chapter 7

When Zollin slowly started to wake up, he felt heavy, as if his arms and legs, and even his eyelids, were weighted down. His head hurt, and his back felt like it was on the verge of cramping. He was thirsty, very thirsty. He started with his lips, even though they felt swollen and stuck together. He moved his jaw a little, and his tongue slowly pulled lose from the roof of his mouth.

He tried to move his arm and realized he was under heavy quilts and blankets. He turned his head to the side and groaned. His throat was so dry the sound came out more like a croak. He tried again to open his eyes and found that they parted slightly.

"He's waking up," Brianna said.

She had returned to the little cabin after collecting Zollin's things. She knew that Zollin wasn't dead, but it still angered her to see the almost festive atmosphere of the townspeople. Kelvich had been right; they didn't need proof of Zollin's death. They were all too happy to be rid of their wizard and his extraordinary powers. The news had spread through the town like a wildfire through a dry forest. No one even seemed sympathetic, despite the fact that it was obvious she was distraught. They were smiling and going about their daily chores as if nothing had happened. In a way it disgusted her, but in some small way she understood. They had their little lives and were content to live in them, hoping that no one came along and shook them up. Zollin had done that, and now they were happy that he was gone.

Brianna knew instinctively that the town would soon turn on Quinn and Mansel, as well. She knew that Zollin secretly hoped his father could make a life for himself in Brighton's Gate. He had never spoken of it, but she knew it was true. He took so much blame upon himself. She knew better though. Quinn would stay with Zollin, and Mansel, too. She had seen Mansel's admiration grow for Zollin. He would never admit it, but he was awed by Zollin's powers and counted himself lucky to be on a great adventure, even though he'd nearly been killed on the journey. Still, he understood her own need to see the Five Kingdoms, to live a life that really mattered, not merely to find a home and husband. She didn't want to just exist, that wasn't living to her. Zollin would probably scold her for such thoughts, especially since their adventure had been a harrowing race against death itself, but she had no regrets.

Kelvich walked over and let some water trickle onto Zollin's lips. Zollin felt the water and licked greedily at it. His tongue was sluggish, but the water worked its way into his mouth, and he felt better immediately. His eyes opened, and he could see Brianna's beautiful face looking down at him.

"Are you okay?" she asked.

"More...water..." he said, his voice barely more than a rasp.

"Thought you'd be thirsty," Kelvich said. "All day and night with no water is serious business."

He poured a little more water into Zollin's mouth. It was cold and tasted as sweet as honey to Zollin. He held it in his mouth for a moment, letting it soak into the dry flesh, then he swallowed it down.

"Better see if we can sit him up," Kelvich said. "He'll need some more water, then maybe a bit of wine. Let's see here."

Kelvich took hold of Zollin's left arm, Brianna held his right and supported his head, which felt abnormally heavy to Zollin, as if his neck wasn't working anymore. They situated cushions behind him and then set him back.

"There, that's better. I've got broth boiling," Kelvich said pleasantly. "Should be ready anytime now. Here, Brianna," he said, handing her the cup of water. "Give him small sips. He doesn't need to choke. His muscles will take longer to recover from the Gypsum flower than his senses."

Brianna took the cup and gave Zollin another sip. He could feel it run all the way down his throat and into his stomach, which growled. He smiled at Brianna, who favored him with a smile of her own.

"Did they buy it?" Zollin asked her.

"Oh yes, they are probably getting drunk in jubilation right now. I don't know how your father can stand to be there."

"They're happy I'm dead?" Zollin asked, more to himself than to Brianna. "I knew they weren't fond of me, but I didn't think they'd celebrate my passing."

"They were very merry, and none more-so than that vile creature, Henrik," Brianna said.

"Oh, he's not so bad," Kelvich said. "Just old and set in his ways."

"He's a coward," Zollin said.

"Most men are," Kelvich assured him. "Now, sip on this broth, then we'll see about that wine."

Kelvich handed Brianna a bowl and spoon. The broth was made from boiled chicken, but it tasted divine to Zollin. He ate the entire bowlful, and the hot liquid filled him with a contentment that seemed to relax his muscles. They no longer felt heavy, just tired.

"How can I be sleepy after sleeping so long?" he asked.

"Your body is just responding to the drug," Kelvich reassured him. "It takes a while to work through it. Better say good night to Brianna, she'll be heading back to the inn in the morning, probably before you're up and around."

"Can't she stay here, with us?" Zollin asked, and he noticed that Brianna was staring into the empty bowl in her hands.

"There's no need for her to stay here," Kelvich said. "It'll only make people suspicious. Besides, she'll be much more comfortable at the inn. We've only the one room and the one bed, remember."

"But she can visit," Zollin said between yawns.

"Perhaps, that might be nice," Kelvich said. "Here, take a little wine."

The wine was strong and made Zollin grimace, but he swallowed it. It burned its way down his throat in a completely different way than the hot broth had. His eyelids were drooping, and he sagged on the cushions.

"Go to sleep now, Zollin," Brianna said. She had hoped their time together would have been longer, but she knew he needed rest. She had seen him awake and okay, it would have to be enough to sustain her through the long weeks ahead.

"Okay," he said sleepily. Then he drifted away and dreamed of warm summer days.

* * *

Three days later the bird reached Isos City. It flew directly to the inn where the Mezzlyn leader was ensconced. Branock had not been with him when the bird arrived, but the assassins wasted no time in gathering their things. They had been gathered together for what was a very important job. Now it was over, and the death dealing agents were being sent on other business around the Five Kingdoms.

When Branock returned from his walk around the harbor, he was surprised to find Owant preparing to leave. The vile man traveled in a large, black carriage pulled by two draft horses that were so massive their hoofs seemed to make the ground tremble, as if it were afraid of being trod upon by such beasts.

"Where are you going?" Branock asked.

"Our job is done, and I am returning to Osla with all haste. Don't get me wrong, Isos has its charms," he said, caressing one of the serving girls, who appeared to be supporting the gaunt man's weight on her own narrow shoulders. "But I prefer a more civilized home."

"Your job isn't done," Branock said angrily. "The boy lives."

"Oh, I'm afraid not," said Owant. "I received a bird just a few short hours ago. The boy was killed by my agent's poison dart. You can question the man when he returns here. I'll leave word for him to find you."

"You fool, I can feel the boy's power. He is not dead, your agents failed."

"It is you who are mistaken," said Owant in an icy tone. "My agents never return unless they have fulfilled their mission. They will kill or be killed, there is no alternative. Now stand aside, I grow tired of your company."

"You grow tired of me?" Branock sneered. "I have choked on your insolence long enough."

There were four Mezzlyn assassins in the small courtyard. They moved immediately, drawing razor-edged daggers from the voluminous sleeves of their cloaks. Branock merely smiled at their leader as the assassins raised their blades to their own throats, their faces flushing as they fought against the wizard's control of their own bodies.

"Shall I have them slay themselves for your vanity? Or perhaps the girl? No, that won't do, she means nothing to you. I think I'll have them slay the horses."

"No," shouted Owant, suddenly very worried by the wizard's threat.

"I would slay you where you stand, cur, but I may have use of you. Go on your way, tell everyone you meet you have succeeded. But be warned: do not return to the Torr for your final payment. The master has no fear of you or your brigands, and the price of failure is death. Are we clear?"

Owant's eyes narrowed, but he nodded.

"Go instead to Orrock and wait for me there."

"Do you have payment?" the Mezzlyn leader asked in an arrogant tone.

Branock pulled his bulging purse from its place on his belt. He held it out toward the pale man and then dropped it into the muddy snow.

"Do as I say, or you shall not live to regret it."

Owant nodded and pushed the girl after the money. She scooped it up, and they climbed into the carriage. The four assassins took their positions on the lumbering wagon, two on the driver's bench, two standing on pedestals above the rear wheels. There was a slap as the leather reins popped against the big horses' rumps. They set out of the courtyard, the carriage rumbling as it rolled over the snow encrusted cobblestones.

Branock spun on his heel and walked quickly away from the noisy inn where he was staying. He would need to find Whytlethane and inform him of the Mezzlyn's mistake. It would play perfectly into his plans. The elder wizard would see this as their opportunity to make up for the mistakes they made at Tranaugh Shire. They could capture the boy and return to their master's good graces. Although Branock had no intention of returning. He had bigger plans, and the elderly wizard was about to fulfill his part. Branock smiled as he walked. All he had to do now was wait on the winter snows to thaw. It was fast approaching the winter solstice, and then the days would grow longer, the weather warmer, the seas calmer. Then his plan could begin in earnest. Once he had Zollin under his control, his first item of business would be making the idiot Owant suffer for his insolence. Zollin hoped the man would heed his warning not to return to Osla, but if he didn't, he would get his just dessert. Branock was certain that Zollin was not dead. In fact, at that very moment, he could feel the young wizard's power. It was pure and strong and growing more powerful every day.

* * *

"Blast!" Zollin said in frustration, watching the misshapen lump that used to be iron ore glow red once more. He would have liked to see it burst apart, but the metal was too dense.

"Concentration is more than just thinking about something without distraction," Kelvich said. "You have to push your mind into the object and become master of it."

"It's so difficult," Zollin complained.

"Aye, it is difficult, but not impossible. You do this quite well when you are attempting to heal a wound."

"That's because the flesh is so pliable."

"Well, there's a reason blacksmiths use fire and hammers to shape steel. It isn't easy."

Zollin had been reading a lot since he had woken up after his fake death. His body was still tired, it was as if the drug still lingered in his muscles. He had considered trying to heal himself, but it was an impossible task. The Gypsum flower had infiltrated every fiber of ever muscle, and Kelvich was convinced the only way to overcome the plant's effects was through exercise. The first muscle to be purged seemed to be his mind.

"Dig deep. You know how the process works; rearrange the metal on the deepest level, then you can manipulate its shape." Kelvich was pacing now. "You have the raw material; iron is forged into steel by mixing the iron and carbon together. Smithies use fire, you use magic. It takes concentration and control, not to mention a good amount of magical power. In the olden days, the most precious metals were mined by the dwarves and molded by wizards to make the greatest weapons."

Zollin focused his mind on the lump of iron again. He knew there were other materials in the metal, he could feel them. They were like grainy oats in a silky dough that he was kneading with his mind. He could feel the impurities, but the metal was so tight, so unpliable that it seemed impossible to separate them out. He pushed his mind further and further into the metal. He could sense the individual components, there were thousands and thousands. Each one spinning like moons around a sun. The iron had 26 moons, while the carbon only had 6. He needed to separate the iron from the carbon, then reintroduce the carbon in a controlled amount. But it was like trying to hold water in his hands; the carbon was being pulled back into the iron faster than Zollin could pull it out.

"I can't do it," he said, panting.

"Tap into your power," Kelvich explained. "You have to apply greater force to the spell."

"But I thought you didn't want me to use that power too much."

"Why do you question everything I tell you and then remind me of what I've said?" Kelvich asked. "You can't hide from your power."

"I'm not hiding," Zollin said. "It's just that I don't want to lose control."

"You learn control through practice," the sorcerer explained. "You can't learn it if you're always avoiding it."

"But you said I was getting out of control the last time I tapped into that power."

"You were," Kelvich said, "but there were people pushing the limits of your patience then. Now it's just you and me, no one to smash like a bug... I hope."

"Alright," Zollin said.

The truth was, he didn't mind opening himself up to his power, it was intoxicating and thrilling at the same time. But in most cases it was accompanied by a sense of malice and superiority that he didn't like. He felt as if he could lose himself in the thrill of his abilities, and that scared him. He released the power and felt the flames of magic engulf him. His mind shot into the lump of iron ore like an arrow, and he knew that if he wanted to destroy the metal now, he could do it. He could break it apart like a child smashing a sand castle.

"Now separate the impurities," he heard Kelvich say.

Zollin felt the carbon and traces of other impurities. He pulled them apart, his will now much stronger than the natural forces that wanted to hold the ore together. Slowly, he let the carbon slip back into the metal. He felt it strengthen. He played with the balance until he felt the carbon begin to weaken the metal again. He removed a bit more and then cast the impurities into the fireplace with a thought.

Kelvich could feel the power radiating from Zollin, as if he were standing next to a baker's oven. The sweet aroma of the boy's magic was as delicious to Kelvich as any honey cake. He stared at the lump of metal which was hovering in front of Zollin. It shimmered and rolled like liquid metal, although it didn't look molten as it would in the blacksmith's forge. When Zollin cast away the impurities they sputtered and popped in the fireplace, and then the metal extended. It had been a rock the size of a grapefruit, but now it extended, growing long and slender. Kelvich was in awe of Zollin's power. He was playing with the iron ore as if it were clay. He molded it into different shapes: first a short, two edged sword like his father's, then a longer sword, slightly curved, a cavalry saber. Then the sword pulled back and separated into two long daggers with blades that tapered down into a point. Then they settled back down onto the wooden table.

"What do you think?" Zollin said, as the bright flames of power settled down into glowing embers that he could control.

"Excellent," said Kelvich. "That was better than I had hoped for."

"What had you hoped for?" Zollin asked.

"I had expected that you could separate the impurities and perhaps fashion a crude weapon, but the way you molded the steel was a sight to behold."

"Good, we can eat then," said Zollin, his appetite returning.

"First, tell me how you feel," Kelvich said. He had the feeling that Zollin was hiding himself from the sorcerer somehow.

"I feel hungry," Zollin said, smiling. "Why?"

Kelvich didn't answer right away. He was pondering the situation. Was it possible that Zollin could hide his power from the sorcerer; that he could somehow keep Kelvich from accessing his magic? If so, was it possible that he could vanish completely from the inner sight that other magic users shared? It was something he wanted to ponder.

"Just wondering, I've never taught anyone as powerful as you," Kelvich admitted. "It makes me wonder just what you can do."

"I can do anything," Zollin said, smiling.

"There is more than power, Zollin. You need knowledge, you need strategy."

"I don't need anything," the young wizard said smugly.

"Why do you get so angry when you tap into your own power, I wonder?"

"I'm not angry, I'm just certain."

"Certain of what?"

"Of everything."

"Come on now, Zollin, you aren't making sense."

"Sure I am. My whole life, I've lived just below the surface. When I was little, I was passed around from wet nurse to hand maid, because I didn't have a mother. Quinn took care of my needs, but I was always different. When I went to school, I stayed behind the others. When I went to work, I struggled. I thought I was broken, but I just hadn't found the right fit. When I discovered magic, I tried to hide it. I wasn't ashamed, just afraid. My whole life, I've been afraid, but not anymore. When the wizards from the Torr came for me, I let others fight my battle. I could have killed them all, but I was afraid. I'm not afraid anymore. I know what I'm capable of and where I fit."

"Where is that exactly?" Kelvich asked.

"Wherever I choose," Zollin said with a smile. "The townspeople are scared of me, so what? They can't do anything about it. If I want to go down there and smash their homes one by one, I'll do that. And there is nothing they can do about it."

"You realize you don't sound like yourself, right?"

"No, I sound like my true self."

"So, why is it so different than when you aren't tapping into the power?"

"It isn't my power that gives me confidence, old man. It's the connection."

"What connection?"

"The connection to freedom, to truth," Zollin said, his eyes flashing.

"What if I said that I think someone is manipulating you?"

"I'd say you're crazy. No one can touch me."

"I can take over your power anytime I want," Kelvich threatened.

He knew he was taking a terrible risk, but if his theory was right, then someone was influencing Zollin whenever he tapped into his magic. It was a magic he was ignorant of, but that wasn't surprising. He knew enough to know that there was a lot he didn't know. He wanted to test his theory that Zollin could withdraw his power, and his hope was that it would sever the connection he was having with whoever or whatever was making him so brash and prone to violence. Of course, he was running the risk of making Zollin angry and getting killed—or worse, getting a taste of the boy's heady power and being unable to let go of it. But if he was right, he knew that he needed to free Zollin from the influence of whoever was trying to control him.

"I'm going to try something," Kelvich warned. "Why don't you see if you can stop me?"

Zollin smiled. "Go ahead."

Kelvich thrust his will onto Zollin suddenly, he didn't want the boy lashing out and hurting one of them. He felt the power surge into him, so bright and powerful that it was like climbing out of a cave and standing in brilliant sunlight. Then, just as quickly, it was gone. Kelvich felt desperate, as if he were naked without the power. He reached for it mentally, but there was a wall, a strong wall, an insurmountable wall, between him and Zollin's power. He could still feel the magic, it was dancing and jumping like a bonfire, but it was beyond his reach now. He strained to touch it, but he couldn't. He pulled back and looked at Zollin. His face was relaxed now, and he seemed happy.

"How do you feel now?" Kelvich asked.

"Fine, a little hungry maybe," Zollin said.

"I can feel your power, but I can't touch it," Kelvich confided. "That's very good. How are you doing it?"

"It's hard to say. I'm guarding it, sort of creating distance between it and everything else."

"You said a minute ago that you could do anything, do you still feel that way?"

"Yeah, I guess. I mean I feel strong, not just magically strong, but strong, confident and happy."

"What about destroying people?" Kelvich asked. "Do you still feel your desire to destroy the town?"

"No," said Zollin. "In fact, I'm embarrassed that I actually said that out loud."

"I need to tell you something, Zollin, something important. Does guarding your magic that way take a lot of effort?"

"No, not really. In fact, I kind of like it."

"Most people can't do that. Most wizards aren't as powerful as you. They make things worse by depending on magical objects to strengthen their abilities, and that ends up making them weaker because they never develop their own true strength. But even powerful wizards are susceptible to a sorcerer's control. I've never heard of anyone who could block a sorcerer's efforts the way you're doing right now. But I think it's good, because I think you're being influenced by someone or something when you tap into your magic."

"Really? How?"

"You know how you said when you first tapped into your power that you felt as if it were evil. Well, I think that feeling was coming from someone else."

"And how is that possible?" Zollin asked.

Kelvich was pacing, not that there was much room to pace, but his mind was working feverishly.

"When you tap into that power you shine like a bright star. You know how you can feel the magic in other wizards? Well, I think when you unleash your full magical potential, it's noticeable, even from far away. I think that somewhere, someone is trying to control you."

"Then I shouldn't use my magic," he said in alarm.

"No, that's not the answer. I think, instead, you have to work on developing your defenses. You kept me out, but we're experimenting. The question is can you keep up that level of defense when you are busy doing other things. I think from now on I'll test you periodically. I want you to resist me, but also tell me when I'm attacking. Hopefully, you'll be able to tell when someone is probing your defenses."

"I could feel you trying, but no one else," said Zollin.

"Yes, well, it's probably because they are too far away. On the other side of the Highland Mountains, at least. Otherwise they would have taken control of you, not just influenced you."

"I guess that makes sense."

"Well, we'll learn together," Kelvich said, smiling. "Let's start dinner."

* * *

Gwendolyn was confused. Her hold on the bright spark had been lost. She and her sister, Andromina, had been traveling north slowly, following the bright pulses of light that were far in the north, like the ancient story of Magi following a star that lead them to their lost king. Gwendolyn was sure that the bright spark was no king, but he was intriguing, almost alluring. She closed her eyes and channeled all of her sister's power, but the spark was gone. She had lost control of it before, but not like this. Before, she could still feel him even when his spark was dim, but now he was gone. Was it possible that he had been killed? It didn't seem likely, but there was no other explanation. She needed more information.

"Mina, we're going to Lodenhime," Gwendolyn announced.

They were just north of Olsa, at Miller's Crossing, one of the more important cities of the southern kingdoms at the crossroads between Falix and Ortis. The inn where they were staying was crowded, and Gwendolyn was glad to be leaving. She preferred small places where she and her sister could be alone. It had been years since their master had sent them out of the Torr.

90

She felt exposed and frustrated by the constant options that beset her. Andromina was no help, her power was strong, but she couldn't help her sister with any of the practical matters. Their mother had said that Gwendolyn and Andromina were two sides of one coin. It made sense; they were perfectly identical, only the blank look in her sister's eyes was different.

Gwendolyn rushed around the small room they shared at the inn. She stuffed their belongings back into their trunk and rang a small bell. The inn keeper came to their room at a run. He was anxious to please his lovely guests and had locked his wife away in a cellar so that she wouldn't interfere with his plans.

"You need something?" he asked through gasps of breath.

"Prepare the carriage," Gwendolyn said. "Mina and I are leaving."

"No," said the inn keeper desperately. "You can't leave, please stay."

"We're leaving! Now prepare the carriage."

The inn keeper fell to his knees. "Please, don't leave me. I'll do anything."

Gwendolyn swung her hand and knocked the man back into the hallway with a wave of magic. He cried out as he crashed into the wall. Men from the inn's main room came running to see what had happened. The inn keeper was weeping now, holding the back of his head.

"Bron," Gwendolyn said, pointing at one of the men. "Prepare our carriage. Mina and I are leaving."

This news was met by a chorus of shouts and boos. The men were begging them to stay, but Gwendolyn pointed at two of them and ordered, "Fetch our trunk!"

The men complied.

"Come along, Mina," Gwendolyn said in a haughty tone. She pulled her sister through the throng of men who were reaching out to touch the sorceress.

Outside, they climbed quickly into the carriage, which was plain, but comfortable. There were cushions inside and curtains to block out the world. Gwendolyn preferred the solitude and had no desire to see the landscape they traveled through.

"Bron, drive us to Lodenhime!" she demanded.

Bron was a big man, with a wife and three small children at home. He hadn't seen them since he had met Gwendolyn. She was so beautiful, he thought, although he couldn't say precisely why he thought so. In fact, he couldn't really think when he was around her. All he knew was that he wanted to stay with her, to love her and make her happy. He climbed up onto the driver's seat and whipped the reins to get the horses moving. The crowd at the end stumbled along after the carriage; it was a sight that no one in the town of Miller's Crossing had ever seen before. The women looked away, not wanting to be enslaved as so many of the men had been.

As the carriage rolled out of town, Gwendolyn once more reached out with her sister's power in hopes of touching the bright spark. She did not know the wizard, but she been given strict orders. She wasn't to see or speak to the young wizard, only influence him or control him if she got close enough. Her master wanted the boy, she knew that, but a tiny part of her wanted him, too. He was lovely, she thought, so bright and pure. It made her happy to feel him, even though their connection was tenuous at best. Now he was gone. She still could not feel him, and the thought put her in a melancholy mood. Perhaps in the old temple at Lodenheim she could find some answers to this riddle. She sat back in her seat and pouted. Andromina stared out the crack between the curtain and the window sill. Her face didn't register the emotion she felt, nor did she know how to articulate it, but it was there. They were moving further away from the master, and that was good.

Chapter 8

Freedom! That was the only word to describe flying. The dragon had slowly ventured out of his cave. He didn't mind the cold; it was always cold when he flew high in the air. And he didn't mind the sun, which was starting to turn his soft, white scales red and eventually black, which was stronger than steel, as was the case with his kind. No, what made him leery of leaving his cave was the energy it took. Magic was awakening in the land, but it had not yet taken hold, and more than anything the dragon thrived on magic. In days gone by, his thick, forked tongue could taste it dancing in the air, but now there were only echoes.

He soared up over another spiny ridge and found what he was searching for. There were only three things in the mountains that concerned the dragon. Men, of course; men sometimes scurried over the unforgiving rock, as out of place, in the dragon's mind, as the moon in daylight, but occasionally it did happen. The hairy men from the north raided down through the mountains, and the southern men were always digging. The dragon could think of many places that would have been easier to dig into, but the motives of men were not his concern. In time, he would need them to supply his one basic need, but until then they were nothing more than food.

The mountains were also home to a very hearty species of ram, which was the dragon's preferred meal. They weren't as tasty as humans, but they were much easier prey and they usually traveled alone. He wasn't ready to take on a party of humans intent on slaying him. He could fly, and, of course, his fiery breath was deadly, but his scales were soft and susceptible to man's iron weapons. He needed time in the sun to harden his scales and more magic to give him energy so that he could venture farther from the source of his power. The gold in his cave sustained him, but more was needed, more was always needed to keep him strong. The only other substance that lent him strength was magic, only he had none of his own. But he was like a metal rod in a thunderstorm; he channeled magic, attracted it to himself, and consumed it the way men did fermented drink. In time, as magic returned to the land, he would fly south, laying waste to the country side and striking fear into the heart of all those who saw him. He would terrorize the humans until they gathered their precious gold and hauled it into the mountains for him.

Those things were always on his mind, as were the eagles that also lived high in the mountain peaks. He was larger than the eagles, but they alone were unafraid of him. They attacked him in the air, and their wings were powerful enough to take them high out of his reach. Their wicked talons could harm him now, but once his scales hardened they would be of no concern. He needed food, so he risked the exposure. The magic had woken him from his hibernation, and he needed meat to restore his body to its glory.

The air filling his wings was delicious. It stretched his muscles and gave him a feeling of invincibility. He loved flying and swooped through the air as gracefully as a swan gliding across a forest pool. It was an incredible sensation, the beast thought. He was slow and lumbering on the ground, but in the air he was fast and sleek. He exhaled lightly, igniting his breath so that the flames rolled back over his body, warming the icy scales. He flapped his wings to slow his descent as he approached a towering peak that would give him a good view of the surrounding mountainsides. He landed, with his powerful hind feet gripping the icy pinnacle, and sunk his talons into the ice and stone to secure his hold. He wrapped his leathery wings around him to hold in the body heat. The wind, high up on the mountain, was bitterly cold, but the dragon didn't want to attract attention to himself by using his fiery breath again. The hunt required patience and fortitude, two virtues he had in plenty. He settled in to wait for his prey to appear.

His eyesight was unrivaled. Muscles around the large eyes could contract and squeeze the eyeballs, allowing him to focus on objects very far away, but the muscles could also relax and give the beast a panoramic view. It was a necessary skill for a creature who flew so high into the air. He also had a very highly developed sense of smell and, with his forked tongue, could taste the chemical trail left in the air by other creatures. But, being high up on the mountain, his sight was his greatest asset.

The morning waned, and in the early afternoon, he caught sight of movement at last. It was slow, down in a crease of the mountain. He watched intently, waiting for his prey to reveal itself. He had hoped that it would be one of the big, horned sheep, but instead it was a man. No, it was many men, the shaggy humans from the north. The dragon waited and watched. It was more than just a tribe or raiding party. It was a large force, an army of men, moving south. This was interesting to the beast. The Skellmarians were moving toward the magic. They would be in the valley soon, perhaps two or three days at the pace they were traveling. War was almost as delicious to the giant serpent as magic. He thrived on chaos and death. Soon he would have his fill of man flesh, and he could venture south into the warmer lands that lay beyond the mountains.

He was still hungry, but the beast was giddy with anticipation. He had gained something much more valuable than food; he had knowledge and his appetite had been whetted for even more. He arched his neck so that he was looking down his sleek body. Most of his scales were red, but he needed them to be black. It was the one thing he couldn't manipulate. As he aged, his hide took longer to harden. He blew out a plume of welcome flame, melting the ice that had formed on his wings and warming his body nicely. It wasn't necessary, but it felt sublime and it attracted the attention of the rock lovers in the valley far below. He jumped off the mountain and circled the peak several times, billowing flame and roaring. His voice, rough and deep, echoed off the rocky mountainsides, creating a cacophony of sound. He had let the Skellmarians see him; they would take it as a good omen from their gods. The dragon smiled as he flew behind the mountain and disappeared from their view. He was the only divine being in the mountains, but playing on the Skellmarian's beliefs would give them courage. His time had come.

* * *

Over the last two months, Zollin had learned various skills, such as accelerating growth, sensing hidden objects or substances such as poison, and controlling his power. It hadn't taken him long to grow accustomed to keeping his inner defenses up. Kelvich could still feel his power, but he was completely unsuccessful in breaching Zollin's magic again, let alone usurping his control. He had never been thwarted in his efforts to control another magic user, and he was both relieved and confounded. His curiosity was insatiable, but Brighton's Gate was no place to research the old ways. He needed to visit the great library at Lodenhime or the Chronicles of Osla, both were the best sources of ancient history, but they were far to the south. Eddson Keep had a library, it was mainly regional history, but perhaps it might shed some light on Zollin's abilities. Kelvich doubted that this was a new power, but so much knowledge had been lost in the dark years of the Torr's power that it was certainly new to him. The snow was steadily receding now, with the temperatures still cold, but above freezing, and with lots of sunshine. The river beyond Brighton's Gate was swollen with the melting snow, and the town was slowly coming back to life.

Zollin had been successful at manipulating matter and transforming just about anything. Most wizards struggled with heavy metals, such as lead and gold, but Zollin had no trouble with them at all. Unfortunately, Kelvich didn't have much of either substance to work with. It was one thing to transform the shape of something, which was a bit like rearranging wooden blocks. Zollin could even identify the blocks, separate them, and put them back together again. Even more impressive was his ability to tear the blocks apart and remake them. It was a feat only the most powerful wizards had ever been able to achieve, and only after years of training and practice. Zollin picked it up in a matter of weeks. He not only had the magical strength, but his mind seemed to grasp the abstract principles easily. Once he got a feel for a certain substance, like gold, he could transform just about any other material into gold, not just lead, but anything. The amount of power that it took was staggering, and Kelvich was often forced from the room when Zollin was practicing.

Food had been an issue as well. Zollin had been forced to learn to hunt, just so that he had enough food. He would often go out at night, despite the cold, and locate rabbits, big, horned sheep, and even elk, using what he called his inner sight. He could push his senses out in any direction and identify wildlife, flora, and even minerals buried under the ground. Sometimes he claimed he could hear singing, not with his ears, but rather like feeling the vibration that sound makes, only he could feel it by magic. Kelvich was absolutely fascinated, but the last week or so he had been depressed by the approaching wizards.

Zollin could feel them, too, moving steadily closer. He even thought he recognized them, although he wasn't sure. He was certain, however, that they were coming for him, and that they were traveling up the valley, which meant they had taken a ship into Whistle Bay. Zollin's first thought was that he could escape back through Telford's Pass, but the snow higher up in the mountains wasn't melting as quickly as it was in the valley.

Brianna had brought news from town on her occasional visits. She was frustrated by the fact that Quinn and Kelvich thought it unwise for her to come more than once every other week. And when she did come, the old sorcerer rarely let her stay longer than it took for her to deliver the latest news. She and Zollin shared a few moments alone together each visit, but it was never enough for either of them. For her part, Brianna had honed her archery skills and spent most of the winter doing odd jobs around the village. She had worked with the tailor, but also helped at the inn, where she stayed with Quinn and Mansel.

The Gateway had reopened and, while there was still work that could have been done, the townspeople were making it clear that the little group should push on now that the snows were melting. No one seemed keen on hiring Quinn, and their money was just about used up. Had it not been for the money they made selling the sled and dogs Mansel had retrieved, they would have been desperate. They had spread the word that they were spending the day preparing Zollin to be buried, but no one from the town even pretended to be interested in joining them, except for Ellie, but her parents forbade her.

Several of the young men of the town had begun showing interest in Brianna. In fact, Quinn had even gotten several offers for her hand in marriage. He had turned them all down, which probably only made the people of Brighton's Gate more suspicious, but it couldn't be helped. Brianna simply wasn't interested, and Quinn had no reason to try and force her to marry someone from Brighton's Gate. He knew she favored Zollin, and he felt both good and bad about it. He was, of course, happy for his son, who he knew had feelings for Brianna, even if they were tainted by his friend Todrek's death in Tranaugh Shire. On the other hand, he also knew that Zollin was not like most people. Settling down and starting a family wasn't in his son's future, as far as he could see. He didn't want to see Zollin's heart broken and, truth be told, he had become fond of Brianna, as if she were his trueborn daughter. He only hoped that neither of them ended up hurt as they navigated the uncertain waters of their future.

Mansel was the only member of the group that the town seemed truly interested in. He was remembered as a hero from the Skellmarian attack and the man who had single handedly slain the miner Trollic's enforcer, Allistair. Of course, that wasn't exactly true, Zollin had played a big role in both the invasion and in subduing the miners, but the townsfolk were all too happy to forget about the wizard. The young girls, many of marrying age, spent all their time trying to get and keep the young carpenter's attention. But Mansel's true passion was the sword. He'd become very skilled in swordcraft through the winter, learning more than just carpentry from Quinn. Mansel had no intention of settling down and would have set out to see the world even if Zollin wasn't being pursued. He wanted adventure and was intent on getting it.

Quinn, Mansel, and Brianna had ridden their horses up to Kelvich's cabin to "bury" Zollin, but in reality, they had come to talk about what to do now that the snows were melting.

"I'm sure I could escape through the mountains," Zollin argued. "I know the snows haven't melted, but it's not like I can't burrow through the snow."

"You would need to use your magic," Kelvich argued.

"I've been using magic all winter long."

"Yes, but they knew you were here. There was no reason to hide the fact. But if you go on the run, every time you use magic, they'll know it. It will lead them right to you."

"What options do we have?" Zollin asked.

"We can fight," Mansel said. "It's only two wizards, right?"

"Two that we know of," Quinn said.

"He's right," Kelvich agreed. "We can sense the two wizards approaching, but not the people they have traveling with them."

"And they didn't come alone last time," Brianna reminded them.

"What if we try and sneak past them?" Quinn asked. "Is it possible that we could, perhaps, skirt the valley without them knowing it? I mean, if Zollin doesn't use his magic?"

"No, I'm afraid not. They can feel Zollin, just as we can feel them."

"But they may not know about you," Zollin chimed in. "You've been hiding here for years, unnoticed."

"Yes, your power is probably masking mine," Kelvich agreed. "That would certainly give us an advantage if we decide that fighting is the best option. I could take control of one of them, as long as I can get close enough and maintain concentration."

"With one out of the way, I can battle the other," Zollin said.

"But isn't that dangerous?" Brianna asked. "I mean, these are experienced wizards, right? They'll be looking to take you out this time and..." her voice trailed off.

"But it won't just be me," Zollin said. "Kelvich can take control of one of the wizards so that it will be two against one."

"That's a sound plan, but we can't commit to it until we know what we're up against," Quinn said.

"So how do we find out?" Mansel asked.

"I suppose we need to do some reconnaissance," said Quinn. "Mansel and I could go, see what there is to see, and report back."

"I think that would be wise," Kelvich said. "Brianna and I can get everything ready for us to leave, in case we need to make a hasty exit from Brighton's Gate."

"Why would we need to do that?" Mansel asked.

"Because if the townspeople get ugly, we want to leave rather than fight them," Zollin said. "Once they find out I'm alive, you may not be welcome there anymore."

"Oh, yeah, I didn't think about that," Mansel said, grinning. "You might scare half of them to death, as skittish as they are about you."

"So we all have something to do," Quinn said.

"Not me," Zollin interjected.

"Oh, you'll be busy," Kelvich said. "We'll need coin if we're going to charter a ship to take us out of the valley. I want you focused on turning these mineral samples into silver coins."

"Silver?" Zollin asked. "Why not gold?"

"Because silver is more common and easier to spend," Kelvich said. "Besides, gold would only attract more attention to us, and we want to avoid that."

"Are you saying Zollin can make money appear out of thin air?" Mansel asked.

"No," Kelvich snapped. "But he can turn other metals into gold. Not that it's any of your concern."

Zollin noticed that Quinn, Mansel, and Brianna were all looking at him with excited expressions. He had forgotten that there was so much they didn't know. He wasn't used to being the person who knew things that others didn't. His whole life his father had been showing him how to do things. Now he was coming into his own, and, in fact, he had spent a good part of the winter reading and learning. His mind had become a sponge. He had never enjoyed learning before; it was all just random information that got jumbled in his head. Now, however, what he was learning was important, practical stuff that he could use every day. And although he learned a lot by reading, everything he learned in a book he also practiced in real life, using amazing magical skills that he had never dreamed of before.

"Alright, we better get to it. I don't know how much longer folks in Brighton's Gate are going to welcome us," Quinn said.

"The other wizards aren't far. Perhaps two days out, I'm guessing," Zollin said.

"It looks like the adventure continues," Mansel said, smiling with excitement.

"Yes, well, let's just hope we all live to enjoy it," Kelvich said sourly.

Chapter 9

The cold was insufferable, Branock thought. It wasn't that he couldn't tolerate the cold, like an infirm, old man, but rather that he was tired of it. He was tired of snow and mud and being outside, but most of all he was tired of being cold. He and the small army Prince Simmeron had sent to him had taken four ships from Isos. He was now leading an entire legion of troops. They were spread out across the valley about half a day's walk behind Branock and Whytlethane. There were two hundred archers, all longbow men with fat quivers and stout bows which could rain down death on an enemy from over 200 yards away. There were 650 foot soldiers, each carrying a large, round shield made of yellow birch and banded with iron. For a soldier fighting hand to hand, the shield was his most valuable weapon. Without it, he was dead; armor and chain mail, which very few soldiers possessed, didn't count for much without a shield. Great swordsmen could defend themselves with a sword, but in a mass of men struggling and fighting, there was simply no room for defensive work. So the shield was the only thing that stood between the foot soldiers and death. They carried the shields everywhere they went, no matter what task they had been set or how tired of the shield's weight they became. They also carried short, double edged thrusting swords and curved daggers.

There were 100 mounted cavalry, all with heavy armor, lances, short recurve bows, and battle axes or maces. They also carried longswords and small shields. There were a dozen or so knights, with their pages and squires, servants and military staffs. The knights were all sons and nephews of high ranking nobles. They served as officers, each commanding sections of the army, and a few of the most experienced knights led as generals. It was an impressive army, but it reminded Branock of a swarm of ants. They crawled over the land, consuming everything. The small towns in the Great Valley struggled to find enough resources to feed a thousand hungry men. The winter was over, but it would be a long time until harvest and, although news of the Skellmarian attack had trickled down the valley, most of the inhabitants felt no credible threat from the north men. Certainly not enough to warrant the impoverishment that the soldiers created as they passed through.

Officially, a knight named Orbruk, from Eddson Keep, was in charge of the legion, but Branock was in control. Prince Simmeron had spoken to Orbruk personally. Although their official purpose was to oppose the Skellmarian threat, Branock was going to leverage the army to ensure that he brought Zollin under his control. It was a brilliant plan, with only one vexing caveat: he needed to somehow find a way to destroy Whytlethane. The elderly wizard had been on his guard since the Mezzlyn had pulled out of Isos. He'd seen the opportunity they had to redeem themselves, but when Branock had mentioned the army, he had actually seen Whytlethane's guard go up. The animosity between the two rivals was no secret and, while the elder wizard didn't know Branock's plan, he was aware that one was in motion.

"The wind has finally turned," said Branock. "At least we don't have to smell their filth now."

"No," said Whytlethane, who was even tighter lipped than usual.

They were riding horses and were closely followed by a small group of men who had been employed to serve the two wizards as they traveled. They brought tents from Isos, complete with furs and braziers to keep the small shelters warm. They were in charge of packing and setting up the camp, as well as preparing meals and seeing to the horses. It was a much more comfortable way to travel. They would stop each day at sundown and send someone back for news of the army.

"Let's make camp," Branock said. "We are getting close, and I want the army with us when we approach the town."

Whytlethane looked at Branock suspiciously and nodded.

They were on a small hill, and Branock stepped off of his horse, the scar tissue that ran just under the skin all along his left side was stiff. It was like wearing clothes that were too small, but he managed to get off the horse on his own. The elder wizard merely sat and waited. One of the servants ran up with a large, wooden box that was tiered like steps. He sat the box on the ground beside Whytlethane's horse and then held the reins. Another servant hurriedly set up two canvas camp chairs with cushions. Another set a brazier between them. The servant had carefully tended to a small number of coals all day as they traveled. The brazier didn't do much to heat the two wizards in the open air, but it was something to warm their hands by.

"Get a fire going," Branock said in haughty tone.

The truth was he enjoyed having people to wait on him hand and foot. It was the least he deserved as a powerful wizard, or so he told himself. Their master disagreed and preferred to keep only a handful of mute eunuchs to serve their basic needs. He was old, even for a wizard, and paranoid, seeing spies and traitors everywhere. Whytlethane didn't seem to mind the servants, which gave Branock a strange sense of peace about the murder he was planning to commit. At least the elder wizard's last days would be as comfortable as possible.

The servants were bustling about. Branock felt that gold was the ultimate motivator, not pain or fear. Greed drove these men to see to his every need and to do so with a smile. He was now their master, not because they had no other choice, but because they loved his money. The fact that he alone was able to produce the gold ensured his safety. If he were merely a wealthy merchant with a hidden trove of wealth, they might betray him in hopes of getting the treasure for themselves. But Branock had no treasure; he had shown the men the truth of it once they agreed to his terms. He had spent himself to the point of total exhaustion transmuting a small portion of lead into gold. He had given it to the men, allowed them to test it and to spend it. Now he was their god, and they would guard him with their very lives to ensure that nothing came between them and the one person who could make them rich.

"Do you prefer to return to Osla overland or by sea?" Branock asked. He had no intention of returning until he had conquered the other four kingdoms and was leading the largest war host ever seen in the Five Kingdoms, but he wanted to engage his fellow wizard in conversation.

"I prefer the sea," Whytlethane said.

"It will be colder on the water," Branock argued.

"Not colder than sleeping on the ground or in some flee infested inn."

"Oh, I'm sure you're right. I'll be glad to be out of the saddle for a while. I feel the winter spent in Isos has made me soft."

Whytlethane merely grunted. He was disgruntled, but that was to be expected. His time was short, Branock reminded himself. He could endure for a while longer.

The tents went up next, as a servant gathered wood for a fire. Then Branock set the wood ablaze with his short staff. It was a finely carved staff of desert ironwood that looked more like a cane than a wizard's staff. Soon they had steaming cups of mulled wine in their hands and their boots were warming nicely by the fire. It was not what Branock considered comfortable, but it was less uncomfortable than before.

"What is your plan?" Whytlethane asked suddenly, shaking Branock out of his daydream of life in Orrock City as supreme potentate of the Five Kingdoms.

"Plan for what?" Branock said a little defensively.

"For bringing in the boy, of course," Whytlethane said, without trying to hide his agitation.

"It has not changed; we threaten his family and the city if he does not come along. We leave the army behind so that he knows what will happen if does not cooperate. It is just the stroke of good fortune that we needed."

"Yes, a little too good, in my experience."

"Don't worry," Branock said. "You worry too much."

"And you not enough. I should think you would be much more cautious, since your last encounter with the boy almost lost you your life."

"It was a fluke. A mystery that I plan to solve, but nothing to be worried about."

"I'll be watching you," Whytlethane said.

"And what does that mean?" Branock said angrily.

"It means I don't trust you."

"You are a jaded, old man," Branock said. "You should use a rejuvenating spell."

"I don't need you to tell me what to do."

"Perhaps..." Branock let the thought trail off as they watched a horse come into view.

It was a single man on horseback, cantering through the mud apparently without a care in the world. He rode close to the river and seemed oblivious to the camp being set up on the hill. When at last he appeared to notice them, he changed directions and rode toward them.

"This could be useful," Branock said.

Whytlethane merely nodded. They waited patiently for the man to arrive. He shouted his greeting as he approached, still on horseback.

"Halloo, my lords, is everything aright?"

"Yes," Branock replied coolly.

"You may take shelter in Brighton's Gate. A hard ride will see you there by nightfall," the man claimed. "The Gateway Inn's been reopened, and the wine is the finest in the Great Valley."

"I see, but we are not interested in wine," Branock countered. "We come in search of our kin. A man and three young people, one a handsome young maid."

"Ah," said the rider, his face darkening. "Well, there's no good news there. They remain, but only just. One was slain by an assassin. They'll be pushing on soon."

"Well that's good to know."

"News in the Valley is rare," said the man. "Any little bit's a treasure," he said, hinting for payment.

Branock felt the magic in his companion churning angrily.

"Right you are," said Branock before Whytlethane could act. "Here's a coin to ensure your successful journey," he said as he flipped a gold coin high in the air. The man looked up, watching the glinting metal as it flashed in the cold sunlight.

He didn't see Branock wave his hand, but he heard the horse's legs on its right side snap and the horse's wailing neigh. It toppled over and landed hard on the rider's leg, pinning it under the weight. Branock raised his staff and the cold coin flew back into his hand.

"Slay him," Whytlethane said stiffly.

"Not until I hear everything about our young wizard."

"He obviously knows nothing. He thinks the boy is dead."

"Yes, well, I would like to know about the others, at least. I doubt that Zollin would willingly leave them. They are the key to this entire plan. For all we know, the boy could care less about the village, which would render the army useless to us."

"We don't need an army," Whytlethane insisted.

"Don't be so hasty," Branock mocked. His fellow wizard of the Torr was anything but hasty.

"Ow, sirs," cried the rider. "I'm pinned, and the beast is wallowing my leg something fierce. Can you help?"

"Indeed," Branock said, using his magic to enhance his voice.

He raised his staff and the horse rose in the air. The rider was so surprised that he failed to move. Branock let the beast fall back onto the man, who now had both legs pinned under the horse and was crying out in pain.

"Tell me about the wizard's companions."

"I've told you," he cried, even though he was panting and there was sweat popping out on his forehead. "They've rebuilt the Gateway Inn. Stayed busy all winter, but they aren't welcome to stay."

"And you're sure the boy's dead?"

"They went up to bury him today," the man said.

"Up where?"

"To the hermit's cabin. Not far from the pass."

"Telford's pass?"

"That's...right..." the man said, gasping.

Branock lifted the horse again and dropped it beside the rider instead of on top of him. Then he broke the horse's neck and walked down toward the man.

"My leg's broke, I think," said the man.

"Could be," Branock replied, but there was no concern in his voice. "You said the family was leaving the valley. Could they get out through Telford's Pass?"

"N...no my lord," the man said through clenched teeth. "The snows haven't melted in the mountains."

"Good, now tell me how the boy died."

"He was poisoned," the man said, groaning. "He died in his sleep. I didn't see it, but there were a lot of people who did."

"Tell me about his companions."

"The girl is an arrogant little wench, too good for our boys, is what I'm told. The father has tried to make a good impression. He built the new drawbridge with his sons, but no one wants him around. He's a good fighter though. Challenged the Skellmarian chief to single combat and managed to kill the barbarian. They say he was King's Guard, but I can't say for sure."

The man was trembling from the pain in his leg, so Branock used his power to block the nerves that were sending pain messages to the man's brain. It was a simple spell, one he had used many times when he was interrogating prisoners of the Torr. He had found that by relieving pain, he was able to get much more cooperation than by inflicting pain.

"Oh..." said the man, his head rolling back onto the muddy ground in relief. "My, my leg is better."

"Yes, I thought a little relief might help your memory."

The man looked up again. "The other boy's a swordsman, if ever I seen one. He carries a long sword, and they say he can use it. He killed Trollic's right hand man in single combat. He's one to watch out for."

"Indeed, what else can you tell me?"

"Just rumors is all, my lord. Some say the old man Kelvich is a devil worshiper. They say he can channel the dead, and that's why he volunteered to keep the wizard's body at his cabin. Other folks say he's doing evil things to the body. No one knows really, no one goes up there except the girl. She goes every couple of weeks to check on the body, at least that's what she tells folks."

"You said they aren't welcome to stay at your village. Will the people give them up, you think, if the town is threatened?"

"I'd say so."

"Do you think they'll be run out anytime soon?"

"Not as long as they still have coin, I don't suppose."

"Good, that's very good to know," Branock said, smiling. "Anything you want to ask him, brother?"

"No," Whytlethane said.

Branock turned his back on the rider, who was now writhing in the mud from the pain that had suddenly returned as the wizard ended his spell. The man was groaning and begging for help. It wasn't a lovely sound, but in a way Branock enjoyed it. He returned to his seat.

"I think they faked the boy's death to keep the assassins at bay," Branock said. "Someone in that little group has brains."

"I hope it's the boy," Whytlethane said, his voice barely above a whisper. "Then he'll see through you."

"You do me disservice, brother. Your attitude is as icy as the weather."

"Are you going to let that pathetic thing moan all day?"

"I'm sorry, is it bothering you?" Branock asked sarcastically.

Whytlethane waved his arm, and there was a loud crack as the man's neck snapped cleanly in two, killing him instantly. The spell took a heavy toll on the elder wizard, but he tried not to let it show. Unlike Branock, Whytlethane kept no staff; instead, he utilized a medallion which he wore around his neck and kept secret. The stone was black onyx and polished so that it gleamed in the light. It had been a powerful stone, but since their first encounter with Zollin at Tranaugh Shire, when the young wizard had blasted them unexpectedly with the energy from his staff, the stone seemed to be steadily weakening. Whytlethane had worked all winter to restore the stone, but nothing seemed to help. The elder wizard needed to find another powerful object to supplement his own magic, which had grown weak through the years, but he had no opportunity to search for one without Branock knowing. And Whytlethane had no intention of showing his rival any weakness what-so-ever.

"The end is near," Branock said airily.

"Let us hope there are no more surprises," Whytlethane said.

"We have an army at our disposal. What could go wrong?"

"What indeed?" Whytlethane said under his breath.

Chapter 10

Zollin was a little disappointed. He sat at the small, wooden table looking at the metal that he'd been given. It was scrap from the smithy's shop, but it was suitable. It only took an hour to transmute the scrap metal into silver coins. Zollin tried his best to make them look distressed, rather than new. Now he had nothing to do but sit around in the little cabin and wait. Patience was not his strong suit, especially when he felt the dread of the Torr wizards so strongly. He was convinced they were close, perhaps only days away. The more he used his power, the more acutely he could sense the others wizards. The magic inside of him was not only more accessible, it seemed to be growing. In fact, he could feel it coursing through his body like blood, glowing in every fiber and sinew. Even though he rarely tapped into the deep well of magic, he had more power on a regular basis just using what Kelvich called the overflow.

They had spent time exercising through the winter, and Zollin had noticed his body changing. He was still thin, despite his ravenous appetite, but he had begun to develop some pronounced muscle tone in his chest, arms, and shoulders. He was still nothing like Mansel, whose constant sword practice had hardened the bulky muscles he already had so that he looked like he could burst the seams of his shirt with one flex. But the changes in his physical body had at least corresponded to the changes in his magic. He felt stronger, smarter, and more in control. He no longer needed his staff, but he still carried it whenever he left the cabin. It felt more like an old friend than a tool. The staff may have been dead wood, but the magic it contained was real enough.

It may not have been alive in the same sense that Zollin was alive, but it certainly had a will and reacted to his emotions.

He had already packed his things into a small pack that could be slung over his shoulder. He didn't have much. Some clothes, although he wore the outfit that Brianna had made him practically every day. He had the pathfinder that his father had given him for his birthday and the medallion that he had bought at Tranaugh Shire. He'd given away the other things he'd made using his magic. The curved daggers had been sold, the gold hidden away by Kelvich. He wasn't sure if was more anxious to leave Brighton's Gate because of the dread he felt about the wizards approaching, or just to spend more time with Brianna.

He'd found peace over his guilt. Todrek's death had wounded Zollin deep in his soul, but Brianna was free now to make decisions about who she wanted to be with. He'd tried his hardest to distance himself from her, and thereby honor his friend, but she had not been deterred. She liked him, as absolutely unbelievable as that sounded to Zollin, he had to admit that it was true. He wanted to be with her, the truth was that he had always wanted it, but now he was willing to allow it. He had fallen in love with her, and not just because of her beauty. She was strong in a way that he had never known before. She was courageous in the face of danger and adventurous, with an openness to any new challenge. They had shared a few moments together since the attack by the Skellmarian's, but none as long or as satisfying as the night the assassins had come. He was anxious to be alone with her again, to look into her eyes by firelight, to lie side by side and stare up at the sky, sharing their hopes and dreams.

He could feel his magic hum as he thought of it. It was as if the magic mirrored his emotions, sometimes giving them a much needed outlet and at other times magnifying them. There was so much he didn't know about his power, despite the fact that he had learned so much. He had refined his defensive spells and honed his reflexes so that he could throw up a magic shield in an instant. He could feel physical projectiles, such as a knife or even an arrow, and deflect their flight with just a thought. Every object around him became a weapon. He could ignite the air around him, channel lightning through his body, transmute practically any substance, and lower temperatures to below freezing. He could heal wounds in humans and in animals. He had learned about magical plants and how to identify the magical properties of minerals. His medallion was the sole exception. Whenever he delved into its depths, all he could feel was darkness. Kelvich had refused to help him discover the mysterious object's true nature.

His mind swirled with all these thoughts as he waited for people to return. Brianna and Kelvich had gone to town to fetch the other horse and pack up what little belongings they had. They also needed supplies for their journey. They would be leaving Brighton's Gate abruptly, and there would be no time to collect what they needed once they had confronted the wizards. Zollin didn't know exactly what to expect from the confrontation. It was possible that with Kelvich, they could turn the tables on the wizards so quickly that the sinister agents of the Torr would simply surrender, but Zollin doubted it. He knew from experience that magical battles were not easy, but he felt confident that he could do much better than before. He knew what he was doing now and had more control over his growing power. It was exciting, although he told himself repeatedly that the approaching confrontation was no game.

He was too anxious to sit around and wait any longer. He decided to go on a quick hunt. Many of the animals that had hibernated through the winter were stirring now. It only took a short walk into the woods that surrounded Kelvich's home before he could feel the movement of woodland creatures. He took his time and finally came upon two fat rabbits that were searching for food. He focused on thoughts of drowsiness and pushed them toward the two small animals. He also gave them a sense of safety and security. They were soon asleep, and he lifted them into the air with his magic. He could feel an unwelcome desire creeping up through the hot wind of magic. He could crush their skulls, or block their tiny windpipes so that they suffocated. He had to push the cruelty away. He'd found that it was much easier to control when he wasn't emotionally charged, but the giddy sense of power that arose whenever he used his magic was always there, just under the surface, as if it were searching for a breach in his control to exploit.

He took hold of the rabbits that he had levitated. They were still asleep and never felt the razor sharp knife that opened their throats. He returned to the cabin and skinned the animals, which were a bit on the lean side after the long months of winter. He cut the meat off the bones and made a stew with potatoes, onions, carrots, and celery. Kelvich had herbs, which Zollin used to give the stew a savory flavor. He could still feel the presence of the approaching wizards, but cooking the meal gave him something to focus his mind on. His mouth was watering, and he had just about decided to eat alone when he heard horses approaching. He stepped out on the small, covered porch and saw Kelvich and Brianna dismounting. He hurried to help them with their packs, but the sorcerer waved him off.

"We'll leave them for now," Kelvich said. "No sense unpacking these items just to have to repack them again when we leave. Any word from your father?"

"No, he and Mansel haven't returned yet."

"Well, it shouldn't be too long. They won't be able to do much scouting in the dark."

"I've got a stew on," Zollin said. He was talking to Brianna, but Kelvich replied.

"That sounds great. I'm famished. Let's eat."

* * *

Quinn had spotted the smoke from the campfire before they were close enough to be seen by the wizards. He and Mansel had tethered their horses and made their way stealthily toward the camp. They were now laying flat on a small rise where they could see the camp on its small hill. They had watched the wizards for some time, noting the body of the slain horse, which their servants had slaughtered downwind of the camp. They had also carried off what looked like a man's body. Nothing else of importance had occurred, and they were about to head back to the little cabin in the woods when the officers on horseback came into view.

"Who do you suppose they are?" Mansel asked.

"I don't know," Quinn said. "We're too far out, and I can't really see the arms on their banners. But it's safe to say they're leading a war band."

"A war band? Why?"

"Can't say," Quinn said thoughtfully. "Perhaps for us. At this point that wouldn't surprise me."

"I don't think we can take on a full war band," Mansel said in frustration.

"No, we can't. We need to see what these riders do and if they have more men with them."

They waited as the riders made their way toward the hill where the wizards were camped. Soon they saw the armored cavalry. The riders began to spread out, looking for dry places to pitch their tents for the night.

"How many would you say?" Mansel asked.

"I don't know. It looks like a full regimen. I can't imagine why there would be that many heavy horses here."

"How many are in a regimen?"

"One hundred."

Mansel was silent after that. Just watching the heavily armed men moving around on their horses made him nervous. Running from a small band of mercenaries had been frightening enough. He couldn't help but think of his encounter in the woods. He'd been wounded by the mercenary's horse, but he'd survived. Still, he remembered how defenseless he felt as the soldier toyed with him. He had no desire to repeat that experience.

"Oh damn!" Quinn said under his breath.

The foot soldiers were coming into view. They could hear the sound of their marching as the soldiers came slowly up the road that ran parallel to the river.

"There's more?" Mansel said in surprise.

"That's no war band, that's a full army legion," Quinn said grimly. "There'll be archers next and then the supply train."

He was right, and they stayed until after dark, watching the soldiers make their camp. They spread all across the valley, their dirty, little tents popping up like mushrooms. They made fires from the damp wood they collected from the forest. The smoke soon settled in all around them like a thick fog.

"What do we do now?" Mansel said.

"One of us needs to stay and see what they do tomorrow. They're close enough to Brighton's Gate that they won't break this camp. They may move against the town, but I just don't know. I simply can't imagine why so many men are here, it doesn't make any sense."

"What do we do?"

"I don't know," Quinn said honestly. "We can't fight an army. We need to regroup and make a new plan."

"Alright, then, I'll stay," Mansel said. "You need to talk to the others and decide what our next move is. Besides, I'm not sure I can find my way back to the cabin in the dark."

"Okay, but be careful. Don't do anything that would draw attention to yourself. Make a small fire well out of sight of the army. You need to be able to see if anyone approaches the town tonight. If they do, ride to us immediately. Just shout when you get close to Kelvich's cottage. We don't need any surprises. You think you can stay awake all night?"

"Yes," Mansel said. "You can count on me."

"I am," Quinn said. "Be careful. If something happens, don't try to fight. Run. We need you alive, understand?"

"Yes, sir."

They crawled off the hill they had been spying from and hurried to their horses. Quinn gave Mansel all of his extra rations. Then he set off for the little cabin in the woods.

Chapter 11

They had settled around the fire and had their first bowls of stew as night fell. Brianna looked tired, and Zollin felt for her. He wished he could do more, but the warm stew was all he had. Everyone was too nervous waiting for Quinn to return to carry on an actual conversation. As the night dragged on, Zollin began to pace. Kelvich dozed fitfully in his rocking chair. Brianna stared into the fire.

"What could be taking them so bloody long?" Zollin wondered aloud.

"I'm sure they're fine."

"They've run into something they didn't expect," he said. "I should have gone with them."

"If you had, we'd just be sitting here worrying about you."

"I could have protected them," he argued.

"Quinn and Mansel can take care of themselves. Our highest priority is to keep you safe."

Zollin's pride boiled at that thought. They were all endangering their lives because of him. He didn't know what he would do if something bad happened to Brianna, just the thought of it made the magic inside of him almost uncontrollable. He was still pacing when they heard a horse come galloping up to the cabin.

Zollin and Brianna rushed to the door, and Kelvich staggered to his feet. The light from the cabin spilled out into the darkness and illuminated Quinn's pained expression.

"Is Mansel okay?" Brianna said, searching the darkness for a second rider.

"He's fine, but we have a big problem."

"Come in," Kelvich said. "Zollin, get your father a bowl of stew. Brianna, get the ale."

Kelvich had a small keg of ale, Brianna hurried to find a cup. Quinn came in and slumped into a chair by the fire.

"We found the wizards," Quinn said. "They're camped about an hour's hard ride down the valley. But they aren't alone. They have a full King's Legion with them."

"A legion?" Kelvich said in surprise.

"That's right. There's no way we can fight them. We need a new plan."

"Are you sure the soldiers are with the wizards?" Kelvich asked.

"Positive," Quinn said around a mouthful of stew. "The officers are camped with them. I can't imagine why they're here."

"Zollin," Kelvich said matter-of-factly. "In the days before the Torr, every kingdom had a wizard to supplement its army. A powerful wizard would be a huge asset to any of the Five Kingdoms."

"Well, I have no intention of seeing Zollin become a slave to a war mongering king," Quinn said angrily.

"What do we do?" Brianna asked.

"Nothing has changed," Kelvich said.

"Are you out of your mind?" Quinn asked. "Everything has changed. We can't take on the wizards with an army supporting them."

"And we can't hide from them either," Kelvich said.

"I could surrender myself-"

"No!" Kelvich and Quinn shouted at the same time.

"Don't you see that there is more to this than just you, Zollin?" Brianna said. "I don't understand it all, but one thing is clear. You cannot allow these men to take control of you. They obviously think that you will be able to do something that is vastly important to them. We've already seen that they are wicked and cruel, you can't add your power to theirs."

"But if I don't, you could all be killed," he said.

"Never give up before the battle is over," Kelvich said. "We don't know what they will do yet, so we'll have to wait and see. We'll all take our chances and look for a way to escape."

"I expect they will stay where they are and send a delegation to Brighton's Gate," Quinn said. "They'll demand the town turn us over to them and then use us to get Zollin to surrender himself."

"That's a good plan," Kelvich said. "The people of the Gate won't hesitate to throw you to the wolves. They'll be glad to be rid of you, I would expect."

"Ungrateful bastards," Zollin said angrily.

"Zollin!" Quinn said.

"Don't let your emotions get the best of you, my boy," Kelvich said. "Desperate times call for cool heads and good decisions. Let's see what the army wants, then we'll know what we can do."

"I think Brianna and Quinn should hide in the woods," Zollin said.

"No way!" Brianna said loudly.

"That won't help," said Quinn. "She's just as safe here in the cabin as she would be alone in the woods."

"But the townspeople might come here looking for her," Zollin said.

"And if that happens, we'll deal with it," Quinn said.

"I can take care of myself," Brianna said.

"All of this is wasted emotion," Kelvich said. "We should get some rest. Tomorrow we'll know what we should do."

"I'll keep first watch," Zollin said. "I don't think I can sleep right now anyway."

"Alright," Quinn said. "Mansel is keeping an eye on the army. If they send people into town tonight, he'll let us know. If he hasn't come in by morning, I want to be back out where I can keep an eye on the army at first light."

"I'll take the second watch," Brianna said.

"And I'll take the third. I'll wake you an hour before dawn," Kelvich assured Quinn.

They all settled down for the night. Quinn and Brianna stretched out by the fire. Kelvich retired to his small bed. Zollin went outside, letting his eyes adjust to the dim light of the starry sky that filtered down through the tall pines and cedar trees. It was cold out, but his emotions, which were agitating his magic, heated him from the inside out. He couldn't sleep anyway, so being on watch suited his mood. After an hour or so, he heard the door open and saw Brianna step outside with a blanket wrapped around her shoulders.

"It's not time for your watch yet," Zollin whispered to her.

"I know, but I can't sleep," she whispered back. "Do you mind if I join you?"

He shook his head. Brianna crept out to the side of the porch were Zollin was leaning against one of the support posts. She stood close, shoulder to shoulder with him, a fact which Zollin was very aware of. He liked being close to Brianna. She had a way of calming him simply by being close.

"Aren't you cold?" she asked quietly.

"I've got my heavy cloak on," he whispered. "But the magic is also pretty hot, so I stay comfortable. I'm worried about you though."

"I'll be okay," she said, although she was already shivering. The snow was melting steadily each day. There was none on the trees, and the only snow in the valley was in the places that didn't get much sunshine. But at night the temperature still plummeted well below freezing.

Zollin bent down and picked up two rocks, each about the size of a chicken egg. He concentrated on the movement of the rocks' tiny particles. They were in constant movement, but as he focused his mind, he felt the magic flow into the rocks, felt the particles speed up and produce heat. He handed the rocks to Brianna.

"These should keep your hands warm for a little while," he said. "Let me know if they get cold again."

The warm rocks felt heavenly in the freezing night air. She held them close to her chest and could feel their heat through her clothes, warming her skin.

"Thank you," she said sweetly. "You take good care of me."

"It's the least that you deserve. You should be in a castle, with the finest clothes and food. And servants to wait on you hand and foot."

"No I don't," she said. "You say the strangest things."

"Well, that's the way I see it."

"There's nowhere else I'd rather be right now than here with you," she said.

"Even though it's freezing?"

"I'm not cold, thanks to you."

Zollin felt his own temperature rise. What he really wanted to do was take her in his arms and kiss her. Not that he had the first clue how to do that, but it seemed like the natural thing to do. Still, he knew that if he got distracted, she could be hurt, even killed. He focused on the forest around them, letting his perception flow out so that he could sense every creature around them. They settled into a comfortable silence as the night wore on.

* * *

Across the river, just out of sight in the foothills, another army was camped. This one had no fires, no horses, no little tents to shelter in. They were big men, and even some women, all wrapped in thick, furry hides, and many huddled together for warmth. Toag was the High Chieftain, and he stood on the crown of the hill that hid the army from the town of Brighton's Gate. He was a massive man, with thick arms and a barrel shaped chest. His long beard hung down like a curtain over his chest, and he had a large, white, bear skin wrapped around him.

"We're ready," said the man who had come up behind him. The man was shorter and had a thick brow ridge. His hair, what little was left of it, was dirty grey and hung far down his back.

"Is the bridge ready, Bozar?" Toag asked.

"It is, Great One."

"Good, I want to crush this little village and feast on their blood at first light."

"As you wish, Great One."

They stood in silence; the great chief of the Skellmarians was accustomed to the night and to the cold. They were like old friends who were there to visit and encourage the warlord before his conquest. Toag had ambitions, not like the last High Chieftain, who was shrewd and cruel, but content to let the southern infidels, with their lonely god, grow rich and fat. Toag had slain the High Chieftain to take the man's position and had immediately sent raiding clans south through the mountains. All had returned, save one. Skollack's clan had been almost wiped out. Those that returned told stories of a devil who had cracked the ice and drowned their kin in the icy waters. Toag hoped to find this devil and sacrifice him to Quotar, the High Mountain God, who had sent them the sign of the dragon. Success was assured, but whether Toag could find the devil was still to be seen.

"The wives await you, Great One," Bozar said at last, shaking Toag from his visions of conquest and blood.

"May your blood run hot," Toag said to his companion.

"And yours, Great Chief."

Toag returned to where his people lay resting before the battle. Most were already asleep, but sentries had been posted. Toag doubted that the infidels even knew they were coming; he'd made sure their sentries did not survive to send word back to the village. Once Toag had Brighton's Gate for his base of operations, he could raid south through the pass and grow fat on the blood of the southerons. Their lonely god would not save them from the Skellmarian's strong arm.

He approached what passed for his pavilion. There were two large casks of fermented goat's milk and huddled on the ground were no less than 10 of his wives. He kept them well fed, and their naked bodies would warm his blood before battle.

He pulled off his clothes and draped them over the women, then burrowed into the middle of the little crowd. They were warm and huddled even closer to him. He followed the ancient custom of abstinence before battle and closed his eyes. He was the

High Chieftain of the Skellmarians, and tomorrow he would become the scourge of the Great Valley and beyond.

Chapter 12

The third watch came early for Kelvich; he had grown accustomed to sleeping late in a soft bed. Isolation suited the sorcerer, but he knew that Zollin's coming was no accident. He would not leave the boy on his own, even if going with him meant death. For too long he had hidden himself away, fearful of the Torr, but now there was a chance that everything could change. He could feel the world waking up around him, feel the power of magic growing in the land once more. He needed to be part of that, and so he would go with Zollin, wherever their road took them. If that meant waking in the wee hours of the morning to stand watch, so be it.

Brianna had gently shaken him awake, now she lay stretched before the fire, wrapped in a long blanket. When Kelvich stepped outside, the cold air was like a slap in the face. It was bitterly cold with a northern wind that rushed up the valley and chilled his bones. At least he wouldn't have any problems staying awake, he told himself. That was one good thing about the cold. Zollin was waiting outside to be relieved.

"Why didn't you go in after your watch?" Kelvich asked.

"I'm too keyed up to sleep."

"You should get rest whenever you can; you never know when you might not have that chance again."

"I'll try," he said, stretching. "You want me to warm some stones for you?"

"No, the cold will help me stay awake."

"Should I wake my father?"

"No, not yet. I'll wake him an hour or so before dawn. Judging by the position of the moon, there's a couple hours before that still."

"Alright, if you get tired come get me. I'll stand watch with you," Zollin said.

Kelvich nodded. He'd been having a nightmare when he was woken up. He didn't remember the dream, just the sense of fear and foreboding that had lingered. Now he sensed that fear again, only more strongly than before. It was as if there was something palpable in the air that foretold of something ominous. The elderly sorcerer assumed that his dread was because of the danger they were in. It was a feeling he would have to get used to. He knew that while Zollin's power was a wondrous thing, it also made him a target. He would be hounded and hunted all his days. People would manipulate him and use him, always striving to control him and use his abilities for their personal gain. He was glad that Zollin had people around him that loved him and knew him as a person first, not just as a wizard.

A magical life may seem wonderful and full of adventure in a bedtime story, but the reality was a lonely existence. Zollin needed to survive the dangers he faced and remain independent, his magic allowed to grow and revive the magic of the world around him. He needed to move through the Five Kingdoms, bringing life back to the world. He couldn't do that with the Torr hounding his every step. He would have to be strong, to resist the urge to give into the bribes and seduction of the rich and powerful. He would be the flame that draws every magical creature, good and bad, from their place of hiding and into the world. He would need help, and Kelvich was determined to give him all he had.

The moon was dropping rapidly toward the mountains, and Kelvich watched it descend. He was cold and his bones ached from it, but it kept him alert. Not that there was really anything to be afraid of. Mansel was watching the army, Zollin would feel the Torr wizards approaching. The townspeople were blissfully unaware of the precarious position they were in. Kelvich envied them their ignorance. He had often wished that he could have been normal, just living a single lifetime, but that one life filled with love and happiness. Of course, he was wise enough to know that no life is without trials and hardships, but the thought of having a family, a loving wife, children, even grandchildren, was a happy thought.

Once the moon had disappeared behind the northern mountains, Kelvich went inside and started heating water over the coals. He wanted some hot coffee, and Quinn probably would, too. He went back outside to check everything, but it was dark and quiet. It seemed that even the forest creatures had finally taken to their beds.

"I'm the only one foolish enough to be awake at this hour," he said quietly.

He went into his little shed, where they had stabled the horses. They had all left their gear on, but the girth straps had been loosened so the horses could rest comfortably. None of them seemed to be asleep when Kelvich came inside. It was cold in the little shed, but the horses' body heat kept the cold to a tolerable level. Kelvich rubbed down Quinn's horse and then tightened the saddle, before leading it out to the front porch. The horse snorted in the cold air, its breath puffing little clouds around his head. Kelvich lashed the horse to the front porch post and went back inside. He gently shook Quinn awake, then poured a large basin of water for the carpenter to wash in. While Quinn splashed the cold water on his face, Kelvich quietly made coffee. He poured himself a large cup and then put the rest in a metal flask. He then wrapped the flask in wool. He also sliced some bread and apples.

"It isn't much," he whispered to Quinn. "But the coffee's hot."

"Good, that's enough for me. I haven't had coffee in ages."

"It's hard to come by," Kelvich agreed. "Especially this far north. Hopefully it'll give us both a little pep in our step today."

"Aye," Quinn agreed. "I'll be back as soon as we determine what the army is going to do. Have these two up and ready."

"Sure, no problem."

"And pack any more of that coffee, if you've got it."

"Already done," Kelvich said with a smile. "Be safe."

Quinn nodded and then headed outside. The cold was waiting for him, searing any exposed flesh it could find. He wrapped his cloak tightly around him as he settled into the saddle of his horse. He took the reins in one hand, and the flask of coffee in the other, before setting off through the woods. He rode as swiftly as he dared in the darkness. The stars were mere pinpricks in the heavens above him, giving no light to the road he was trying to find through the woods and out of Brighton's Gate.

The coffee warmed him as he rode, and he was truly grateful for it. He'd gotten used to the warm bed in the Valley Inn and forgotten just how cold it was out on the trail at dawn. When he finally found Mansel's camp, there was just a hint of lightening to the sky.

"Anything?" Quinn asked his apprentice.

"Nothing, they haven't left camp yet. But they're forming up. I was just getting ready to ride out and find you."

"Who is forming up?" Quinn asked.

"Everyone."

"The entire legion?" he asked.

"Yes, they've been taking positions and getting ready to march."

"Good God, they're moving on the town. We've got to go. Come on."

They rode through the gloom just prior to dawn, but they weren't the only ones.

* * *

Toag rose early. He had hardly slept, he was just too excited. He'd led his own clan on many raids, but this was no raid. This was an invasion by a Skellmarian army, and it hadn't been seen in his lifetime. He met with the other clan leaders. His plan was simple. They had constructed a narrow bridge, not much more than a reinforced, plank walkway, wide enough for one man at a time. Toag doubted that it would hold his own weight, certainly not two men at once. One clan would take the bridge upriver, where it would reach safely from bank to bank and where they would be safe from the sight of the townspeople. The clan would cross and make their way back downriver, take control of the drawbridge, and lower it so that the rest of the army could cross. They would then invade the town. It was a solid plan, but it all hinged on the clan that was chosen to make the initial crossing. He needed men with the unique combination of strength, intelligence, and small stature. He and his army would be trapped on this side of the river if the crossing clan failed. They might risk the freezing waters, but the current was too swift with snow melt-off for them to risk it. They might lose as many as half of their strength just trying to get across the river, and they would all be washed far downstream. The crossing clan was their only chance.

Toag looked at his clan leaders before making the announcement. They all looked anxious to be chosen, but he had already made up his mind. The rest would have to win glory through battle.

"Ruggle Clan," he said. "You are chosen."

"Ruggle Clan will make you proud, Great One!"

"Good, we will wait for you to lower the bridge, then we will begin our conquest. May your blood run hot!"

"May your blood run hot!" echoed the other chieftains.

"Go, prepare your clans," Toag ordered. "Our time has come!"

* * *

As dawn broke over the mountains, three things happened at once. First, Zollin awoke to the realization that the wizards from the Torr were on the move. He and Brianna hurriedly readied themselves and, with Kelvich in the lead, they began making their way toward town. They didn't want to reveal themselves, but they knew something was happening and they didn't want to be caught waiting around when it did.

Second, the King's Legion, led by Branock and Whytlethane, marched on the town of Brighton's Gate. Branock had every intention of bringing Zollin under his control, but he also needed to eliminate his rival. He'd given Orbruk secret orders to have his archers fire on Whytlethane at Branock's signal. If the arrows didn't get past the elderly wizard, Branock planned to use the distraction to kill him personally.

Meanwhile, the Ruggle Clan used the bright, spring sunlight to ensure they made it across the river safely. There were twelve men in all, each with a curved, short sword and a small pick axe. They moved swiftly, but silently, toward Brighton's Gate, where the townspeople were just starting to stir from their homes. Fires were being kindled and breakfasts were started.

Zollin, Kelvich, and Brianna had just caught sight of Quinn and Mansel when the first of the Skellmarians came within sight of the drawbridge. It was guarded, one of Quinn's ideas that the town hadn't neglected yet, but the two men on duty were half asleep and totally unaware of the threat. The Skellmarians waited until the entire clan was in position and then slowly started moving toward the bridge.

"What are you doing here?" Quinn asked.

"I felt the wizards moving," Zollin said. "We couldn't wait."

"It's not just the wizards," Mansel added. "The whole army is marching."

"What are we going to do?" Brianna asked; Zollin couldn't determine if she sounded fearful or excited.

"If we sneak away, the wizards will know it and the town will be totally defenseless," Kelvich said. "They don't deserve that, even if they haven't been honorable."

"I agree," said Quinn. "But I don't want to move into a position where we might be trapped or cut off, either."

"Then we should ride down," Zollin said. "Wait for the army before they get to the town."

"No, we'll be trapped there," said Quinn. "We need better ground if we're going to make a stand."

"What if we cross the river?" suggested Brianna. "We can negotiate from a position that makes a big part of their army useless."

"That's a good idea," said Quinn. "We can reveal ourselves and still have a good escape route if they won't see reason."

"And if they still attack the town?" Kelvich asked.

"Why would they?"

"To force Zollin to surrender."

"If we ride away," Brianna suggested, "and pretend not to care about Brighton's Gate, they'll have to decide between killing their own people and pursuing us. We can't fight an entire army, and it might be the best way to ensure the town's safety."

"I don't have any better ideas," Kelvich said.

"Alright, let's go," Quinn agreed.

They rode swiftly toward the town, but at the same time the Skellmarians attacked the guards at the drawbridge. They crept toward the unsuspecting men and stabbed them from behind, covering their mouths as they fell so that it was an almost silent attack. The remaining clan members spread out to protect the two who were trying to figure out how to lower the bridge. Quinn and the others rode swiftly through the town, their horses kicking up mud and causing curious townsfolk to peek out their windows.

The Skellmarians had just begun lowering the bridge when Zollin and the others rode into view. They pulled their horses to a sudden stop in shocked disbelief, not only at the shaggy barbarians lowering the drawbridge, but at the army of Skellmarians that was forming up on the far bank.

"We've got to stop them!" Quinn shouted.

He spurred his horse forward just as the other ten Skellmarians charged forward. Quinn reined back on his horse hard, causing the beast to rear suddenly. Quinn toppled out of the saddle and fell into the muddy street. Zollin was about to stop the drawbridge from lowering when he realized his father was in trouble. He had to decide between saving Quinn and stopping the drawbridge. He didn't hesitate, but released the flaming magic within him and lifted his father out of the road. Mansel and Brianna were ready, with arrows nocked and drawn. As soon as Quinn was clear, they shot the two leading Skellmarians. The others didn't hesitate, but jumped over their companions and continued forward. Brianna had just nocked another arrow to her string when Zollin set Quinn down on her horse just behind her. She fired her second arrow, which found a home in a Skellmarian's leg, then turned her horse. The others followed her, racing back to the town, shouting a warning to the people as they rode.

The bridge was down now, and the Skellmarians were swarming over, their battle cries echoing off the mountains.

"Zollin, see if you can slow them down," Quinn yelled. "Mansel, ride out to the army. They have to know the town is under attack."

Mansel angled his horse away from the main street that ran north and south through the little town. He whipped the reins and shouted for the tired horse to run faster. Quinn and Kelvich began shouting for the townspeople to take up arms. They needed to hold back the advancing horde until the army could arrive. It might take several minutes before they got any relief, and although the drawbridge was narrower than the original structure, it would only take a few moments before the entire war host was across the river and advancing on the town.

Zollin slid off of his horse and raised his staff over his head. Lightning cracked and popped up and down his arms and body, before shooting out and blasting three of the Ruggle clansmen off their feet. The other four stopped for a moment, pondering whether attacking was the right idea, while their chieftain ran past them, bellowing a war cry. Zollin lifted the man high into the air and then set him ablaze. The clan leader screamed in agony, a high pitched warble that made the barbarians' blood run cold. Then came Toag, shouting encouragement to his hesitating army before throwing a pick axe with all his might. It arced over the Ruggle Clan, who were frozen in the street, watching their clan leader burning to death in the air above them.

Zollin saw the ax and deflected it easily enough, but the act of valor had restarted the Skellmarians' courage. They resumed their charge. Zollin dropped the flaming Ruggle chief on top of his clansmen and then turned and hurried back into town. Archers had taken position and were shooting arrows toward the barbarians, but at extreme range there was no way to take good aim. Quinn was busy lining everyone up. The women, with their bows, behind the men, who were firing longbows, but also had swords and axes.

The road on either side of the bridge was open ground, muddy, but passable. The barbarians spread out, shouting and taunting the townspeople. There were almost two thousand Skellmarians. They all wore shaggy animal skins, their faces dark with dirt and oil, their weapons of choice curved swords of varying size and ice picks that were more climbing tool than weapon. They had no shields, but the thick hides they wore would stop an arrow unless it was fired directly at a specific target and from fairly short range, as Brianna's and Mansel's had been.

"Hold your fire!" Quinn shouted. He was limping from his fall, but he was still moving. He had his sword in hand and was standing in front of the town's defenders. "The King's army is near," he shouted. "You only need hold them off for a few minutes. Hold your fire until they are closer and aim true. Wait until I give the order, and perhaps we can push back their first charge and give the army time to arrive."

The townsfolk were murmuring as Zollin hurried back up to his father. Brianna had taken up position with the other women, behind the men, but she had her bow ready, an arrow nocked and a determined look on her face.

"Zollin, we have to find the wizards," Kelvich said.

"But we can't leave these people."

"We've done all we can for them. We can't let you be taken unaware."

"Alright," Zollin admitted.

He gave Brianna one last look, and she nodded at him. Then he ran after Kelvich.

* * *

Mansel saw the army marching slowly ahead. The town was blocking their view of the Skellmarians. He galloped toward the group of riders with long lances and banners flapping in the morning wind. He was waving one arm and shouting at them. They did not respond until he came to a skidding halt a few feet away from them.

"The Skellmarians are attacking!" he shouted.

"What? Where?" demanded Orbruk. He was a big man, with a curly, black beard and a puckered scar on his cheek that cut through the whiskers to his chin.

"On the far side of the town," Mansel explained. "It's an entire army."

"A raiding party more like," Orbruk said in haughty tone. "Billips!"

"Yes, sir!" said one of the other knights.

"Take charge of the legion. I shall take a few of the cavalry and mop up this rabble."

"But, sir, there are hundreds of them!" Mansel said in shock.

"Oh yes, I'm sure, the hills are alive with them," Orbruk said with a sneer. "Carry on, Billips."

Orbruk spurred his horse forward and turned down the line of soldiers. Mansel followed. When they reached the cavalry division, Orburk called out several names, seven in all. They fell in behind their leader and galloped toward the town. Mansel tried to keep up, but his horse was simply too tired and he fell behind. When the knights rounded the buildings on the outskirts of town, they found over a hundred Skellmarians moving to flank the town's defenders. The two groups were surprised, and while the mounted soldiers were able to cut down three times as many Skellmarians, they were quickly overwhelmed.

Mansel wanted to ride to their aid, but he could see that it was suicide. Orbruk was hacking furiously with his long sword, but the Skellmarians were smart enough to fall back, first on one side and then the other. One group feinted forward, while the group on the opposite side attacked. They caught the knight unaware. Some grabbed him and began pulling him down from his horse. Another hacked the horse's neck, sending the animal crashing forward to the ground. The barbarians didn't hesitate, even though Mansel heard the knight calling for mercy. They slammed their curved blades under the plates of armor again and again. They were totally caught up in the blood lust and, after hacking the bodies of the soldiers to pieces, they looked up for their next foe. Mansel rode along the edge of the group of

Skellmarians, using his sword deftly, and taking full advantage of his horse's momentum, both to give strength to his blows and to actually trample down two of the barbarians. Then he turned and galloped back toward the army. The enraged Skellmarians followed him, and the army at last saw their foe.

"Left wheel turn!" ordered Billips. "Sound the charge for the cavalry!"

The other officers were shouting orders, and the army began to turn. They were slow, too slow to make much difference to the villagers, Mansel saw. But the mounted soldiers were riding to his aid at last. Several galloped past him, cutting into the thinning group of Skellmarians, who at last turned back toward their war host.

"What has happened?" cried one of the soldiers.

"There are hundreds of Skellmarians attacking the village right now," Mansel shouted at the man.

"Where is Orbruk?"

"Dead!" Mansel told him in a grim voice. "And all the villagers will be, too, if you don't do something."

"Fin, Lorek, scout the situation, but don't engage," the man ordered.

"You have to hurry!" Mansel told him.

"I can't rush into a fight with no intelligence. We'll all be slaughtered."

It only took the scouts a few moments to return.

"The boy's right, Joren," said the one named Fin. "Biggest gathering of Skellmarians I've ever seen. Orbruk managed to disrupt the group flanking on this side, but if they sent another group to the far side, the townspeople will be slaughtered."

"Take the rest of the division and ride to the other side. If there is a flanking party, stop them. Otherwise hold your position until I arrive."

"Yes, sir," said the soldier, saluting. Then he snapped his visor shut and shouted for the other cavalry soldiers to follow him.

Mansel and Joren turned and rode back to the officers. Joren reported, and Billips gave orders for the foot soldiers. He sent five hundred into the town proper at double quick to protect the villagers. The other hundred and fifty were ordered to move toward the edge of the village where Orbruk had been killed. The archers followed the smaller group. Joren was sent with another knight to command the cavalry on the far flank. Once the foot soldiers were in place, the horsemen were to sweep them toward the other flank and smash them into the soldiers and archers. It would have been a good plan if there had only been a few hundred Skellmarians, but the legion was out numbered, and, by splitting their forces, they became even more vulnerable. Mansel turned his horse and rode as fast as he could back to the front line to report to Quinn.

Chapter 13

Branock had wasted no time once the report of the Skellmarians came in. He spurred his horse forward to find Zollin. He could feel the boy's power; it was as potent as freshly cut hay in summer time. Whytlethane followed him, and they made their way into the town proper. They were well back from the line of defense set up by the villagers when they came upon their quarry.

Zollin was standing in the street. He had his staff in one hand, angled across his body. He was looking straight at the two wizards, who approached slowly. Kelvich was hidden in a small house, watching the scene from the window. He could tell the power of the bald wizard was greater than that of the elder wizard. Still, he waited to see what would happen before using his own unique magic to control the one closest to him.

"Zollin, we meet again," Branock said in a jovial voice. "You are looking well."

"I'm sorry I cannot say the same about you, Branock," Zollin replied.

"It is a drastic change, but not an unwelcome one, I assure you. Will you come with us? We really must insist that you do."

"Never," Zollin replied coolly.

"Must it come to blows? I mean, really, you can't honestly hope to destroy us both."

"Turn and ride away—or, better yet, help the people here. I have no wish to fight you," Zollin said.

"You will come with us, boy, or I will destroy you," Whytlethane said angrily. "I grow tired of your prattling on as if you were an equal. We are wizards of the Torr, bow to us or die."

Zollin merely shook his head no; he could feel the power building up inside the elder wizard and, for an instant, he wondered if his defense would stand up to the magical blow he knew was coming. He had practiced with Kelvich, but the sorcerer couldn't replicate the power that these two wizards possessed.

"As you wish," said Whytlethane quietly.

"Whytlethane, don't!" shouted Branock, but it was too late.

The elder wizard held out his hand and produced a pillar of green plasma energy. It wasn't like the blue lightning of Zollin's staff, nor was it fire. It looked like molten lava, only the color was different. It was energy in a liquid form, and Zollin recognized it immediately, even though he'd never seen it before. His shield was up, an invisible barrier that separated him from the other wizards. The plasma hit the magical wall and was stopped cold. It spattered and burned whatever it touched before fading away.

Kelvich made his move, usurping Branock's control before the wizard knew what was happening. He raised his hand, attempting to levitate Whytlethane out of his saddle, but the elder wizard was ready. His defense caught the spell and sent Branock sprawling off of his horse. The animal reared, neighed loudly, and pawed the air before crashing back down. Its right hoof landed squarely on Branock's left arm, shattering the twin bones in his forearm. The pain sent Kelvich reeling backward. He tripped over a stool and fell, hitting his head on the thick edge of the wooden table and knocking himself out cold.

Branock was in shock at the pain, but he was in control of his body and magic once again. He didn't know if the controlling spell had been from Zollin or someone else, but he was able to disconnect his mind from the pain in his arm and scramble to his feet. He was dizzy and he staggered backwards.

Zollin had been watching and waiting for an opening in Whytlethane's attack. It didn't come; the elder wizard was focused and ready for anything. Zollin got the impression he'd been expecting Branock to attack him, and that's why Kelvich hadn't caught the wizard off guard. Whytlethane returned all his attention to Zollin, funneling more power into the plasma blast and driving Zollin back.

"You may be strong," Whytlethane said. "But you are no match for me, boy. I've trained for over a century. I'll find your weaknesses and exploit them."

"Fair enough," said Zollin. "But I still won't go with you."

He said the last words as he pushed back against the blast. His defensive spell was strong, but Whytlethane's offensive spell was made to drive his opponent back. It was unrelenting, and Zollin knew he couldn't overcome it straight on. He needed leverage, or an angle, to make it a fair fight. He moved toward the corner of the nearest house, but Whytlethane was ready for that move, too. He used his other hand and sent a blast of energy at the house, which burst like a clay pot dropped on a stone floor. The house shattered, and the force knocked Zollin back into the street. His defensive spell faltered for a second, but it was enough for Whytlethane to break through the magical barrier. Fortunately, the plasma wasn't quite on target, and Zollin did the last thing Whythlethane expected. He rolled forward, under the pillar of plasma energy, and began deflecting it at an angle, so that the beam ricocheted up into the air.

The force of deflecting the magic took much less energy, and Zollin was able to spook the elder wizard's horse. The animal reared, causing Whytlethane to break off his attack and grab desperately at the saddle horn and the horse's mane to keep from being thrown off. The horse kicked out, then hopped to the side, before wheeling around and running back out of town. Zollin saw Whytlethane lifting himself, magically, from the saddle, but then Branock was casting a spell at Zollin. It was wave of drowsiness, but Zollin shook it off quickly and sent a water pot flying at the wizard's head.

Whytlethane was stalking back down the street, and Zollin could no longer feel Kelvich. The older sorcerer hadn't winked out of existence, he had simply gone away. Zollin felt abandoned, it was as if his mentor had run away from the fight and left him all alone. He sent a blast of energy first at Whytlethane and then at Branock. Both blocked the spell, but it bought him some time. Branock was the stronger of the two wizards, but Zollin could feel the dull ache of pain radiating from him.

Whytlethane attacked again, but Zollin was ready this time, angling his defensive shield so that the green plasma bounced away from Zollin and toward Branock. The energy caught the wizard off guard; he was barely able to raise his own shield, and the shock of the blast knocked him off his feet. Unfortunately, it also set the house that Kelvich was unconscious in ablaze. Branock scrambled back to his feet as Zollin tried to sweep Whytlethane's feet out from under him, but the elder wizard was too canny. He deflected the clumsy attack easily enough.

"Branock, get in the fight!" Whytlethane shouted.

Branock was shaking his bald head to clear the cobwebs. He had been caught totally unaware, first by Kelvich and then by the horse who had trampled his arm. His body was going into shock, and he felt weak. He stumbled back, bracing himself against another house.

Whytlethane snarled and sent an invisible shove straight at Branock, who was just then stepping away from the stone wall of the home. The shove slammed Branock into the unyielding stone wall and knocked him unconscious. Zollin was startled by this turn of events, but Kelvich had told him that the other wizards were not to be trusted.

Whytlethane renewed his attack on Zollin, alternating blasts of energy with flying objects, levitating spells, and mental suggestions. Zollin batted each one aside, but he knew he needed to shift the momentum. Suddenly he caught a movement inside the burning house. Kelvich was coming to, but he was trapped by the fire. Zollin knew if he didn't act soon, his mentor would be killed.

Digging deep into his well of power, Zollin kicked up a layer of mud from the street. The mud and clay absorbed Whytlethane's blast and blocked Zollin from his sight for just a moment. It was the distraction Zollin needed. He dropped to his stomach and reached out with his magic. Whytlethane felt the surge of power from his foe speeding toward him and raised a powerful defensive shield in front of himself. But Zollin was reaching past the elder wizard. There were loose rocks and debris nearby, Zollin grabbed them and sent them hurtling into Whytlethane's unprotected back. One of the rocks slammed into the wizard's head and knocked him down. He was still awake, but the rock had cracked the wizard's skull.

Zollin rushed to the burning house and kicked in the door. It burst into smoking shards. The heat wave beat against Zollin and threatened to drive him backward, but he pushed against the heat with his magic. It was difficult, since the heat wasn't a solid object, it was like pushing water with his hands; it kept trickling through his defense and singeing him. Still, he pressed into the house. The roof was blazing and dropping flaming shards down all around the room. Zollin saw Kelvich on the floor and, using magic, pulled his friend out of the burning house. Kelvich was coughing from the smoke, his head, hands, back, and legs burned from the falling bits of timber raining down inside the house. But he was alive, and he looked up at Zollin though watery eyes, still coughing, but nodding that he was okay.

When Zollin looked up, he saw that Branock was nowhere to be seen, while Whytlethane was using all of his remaining strength to heal from the attack. His skull was already mending, and soon he would be back on his feet, perhaps even able to attack again. Zollin knew instinctively that he needed to stop Whytlethane, but he didn't relish the idea of killing a man who was at that moment incapacitated.

"Do it!" sputtered Kelvich. "If you don't, he'll try again."

Zollin walked over to the elderly wizard. There was blood matted in the long, grey hair. Several shards of wood had lodged in the wizard's back. It was actually a miracle that he was alive at all. Zollin touched Whytlethane with his staff and sent electrical energy shooting through the wizard's body until he felt the magic wink out. It made him sick, even more than seeing the body twitch and jerk and smoke from the attack. It was over, and for that Zollin was thankful. Then he felt a magical movement behind him, and he twirled, with his shields raised. The blast wasn't aimed at him, though; instead it hit his mentor and sent Kelvich sprawling in the mud.

Branock was back, Zollin saw. Only he wasn't alone.

* * *

The Skellmarians had waited patiently, ranged along the river, just out of bow range. Toag had sent two parties to circle around the line of defenders and attack from the rear. He could have pressed the attack and trusted in his numbers to defeat the townspeople, but they were armed with bows, and he knew that a frontal assault would cost him many warriors. He was as blood thirsty as any of his clansmen, but he was also smart. He wanted as many warriors to raid down the valley and through the pass into the rich southern lands as possible. If he could hold the town through until the next winter, it might be possible to entrench here and create a permanent stronghold to raid from year after year.

When his flanking clans failed to attack the town's defenders, he realized he was facing a larger force than he had expected. Still, he did not want to rush into a fight that he did not understand. His warriors were growing restless, but still he hesitated, not out of fear, but hoping for an advantage. Suddenly, the town's defenders fell back. The town seemed ripe for the taking, but to Toag it felt like a trick.

"They've fallen back to fight our clansmen," one of the warriors near Toag shouted, but there was no sign of fighting.

"We must attack!" screamed another.

"No!" shouted Toag. "It is a trap. There must be more horse soldiers in the town."

"We do not fear the horse!" shouted another warrior, and there were echoes and battle yells up and down the line of shaggy warriors.

Toag knew he was losing them. His only option now was to give his people what they wanted.

"Attack!" he bellowed.

The full Skellmarian force screamed and then charged forward.

Quinn saw them coming. He had moved back, past the King's army that was now shuffling through the buildings of the little town and taking up positions along the street. Their commander should have positioned them between the buildings, to nullify the Skellmarians' superior numbers, but there was nothing he could do. He needed to find Zollin and use the battle as a distraction to get his family out of Brighton's Gate.

The townspeople were afraid and confused. It was sad to see them so disorganized. They had held up well at the beginning, but as soon as the first of the soldiers arrived, they had retreated. Now he watched as the Skellmarian army ran across the empty ground. Arrows suddenly rained down from their right flank. Many were hit and fell screaming in the mud, but their companions kept running. The King's archers, positioned on the flank, had time for one more volley before the Skellmarians reached the town buildings and threw themselves against the army's shield wall.

Quinn moved quickly now, he had neither the time nor the authority to help stop the invasion. He searched desperately for anyone he recognized. Mansel had not returned from his errand, and Brianna was nowhere to be seen. Zollin and Kelvich had gone to confront the wizards, and Quinn guessed that Brianna had gone seeking his son. If he could find Zollin, he was sure to find the others as well.

He ran past several small homes, keeping his sword down so that he didn't accidentally hurt anyone. The noise from the battle, mixed with the panic of the townsfolk, made it impossible to hear anything. Quinn shouted for his son and for Brianna, but he could barely hear his own voice. He knew it was useless to keep shouting, but giving up simply wasn't in his nature. He had sent a young boy with his horse to the stable at the Valley Inn. If he could get there and get mounted, he'd be able to see, and be seen, better.

He hurried through the muddy streets. Brighton's Gate had two main streets. One ran north and south, from the bridge back to Telford's Pass and through the mountains. Crossing the first road was a major street that ran east and west through the heart of the Great Valley. Both inns were on this street, as well as several shops and a few homes. Scattered all around these buildings were homes, shops, storage sheds, animal pens, gardens, and wells. Quinn hurried through the maze of buildings and came to the inn from the rear. He made his way to the stable, which was shielded from the main street by the building of the inn.

Quinn ducked inside and found his horse, the mare that Brianna had been riding, and Kelvich's horse. They were still saddled, their reins tied to a support beam. The horses were nervous, shuffling around in the dark building. It occurred to Quinn that he should be nervous, too, a queer sense of dread had come over him, but he assumed it was just fear for Zollin and the others. Had he taken the time, he might have realized it was something more, but he was too intent on his task. He untied the reins of all three horses and led them outside. He climbed up into the saddle of his horse and led the other two. If Mansel had managed to stay with his horse, they could double up and get out of town. But even as Quinn was thinking through his options, there was a terrifying roar that rang out louder than the sounds of fighting, louder than the cries of panic. It echoed off the mountains and made the horses almost impossible to control. They bucked and pulled as the reins, almost unseating Quinn, but he quickly wrapped the reins around his saddle horn and turned his mount to face the mountains across the river. What he saw there stopped his blood cold.

Chapter 14

The dragon had watched the battle with interest from a high mountain peak. The cavalry sent to stop the flank attack had succeeded, but being caught between the buildings had reduced their advantage considerably. All but two dozen had been killed or dismounted. Horse flesh would be a nice contrast to the humans the dragon would consume. He would soon feast, but first he watched to see how the scene would play out. He had watched the magical battle with some interest, letting the waves of magical power wash over him and strengthen him. Wizards were powerful creatures, but working their magic only made the dragon stronger and very few of their spells had any effect on him. He had stretched his wings in anticipation of taking flight and raining down terror on the unsuspecting armies.

The shield wall of the southerners was breaking and being overcome by sheer numbers. The archers had fallen back, and the soldiers on the flank were now battling for their lives, as well. Gone unchecked, the dragon was sure that the shaggy men from the north would have won the day, but he had other plans. He wanted them all!

He roared out his intentions, it was a battle cry of sorts. It had an amazing effect on everyone, causing them to stop and stare. The dragon jumped high into the air and then rose higher as it flapped its leathery wings. Then it dove forward, racing down toward the valley, its mouth open wide, flames licking the sides of its scaly head. There were screams of panic and people began to run. Weapons were forgotten, enemies ignored, plunder left untouched in their need to escape the beast. The dragon's heart was filled to bursting with the panic he'd caused, and it was only the beginning. His reign of terror would stretch far and wide, across the desert and the ocean, filling everyone who saw him with fear. Fire shot from the dragon's gaping maw and set several buildings ablaze. Black smoke billowed into the air as the dragon made a long, looping turn.

The smell of burning flesh filled the dragon's nostrils and made his mouth water. His turn complete, he made a second dive toward the village. This time dropping low enough to snatch a fat man from the street. He felt the blood flood his mouth as his razor sharp teeth cut the man to ribbons. He sucked the juices before chewing the flesh and bones and then swallowing him down. It was succulent, but he didn't savor the man flesh. He didn't have to. They were spread out before him now, like food on a platter, waiting to be snatched up. He didn't hesitate, but dove again, this time snatching one with each talon while roasting several more with his fiery breath. As he rose in the air, he tossed up one screaming Skellmarian and then the other, snatching them out of the air with a striking motion, like a viper attacking its prey. He swallowed the people after only a few bites and then turned back for more.

* * *

Zollin couldn't believe what he was seeing. Branock had seemed so weak, so afraid and fragile, but now he stood straight and tall. His eyes were clear, and in front of him stood Brianna. She looked frightened and angry; Branock had his hand around her throat. His other hand was held out in front of him, palm facing Zollin. It was both a gesture of peace and a threat, since Zollin had seen Branock blast plumes of fire from his hands. His short staff was under his arm, and he was smiling, as if he knew something Zollin didn't.

"Now, you've done me a great service, and I'd like to repay the favor," Branock said. "You killed Whytlethane, which I had been planning to do for some time. So, why don't you come with me and learn real magic. That broken old man at your feet doesn't know anything, except how to manipulate and steal your power."

"He was strong enough to control you," Zollin said, his voice tight.

"Yes, and look at him now."

"Brianna, are you okay?"

She nodded, short, little bobs of her head, but it was enough. Zollin could see that Branock's knuckles were white, his long fingers digging unmercifully into her neck.

"If you hurt her, I'll kill you."

"Yes, I'm sure you would like that. I imagine your power pushes you in that direction. Don't let it rule you, Zollin. I can teach you to control it."

"Let her go, and you can leave the valley," Zollin said.

"You're in no position to make demands. I have what you want, not the other way around."

Zollin was stuck. He couldn't attack for risk of hurting Brianna. She still wore the white azure ring he'd given her, which should protect her from magic. Anything he tried to do to Branock would probably rebound onto himself, just as the Torr wizard's fire spell had done in Peddinggar forest. But there was a chance that the ring also rendered Branock powerless while he held onto Brianna. It was obvious that Branock had done some healing work on his arm, otherwise he couldn't have held it outstretched. But how good a job could he have done in such a short time. Zollin was betting that, at the very least, it was sore. If he could get

155

Brianna to hit the arm, Branock would probably release her and she could escape.

"How's the arm, Branock?"

The wizard only glared at him.

"His left arm is broken, Brianna," Zollin said.

"I healed it, you fool," Branock snarled.

"Get away from him as fast as you can. Don't stay between us."

"I'll kill her," he said bitterly. "I may not be able to hurt her with magic for some reason, but I can still snap her neck."

"With one hand?" Zollin said, having to shout now as the two armies collided not far away.

"That shows how little you know about magic, boy," Branock said, spitting the last word as if it were a curse. "I can boost my physical strength with a thought."

"Don't believe him, Brianna, he doesn't know what he's talking about it."

"Fool!" Branock screamed. His face was red, and Zollin could see blood vessels turning dark through the white skin of his bald head. "I've been a wizard of the Torr for over a hundred years. I will show you my power."

He started to squeeze, cutting off Brianna's air supply. She clawed at his right arm, the one holding her neck, but he only squeezed tighter.

"Shall I kill her now?"

"Hit his other arm!" Zollin shouted at her.

She lashed out, and Branock tried to avoid the clumsy blow, but he was holding her too close. Her hand slapped his forearm, and he cried out in pain, grimacing but not letting go of her.

"Hit him again!" Zollin screamed.

This time she hit his arm, which he was now holding at his side, with a solid blow. He released her neck and dropped to one knee, cradling his broken arm. Unfortunately, Brianna ran straight for Zollin. He snatched her up and turned his back to Branock, throwing up a shield around himself, Brianna, and Kelvich. The blast he expected didn't come. Just as he was turning around to face his opponent, the dragon roared. Like everyone else, Zollin turned to the mountains. What he saw staggered him like a body blow.

A great, red dragon was rising from a mountain top on huge, bat-like wings. It had a long neck, with a squarish head and what looked like small horns above each eye. The body was large and muscular, and the tail whipped back and forth behind the beast. Zollin watched it rise up and up, then turn and dive toward the village. It was traveling so fast there was hardly time to think.

"Inside!" Zollin shouted.

He grabbed Kelvich and half dragged the old sorcerer into the nearest building. It was the tailor's shop. There were neatly folded bolts of cloth and several garments in various stages of completion. Zollin didn't wait, but pulled Brianna and Kelvich through to the back of the shop and out the rear door. He turned to his right, heading toward the next building.

"Stay low," Kelvich croaked.

They ducked between the buildings and saw Quinn come riding out from around the Valley Inn. He was leading two other horses and towering above the townspeople and soldiers who were running for their lives.

"Dad!" Zollin screamed, but in the pandemonium, Quinn didn't hear him. "Dad get off the horse!"

Quinn used his heels to get the horses moving down the street. He hadn't seen Zollin or the others, but was looking frantically for them. The soldiers were in a panic, running over townspeople, dropping their shields and swords and running through the town toward the southern range of mountains. He maneuvered the horses through the throng, a bit surprised that no one was trying to get the other horses away from him.

The dragon was now behind Quinn, who didn't see it coming. It was swooping down, igniting the rooftops with fire and flying straight for Quinn and the horses. Zollin looked up and saw the beast closing in. There was no time to warn his father, even if his voice had been able to carry over the sounds of panic all around them. Instead he looked at Brianna so that she could read his lips, even if she couldn't hear what he was saying.

"Stay here," he screamed. "Stay safe!"

She nodded, taking hold of Kelvich, who was slumped against the wall of the nearest building, coughing uncontrollably. Zollin stepped out of the narrow space between the buildings and held up his staff. His first spell was an effort to knock the dragon off course. The magic inside of him was an inferno. His fear for his father's life seemed to feed the magical power, and he sent an invisible shove at the huge beast that nudged it off course a little. It wasn't enough to hurt the creature, but it did succeed in getting the dragon's attention.

The dragon felt the push, the magic power leached into him like a cool breeze on a hot summer day. The wizards had turned to him now, using their puny skills to try and scare him away. The chuckle that thought inspired brought a billow of black smoke from the dragon's nostrils. It was a frightful sight, and the dragon flapped its wings in a way that made the beast stall in mid air. It opened its mouth and belched out a plume of fire.

Zollin saw what was about to happen and sprinted away from the alley where Brianna and Kelvich waited. He knew he couldn't outrun the flames, but he wasn't sure how strong the force of the blast was going to be. He didn't want the fire to overlap his shield and burn Brianna or catch the buildings she was hidden between on fire. He slid to a stop in the mud and brought his staff up across his body, mimicking the magical shield he had thrown up between himself and the dragon. The fire rebounded up into the air.

The dragon was not surprised to see the wizard deflect his attack. In fact, the fire had been more of a distraction than an attempt to take the human out. Now, the wizard was in a fixed position though, hopefully too intent on his puny spell to notice the dragon's tail, which he was now whipping toward Zollin.

The oily smoke made seeing difficult, the dragon was shrouded in the dark clouds, but Zollin sensed the attack. It was physical, and Zollin didn't expect his power, raging though it was, to be strong enough to counter the beast's move. Instead he dove, face first, into the mud. The dragon's tail whipped harmlessly over him and slammed instead into the Gateway Inn. The two story building started to collapse inward, and Zollin saw his chance. He reached up with all his magical strength and pulled the building down on the dragon's tail.

Normally the dragon would have shattered the building with his hardened scales, but they weren't yet solid. The red scales were still too soft, and the force of the building's shattered timber pierced the beast's tail in hundreds of places. The bone inside cracked, and the dragon roared angrily. He flapped his wings fiercely, causing a downdraft that sent debris flying. Zollin was forced to remain in the mud, covering himself with a protective shield.

The dragon tugged its tail, causing pain to shoot through the tail and up into the beast's shoulder and neck. It was agonizing, but the dragon had to somehow get free. It recognized that the wizard had caused the structure to collapse on it, and it wanted revenge. It also needed to land and use its powerful legs to pull its tail free of the rubble. He looked down and spotted Zollin lying prone in the mud. He dropped toward the wizard, but Zollin was able to leap away. The dragon struck at the boy like a snake, but Zollin was ready and sent a sizzling ball of crackling, blue energy from his staff straight into the dragon's mouth. The beast howled in pain and jerked its head back even faster than it had struck.

Zollin didn't wait to see what would happen next. He turned and ran as fast as he could, hoping that Brianna and Kelvich had moved out of the little alley now that the dragon was on the ground. Quinn had finally spotted Zollin and was waving his arms to get his son's attention. Zollin ran straight to his father and at the last minute jumped, boosting himself through the air and then softening his landing in the saddle of one of the horses his father held.

"Where are the others?" Quinn shouted.

"This way," Zollin said, gesturing with one hand.

He turned the horse and moved around the side of one of the shorter buildings. He could see the dragon over the building's roofline. It was incinerating the remains of the inn to free its tail. Zollin slid off the horse and motioned for Quinn to do the same.

"You stay here with the horses," Zollin said. "I'll go get Brianna and Kelvich."

"Have you seen Mansel?" Quinn asked.

"No, we'll find him next."

"Alright," Quinn nodded. "Hurry!"

Zollin sprinted away, his back bent and his head low. He was keeping the buildings between himself and the dragon, while trying to search for Brianna and Kelvich at the same time. Surely, he thought to himself, they hadn't stayed in the alley where he had left them. He didn't see them anywhere else, though. He slowed his movements as he approached the alley. He pressed his back against the cold, stone wall of the building and then peeked around the side into the alley. He could see the dragon's glistening, red, scaly leg in the open street beyond. There was no sign of Brianna, but Kelvich lay face down in the mud. Zollin lifted his mentor without looking and levitated the sorcerer out of the alley. He set the old man down in front of him.

Kelvich had been knocked senseless. There was blood on the back of his head, but as Zollin probed with his magic, he found the skull intact, the brain undamaged. He gently shook Kelvich and the sorcerer's eyes fluttered open.

"Kelvich, where is Brianna?"

The old man, who was filthy and glassy–eyed, looked around him as if he expected her to be close by. Then he said, "I don't know."

Zollin pulled Kelvich to his feet and led him back to where Quinn was waiting, supporting the older man's weight as much as possible.

"He's hurt," Zollin explained, "but not too badly. Help me get him on one of the horses."

They boosted him up, and he sat in the saddle but leaned against the horse's neck.

"Where is Brianna?" Quinn shouted.

"I don't know. She was supposed to stay with Kelvich, but someone hit him over the head. I think someone must have taken her."

"Who?"

"I don't know," Zollin said, but he had an idea.

Just then the dragon broke free of the collapsed building and, with a roar, jumped back into the sky, flapping its wings through the billowing smoke of burning buildings to get airborne again. Then it turned and flew back toward the northern mountain range.

"Let's mount up and find our people," said Quinn.

Zollin climbed up behind Kelvich and held onto the sorcerer to keep him from falling out of the saddle.

"Where should we look?" Quinn asked.

"Let's start with the army," Zollin said angrily. They were with the wizards from the Torr, and he expected that Branock was behind Brianna's disappearance.

Chapter 15

The army was in total disarray. The soldiers who hadn't been killed by the Skellmarians had scattered when they saw the dragon. The group of foot soldiers and archers on the enemy's flank had broken and run for cover, including many of the officers. Mansel, though, was in a fit of blood fury and had continued fighting   He was still on the plain between the river and the town, cutting down the Skellmarians who were retreating toward the mountains.

Toag had seen first that his warriors were overrunning the foot soldiers' shield wall. He had been confident of victory until the dragon appeared. At first the Skellmarians saw it as a sign that the mountain gods were blessing their invasion. Then the dragon attacked, and they, too, had been stricken with fear. They ran for cover or retreated back across the bridge. Toag had taken a place of safety, but when the dragon flew away, he began trying to rally his people and press the attack.

Mansel had seen the big warrior and, without hesitation, had spurred his horse straight toward the small cluster of Skellmarians gathering around their leader. The horse's thundering hoofs alerted the crowd and most of them scattered out of Mansel's way, but a few were too slow or too stupid to move. Mansel cut through one with his sword, another fell under his horse, and a third was kicked in the face by Mansel as the horse charged past. He wheeled and turned back to find that the group had spread out and were urging their leader on.

Toag was waiting for the mounted warrior. It was not the first time he had faced an enemy on horseback. He knew the horse would give the warrior strength and momentum, but there were ways to counter those skills. He braced himself and raised a huge scimitar, shouting curses that his foe could not understand.

Mansel urged his horse forward, but not too quickly; instead of charging past, he reined up short of the chieftain and caused the horse to rear on its hind legs. The horse pawed the air, forcing Toag to leap backward. Then Mansel spurred the horse away from the big warrior. He slammed instead into the unprepared Skellmarians who were watching the battle. He pushed his horse into the mass of bodies, causing them to stumble back. Many fell, some were trod upon by Mansel's horse, others by their own people, who were desperate to get out of the way. Mansel cut down any unfortunate soul unlucky enough to come within range of his long sword.

The Skellmarians were not horsemen, and most harbored some type of superstitious fear of horses. In open combat, they could find the courage to face a cavalry soldier or knight, but surprised as these Skellmarians were, they gave into their fear and scattered. When Mansel at last turned his horse, he found the big clan leader hot in pursuit. He pulled hard on the reins again, causing the horse to rear back and buying Mansel a few seconds. It also caused Toag to hesitate and slow his charge.

The big Skellmarian High Chief was outraged at what he considered a cowardly act. In his culture, to make a challenge and then turn away was the greatest form of cowardice. In his rage, he charged after the horseman, only to be stopped in his tracks by the animal's flailing hooves. He swung his big sword in a level arc, but the horse danced back out of reach. He jumped forward with his sword over his head and brought it down in a mighty blow that should have cut the soldier in half, but Mansel parried the strike with his own sword.

Quinn had taught Mansel about angles, and how to use one blade to deflect another without taking on the force of the blow. Still, it was all he could do to hang onto his sword after blocking the barbarian's cut. The horse now sidestepped back out of reach, but Toag was in no mood to fight fair. He pulled his pick ax from his thick, leather belt and threw it at the soldier. It should have buried itself in the man's back, but, instead, it stopped in mid-air as if it had hit an invisible wall.

Zollin and Quinn had come around the last building in time to see Mansel block the vicious strike from the Skellmarian leader. They saw his horse dance away and then the ax was thrown. Zollin acted without thinking. He pushed out a defensive spell to block the ax and then shot crackling, blue energy at the barbarian.

Toag realized that one of the riders approaching must be the devil who had slain his kinsmen, but before he could act on this knowledge, the wizard was casting a spell at him. Toag dove out of the way, sliding in the mud, which was now watery with blood. He rose hurriedly to his feet to see the mounted warrior riding after him again. Toag started to swing his sword at the rider, but it seemed to freeze in mid-air, just like his ax. The rider's sword didn't freeze, though. It was coming at Toag's head.

The barbarian ducked just in time to avoid the sword, but it went against his instincts to let go of his sword. So his arm was still raised, still tugging on the weapon that Zollin held tightly with magic. Mansel's weapon sliced cleanly through the arm, just below the elbow. Blood fountained into the air as the Skellmarian leader fell back, howling in pain.

Seeing their leader fall brought more of the barbarians rushing forward. Mansel wheeled his horse and turned back toward his friends. They were waiting, and as the barbarians

165

approached, Zollin once again sent a blast of electrical energy surging toward them. Several were hit and burned, some shaking as the energy twisted their bodies into bone-crunching gyrations. Others were blown backwards, slamming into their companions by the power of the blast. They managed to drag their leader away, and Quinn led Zollin and Mansel back from the fighting.

"Where's the army?" Zollin shouted at Mansel.

"The cowards fled," Mansel replied.

"Where to?" Quinn asked.

"Back the way they came, I think."

The valley floor was a rolling plain, so that a slight rise blocked their view. Quinn spurred his horse forward in the direction the army had come from, while hundreds of Skellmarian warriors fled back across the river.

Toag was in so much pain his vision was blurry, but he had the sense of mind to order his men to cut the lines that raised and lowered the bridges. Then he had his men chop down the support pillars that Zollin had set in place. The day had not gone well for the Skellmarians, but the southerners were in worse shape, their homes burned and their army all but destroyed. Toag would return, he swore it.

* * *

"What are you doing with that girl?" Billips asked Branock as the wizard rode into the camp, where his servants were waiting on him.

"Form up your troops, commander," Branock snarled. "Keep your mind on the task at hand. Kill anyone who tries to follow me."

"But where are you going?"

"To report what happened here today to your King. You should establish a base of defense here to keep the Skellmarians from raiding down the valley. The snows will keep them from using Telford's pass for a while, but not long enough. You'll need to hold it as well."

"Against an army that size?" Billips said. "That's impossible. My men were slaughtered by that dragon. You saw what happened."

"Yes," said Branock. "I did see it, and I shall report how you divided your force and were overtaken by the barbarians."

"That's not what happened!" the knight said angrily.

"Oh, yes it is. If the dragon hadn't appeared, you would have been wiped out to the last man. Now, do as I say, or you'll find yourself in the King's dungeons."

"Yes, sir," said Billips. He was angry, but he'd learned long ago that his birth order had left him in no position to give orders. He swallowed his anger and began taking charge of the scattered remains of his legion. Only a quarter of their entire force had returned so far, most of them archers. Still, he would do what he could with what he had.

Brianna was only half conscious of what was going on around her. She had been clubbed from behind, just like Kelvich. Then dragged back to where Branock had left his horse. The poor animal was wide eyed with fear of the dragon, but there was nothing to be done about it. Branock had thrown Brianna across his saddle, a job that took all his physical strength even though she was not heavy. Branock had relied on his magic and neglected his physical strength for years. But no matter what he tried, he could not levitate the girl, so he lifted her. Then, panting from the exertion, he climbed up behind the saddle and rode for his camp.

He was frustrated that he had been unsuccessful in getting Zollin to come with him back to Orrock, but the girl was just as good. He'd seen the way the boy wizard had looked at her, and he was certain that Zollin would follow him now. Right back to where Branock wanted him to go.

"Break camp," he ordered his men. "Make haste."

He didn't stop riding. The servants would follow him if they wanted their gold. He would bolster their stamina and lace the girl's water with drugs so that she stayed manageable on the trip back. If he rode through the day and night, he would be able to take a boat back down the river, which would far outpace any horse. Then he could take a ship down the coast and be within the castle walls, safe and sound, when he faced Zollin again. This time he would not fail, and then, with Zollin firmly in place, he could face his master and bring the old man to his knees.

* * *

They rode swiftly, passing soldiers who were making their way back to their camp. None of the men talked. Zollin focused his energies on healing Kelvich, even though he was exhausted, both physically and emotionally. He didn't blame the older man for Brianna's abduction, but he was angry. Someone had nearly given his mentor a concussion and had taken Brianna. He was sick over the loss, and he swore that he would never forgive himself if something bad happened to her. He probed Kelvich's body. There was swelling around the head wound, but it was only skin deep. He was able to knit the cut back together rather easily, and then he did a more thorough assessment.

Kelvich's lungs were the real problem. They were seared from the heat of the fire he'd been exposed to and were filling with liquid. There was also liquid forming around the sorcerer's heart, making the muscle work harder than it should, and less efficiently, as well.

It was one thing to knit a clean wound back together, or even to mend broken bones, but he wasn't sure what to do about the buildup of liquid. He was forced to levitate it out, a tiny bit at a time, up Kelvich's wind pipe and out of his mouth. It was slow and painstaking work. If he bumped the lung wall or the wind pipe itself, it threw Kelvich into a coughing fit. He was not even half way done when the army encampment came into sight. The wide plain was littered with tents, equipment, and the remains of fires. There were wounded soldiers being helped, and others working to form up the healthy soldiers into some semblance of order.

"Do you know who is in charge?" Quinn asked Mansel.

"It should be a knight named Billips, unless he was killed."

As they came closer, a small group of men came up and blocked their progress. They were haggard looking, their faces and uniforms soiled, their weapons stained with blood.

"You'll have to turn back," one of the men said. "No one's allowed to leave the vicinity."

"We're looking for someone," Quinn said. "A girl, dark hair, thin. I think she was wearing an olive colored dress today."

The men looked at each other with knowing glances, but the one who had spoken before was the only one to respond.

"I'm sorry, there are no women here. You'll have to go back."

"There are no women here now," Zollin said. "But have you seen her?"

"My orders are to hold the road, not to answer questions, now you'll have to turn back."

"The hell I will," Zollin said angrily.

169

"Don't bite off more than you can chew, boy," said the solider. He was flexing his grip on his sword.

"He's not a boy," Mansel said with a smirk. "He's a wizard, and he just fought off the dragon. I don't think he's worried about you and your companions."

The soldier's face drained of color.

"We aren't looking for a fight," Quinn said, as much to Mansel and Zollin as to the group of soldiers. "We're trying to find the girl. Her name is Brianna, and we mean to find her. If you don't want to answer our questions, then take us to someone who will. Is your man Billips still in charge?"

"Aye, he is," said the soldier. "Follow me and I'll lead you to him, but you'll have to turn over your weapons."

"That's not a problem," Zollin said.

Mansel didn't look so sure, and Kelvich was just struggling to stay in the saddle. They rode toward one of the larger pavilion tents. It had several pendants fluttering in the morning breeze. Two more soldiers stood guard outside the tent. Quinn and Mansel handed over their weapons, and Zollin gave the men his staff.

"Is there a place where our friend can rest out of the cold?" Zollin asked.

"Sure, I'll take him," said the guard.

Kelvich was led toward another tent, not far away. Quinn turned to Zollin and Mansel.

"Let me do the talking. It won't help us to lose our tempers."

Zollin and Mansel both nodded. They stepped inside the tent and found several knights standing around a table. There was a chart of the valley spread out on the surface, and men were pointing to various spots while they discussed the arrangement of their men.

"Who are you?" asked one of the knights.

"My name is Quinn, and I'm looking for my daughter."

"There are no women here," said the knight. He was tall, with thinning hair and a large, hooked nose that had obviously been broken in the past.

"We believe she may have been kidnapped and brought here," Quinn said in a gentle voice that Zollin recognized. His father used the same voice when Zollin was younger and had been caught doing something he shouldn't have.

"And I said there are no women here," said the hook nosed man. "Now be gone, before I have you thrown into stocks and beaten."

Quinn sighed and spoke again. "Are you Billips?"

"No, my name is Aquil, and I've no time for questions from pathetic villagers. I've an army to assemble, and a war host to fight. Now get out of my camp, that's you're last warning."

"I'm looking for Billips," said Quinn.

"Old man," said Aquil angrily, drawing his sword and stepping forward menacingly, "get the hell out of my sight."

Zollin's magic was churning and flashing inside of him. He couldn't believe he was standing back and letting someone threaten his father that way, but Quinn had quietly gestured for Zollin and Mansel to move back, which they had done. But it was all Zollin could do to contain his desire to blast the arrogant knight into a smoldering heap.

"We're not leaving," said Quinn in a steady voice.

"We'll see about that," the man called Aquil said viciously.

He stood still for a moment, eyeing Quinn, who looked as calm as a man inspecting fruit at market. Suddenly, Aquil jumped forward, thrusting his sword straight toward Quinn's stomach. But Quinn was faster, spinning out of the way and bringing his fist around in a punch that landed squarely on Aquil's jaw. His other hand grasped the knight's sword hand as Aquil fell to the ground, his body stiff and his eyes rolling back so that only the whites showed.

Quinn held up the sword by the blade with one hand, and the other hand was held open, palm facing out toward the other knights in a conciliatory gesture.

"We aren't looking for trouble," Quinn said in a tone of command. "We want to speak to Billips, and we want to find our friend. That is all."

"I'm Billips," said one of the other knights. "Your friend was taken by Branock of the Torr, but we can't let you pass."

"You're King's soldiers, aren't you?" Quinn said. "Why are you letting this man take a young girl by force?"

"Our orders were to give Branock any assistance he might require and to follow his orders. Prince Simmeron gave us these orders personally. I may not like them, but I will follow them."

"Let's go," said Zollin. "They can't stop us."

"I'm afraid I can," said Billips.

He made a hand signal, and six soldiers entered the tent, all with weapons drawn. They blocked the entrance, and the knights drew their weapons as well. Zollin, Quinn, and Mansel were outnumbered more than three to one, and none of them had weapons except for Quinn, who still held the sword he had taken by the blade.

"Wait," said Quinn, speaking to Zollin. "There's no need to hurt these men, and the villagers are going to need them."

"I'm not waiting," said Zollin. "Branock can't be that far ahead. We've got to rescue her."

"Take them away," said Billips to his men.

"Don't kill them," Quinn shouted.

Zollin was already acting. He didn't move, but he pushed out a wall of magic that he formed around his father, Mansel, and himself. The magic jumped out, as solid as a wooden beam as it slammed into the unsuspecting soldiers. They were all knocked off their feet.

"Wow!" Mansel said.

"Let's get moving," Quinn said, "before they have time to recover."

Outside the tent, they found their weapons in a pile. They scooped them up and swung onto their horses. The men inside the tent were stirring, the knights shouting orders to detain Zollin, Quinn, and Mansel.

"If we stay here, people are going to get hurt," Quinn said.

"We can't leave without Kelvich," Zollin replied.

They turned their horses and rode to the nearby tent, where Kelvich had been taken.

"I'll get him," Zollin said.

He jumped off his horse and ducked into the tent. He never saw the wooden club that hit him. He fell into the mud with a grunt.

"Zollin!" Quinn said when he heard the blow. "Son!"

Mansel spun his horse, drawing his sword, but there were over two dozen men at arms surrounding them. Quinn rushed inside the tent, but was immediately disarmed and dragged back out. Billips came striding over to them.

"You were duly warned," he said.

"Don't be a fool," Mansel said to Billips. "We only want to save our friend."

"You've attacked the King's officers," he said in haughty tone. "You'll have to be detained and tried for your actions."

"This is a mistake," said Mansel.

"We'll see about that," said the knight. "Put them in chains and hold them by the river."

Chapter 16

When Brianna came to her senses, her head was pounding with pain. She was lying across a saddle, her legs numb, her hands tied behind her back. She could feel the crustiness of dried blood on the back of her head and on her neck. Her head felt like it was being hit like a drum with every jarring step the horse took. And there was a sharp, stabbing pain in the back of her head.

She had seen Zollin move away from the building they were hiding between. The air around her had been blowing hard from the dragon's flapping wings and was searingly hot from the fire the beast had belched at Zollin. She had been paralyzed by fear for Zollin, even more afraid then when Branock had snatched her off the street and used her as a hostage. The dragon was so big, so incredibly powerful, and Zollin was facing it all alone.

Then, suddenly and without warning, her world had gone black. She didn't remember anything else until she woke up stretched across the horse. She moaned and tried to move, but her body was too weak.

"Ah, you're awake," came a voice that sent icy chills down her arms and back. She could feel the goose bumps rising on her skin and tingling up her neck.

"If you will cooperate, no more pain will come to you," Branock said. "If you struggle or try to escape, I'll beat you or drug you. Do you understand?"

Brianna did understand. She was powerless to do anything about her awful predicament, and fighting was of no benefit. Even if her captor weren't a powerful wizard, she simply was in no shape to do anything. But what she desperately wanted was for the pain to stop. She wanted to lie down, untie her arms, and rest. Still, she didn't think that was going to happen either.

"Let me go," she said in a weak voice.

"Oh, I can't do that," said Branock. "No, that would not serve my purpose at all. I need you, so you'll have to stay with me. But there's no need to be trussed up like an animal. I'll cut you loose and let you ride with me, if you promise not to do anything stupid. We have to ride fast to stay ahead of your friends. Once we find a suitable vessel, we'll travel down the river, which will be a much more comfortable way to travel, for both of us."

"I won't fight," said Brianna, and she meant it. She only wanted the pain to stop.

She felt the cold steel of the knife slide between her wrists and felt an overwhelming sense of vulnerability that made her want to cry. She hated feeling so weak, but there was seemingly nothing to do about it at the moment. But she refused to let Branock see her tears. She held them back through a tremendous act of will.

The knife cut her bonds easily, and Brianna wanted to scream as her arms flopped forward. They were so numb she couldn't move them. They felt as if they weighed a thousand pounds each, and she was surprised their weight didn't pull her off the horse head first. As the blood began to flow through her arms again, they tingled and burned and ached almost as painfully as her head. Every bounce in the horse's gait brought fresh waves of agony. Tears burned her eyes, but she didn't make a sound.

Then Branock grabbed her arms and wrenched her upward. He wasn't strong, but she had always been thin and didn't weight very much. He huffed and puffed, out of breath from the exertion of lifting her upright. She sat sideways in the saddle, and only his hand on her arms kept her from toppling off the horse. Now the blood was running back through her legs, and her whole body felt as if tiny ants with red hot feet were running up and down her body.

"I'd help with the wounds, but for some reason you're immune to my power," Branock said. "It's a bit of a mystery, but isn't that what makes life so grand? We can't know everything, and every new discovery is a triumph. I'm looking forward to solving the riddle you pose."

Brianna wanted to spit in his face, but she still couldn't control her body yet. Her arms were slowly becoming less painful, and her head, now that it wasn't upside down and flooded with excess blood, wasn't aching quite as much. She looked around and noticed that they were still in the Great Valley, with towering, razor sharp looking mountain peaks on either side. They were on a road, or at least what passed for a road. It was still muddy, but more of a packed, clay-like mud rather than the watery brown quagmire of the plain. The forest grew closer to the river here, where the rich soil hadn't been cleared for crops. The river was muddy, too, brown with white bubbles that looked like spit. It was running fast and looked to be about as wide as it had been in Brighton's Gate. She decided they hadn't gone that far, and she chanced a look back over the wizard's shoulder.

"How sweet," he said in a mocking tone. "She hasn't given up hope that her savior will come swooping down to rescue her. Are you imagining that you are Princess Everdale and the Falcon King will save you and make you his bride?"

She ignored him. She wasn't strong enough to make a break for freedom herself. But Branock had said that she was bait to draw Zollin in, so she was relatively sure that he was still alive. She hadn't seen what had happened to the dragon, or who else had been hurt. Had Branock killed Kelvich when he'd kidnapped her? She didn't know, and the questions were like festering, open wounds that she was powerless to mend.

"The soldiers will at least slow him down, and I doubt his mount can keep up with us. I may not be able to help you, but our horse can benefit from my power. He'll keep up this pace all day and night. I don't think your young suitor can replicate that nifty trick. Zipple Weed doesn't grow this far north; it's not a fan of the cold. And neither am I. I'll be glad to get back to a warm bed, a roaring fire, and plenty of mulled wine. Doesn't that sound better than tramping through the mud and muck?"

Brianna ignored him once again. She felt like throwing up, partly because her body was still in shock from its poor treatment, but partly because she hated being so close to the dark wizard. He may have spoken like a gentleman, but she could sense that he was anything but. He felt cold, not just physically, but deeper down. It was like being near ice, the cold seemed to penetrate, and it felt like no amount of warmth could touch it.

"You're a quiet companion, much like my last one. He underestimated me, but that was to be expected. He underestimated everyone and overestimated himself."

"What happened to him?" she asked in a quiet voice.

"Zollin killed him," Branock said with smile. "It was a fantastic battle, really. You would have been proud. He's improved quite a bit since we last met in the forest. A bit raw still, perhaps, but he's learning, I'll give him that much."

"You didn't help your friend?" Brianna asked.

"Oh, he wasn't my friend. No, not at all. Just an inconvenient problem that young Zollin helped me to eliminate."

"He defeated you, too," she said, trying to sound more confident than she was.

"Ah, well, that may be true, but there were extenuating circumstances. The dragon was not expected, and I've no doubt that it will be a wrinkle we'll have to deal with in the future, but that can't be helped. For now, we need your young friend to join us at Orrock. I wish you would believe me when I tell you I don't wish Zollin any harm."

"No, just those around him, like me."

"I haven't harmed you," he said as if her words had hurt his feelings.

"You threatened to break my neck if he didn't do what you wanted," she said.

"Empty words," he said playfully. "I couldn't hurt you, now really. What kind of man do you take me for?"

"I don't take you for a man at all," she said. "More like an empty shell filled with evil."

She had meant the words to sting him, but he only laughed and urged the horse to pick up its pace.

* * *

The soldiers carried Zollin, still unconscious, to the riverbank and dropped him in the mud. They chained his hands and feet together, then drove a long, wooden stake into the ground and chained him to that. They did the same with Quinn, Mansel, and Kelvich, all along the riverbank. The water had risen and was continuing to rise as more snow melted. It was only a few feet below the bank now, in a few more weeks it would over flow its boundaries and spread across the plain. Brighton's Gate had been built on a small rise that would probably keep the ruined buildings dry while the floods brought fresh soil and minerals to the plain and allowed the farmers to raise their crops.

Of course the town was now a smoking ruin. More of the buildings had caught fire, Quinn was sure of that from the amount of black smoke continuing to rise into the sky. They were an hour's ride from the village, but the devastation was marked clearly by the oily smoke.

Kelvich was motionless in the mud where the soldiers had dropped him. It was cold enough that being wet and muddy made them miserable. Quinn could only guess what the cold was doing to the old sorcerer's injuries. He hadn't heard exactly what had happened to Kelvich, but from the way Zollin was treating him, it couldn't have been good. And the knock on the back of his head hadn't helped.

Quinn felt his anger rising up like bile in his throat, but he swallowed it back down. There was nothing they could do now, not until Zollin woke up...if he woke up at all. A blow to the head could kill a man or make him senseless the rest of his life. Quinn had seen it, and although he hadn't seen how Zollin had been hit, he had seen the club. It was a big, knobby piece of hardwood that could kill a man easily enough.

"Quinn," Mansel said. "What do we do now?" He was holding up his wrists, which were chained together, as if he expected Quinn to snap his fingers and make the chains fall into a heap at his feet.

"We wait," said Quinn. "And hope Zollin wakes up."

"Zollin," Mansel said, calling to the young wizard. "Zollin, wake up."

But Zollin didn't move. His face was out of the mud, but there were very few signs that he was alive. He was breathing,

Quinn was sure of that. He had stared at his son's chest, making sure he wasn't just imagining the slight movement he saw there.

"That won't help," said Quinn. "They bashed him with a club. We'll just have to wait and see."

Mansel and Quinn stood as long as they could. Mansel had been awake all night and finally succumbed to his aching muscles and the fatigue that was creeping through his mind like a low cloud. Quinn was tired, too, especially as the adrenaline from the battle began to fade. He sat down reluctantly on the ground as the wet mud soaked into his clothes. He still had his chainmail on under his over shirt, and the metal seemed to absorb the cold and chilled his bones. The sun was bright, but added very little warmth to the day. Quinn watched it inch across the sky, dividing his attention between the activity around the camp and checking on Zollin.

The soldiers had broken their camp and set up on the small hill where the wizards had stayed the night before. They piled the excess supplies from their fallen comrades into a large heap near the hill, and they set up shelters for the surviving soldiers all around the hill. They also placed a picket line across the valley. The horses were kept in a stand of trees that were close to the hills. Quinn imagined that some of the cavalry soldiers had been sent to round up any that had survived the battle, but there were only a few dozen. The Skellmarians attacked horses as viciously as they did men. Their own horses, including their mare, Lilly, which Zollin had won from a traveling magician in Tranaugh Shire, had been added to the army's herd.

Food had been prepared, but none had been given to Quinn or Mansel. Kelvich was in and out of consciousness, and his breathing had grown even more labored. Zollin still had not moved. Worry nagged at Quinn like termites gnawing their way through wood. He felt a hollowness inside of him that was filling up quickly with fear. He couldn't imagine losing his son, and he was desperate to see Zollin respond. The fact that he was chained so far away from his son was painfully difficult. He wanted to comfort him and perhaps find a way to warm him up, but there was no chance of that. He had spent a large portion of his strength trying to pry up the stake that held him in place, but it had been hammered into the ground with big, wooden mallets, and it refused to budge no matter how hard he tried.

Finally, just as the sun was setting, Zollin started to stir. Quinn felt a wave of relief, but he knew that his son could still have been permanently injured. Quinn sat waiting, watching his son, until Zollin rolled over and looked at him.

"Are you okay?" Quinn called out.

"My head hurts," Zollin said. "What happened?"

"Someone clubbed you when you went in the tent to get Kelvich."

"Oh," Zollin said. In truth, he was still trying to put everything together. His mind was a patchwork of unrelated memories that he couldn't quite get into order yet. There was Brianna, as beautiful as ever in an olive colored dress that seemed both warm and utilitarian. There were images of frightening looking Skellmarians, shaggy in their thick animal skins and waving their curved swords. Then another image, this one of Branock and his compatriot from the Torr, Whytlethane. They were on horses on the main street of Brighton's Gate. There was an image of a Skellmarian warrior, bursting into flame, high above the others. Then the dragon, with red scales, huge, leathery wings, and a snake-like head. Then an image of Branock again, this time holding Brianna, and everything fell into place.

Zollin sat upright so fast he got dizzy and had to close his eyes. Without even consciously thinking about it, he probed the knot on the back of his head, checking the skin and then deeper, just as he had done with Kelvich. The blow had caused some swelling and pushed the bones in his neck out of alignment. He corrected them quickly with a gentle push of magic. His stomach was empty, and he was ravenously hungry. He felt tired, but the realization that Brianna was gone, probably taken by Branock, fired adrenaline into his veins and got him moving. He saw that his companions were trussed just as he was, and he nodded to his father.

"Let's wait until dark," Quinn said.

"But what about Brianna?" Zollin said.

"I've been thinking about that, and I don't think we should go after her."

Zollin was about to shout how crazy that was, but Quinn raised his hand. It was a gesture that he had used Zollin's whole life to say, wait a second, I'm not finished. Zollin shut his mouth and waited.

"Look, we've been running and playing things off the cuff since this started," Quinn said. "Two things seem obvious to me. First, Branock has Brianna, but he's using her as bait, which means she's safe. I know," he said, holding up his hand again. "I don't like it anymore than you do, but let's be smart about this. Getting her back is my highest priority, but we don't have to play by their rules. The other thing I'm fairly certain of is that he's taking her back to Orrock."

Zollin looked perplexed.

"Think about it for a minute, why are these soldiers here? There was no reason to send out an entire legion to quell the Skellmarians. The mountain clans haven't come together in such numbers in over a century. No, those soldiers were here for you. And you heard yourself what that fool Billips said. Prince Simmerion ordered them to do whatever Branock told them. Either he's bewitched the Prince or he's struck a deal."

"But he's a wizard of the Torr, not of Yelsia or Orrock," said Zollin.

"No, in the past each kingdom had powerful wizards, but since the Torr came to power, no single kingdom has had any wizards. But what if Branock has changed that? What if he made a deal to be the wizard of Orrock?"

"Can he do that?"

"I'm sure the other wizards at the Torr wouldn't approve. But there is more to this than meets the eye."

"Yes, but what does that have to do with Brianna?"

"Well, first of all, he's got almost a whole day's lead on us, and we've got an injured man. We can't leave Kelvich behind, there's nowhere for him to go, no one to take care of him. From the way things looked earlier, I'm guessing that most of Brighton's Gate is gone, burned to the ground. He's still got his little cabin, but without the support from the town, and with no one to take care of him, his chances are slim."

Zollin looked over at his mentor. Kelvich was wheezing in rough, wet sounding gasps that sounded serious. Zollin reached out with his magic, the fluid buildup was getting worse around his heart, and his lungs had refilled with the thick mucus that Zollin had been trying to get out earlier in the day.

"No, he needs a lot of work or he's going to die," Zollin agreed. "We can't leave him behind."

"Okay, so let's do this on our terms. Let's go to Orrock City by a different route."

"But the mountain pass hasn't opened up."

"You said you could tunnel through, didn't you?"

"Yes," Zollin admitted.

"Okay, so we go south, though Telford's Pass and back through Peddinggar Forrest. We may not be able to catch this wizard completely by surprise, but we can keep him guessing. Everything we can do on our terms will give us a better chance at getting Brianna back without losing you or anyone else."

"Alright, we wait until dark. I'm starving, have you got any food?"

"No, they didn't feed us."

Zollin was disappointed to hear that, his ravenous appetite was almost as strong, at that point, as his desire for revenge on the soldiers who kept him from going after Brianna. That thought made him feel ill. Just the thought of going in a different direction was almost more than he could bear. He felt as if he were abandoning her. And what if Quinn was wrong? It would take twice as long to get to the Torr overland as it would traveling by sea. If Branock caught a ship going south, it might take months before Zollin could find Brianna and rescue her. He felt hopeless. Despair rose in his heart as the sun set and cast the long, dark shadows of twilight onto the valley plain.

"I think it's time," said Quinn, waking up Mansel.

"Good," said Zollin, as the magic flared up inside of him. "Try not to move, I don't want anyone to get hurt."

Chapter 17

Zollin started with his father's shackles. They were made out of steel already, so all he had to do was transform them. Quinn felt heat on his wrists and around his ankles. He looked down and saw that the metal was quivering. It was an unnatural sight, and it made him nervous, but then the metal seemed to liquefy and flow away from him. The metal all came together and reshaped into several objects. First there was a short, two edged sword, just like his old one. Then three of the short, thin throwing knives Quinn was adept with. Finally, there were three round bands. Quinn was puzzled at first, but then the wooden stake he'd been chained to flowed up out of the ground in a brown, molten blob, then it settled around the metal bands and resumed its solid form.

"That is strange," said Quinn, a little unsettled.

"Just think of it as carpentry," Zollin joked.

It wasn't quite dark yet, but they were in deep shadow and the soldiers were mostly around bright fires, so Quinn judged it was safe enough to give the weapons a try. Zollin was already working on Mansel's bonds, so Quinn picked up the shield. It was lighter than he expected, but felt solid enough. The short sword was perfectly balanced. He lifted the throwing knives and was surprised at how perfect they felt. He slipped them into his belt and walked over to where Mansel was inspecting his own set of weapons. Zollin had fashioned the older boy a shield like Quinn's, but his sword was longer, with a two handed grip. Not quite a broadsword, it was amazingly light, but had just enough heft to make it deadly from the saddle as well as on the ground. The other weapon for Mansel was a thick knife as long as his forearm. It was obviously made for utility as well as defense. The young warrior nodded in appreciation to Zollin.

"Will these weapons hold up?" Quinn asked, although he felt confident they would. He'd handled enough weapons to know the feel of finely made steel.

"They should be as strong as anything they come against," Zollin replied.

He had simply unlocked his own chains and those of Kelvich. He had hurried over to the older man, kneeling down in the mud to look at his friend.

"He's burning up with fever," Zollin said. "We need to get him back to his cabin."

"We'll need our horses," Quinn said.

"I wouldn't mind a little payback, too," Mansel added.

"These soldiers aren't our enemies," Quinn said. "They fight for Yelsia."

"But they just about killed Zollin and helped the wizard make off with Brianna."

"Still, they were just following orders. If we kill them, we truly will be outlaws. Not to mention that we'll be making the Skellmarian's job that much easier."

"You think they'll be back?" Mansel asked.

"Yes, they weren't defeated by the army or even by us, really. You maimed their chieftain, but I saw them cutting the drawbridge support lines. They're coming back. This army is the only thing between them and the rest of Yelsia."

"Okay, so how do we get our horses back and escape without killing anyone?"

"Getting away shouldn't be too difficult, we just need to get past a few sentries," Zollin said. "I can deal with them, then

Mansel and I can double back and get the horses. We'll come in from the woods. There may be more guards, but we'll have cover."

"I wish I had my bow," Mansel said.

"Give me a minute," Zollin said.

Suddenly the wooden stake that had anchored him to the ground was floating up and shaping itself into a sturdy looking longbow. It took several minutes of intense concentration to transmute the wood into string. He conjured up Kelvich's stake and changed it into a dozen arrows, with wood shavings substituted for fletching feathers. He shaped some of the discarded chain into triangular arrowheads and bonded the wood and metal together.

"Man, you are handy to have around," Mansel said, admiring the bow and arrows.

"Thanks, we better move," said Zollin. "I've got to eat, or I won't be able to keep this up."

Quinn led the way. Kelvich was awake and on his feet, although he was so groggy he wasn't much help. Zollin and Mansel had to practically carry him between them. They encountered one sentry, who Zollin was able to distract by creating sounds across the river. The guard was so intent on what he thought was happening on the far side of the river that Quinn was able to lead them safely around the man and into the growing darkness of the valley beyond. They were now between Brighton's Gate and the army, far enough out that no one could see them. They carried Kelvich all the way to the edge of the woods. Then they sat him down. He was coughing and hacking on the mucus in his lungs, but lacked the strength to actually move any of the thick liquid buildup out of his chest.

"He needs help," said Quinn.

"I can help him, but I've got to have food."

"I'm hungry, too," said Mansel.

"Okay, look, you all wait here. I may not be able to get the horses, but I can get some food," Quinn said.

"How?" Zollin asked.

"I'll just blend in. I know how to do that, especially in the army. I doubt anyone will even question me."

"Okay, but be careful. I..." Zollin couldn't finish the sentence. He felt tears welling up unexpectedly in his eyes. After losing Brianna and seeing Kelvich so sick, he didn't think he could take it if something happened to his father.

"I'll be fine, I promise," he said, then he disappeared into the night.

Zollin began the tedious work of clearing out Kelvich's lungs, although he was growing more and more worried about the fluid building up around the sorcerer's heart. Mansel stood guard, just in case.

Quinn made his way quickly along the tree line. He began swaggering a little as he approached the lights from the camp. He knew he would be challenged by the sentries, and he was ready for them. The first one called out as soon as he saw Quinn.

"Hey, what are you doing out there?" said the soldier.

"Just looking for a place to relieve myself," Quinn said. "I needed a little privacy, if you know what I mean."

"Are they cooking that squalid meat from the bay again?" the soldier asked. "I was sick all night long the last time they cooked it."

"No, I just ate a little too much, I guess."

"Good, I don't even want to think of that nastiness again."

"I know what you mean," Quinn said, moving on and leaving the soldier to his duty.

He wasn't challenged after that. He stayed to the shadows, not wanting to risk his face being seen again. He could smell the night's dinner being cooked and dished out, but that wasn't what he was after, either. Hot food would be more than welcome; after not eating anything more than Kelvich's flask of coffee, because he'd saved the food for Mansel, he was light headed from hunger, too. But there was no way to get enough of what was being cooked back out to his boys, and he refused to eat a hot meal while Zollin and Mansel sat waiting for him to return.

He circled around the large cooking tent and the big fires there and made his way to the supply wagons. There were a few, but they were loaded with staples like hard-crusted bread and dried beef. He got lucky and found a barrel full of apples. He filled a sack with food and started back out into the dark.

"Where are you going?" said a gruff voice from behind.

"Just taking some food out to the sentries," Quinn said pleasantly.

"Since when do we feed them when they're on duty?" said the man.

Quinn had turned around, and now he could see the man accosting him. He was older than Quinn, with a scraggly, grey beard, a round belly, and a nose that no longer had a normal shape. He had some nasty scars, too; one that ran up across his forehead was bright pink, as if it wasn't more than a few months old. Quinn recognized the type; he'd probably spent his whole life in the King's army and was used to bullying the newer recruits. Not that he was a coward, his experience in battle was written by the scars on his face, but Quinn didn't plan to be pushed around.

"Since they fought hard this morning," Quinn said, not intimidated by the man.

"That so? I'm surprised I haven't heard about it."

"Well now you have."

"I suppose, but I can't get loose of the feeling that you're taking that food for yourself and planning to desert."

"I'm not deserting," said Quinn.

"Well, why don't you let me take that food out to the sentries then?"

"Go ahead," Quinn said, fighting to keep his temper in check. The last thing he needed was to raise his voice and attract a crowd.

"I think I will," he said, stepping forward, his hand extended to take the bag from Quinn.

Quinn was holding the food in his left hand, and when the man stepped forward, he swung a roundhouse punch that should have knocked the old soldier out cold. But the man had been expecting it and dodged back out of the way just in time to avoid the blow.

Quinn didn't hesitate; he knew that one shout from the man would be the end of his efforts. He didn't think he could talk his way out it if he were questioned by one of the officers. He kicked out at the man's knee, bringing his foot around from the side and crashing it into the older man's knee with as much force as he could muster. The soldier grunted, his leg giving a little, but not completely. The man stayed on his feet and came forward with a straight punch that caught Quinn just as he was trying to move back out of reach. The fist smashed Quinn's lips and staggered him backward, but it hadn't stunned him the way the soldier had hoped.

Quinn was ready for the follow up shot, a hard, left hook that should have connected to his chin, but Quinn swayed back out of reach and caught the soldier's arm by the wrist, using the man's own momentum to twist the arm and wrench it behind his back. The soldier, his back to Quinn now, moved forward, propelled by the pressure on his arm. Quinn didn't follow but instead kicked the man's boot so that it flew over and into his other leg. The man fell into the mud, and Quinn practically jumped on the man's back. He landed on his knees, driving the wind out of the soldier's lungs and causing the older man to gasp. Quinn wasn't sure, but he might have heard some ribs snapping—but he couldn't worry about that now. He drew one of the throwing knives in one smooth motion and used the metal hilt on the base of the soldier's skull. The man was knocked unconscious.

Quinn snatched up his bag of food, hoping that the mud hadn't seeped through to the bread inside, and started walking again. He needed to get past the ring of sentries before someone found the older soldier. They might assume that he was just drunk, but a closer inspection would reveal the man's injuries and raise the security of the camp. He approached the nearest sentry, who stood with weapons at the ready just outside the light from the camp. He didn't hesitate but drew his sword and moved stealthily toward the man. When he was close enough, he hit the sentry on the back of the head with the flat of his sword. The sentry went sprawling, and Quinn hurried out into the darkness.

His lip was busted, and it irritated him that it seemed to hurt more than a major wound. He knew it didn't, but he had trouble keeping his mind off of the sharp pain. His tongue kept probing the wound, which only seemed to make things worse, but the swollen lip felt strange. He hated the coppery taste of blood, and the way his teeth ached. He opened and closed his jaw, which felt different and didn't quite seem to work right.

As he approached the area where Zollin and Mansel were watching over Kelvich, his legs began to ache. The cold made his hands hurt, and his whole body felt stiff. He handed Mansel the bag of food and went to sit down. He leaned back against a tree, his cold chainmail seemed to press the freezing night air into this body.

"We can't wait much longer," Zollin said. "Kelvich needs a warm place to rest."

"Me, too, I'm getting old," Quinn said.

Mansel and Zollin laughed.

"I don't know what you two are laughing at, but I just took a shot in the teeth to get you that food."

Mansel was already tearing into a loaf of the crusty bread.

"You could have picked up something a little more fresh," he said around a mouthful.

Zollin picked up some large rocks and heated them with his magic. He set one by Kelvich, who was propped against a tree. His breathing was a little less labored, and he was awake, but it was obvious even in the dark that he was in bad shape. Zollin gave the other rock to his father.

"Here, that should keep you warm until we get back," he said.

"You boys be careful," Quinn said. "They'll be on high alert at the camp."

"We will," Zollin said.

He was tired, his head still ached, and his stomach was rumbling. His arms and legs felt shaky. At any other time, he would have complained or argued to wait until morning, but he knew that Kelvich wouldn't make it through the night without a warm fire and constant attention. He also needed to find out how to deal with the fluid around his mentor's heart, and he hoped that some of the old texts in the hermit's cottage would shed some light on the condition.

Mansel handed Zollin half a loaf of bread and an apple. He ate the apple first, sucking the juice out of each bite before swallowing. He was light headed, but the food helped. He needed something to drink, and as they passed a trickle of a stream, he stopped and cupped his hands under the icy flow of water. He drank and drank, then tore into the bread as they got closer to the camp. The bread was dry and stale, but it filled his stomach; he felt his strength returning.

They had moved higher up in the woods so that they could observe the camp and the corral without being seen. The horses were all hobbled with simple rope leads between their forelegs. They were also tied on a long lead line. Of the 150 horses that had come into the valley, little more than 40 remained. They were cropping at what little grass had survived the long winter buried in snow.

"Are we picky about which horses we get?" Mansel asked.

Zollin considered the question. He had a fondness for Lilly, but she wasn't worth getting into a fight over. She wasn't a war horse and wouldn't be in danger, even if the Skellmarians attacked again.

"I would like to get Brianna's mare," Zollin said. "But I don't care about the rest."

"And our saddles?"

"Doesn't make a difference to me."

"Okay, if you can distract them, I'll get the horses saddled and ready, then we can ride away."

"Alright," Zollin said. "I think I have an idea."

He let his magic spread out; it was like unleashing his mind or consciousness. He could feel the trees around him, the small animals, and the camp nearby. He found what he was looking for rather easily, and soon pinecones were flying by in a straight line, headed out of the woods toward the river. It was too dark to see the small objects gliding through the air. Once they were far enough away, he sent a pulse of magic and the pine cones ignited, bursting into light. Then he let them fall. They fell in the mud, but continued to burn. They weren't bright, but they had caught the attention of the sentries, who had immediately called for help from the camp. Most of the soldiers had either fallen asleep around their campfires or were lounging lazily. It took them several minutes to muster and head out to face this unknown threat. As the pinecones burned out, a large group of soldiers moved out into the darkness to investigate. Around the camp, more soldiers were standing guard, but only three remained watching over the horses.

"The officers aren't expecting an attack from the woods," Mansel said, a little surprised.

"I guess they figure the Skellmarians would attack from the river."

"Their loss."

"Let's go," Zollin said.

The three soldiers were standing in a small group near the stack of saddles and other tack. They had their backs to the woods, so Zollin and Mansel approached unseen. He could have killed them easily, and the thought went through his mind—it was more like a temptation, the way you are tempted to eat something sweet

195

when you smell it baking. But he resisted the urge. Tapping into his deep well of magic didn't bring the same sense of malevolence since he had learned to raise a magical barrier around it. But the power still sometimes made him giddy at the ease with which he could kill or destroy something. He was afraid of trying to put the soldiers to sleep. He didn't know how long they would stay unconscious and decided instead to send a wave of panic at them. He started slowly, pushing feelings of dread and then fear upon the unsuspecting soldiers. Then, out of nowhere he shouted at them. The soldiers, fully armed and armored, ran from the makeshift corral, screaming like children.

"Well, that was subtle," Mansel said sarcastically.

"Get busy," Zollin said, ignoring the jibe. "I've got something to do."

"Where the hell are you going?"

"I need my staff."

"Why?"

"I just do, now get the horses."

"Wizards!" Mansel said in exasperation.

Zollin ignored him and headed down into the camp. He wasn't sure where the soldiers would have put his staff. It may have been broken up and used as firewood, but he doubted it. Word would have traveled fast that he was a wizard, and fear would have kept his staff safe. Of course, he didn't need it, the long, white branch had only a fraction of his own power, but he felt comfortable with it. It was like a good friend, and he hated to leave it behind.

He moved stealthily up the back side of the small hill the officers had set up their camp on. Most of the soldiers had chosen to set up their tents on the river side of the hill, not wanting to trudge through the mud any further than they had to. Zollin went first to the officers' tent. It was large and well illuminated. Zollin could see the men moving around inside. The pinecone distraction hadn't been enough to take the knights from their comfortable abodes. He looked around but didn't see the staff. He did, however, see two large bottles of wine, tied together with a leather strap meant to stretch across a horse's back. The officers obviously didn't expect that the soldiers would be stupid enough to steal their wine. Zollin had no such qualms though. He picked up the wine bottles and was surprised to find that they were both full. He put the strap across his own shoulders and moved back into the shadows.

It was several more minutes before he spotted the staff leaning against the side of a tent. He didn't see the other weapons but wasn't worried about them. He assumed they would have been mixed in with the army's supplies, and none were as fine as what he'd made earlier in the day. He walked quickly over and picked up the staff, then turned to head back to where Mansel was stealing their horses. As he turned around, he found himself face to face with two surprised looking soldiers.

Without hesitating, he thrust his staff at them; blue energy crackled from the end and shocked both soldiers. They fell back, twitching and unconscious, but Zollin could tell they weren't seriously harmed. His own magical power was rolling inside him like clouds before a thunderstorm. It was as if it were anxious to join the fight, but there were no other threats, so Zollin tamped down his magic and hurried quickly down from the hill.

It took longer than Zollin had expected to get the horses ready, and the soldiers were slowly making their way back when Mansel was finally ready to go. They each mounted a horse and took the reins of another. Mansel had found Lilly, who seemed happy to see Zollin as he took her reins. He placed the wine across her rump, just behind the saddle. They rode back into the woods, then waited to see if the soldiers would raise the alarm. They didn't seem to notice the missing horses; each looked shamefaced and embarrassed at having run away from their posts.

"Let's go," said Zollin.

They rode quietly through the woods, letting the horses pick their way through the darkness. When they got back to the little camp where Quinn and Kelvich were waiting, the stones Zollin had heated for them were growing cold.

Quinn rose slowly to his feet. He hadn't eaten anything, his mouth was hurting too much. All he wanted was a warm place to stretch out and sleep. Kelvich was sleeping, his breathing sounded ragged again. Zollin lifted his teacher into the air and set him on the back of his own horse. He took hold of the sorcerer's hands, pulled them around his own body, and tied them together with a leather strap.

"We're ready," he said quietly.

Quinn led the way back to Kelvich's cottage since he'd made the trip in the dark before. It took almost an hour, and they were all half frozen by the time they arrived. Quinn went straight inside with Zollin, who was levitating Kelvich into the small home. Mansel took the horses into the little shed, loosened their girth straps, but left their saddles on. After he had given them oats and water, he went back into the cottage as well.

Zollin had dumped an armload of firewood from the front porch into the fireplace. With a tap of his staff, the wood burst into flames. Heat roared out of the fireplace to fill the cold cottage. The wood didn't just burn, it was consumed as the heat gushed like an artesian well. Soon the wood was down to embers, and Zollin carefully laid more wood on top of them. He had set Kelvich in his favorite rocking chair before the fire, with a blanket around his shoulders. Quinn had wrapped up in his cloak and lay on the floor with his feet near the fire. He was snoring when Mansel tramped in from the cold. He had both bottles of wine.

Satisfied that Kelvich was okay for the moment, he turned to the old sorcerer's books. He needed to know how to treat the fluid around his mentor's heart. He flipped through the books as Mansel poured himself a cup of wine.

"Oh, my," he said, smacking his lips. "That's good wine."

"Pour me a cup, please," Zollin said. He was hungry again, but waited until he found a way to help Kelvich before he ate.

Mansel poured the wine and handed it over.

"Your old man's snores sound exactly like when he saws wood with that old, wide-tooth saw of his. You remember?"

"Don't remind me. I hated that thing."

"It took a lot of work to cut with that saw, especially when he made us do it by ourselves."

"I thought it was some sort of punishment for a long time," Zollin said without looking up. He was studying a diagram of the heart.

"Do you ever miss it?" Mansel asked.

"Carpentry? Not at all. I always hated it."

"Not carpentry, just life before all this happened?" he said, spreading his arms as if he were gesturing to the last four months since they had fled Tranaugh Shire.

"I don't know," Zollin said. "I wasn't especially happy there, but I hate that we've been in pretty much constant danger since we left. I can't stand thinking about Brianna with that foul wizard Branock."

"Me either, but I don't regret leaving. I do occasionally miss it, but I wouldn't go back. It seems so small to me now."

"The town?"

"No, not the town really, the idea of the world I had when I was there. I always felt kind of trapped, but I just assumed life was the same everywhere. I mean, I knew there were other places, big cities even, but I couldn't imagine them. Still can't, really. I knew there was an army, and that was always an option for me, but it seemed so far away. When Quinn took me on as an apprentice I was thrilled. I was so happy to be out of the stinking tannery, and the work agreed with me. But now, I can't imagine going back to it. I don't know how Quinn managed it."

"You mean leaving the King's Army and going to live as a carpenter in Tranaugh Shire?"

"Yeah, you knew he was in the King's Guard, right? Can you imagine walking away from that? I hear even the knights give the King's Guard a wide berth."

"Love makes you do crazy things," Zollin said, thinking of Brianna.

"It must," Mansel said, staring into his cup.

Zollin found only one text that said anything about fluid buildup in the body. He saw that he could filter it through an organ called the Liver, and the body would dispose of it naturally. He pulled a stool up next to Kelvich and closed his eyes. He reached out with his magic and could feel every part of the sorcerer. He could feel the mucus building back up in the old man's lungs. He could feel the blood pooling around the wound on the back of his head where he'd been hit when Brianna was kidnapped. He could feel the fever, as his body worked frantically to discover what was making him so sick. It all led back to the heart, which was having trouble pumping blood through his veins. As Zollin delved into the sorcerer's heart, it became obvious that the organ was old and growing weaker. The fluid building up around the heart only made it work harder. Zollin gently moved the fluid into the chest cavity and away from the heart. The liver was like a big sponge, soaking up the fluid and moving it into his intestinal track. It took over an hour to get the fluid moved out from around the heart. There was a need for some of the fluid to remain and cushion the pumping organ, but Zollin could tell the heart was working more efficiently and with less effort. He then turned his attention back to the lungs.

He was sweating and tired by the time he finished. His knees were shaky, but Kelvich's lungs were clear. He was breathing much easier, and his fever had gone down considerably. It was only a few hours until dawn, but Zollin needed some food now. He found a block of hard cheese and sliced himself a few pieces. Mansel had almost finished one whole bottle of wine. There was barely a cupful left, but it was enough. Zollin drank it, then draped a blanket over Mansel's shoulders. He had fallen asleep with his head on the table. Zollin went into the small bedroom, which was much cooler than the main room of the cottage where the fireplace was, but he didn't mind. He was hot and tired and ready to fall over. He dropped onto the bed and pulled a quilt over his legs. Inside a small pocket of his shirt, he kept the ribbon Brianna had wrapped his birthday present with. It was thin and made from delicate material that he'd never seen before. Kelvich had told him it was silk from a country across the sea. It must have been the only thing she had brought with her from Tranaugh Shire. Now it reminded him of her as he pulled the delicate ribbon through his fingers over and over. His mind flashed images of Brianna like lightning across a dark sky. He felt tears welling up in his eyes. Now that the danger was over, at least for the moment, he could let his guard down.

He felt like a failure. He had let Brianna go, not forever, but for now. The realization hurt physically, and he squirmed on the bed, begging for sleep to free him from the crushing guilt. He couldn't imagine what she must be thinking. Was she expecting to see him at any minute, riding to her rescue? He had been a fool not to leave everyone else behind and chase the cowardly Branock down. The conniving wizard of the Torr had no honor, and there was no telling what he was subjecting Brianna to. Quinn's argument had been sound, but it still didn't feel right to be safe in bed while Brianna was in harm's way.

Then Todrek's face loomed up, like a ghost. He pointed his finger at Zollin and cursed him. *You see,* the ghost said, *I told you nothing good would come of this. Now Brianna is gone and it's all your fault.*

Zollin could hold the tears back no longer, they spilled down his cheeks as his sobs rocked him to sleep.

Chapter 18

Pain! It had been so long since the dragon had felt pain. Its soft scales had been pierced with wooden shards, and its tail smashed with heavy, timber beams and stone from the falling building. He had not been expecting it, and the pain was a shock to his entire system. His brain had seemed to freeze and revert to some ancient instinct, and he had fled. He'd flown high into the mountains, his tail dripping his precious blood. He had flown until his wings were on the verge of paralysis. Then he had blown his deadly breath on the rocky ridge beneath him until the rock made the cold air shimmer with heat. He had landed and begun the painful process of pulling the shards from his wounded tail, one by one, with his mouth. The wood grated against his teeth and sent chills up and down his body.

The dragon hated weakness and despised himself for allowing the wizard to best him in combat. True, the human had gotten lucky. Had his scales been truly hardened, he wouldn't have been wounded at all, but in this instance, he had been defeated and forced to flee. He had fed, although it was not a true gorging, as he had expected. But he was strong enough to return to his cave, where the gold would have its healing effect on his body and he could sleep for several days before needing to venture out and find food again. And he needed to get more gold; there was no telling how much had been discovered, mined, and turned into coin or jewelry. Gold was the one thing that could be used to control a dragon. A golden headpiece with a dragon's name inscribed on it gave the wearer complete control over a dragon.

Long ago, men had forgotten this fact. It was after the War of Fire, when the dragons had battled in the heavens for men's domination of the earth. Many had died, and the rest had fallen into hibernation to heal from their wounds. In the years that followed, men forgot the dragons and dragon lore. The headpieces were refashioned, and kings began to wear golden crowns on their heads, oblivious to the history that made gold and crowns so valuable. It wasn't the scarcity of the metal, and certainly not the usefulness of it, but the power it contained. Gold, pure gold, that was mined from the earth where it was hidden in creation, held power over the most formable creatures in the world. Since then, the dragons, upon waking from their long sleep, had been hunted by men as monsters, their mutual alliances forgotten. Most had perished until only a few remained, perhaps only one.

The dragon roared as it swung its wounded tail, the pain reminding it of the hatred in its heart for men. They were weak, pathetic creatures, with short lives. But they were deadly, too. No matter how hard his scales became, there was always one soft spot on a dragon's stomach that was vulnerable to their steel. He would need to find a *familiar,* someone whom the dragon could dominate and force to do his bidding. Then he would begin a reign of destruction that would force the Five Kingdoms to their knees. They would bring their gold to him, and he would let them live...mostly. The thought made the dragon smile, an expression that revealed rows of fangs and short, pointy teeth. It was horrific, and he knew it. Then a troubling thought crossed his mind and a baleful expression returned to his reptilian face. He would have to do something about the wizards. They were no longer satisfied serving kings and maintaining the balance. Their thirst for power had turned their attention to ancient lore, and, if left to their own devices, they might discover how to control him. The dragon vowed to never let that happen. He would crush the dreams of man, one way or another, and no wizard could stop him.

* * *

Zollin woke suddenly. He'd been dreaming that Branock was torturing Brianna. Sunlight was filtering in through the small window. He wasn't sure how long he'd been asleep, but it wasn't long enough. His body was crying for more rest, but he shook it off. The last thing he would do was sleep while Brianna was being carried further and further away. He sat up on the small bed and rubbed the sleep from his eyes. They were swollen and puffy, partly from sleep and partially from the tears he'd cried the night before.

He stood up and stretched, his muscles ached and his stomach growled. He ignored both and went into the main room of the little cottage. Mansel was still asleep at the table, and Quinn was snoring softly on the floor. Both would be very stiff when they woke up, Zollin thought, but he didn't wake them up yet. Instead he checked on Kelvich. The sorcerer's hair was damp from sweat, his fever had broken and his breathing was much easier. Zollin added more wood to the fire, which was now little more than a few coals among the pile of ashes. He sent a little command of magic, and flames licked up over the wood and began popping and crackling merrily.

Not long ago, Brianna had been here, he thought. He had stood with her near the fireplace, and he could still remember the way her hair smelled, clean and fresh. He was tempted to saddle his horse and head out on his own. He could move faster that way, and he didn't need the others to defeat Branock, but his father's idea about running into a trap lingered in his mind. He found some bread and eggs that Kelvich had in the little kitchen area of the cabin. He was about to prepare breakfast when he heard voices outside. He went to the door and flung it open. A cold gust of wind swept past him into the little cottage.

There was a group of villagers approaching, some with swords and others with bows. A few even had lit torches, which Zollin found odd since the sun was up and there was plenty of light. Then it dawned on him what the villagers meant to do.

"What do you want?" he called out.

"This is your fault," cried one of the men in front. "It's him and the others brought disaster on the Gate."

"Face us like a man," shouted someone else.

"He doesn't have his staff," said another. "What are you waiting for?"

An arrow came flying in his direction. It would have missed him had he done nothing, but he didn't want them to think he was powerless. He reached out with his magic and caught the arrow, arresting its flight but holding it up in the air. He turned it so that it was facing the crowd.

"He's a devil," someone shouted.

"He'll be the death of us all," cried another.

"Burn him," came another voice. "Burn them all."

Zollin heard his father come to the door. Quinn was still wiping the sleep from his eyes, but he'd heard the threats and had come to see what was happening.

"We saved your village," Zollin said loudly. "We saved you from the Skellmarians and the miners and then from the dragon.

"The dragon burned down the village," shouted the man in front again. He'd been frightened by the arrow, but he had found his courage again. "We've no homes to live in. No way to make a living."

"Most of your homes were made of stone," Zollin said spitefully. "I doubt they burned completely."

"We've lost everything," came a woman's voice.

"So you rebuild it," said Zollin. "You aren't the first village to have to do so."

"We will rebuild," said the man in front, "but first we're going to deal with you and your ilk."

"Wait a minute," said Quinn. "Hasn't there been enough blood?"

"You brought the blood with you," someone shouted.

"Don't be fools," Quinn said angrily. "We didn't bring the Skellmarians down from the mountains. If those soldiers hadn't been here to capture Zollin, you'd all be dead or enslaved."

"We think if the soldiers came for Zollin, then we should turn him over to them," said another man. "We don't harbor outlaws."

There was smattering of approval, but not everyone was convinced.

"The army doesn't care about us anymore, they've been tasked with stopping the Skellmarians from getting any further into the Great Valley. You need to set up a camp where you can be safe when the Skellmarians return and work to rebuild your homes."

"And where you propose we do that?" someone shouted. "There's not a building anywhere in the Gate that didn't get damaged in some form or fashion."

"Why not here?" Quinn said, stepping down from the porch. "Zollin, drop that arrow."

Zollin let the arrow fall to the ground but didn't drop his guard.

"We're here to burn this place," shouted the man in front. "And all them in it."

"Don't be hasty, Olihon," said someone else. "We need to build, not tear down."

"But it's them that brought the dragon."

"Zollin was the only one able to fend off that dragon," Quinn said in a steady voice. "We're leaving the valley soon to go after Brianna, who was taken against her will. But we can stay and help you establish a base camp and begin rebuilding your town."

Zollin was dumbstruck. He had no intention of staying in the valley any longer than necessary to ensure that Kelvich was going to be okay. Then he was leaving to find Brianna. He didn't care what his father or anyone else thought.

"What'll we eat?" someone shouted. "We lost almost all our food in the fires."

"The soldiers can help with that," Quinn said. "And we will, too. We'll send help back from the villages south of here. The other towns in the Great Valley will help, too. It won't be easy, but no one has lost their lives from Brighton's Gate. Your sons are alive, your daughters still with you. You can rebuild what you've lost, and we will help."

The crowd was murmuring now, considering what Quinn had said. Zollin stepped off the porch and looked at his father. Quinn was smiling, but he wasn't happy. There was a deep pain behind his eyes, grief over Brianna and fear for their lives. Zollin saw it and softened his tone, but he kept his voice as firm as his decision.

"I'm not staying," he said. "If you want stay that's fine, but I'm going to find Brianna."

"I'm going with you, but we can help these people while we're here."

"I'm leaving today, Dad, there's no reason to wait."

"What about Kelvich?"

"He'll be fine. His fever broke in the night. I cleared his lungs and the fluid buildup around his heart. He just needs a few days rest, and he'll be fine."

"Okay, well, then just give us those few days. In the meantime, we can do a lot for these people."

"These people who were ready to burn us alive?" Zollin asked, his voice as potent as any acid. "I'm done with them. They won't seem to do anything for themselves, so why should I?"

"Because it's the right thing to do."

"I wasn't really asking," Zollin said under his breath as he returned to the porch.

The group of people from Brighton's Gate were now ready to talk some more. Zollin felt for them, but he couldn't understand why they wouldn't stand up for themselves. They were always angry with Zollin, when he and his family had been the only ones willing to do anything to save them.

"There's no shelter here," said one man.

"The cabin is in good shape and the shed out back, too," Quinn told them. "We can use some of the tents from the army for extra shelters, and we can build more. Up here, you're away from the town and not on the direct path of Telford's Pass. If the Skellmarians come back, they may not bother you up here."

"But why is it better here than out by the army?" someone else asked.

"Higher ground, for one thing. The plain where the army is camped will be a bog soon. The only source of water is the river, and you'll have to walk much further to get back and forth from the village. Here you have fresh water and some shelter for the sick. The trees will give you protection from the worst of the weather, hide you from prying eyes, and there are plenty of resources for staying warm."

"What kind of help will you give us?" someone asked.

"As much as we can before we leave."

"Where are you going? You said south, but the pass is still snowed in."

"That's not an issue," said Zollin.

"And what do you want in return?" asked someone else from the crowd of people.

"Nothing," said Quinn immediately. "We aren't here to take advantage of you. You're good people, and we want to see you safe, that's all."

"Not everyone trusts your boy there," said a woman at the front of the crowd. She was still holding a lit torch.

"Don't worry, I'm leaving today," said Zollin. "Just as soon as I can gather some supplies."

The townspeople looked at each other and nodded.

"Go get everyone else," Quinn said. "And we'll get started."

The crowd turned and headed back down toward the village. Quinn turned and looked at Zollin, smiling. His son did not smile back.

"I meant what I said," Zollin informed him.

"I'm not stopping you," Quinn said. "But I can't help you clear the pass, now can I? I don't know how long it will take you, but I'll stay here with Kelvich until he's rested up and ready to ride. You and Mansel go ahead. If you get out of the pass before we catch up with you, take one day to rest and wait for us. After that, use your pathfinder and head southwest. That will take you to Orrock, but be careful. If we still haven't caught up with you by the time you reach the city, give us two days before you do anything. And Zollin, be smart. You can guarantee that wizard will be ready for you."

Zollin nodded, then went to check on the horses. He was still hungry, but he was more anxious than ever to leave. He brought out two of the horses and then went into the cottage to gather supplies. Mansel was stirring slowly, Kelvich dozing by the fire.

"What are you doing?" Mansel asked as he rubbed the sleep from his eyes.

"Packing a few things. You can stay here and help Dad rebuild the town or come with me."

"Quinn's staying? For how long?"

"I don't know for sure. He says he'll follow after Kelvich is well, but he'll probably be happier staying indefinitely."

"Well I'm not staying," Mansel said as he stood up.

"Good, the horses are ready. Help me pack something to eat."

There wasn't much food, but they divided it all in two, packing Zollin and Mansel's share into bags. He left some silver and gold that he had transmuted from other materials.

Then he went to find his father. He was very conflicted. He had wanted his father to stay and find happiness, but he resented the townspeople of Brighton's Gate, too. It irked him to think that they might get to be with his father, they didn't deserve him. And if he was being honest, he felt as if Quinn were giving up on Brianna.

"You ready to go?" Quinn said when he saw Zollin coming.

"Yes."

"Well, be careful. I will be along in a few days."

"You don't have to, you know."

"What do you mean?" Quinn asked, the surprise on his face was genuine.

"I mean, if you like it here, you can stay. I ruined your life in Tranaugh Shire, but you can have a home here. The people will come to respect you, once I'm gone."

"Zollin, I'm coming with you."

"Why? There's really no telling what is going to happen. There's no sense in you risking your life for me and Brianna."

"You're my son," Quinn said fiercely. "And believe it or not, I love Brianna, too. She's become like a daughter to me. I'll be damned if I'll let anyone take my family away from me."

"I don't get it then," Zollin said. "If it is that important to you, why are staying here to help these people? They don't care about us. In fact, they blame us for everything that happened here, and none of it was our fault."

"You're right son, but I hate to leave them without hope. Building things is what I do, it's my magic. Helping them is the right thing for me."

Zollin shook his head in frustration. He couldn't say why he was so angry, perhaps it had nothing to do with his father at all, but deep down he had always resented Quinn's choice to work rather than spend time helping Zollin discover what he was great at. Quinn had spent years trying to help Zollin learn a trade that he would never be good at. Now that he knew his destiny, seeing his father choose to stay and build, rather than leave with his son, was like rubbing salt in an old wound.

"You always help others, but what about helping yourself."

"What do you mean?"

"I mean, it seems like you always choose to help others, and the people who love you pay the price."

"Excuse me?"

"You know what I mean, Dad. You've always cared more about your work than about me."

"That's not true," Quinn said in shock.

"It is true. My whole life I've tried to make you proud and do things your way, but I'm not staying here. I'm not helping these people. I'm going after Brianna, and you might as well just stay here."

Quinn was dumbfounded. He simply didn't know what to say. He was still standing rooted to the spot, watching, as Zollin and Mansel rode swiftly away.

* * *

Brianna hurt all over. Her head was throbbing again, the skin itched where the blood had dried on the back of her head and down her neck. The wound from being hit over the head was sharp, especially in the freezing cold, night air. Her back and legs were aching from being on the horse all day and then all through the night. They didn't stop to eat or rest. Branock was using some type of spell to keep the horse going, but he did nothing to help Brianna. She tried to sleep, her head drooping forward until her chin bounced against her chest, but she could never do more than doze lightly, and her neck was now in a major kink that hurt whenever she turned her head. As the sun rose, they could see a small homestead in the distance.

All she could think about was stopping and getting off the horse, which she had come to hate. Hunger and lack of sleep made her thoughts murky. She was shivering from cold and exposure through the night, but most of all she was heart sick. The only thing she could imagine that would keep Zollin from riding to her rescue was that he'd been hurt. He'd been battling the dragon, which was absolutely horrifying and at the same time seemed impossible. She'd heard stories of dragons, but she'd never believed they were anything more than stories. Now she had seen one, seen it diving down and devouring people, destroying buildings and fighting Zollin, but it was hard to accept as reality. Everything seemed like a bad dream to her exhausted mind.

"Mind your manners, and we'll be off this dreadful beast soon," Branock said conversationally.

Brianna hated the wizard so intensely, but she felt powerless at the moment to do anything more than grunt. She had to admit, getting off the horse sounded divine, but she didn't want to give Branock the satisfaction of her affirmation.

They approached the small home. Unlike the village at Brighton's Gate, which was built well back from the river's edge, this building was constructed right on the bank. It had a set of wooden stairs that led down to a pier. There was a good size fishing boat moored to the stairs, since the river had risen so high. Unlike most of the small boats Brianna had seen on the river, this boat had a wide deck and a small enclosed cabin.

People from the home came out to greet them, but Brianna could see the nervous look in their eyes. The sight of the bald wizard, with his scarred face and milky eye, was not welcome. Still, the people tried their best to be courteous. Branock didn't try to bargain, he simply threw the man who greeted him a small pouch of gold coins.

"What's this?" the man asked.

"We need passage downriver to the bay," Branock said.

"Oh, well, I suppose we might help with that," the man said.

"Of course you can."

"I'm Drogan, and these are my sons. We'll need a little time to gather supplies for a voyage that long. Would you like to come in and warm yourselves by the fire?"

"Yes," Branock said. "We need wine and food, too. You can keep the horse."

"Yes, sir," Drogan said, and then ordered one his sons, he had four of them, to take the horse.

Branock swung down from the horse, and Brianna was left swaying in the saddle. He stretched his back; the scar tissue was stiff from disuse, but he had been successful in using the Zipple Weed to keep his strength up. To Branock, Brianna was like a black hole of magic, sucking all his powers away. If he so much as touched her, he was powerless. It had been a difficult chore to use the Zipple Weed while on the horse, but he had managed it. He reached up and pulled the girl down. He didn't bother trying to catch her. Years of using his magic to do the simplest chores hadn't left him with much physical strength, and he saw no need to strain himself. The ground was muddy, and he let her fall.

Brianna felt his arm and the slight tug that sent her toppling to the ground. She tried to brace her fall, but her arms simply didn't have the strength. She landed on one shoulder, and the air was knocked out of her lungs. She lay gasping as the horse shied away from her. She rolled onto her back in the mud, which was covering her clothes and clinging to her hair.

"Bring her inside," Branock ordered.

The women from the homestead were watching the scene in horror. They simply couldn't believe anyone would treat a woman that way. Branock seemed oblivious to their disapproval. He walked into the home without waiting.

Drogan began giving orders to everyone. Two of the boys lifted Brianna gently to her feet and helped her inside, where one of the women took her into a side room. The room was warmer than the temperature outside, but not by much. She peeled Brianna's dress off and scrubbed her face and hands clean of the mud. She also washed the mud out of her hair and then braided it while Brianna drank a cup of mulled wine. She was finally getting some feeling in her hands and feet again. They dressed her in thick, wool leggings. Then they pulled on a short dress with long sleeves and high collar. They helped her into the kitchen, which had a roaring fire going. Branock was dozing by the fire, and Brianna was given a plate of food and a stool to sit on. She had trouble staying awake long enough to finish the rich fair. It was smoked fish, eggs and cheese, thick slices of toasted bread with butter. There was more wine, and by the time she was finished, she could hardly hold her head up.

She curled up by the fire and slept on the floor. It was close to midday when the same girl who had bathed her shook her gently. She looked fearful but didn't speak. Only motioned for Brianna to get up and follow her. Branock was waiting by the door.

"Let's go," he said impatiently.

He took her arm roughly and led her outside. The sun was high overhead, and the day had warmed slightly. He pushed her forward, down the wooden staircase that led to the boat. She had to step over the railing of the boat, which was high, but the wool pants she had on protected her modesty. Branock pushed her roughly into the little cabin. He had no desire to see the scenery. He locked the door and looked at Brianna coldly.

"I need you alive," he said coldly. "But I have no qualms about keeping you trussed up like a wild animal, if that is how you choose to behave. Try to escape, and I will make your life miserable. Play along, and we'll have a pleasant voyage down the coast and then set up in the castle at Orrock. You can have servants waiting on you, hand and foot. You might even find a wealthy noble willing to make you his latest wife. No need to thank me, just don't annoy me and we'll get along just fine."

Brianna was on the floor of the cabin, which was crowded with a tiny bed, a stool, and a low table. Her first impulse was to spew threatening curses, but she knew it would just be hollow bravado. She was exhausted, almost too sore to move, and she couldn't swim. If she tried to escape, she would drown, but her captor didn't need to know that. He couldn't have picked a more effective way to ensure that she wouldn't try to escape. She decided to pretend to be docile. Maybe, she thought, she could even lull him into a sense of complacency so that she could escape or at least exact revenge, if the opportunity presented itself down the road.

She lay down on the floor, trying to get comfortable on the rough surface. The rocking motion of the boat lulled her to sleep.

"Good," Branock said, dropping wearily onto the bed.

He took a moment and created a magical seal on the door. It was nothing more than transmuting part of the wood to terracotta, but if she tried to open the door, the pottery would break and fall to the floor, making a clattering racket that would wake him up. Then he stretched out on the bed, hoping that it wasn't too infested with vermin, but too tired to really care.

Brianna couldn't help but think of Zollin and then Quinn and Mansel, and even Kelvich. She worried that they weren't well. Perhaps they had been wounded, or even killed by the dragon or the Skellmarians. She felt tears leaking from her eyes, but she didn't care. She was too tired to even wipe her cheeks as the teardrops rolled down her face.

Chapter 19

Zollin rode up high into the woods, preferring to pick his way forward rather than ride straight up the road. The tall pines and stately cedars seemed like familiar friends, and he liked the feeling of seclusion they gave him. It matched his dark mood. He didn't like leaving Quinn and Kelvich behind, although he had contemplated leaving them all behind to set out in pursuit of Brianna. Still, now that he had actually done it, he felt uneasy. They needed to stay together, where he could protect them, he thought to himself, so why had he gotten so angry and told his father to stay behind? Keeping them all safe was all he really wanted from life anymore.

Mansel rode silently behind Zollin. He was glad that he hadn't been asked to stay and help the people of Brighton's Gate rebuild their town. He liked carpentry well enough and enjoyed the sense of satisfaction the work brought when he could look at a completed project, but his heart wasn't in the work, not anymore. He longed for a good horse, an open road, and the promise of adventure. And he was growing fond of Zollin, too. They weren't good friends, not yet, at any rate. He had always seemed too timid to Mansel, not to mention clumsy. And Mansel had not always treated his younger companion with respect, but he had never meant it as personal dislike. They were just different, that was all. Now he had a great respect for Zollin and the magic the boy could wield. He wanted nothing more that to help Zollin free Brianna, whom he'd come to love just like a sister.

Neither of the young men talked as they rode. Mansel was nursing a headache, and Zollin was too deep in his brooding thoughts. When they were finally forced onto the road that led into

Telford's Pass, they rode side by side. Mansel looked every inch the warrior that he was becoming. He had thick shoulders and a squarish jaw that bristled with stubble. Zollin was the opposite; he was slender, the muscle stretching across his frame like it did his father's. Using magic seemed to burn through calories, and he was on the verge of being too thin, although he had kept himself and Kelvich well fed through the long winter.

Neither of them were surprised when they came around a bend in the pass and found a squad of soldiers blocking their path. The area was V shaped, with the mountains rising steeply on either side of the trail. There was enough room for four men riding side by side on the trail, or for five men with shields to form an effective wall. There were probably twenty men on the path, all foot soldiers with shields and short swords. And another ten archers were scattered up the sides of the mountains so that they could rain arrows down on attackers trying to break through the blockade.

Zollin and Mansel halted their horses and looked at the squad in front of them.

"This is awkward," Mansel joked.

Zollin knew the soldiers couldn't stop him, but the last thing he wanted was to hurt anyone. They were only following orders, and if Quinn was right, they might end up being the only thing that stood between Yelsia and the Skellmarians if the barbarians invaded again.

"You think they'll try to detain us?" Zollin asked.

"Not if they're smart," Mansel scoffed. "Besides, what would they do with us? It would take four or five of them to haul us back to where the army is camped."

"They may want payback for stealing their horses," Zollin said.

"Let them try," Mansel said.

Zollin recognized the bravado. He knew there were more than enough soldiers to take Mansel out if they wanted to. He had been more than brave against the Skellmarians. He'd shown true skill with his sword, especially from horseback, but there was no way to maneuver in the pass, the foot soldiers had the advantage.

"Well, let's go. If they want to pick a fight, I guess we'll just have to deal with that," Zollin said grimly.

They rode forward and one of the soldiers raised a hand to stop them.

"That's far enough," the soldier said in a loud voice. "No one is allowed through the pass. You'll have to turn back."

"We must be allowed through," said Zollin. "Our friend has been kidnapped, and we are going to get her back."

"Yes, I was told you might try. You're the wizard, right?"

"My name is Zollin, and yes, I'm a wizard."

"Can't let you through, we've got our orders."

"You better think that through again, meathead," Mansel said loud enough for everyone to hear. "He'll turn your men into a bunch of toads, and we'll feast on frog legs for dinner."

"Mansel, shut up," Zollin snapped.

The young warrior raised his hands in a playful gesture of surrender.

"We don't want to fight," said the soldier.

"Neither do we, but we are going past, with or without your help."

The soldiers looked at one another, whispering under their breath. They weren't knights or even cavalry soldiers. Most had

221

joined the King's army because they had no other way to make a living. None of them had seen actual combat before the previous day, when the Skellmarians invaded the Gate. They didn't seem anxious to repeat the experience. But one of the archers decided he could deal with Zollin on his own. He was a young man, barely older than Zollin himself. He hadn't seen Zollin battle the dragon, and he acted completely on his own. He loosed an arrow that would have punched through the wizard's chest, stopping his heart instantly. But Zollin felt the projectile coming, and, without a conscious thought on his part, his magic leapt out and caught the arrow in midair. He spun it around and sent it flying back at the archer, missing the boy by mere inches.

"Hold your fire!" shouted the soldier who seemed to be in charge. "Damn it, Garrit! They aren't Skellmarians. You were ordered not to fire on anyone but Skellmarians. How many times do you have to be told?"

"Sorry," came a shaky voice.

"We'll let you pass," the soldier said to Zollin.

"Thank you," he replied, his anger at having been shot at still kindling leaping flames of magic inside his chest.

The soldiers spread out so that Zollin and Mansel could pass riding single file. The soldiers asked if they had seen or heard anything from the village or from across the river. Mansel explained that the townspeople were moving into the forest not far away, and that they would need food. Zollin and Mansel had instructions to inform anyone in the villages they passed to send aid. They explained all of this and then pushed on. They rode upward at a steady pace for another hour before the snow blocked their way. They had seen plenty of snow in the shadowy parts of the mountains, but finally they had reached the point where it was piled up in the pass, where it had obviously fallen from higher up on the slopes. Parts of it had melted and refrozen until it was thick and solid, almost like a block of ice.

"What now?" Mansel asked.

"Take the horses back a short way. I'll see what I can do."

Zollin's first thought had been to simply move the snow out of their path, but it was packed together. Even his magic couldn't lift it, and if he had been able to, there was no place to put it. Instead he kindled fire from his staff. Not the blue, electrical energy, but bright yellow flames. The heat bounced off the snow, and Zollin was soon sweating, but the snow was melting quickly.

He realized he didn't need to melt it all, but rather to just create a ramp that allowed them on top of the snow. It was packed enough that even the horses would walk across it. He led the way, making sure there were no unexpected weak spots on their path. For the most part, it was easy going, but Zollin's damp clothes clung to his skin and made him cold. Just before sundown, Zollin used his power to make a small shelter for the horses between the snow in the pass and the side of the mountain. Zollin and Mansel climbed higher, where the sun had melted the snow. The rocky mountainside wasn't comfortable, but it was better than trying to sleep on the snow. Plus, Zollin used his magic to heat the ground, so that although they had no campfire, they weren't cold.

"It's odd not to have a campfire, at least," said Mansel. "I can handle the cold, but I miss having a fire to look at."

"Don't be so negative," Zollin said. "Try looking up. You can see so much more of the stars without a fire."

They were wrapped in blankets and although they had found a relatively level spot to camp, it still felt like one wrong move would send them rolling down the hillside.

"It isn't natural," Mansel said.

"Just imagine what Brianna must be feeling."

"I don't want to think about that."

"Me either, but it doesn't change the fact that I can't stop thinking about it. We may not be comfortable, but at least we're not prisoners."

"When we were chained up by the river, after the soldiers jumped you, that had to be the worst feeling of my life. I was lucky I was tired really. At least I was able to sleep through most of it."

"I know what you mean. I can't stop wondering what that bastard is doing to her. I wish that I had just gone after her. This waiting around is killing me."

"You did the right thing," Mansel said kindly. "I think Quinn was right. We need to be smart. I'm as anxious as anyone to get Brianna back, but we need to do it on our terms."

"You love her, don't you?" Zollin said, swallowing the huge lump in his throat. He'd been happy to believe that Mansel didn't have feelings for Brianna, but lying there, side by side, in the dark, he couldn't help but ask.

"I love her like a sister," Mansel said. "It might have been different in Tranaugh Shire, but not now. She's got some weird connection with you, and I'm not ready to be in love with any one person. There's lots of pretty in the world, Zollin. I mean to see as much of it as I can."

Zollin took a deep, shuttering breath. Hearing Mansel say that he loved Brianna like a sister was a huge relief. His view of the world was changing, even the way he saw the tanner's son, who had always been his rival for Quinn's attention and approval, but it was hard to think that any girl would choose Zollin over

Mansel. He was rugged and handsome, a man's man and the kind of man that girls swooned over. He wore his sword with authority, and his shaggy hair and sheepish grin only made him even more likable.

"What made you come with us?" Zollin asked. "I don't mean from Tranaugh Shire, but from Brighton's Gate. You were a hero there. Could have had your pick of the town's daughters."

"And died of boredom," Mansel said.

"You could have led the town against the Skellmarians."

"No, that's not my thing. I love the fighting, don't get me wrong. There's nothing I'd rather do than fight, but I'm not Quinn. Strategy isn't my thing. Just give me a sword and point me toward the bad guys, that's what I like. I certainly don't want people looking to me for advice. Besides, the Skellmarians are beaten, they'll go back up in the mountains and not be seen again until we're old men. No thanks, I'd rather ride into adventure than sit and hope it doesn't pass me by."

Zollin pondered this. It made him think about what he really wanted to do. He was a wizard, and he wanted to learn and grow in that power as much as he could—but to what end, he wondered. He'd never really given it much thought. He'd been learning to fight with magic, just like Mansel had with his sword. It was all about survival and protecting those he loved. But what would he do once he'd won Brianna back? Could he disappear the way Kelvich had, live in isolation? He knew he would never leave Brianna, and the thought of the two of them alone sounded wonderful, actually. But he also knew he would get bored. He would need something to do, something to give his life meaning and purpose. But what? He could be a merchant, but that was laughable. He was about as good with money as he was at carpentry, and why bother buying and selling when he could turn the stones at his feet into gold? There had to be something worth doing, something good and honorable, but he didn't know what it was.

"You ever think about home?" Mansel asked.

"Sometimes," Zollin admitted. Mansel had startled him out of his meditation on the future.

"I wouldn't mind passing through on my way to Orrock. Just to let my family know I'm okay."

"Yeah, I don't think I can do that," Zollin said. "It's not really on the way, and I'm not ready to face Todrek's parents. Not while we're still trying to figure who wants me dead and why."

"Oh," Mansel said. "I didn't think of that. It's probably not a good idea, anyway. The bad guys might expect you to try and go back."

"I didn't think of that, but you're probably right."

They sat in silence for a while, the lack of sleep and the extreme amounts of adrenaline that had been pumped through their systems yesterday was taking it toll quickly. Zollin's eyelids were drooping.

"You think she's thinking about us?" Zollin asked.

"Who, Brianna? I'll bet she is. I'll bet she's constantly looking over her shoulder, expecting to see us come riding to the rescue any moment."

"That's what I'm afraid of," Zollin said. "She'll probably hate me for not doing just that."

"No, I don't think so," said Mansel. "She's smart. She of all people would want you to do things the right way. She'll be watching for you, but she'll want you to surprise her and, more importantly, shock the hell out of the coward that took her."

"He's a powerful wizard, but I could have killed him. If that blasted dragon hadn't interfered, I would have."

"Listen to you, talking about a dragon like it was a cow or something. You fought a dragon and managed to drive it away. They'll be writing songs about that before long."

"I didn't kill the dragon," Zollin said.

"No, but you fought one. I didn't even believe they were real until that one showed up. That was scary. I don't know that I could have done what you did."

"I didn't at first. I was trying to run away, but it was too big and Kelvich was hurt. We just couldn't get away fast enough. I didn't want it to hurt them, so I just ran out there without really thinking about it. When it was over, I was so focused on finding Brianna that I never really thought about it."

"That was a big, nasty beast. The neck and tail were so long."

"I know, it used the tail to try and kill me. It almost worked, too. In fact, if it hadn't missed me and slammed into the Gateway, I don't know what would have happened."

"I thought they were supposed to have impenetrable skin," said Mansel.

"Me, too, but this one didn't. Some of those wood shards stabbed right into it."

"It's too bad we didn't kill it. That would have been something for the minstrels to sing about. Mansel and Zollin, slaying the dragon, side by side."

"Well, if it shows up again, I'll remember you said that," Zollin said.

They both laughed and then grew silent. Each lost in his own thoughts. Zollin's mind feverish over Brianna. Mansel dreaming of glory with his sword.

* * *

Brianna was looking at the same stars, only she was forced to view them from the tiny cabin doorway. She was huddled under blankets on the floor. Branock had slept less than Brianna, but he seemed to need very little sleep. He dozed through the day and spent his nights out on the deck, gazing up at the stars. He seemed impervious to the cold and long hours of solitude. Brianna had spent hours working alone in her father's shop or doing chores around their home, but the sound of voices had never been far away. She loathed the vile wizard and had no wish to speak to him, but she missed being around people.

Drogan and his sons worked the vessel but kept to themselves. If they talked, it was in low voices that Brianna couldn't hear. It was obvious that they were afraid of Branock, and why shouldn't they be? He was terrifying to look at. His scarred face and ruined eye were the stuff of nightmares and ghost stories. She had hoped at first that the fishermen might try to save her, but they didn't, and she didn't blame them. They could only guess at what Branock could do, but she knew. She had seen the fire billowing from his hands and rushing out to envelope her. If it hadn't been for the ring that Zollin had given her, she would have been killed.

She couldn't think of dying, the thought brought tears to her eyes. It made her think of poor Todrek, and the way his eyes stared when the life had left his body. His flesh had gone waxy, like the drippings from a candle. It had terrified her and not because he was her husband or because of love—she had never loved him. It was because it was so final. She wondered what would happen to her once Branock had Zollin. She had hoped beyond hope that Zollin would come riding to rescue her, but once they set sail on the small fishing boat, it was obvious that no horse could keep up. Even if Zollin could magically boost a horse's stamina as Branock had done, no animal could keep pace with the rapidly flowing river. The spring thaw had not only flooded the river, but quickened its pace tenfold.

She had no idea where he was, but she hoped that somewhere he was looking at the same stars and thinking of her. She closed her eyes and pulled the blankets closer, trying not to shiver. She was still very sore. It would have helped to walk around and work some of the soreness out of her muscles and joints. Branock had not allowed that, however. She was confined to the cabin, and although her body ached, she didn't mind. He rarely spent time in the small space, and she wanted to be as far from him as possible. Plus, the water frightened her. She remembered seeing Quinn slip and fall into the icy water when he had fought the Skellmarian chief. It was a nightmare beyond imagining and, despite the fact that Zollin had rescued Quinn, it had left Brianna with nightmares for weeks. She dreamed that she was the one falling into the river and being carried downstream under the thick layer of ice, freezing and drowning, until she clawed her blankets as if they were slimy tentacles holding her under the water.

She stretched her sore muscles, which hurt, but felt good at the same time. She adjusted her body on the rough floor of the cabin again. She had to move around a lot to alleviate the constant pain the rough floor caused her. Still, she was alive, and Branock had not hurt her anymore since they had boarded the ship. That was something to be grateful for. She looked up at the stars one more time before closing her eyes.

"Oh, Zollin," she said in a quiet voice. "Where are you?"

* * *

The next morning, just before dawn, Kelvich woke up and stirred from his place by the fire. He had been asleep for most of the day before, only waking briefly as people came into his cabin. He had thought it strange that so many people were coming and going, bustling about the small space as if they belonged, but he was just too weary to care. He felt better, much better in fact, but his body was drained of energy. So he had slept. The fire had warmed him, as had the blankets that were draped over him and his rocking chair.

He rose and stretched the knotted muscles in his back, neck, and legs. His bones popped, but the people, mostly children, wrapped in blankets on the floor didn't seem to mind. They were sleeping deeply as the morning's chill crept into the room. The fire was down to just a few glowing embers, but it was enough to kindle a new blaze. Beside the fireplace, an ample supply of firewood had been neatly stacked, from fat logs to thin shavings used for kindling the fire. He started with the shavings, and once he had them crackling, he added more wood until the fire was warming the small cabin nicely. Then he ventured to the front door.

In the clearing, he found long tables and several cooking fires with spits. There were barrels stacked neatly, and a crew of women were already hard at work preparing meals. Among the trees, which no longer held snow, were the ghostly forms of white tents. Kelvich closed the door quietly and made his way to the rear of the house. His bedroom had been cleared of furniture and converted to a storeroom. There was a faint smell of smoke in the room, which was stacked with bottles of wine, potatoes, loaves of bread, and wheels of cheese. Kelvich opened the back door to find a make shift pen with sheep, dogs, swine, goats, and a few milking cows all separated into their own areas. The smell of the animals was strong and unpleasant. There was also a large saw set up to mill lumber. Kelvich found Quinn looking over the saw.

"What's going on around here?" Kelvich asked him as he stepped out into the cold morning.

"Townspeople set up camp here," Quinn said gruffly.

"Why here?"

"I told them to."

"Why? Why not in the town where they live? I don't recall inviting my home to become a camp and cattle yard."

"No, you weren't well and so I didn't consult with you," Quinn said in a tight, cold voice that betrayed his anger. "These people needed a safe place to rebuild their lives, and this was as good as any."

"They're ruining my property," Kelvich said, not quite sure why he was arguing about it. He didn't really care, nor did he expect to be living here much longer, but the anger in Quinn's voice had put him on the defensive.

"I don't give a damn about your property," Quinn said. "You want to tell me where that dragon came from?"

"What? I don't know what you're talking about."

"The hell you don't. You told us that Zollin was waking up the land, that magical beings were being drawn to him. What you didn't mention were dragons. But since one just happened to show up and destroy the town, I'm guessing it was drawn to him, and you just forgot to mention it."

"Quinn, I had no idea about that or any other dragon."

"But you knew it was possible."

232

"I know that there are many wondrous parts of our world that have lain dormant for centuries. But like anything, you have to take the good with the bad. I didn't know about the dragon, but I'm not surprised by it. I think we're going to see things that will astound us all."

"Oh," Quinn said spitefully. "I'm astounded alright. Astounded by your stupidity. What I can't quite figure out is why you want this so badly. Why do you want to unleash dangerous creatures on the land, Kelvich? What do you gain? Is it just some sort of perverted sense of revenge?"

"Don't be a fool," Kelvich said in a low voice.

"I've been a fool, letting Zollin anywhere near you. I won't make that mistake again."

"Zollin's a grown man, he can do whatever he pleases."

"You'd like that, wouldn't you?" said Quinn. "Unleash his awful power and ride his coattails to power. Is that your game?"

"I'm not playing any games."

"Neither am I," Quinn said, stepping to within inches of the older man and lowering his voice to barely above a whisper. "I see you near him again, and I'll kill you."

"What are you talking about?" Kelvich said loudly.

"You heard me, old man," Quinn said. "I don't care who or what you are. You stay away from Zollin."

Some of the other men from Brighton's Gate had begun to gather around them, a fact that Quinn didn't seem to mind. Kelvich was flabbergasted. He didn't know what was happening, but he didn't like it. Neither did he like the fact that he hadn't seen Zollin in the cabin or anywhere near it.

"Where is he?" Kelvich asked, suddenly very worried.

"None of your concern," Quinn said flatly.

"Quinn, you didn't send him after the girl alone, did you?"

"He's a grown man, he can do whatever he pleases," Quinn said in a mocking tone. "He's not alone. And I'll be joining him in a few days, but you won't."

"I have to," Kelvich said. "He needs me."

"No, this town needs you. Stay here and clean up the mess you created. I can take care of my family."

"I'm not questioning your ability, Quinn, but Zollin needs someone who understands him, who understands the burden of his abilities. He needs me," Kelvich said with a note of desperation.

"More like you need him," Quinn said. "I meant what I said. You go near him, and I'll kill you."

Kelvich watched in exasperation as Quinn turned away and started giving orders to the men watching nearby. Quinn seemed as at home running a refugee camp as he was drinking ale in the village inn. He sent two men for the horses that would turn the big crank that powered the saw. Others were sent to begin cutting trees. Kelvich could only imagine the damage that had been done to Brighton's Gate by the dragon, but it wasn't his fault.

The thought occurred to him that perhaps Quinn was using him as a scapegoat. The people were angry and looking for someone to blame for the loss of their homes. Perhaps Quinn didn't mean what he was saying, but he had no way of knowing for sure. He also felt a tremendous fear that something might happen to Zollin. It was foolish, he knew; he'd been no help to Zollin against the wizards of the Torr or against the dragon. In fact, Zollin had saved his life, not only from the wizards and the dragon, but also healing his heart and clearing the fluid building up in his lungs. He owed the boy so much, but was he really helping? He wasn't sure, but he didn't like the idea of sticking around while

Zollin rushed off into danger. There were things he could do, things that were needed, but that would also provide some space between him and Quinn. He needed to learn more about Zollin's power to block off his magic. He needed to find out who or what was trying to control him, not that it had been an issue through the winter, since Zollin had learned to raise his defenses. But what if that defense only worked from a distance? There were too many unanswered questions and too much at stake.

He hurried back inside the house and found a satchel. He crammed a change of clothes into the bag, along with a few loaves of bread from his own small store in the little kitchen. The meat and cheese were already gone, but that couldn't be helped. He had a small canteen that he filled from the well, and he rolled several of his best blankets together and tied them with a strap of leather. In the shed were several horses, but none were his. He took one anyway. A large horse that he didn't recognize, but he felt confident that it didn't belong to any of the villagers. He saddled the horse and tied his belongs to the rear of the saddle. He used his small back porch to climb up onto the horse's back. Then he rode from the place he'd called home for over two decades.

The villagers paid him no attention. Quinn had them busy, but he wasn't the only one giving orders. Ollie had taken on the role of feeding the refugees, and she had recruited a small army of young girls to help her. There were crews working on the camp, others hauling the milled lumber down to the village, and still more working to remove the rubble. The only other person Kelvich saw not working was Norwin. He'd spent a lot of money rebuilding the Gateway Inn, but now he looked as if he'd lost everything. Kelvich had been knocked senseless while Zollin was fighting the dragon and hadn't seen that he'd destroyed the inn to fend off the beast.   Still, he had a feeling that something like that must have happened.

He rode through the trees and up to the trail that led to Telford's Pass.   He would take Telford's pass through the mountains and then turn southeast and ride for Eddson Keep. Perhaps there he could find some answers. Then he would reunite with Zollin, if that were possible. He had to keep his faith in the boy's abilities.   He was destined to change the Five Kingdoms, Kelvich reminded himself. Perhaps he needed to step back and let the boy do it.

Chapter 20

Quinn was angry, but he was also a little ashamed. He knew that Zollin cared for Kelvich, and he had to admit that he was a little jealous of the attention his son gave the older man. The way Zollin had left things with Quinn was still painful, and he'd taken his frustration out on the older man. He didn't know if Kelvich had actually known about the dragon, but in his mind, it didn't matter. He felt that there was something not quite right about the man, and he'd learned to trust his gut when it came to judging people. He didn't think the old sorcerer was dangerous, but he didn't want the man following Zollin.

He walked to the group of men waiting on him. He wasn't surprised that so many of the townsfolk were taking his lead. He may not be on their council, but he was getting things done, which was more than most. He'd convinced the town to set up a saw to mill the lumber they needed. There was an abundance of material available, and if they all worked together, they could be back in their village by harvest time. It wasn't an ideal situation, but life wasn't perfect. Quinn understood that, perhaps better than most. He'd lost his wife from complications she experienced while giving birth to Zollin. His son, whom he'd worried about for almost two decades now, was a wizard. Life always seemed to come at him from the most unexpected places. The truth was, he would have loved to have stayed and helped the people of Brighton's Gate rebuild their village. Not that they really appreciated him, but he loved the mountains. He loved the snow in winter and the cool weather in summer. He wasn't afraid of violence, but he wasn't drawn to it like some men, either, and he had had his fill of adventure. What he longed for was peace, good friends, and good ale. He had expected to spend his final years around a glowing fire, surrounded by grandchildren—at least, that was what he had hoped for. He had to admit he'd feared that Zollin would not want children. It was hard on a boy to grow up without a mother, and although Zollin had handled it better than most, it had left its share of scars on the boy.

Quinn thought wistfully of how Zollin seemed to shoulder the responsibility for every negative thing that happened around him. That thought led to the realization that Zollin's shoulders weren't as thin as they had been. His son had put on some solid muscle, from the looks of things. He'd been busy through the winter, that much was obvious. It was another burr under his saddle, the fact that Zollin had seemed to respond so well to Kelvich and so poorly to his own tutelage.

He gave assignments to the men waiting on him and then turned to hitch the horses to the big saw that was being used to mill the freshly cut trees. He didn't know how long he planned to stay in the valley, but he could ride hard and catch up with Zollin and Mansel soon. They wouldn't get too far ahead. He wasn't sure how quickly Zollin could make it though the pass, but surely he had enough time to wait another day or two.

When he saw Kelvich riding out of camp, he grew even more uneasy. He trusted Zollin, but if the old sorcerer had his way, he might convince Zollin to run away with him. Quinn didn't think that was likely, but he didn't discount it altogether. He knew Zollin was desperate to get Brianna back, and if Kelvich argued that he could help Zollin with that task, his son might be tempted.

"You look downright hoodwaggled," said an older man. He was one of the farmers who had brought his family up to the camp for added safety.

"It's been an unusual day," said Quinn, not wanting to say too much.

"They say every day is unusual if you just give it a chance," said the man.

Quinn wondered how unusual a farmer's day could be, but he dismissed the thought. He liked this man; his name was Tollver, and he hadn't planted his fields yet, but was helping with the construction of the town. His own home hadn't been damaged, since it lay several leagues to the east of Brighton's Gate. Still, he was working with the townsfolk and so was his wife, and even their three young children.

"The saw's ready," Quinn replied.

"So it is, that's fine. Did you know that sour thoughts can turn a man's stomach? You've the look of something sour."

"Yes, well, that may be true, but I doubt you need to hear about my problems," Quinn said. "We've enough work to stay focused on."

"I've always found that keeping my mind busy helps pass the time of a tedious chore."

"You have to keep your wits about you when you're working this saw, or you'll end up losing an arm or worse."

"Yes, that is true. When the saw is cutting, it gets all my attention. But, when I'm waiting for fresh timber to cut, I tend to notice when my friends are carrying a heavy load. I'm not prying, but I'll help shoulder the burden, if you'll let me."

Quinn thought about the offer for a moment. It was the kind of thing he might have said himself. Friends were the one thing he missed most of all about Tranaugh Shire. Zollin had Brianna and Mansel, but Quinn had no one to lean on. He'd hoped that might change with Kelvich. Truth be told, he liked the old man, but perhaps that was just desperation for someone to help him make decisions. He'd allowed Zollin to stay with Kelvich and allowed them the freedom to do whatever they wanted. Now he wondered what his son's gifts had really unleashed on the realm.

"It's true, my thoughts do seem a burden these days," Quinn admitted. "It's hard not to worry about the future, and things just seem to be getting worse."

"This have anything to do with the dressing down you gave the old hermit this morning?"

"Some, and the fact that a fire breathing dragon is now on the loose. I mean, really, if I hadn't seen it with my own eyes, I wouldn't have believed it. How are we supposed to deal with a dragon?"

"That's a good question, and one I don't have an answer for. But, if the story is true the way I heard it, your boy did a handy job of driving the beast away."

"Well, yes, but it wasn't something a father wants to think about happening again. And to be honest, I think it will. I'm a plain man, I like dealing with things I can see and touch. I don't understand magic, but I do know that trouble is drawn to that boy like moths to a flame. It's enough to drive a father mad."

"Yes, I can understand that. It's hard not to worry about the people we love. What made you send the boy away, if you don't mind my asking?"

"I didn't send him," Quinn said. "He's intent on rescuing Brianna, and I just needed to focus on a problem that I could deal with for a while before I rushed off with him."

"Like rebuilding the Gate."

"That's right. I know I can help here, but with Zollin I just feel like I'm barely able to keep my head above water. He can do things I can't even imagine. I mean, look at this sword."

He held out the sword by the blade to Tollver.

"Do you know much about blades?"

"I do, but I'll admit I know more about plows."

"I'll bet you do," Quinn said, smiling.

"This is a fine weapon. The balance is nigh on perfect, I'd say."

"I know, the edge is keen, the weight of the steel balanced between handle and blade. My son made that out of a plain, steel chain, with no fire, no forge, no hammer or anvil. He made it, standing beside the river, in less than five minutes. He didn't utter a word, but the metal just melted, without even getting hot and without a touch from human hands. Now, how does a father deal with that?"

"You say he made this sword with magic."

"He did, and again, I wouldn't have believed it if I hadn't seen it with my own eyes. I don't know how he does it, or where the power comes from. I certainly don't have it, nor did his mother. But he does, and now there are armies and wizards pursuing him and dragons attacking him. It's enough to boggle my little mind."

"Well, I don't know how you feel, I can't really say I understand any of it. But I know me, and it would be awfully tempting to ease back from it. Family or no, I wouldn't want to deal with something like that."

"True enough," Quinn admitted.

"Still, he is your son, and your only son, am I right?" Tollver asked.

"Yes, his mother passed just after he was born."

"Damn, I'm sorry to hear that. So you've raised him by yourself?"

"Yes," Quinn said.

"Then you can't let it go. It would destroy you. You've got to go and do what you can, even if he doesn't need you. The truth is, you need him."

"I know you're right, but I keep finding reasons not to go."

"There always will be," said Tollver. "But they won't weigh you down with guilt if you shirk them. Your obligation to your boy, though, that's a different matter. I had a son, my first born. He was alive when my wife gave birth, but his body was twisted and crippled. I threw myself into the farm work, told myself it had to be done, but the truth was I knew he was dying. I didn't mind the crippled parts, if he'd lived, I'd have provided for him my whole life, even if it meant going without. But I couldn't stand the thought of seeing him die, and there was just no way his poor, little body could survive in this world. So I stayed busy, and I've regretted it ever since. My wife held him for three days, singing to him and crying over him. But she has those precious memories to keep her company. I left myself with a ragged hole in my heart and, to be honest, I don't think it'll ever heal. Not because I lost him, but because I didn't stay with him."

"There was nothing you could have done for him, you're not a healer," Quinn said.

"No, there wasn't. I don't think there was anything that could ever have been done to save him. But that isn't what eats me up. He was my boy," Tollver had tears in his eyes now, "and I turned my back on him because watching him die was too painful. I turned my back on him, you hear what I'm saying? Maybe he was too young to understand that, but I'll never forget it. That's what I'm telling you. Even if your boy doesn't need you... You need him."

Quinn thought about what Tollver was saying. He certainly felt like their stories were similar. Zollin seemed destined to fight until he was finally overcome. It was a miracle they hadn't all been killed already. And he had to admit that taking out his anger on Kelvich was just an excuse, as was staying at the camp. He didn't want to see his son die, and he was afraid that he was helpless to keep it from happening. But he didn't want to know that he could have been with him. That even if he couldn't stop it, he could ride out and face whatever the future held with his son, so that Zollin didn't have to be alone. He looked at Tollver, who gave him an understanding nod.

"I think perhaps it's time for me to go," Quinn said.

"I understand," said the farmer.

Quinn held out his hand and Tollver took it in a firm grip. They stood looking at one another for a few moments, and then Quinn turned away. He needed to gather his things and let the town council know that he was leaving. If he hurried, he could be on his way by late afternoon. He would be half a day behind Kelvich, but he could catch up with the sorcerer easily enough. He still felt uneasy, but he didn't want to leave things the way he had. He would apologize and then keep a close eye on the man.

* * *

The soldiers had offered Kelvich no resistance as he passed them. He rode slowly, his body still stiff from the ordeal at Brighton's Gate and from spending so much time in his chair. He was well, but he saw no reason to push the pace. It was late afternoon by the time he reached the snow. He hadn't known how

Zollin would break through the clogged passes, but it was obvious when he saw the angled ramp of snow and ice that they had traveled across the top. It was a smart move, Kelvich realized, one that probably allowed them to travel at a much quicker pace than trying to move so much snow and ice.

He urged the horse forward, but it hesitated at the ice. He decided his best bet to move forward would be to dismount and lead the horse himself. The ramp was slick, but he managed the ascent easily enough. The surface was uneven, but felt solid beneath his feet. He'd been walking on top of the melting snow and ice for a little over an hour when he heard the wicker of another horse behind him. He turned and saw Quinn riding on a large, brown horse. They were gaining on Kelvich, and he felt a stab of fear. Quinn had been angry that morning, had blamed Kelvich for the dragon's attack on the village. If he were still angry, he might turn violent. Kelvich could defend himself, perhaps even fend off Quinn's attack, but it was not likely without someone getting seriously hurt. He turned and waited for the other man to make his intentions known.

Quinn had been pushing his mount hard ever since he realized that the snow and ice would not have slowed Zollin and Mansel. They were a full two days ahead of him, and that thought made him ill. The last thing he had told his son was to wait one day if they reached the end of the pass before he did. This meant he would have to ride through the night and hope for the best. When he saw Kelvich ahead of him, he determined that he would extend the olive branch to the older man, but he wouldn't wait on him. He was going to have to ride fast in order to keep up with his son, and he didn't like the idea of Zollin and Mansel getting too far ahead of him.

When his horse approached Kelvich's, he reined to a stop and looked at the older man. It was obvious that Kelvich had been leading his horse for a while, his face was red and there was sweat in his grey hair despite the cold temperature.

"Hello there, Kelvich," Quinn called out.

"Well met," said the Sorcerer. "What brings you so quickly along the path?"

"I'm riding to meet up with the boys. You can join me, if you like, but we'll need to ride fast. I didn't expect them to make such good time through the pass."

"Yes, I'm sure they did make good time, better than us," Kelvich agreed. "But you'll need to walk your horse. This ice is melting more quickly than you might think."

"It seems solid enough," Quinn said. "Look, I know I was hard on you at the village, and I apologize for that. I was angry, I admit it. You're welcome to come along with me, if you like, but we need to make good time. I plan to ride through the night, and you'll need to keep up. I want to catch the boys before they get through the pass.

"I'd be happy to join you," Kelvich said. "But it's folly to ride through the night. You won't even be able to see!"

"The moon and stars will be out, that should be enough to stay on the trail."

"But the trail may not hold up, do you understand that? If any part of it has been exposed to more sunlight, it could have melted through. Your horse could break its leg or stumble and throw you. It isn't worth the risk."

"I understand how you feel, but I'm pushing on anyway. We'll be headed for Orrock. I have a feeling that is where the wizard is taking Brianna. Again, I apologize for blaming you. I was angry, that's all. It's no excuse, I know, but it is the truth. I was wrong to hold you accountable."

"I accept your apology," Kelvich said, feeling relieved to have heard it. He hadn't been offended as much as frightened that Quinn's rage would end in violence. "I still think it's a bad idea to ride through the night. In fact, if you value that animal, you won't ride it at all."

"I understand, but there's nothing to be done about it. I'll see you down the trail."

Kelvich swallowed the rebuke that was on his lips. Quinn was normally a rational man, but lately he'd seemed burdened by something that was clouding his judgment. Kelvich led his horse to the side of the icy trail and allowed Quinn to ride past.

"Be careful," he called after him.

"And you as well," Quinn replied, not looking back.

Kelvich watched him go. The shadows were already growing long. There wasn't much vegetation in the mountains to use as fuel for a fire. Kelvich began collecting whatever he could find. It was going to be a cold night and a long one, too, he was afraid.

Chapter 21

Quinn had been forced to slow his pace somewhat as the night wore on. At first the moon shown through the high mountain peaks, but after a few hours, it dropped behind the mountains, and the stars simply didn't provide enough light. It was very cold, and Quinn felt half frozen in the saddle, but the horse's movement kept it warm and it's body heat was a small relief to Quinn.

He was just coming around a bend in the trail, a few hours before sun-up, when suddenly the ground dropped away beneath him. The horse neighed in terror, but there was nothing it could do to stop the fall. Their combined weight had broken the ice over a small crevice. It wasn't a big drop, nor a large area, but it was enough to snap the horse's right foreleg. Quinn heard it break with a sickening pop as the horse fell. There was a long moment of fear as the world seem to lurch out of his control, and then he was slammed into the solid rock that rose up on one side of the trail.

He was knocked unconscious for a moment, and when he woke up, he found himself pinned at an awkward angle between his horse and the vertical side of the mountain. The horse was writhing in agony over its broken leg. Unfortunately, Quinn's leg was pinned under the animal and was slowly being raked over the rough ice. It felt like his leg was being simultaneously crushed and sliced to ribbons. At that moment, though, his leg was the least of his problems. The horse was battering him in its death throes, and if it didn't stop soon, he would be beaten senseless, perhaps even killed between the animal and the side of the mountain.

He could not reach his sword and was forced to settle for one of the throwing knives Zollin had fashioned for him. He stabbed it into the animal's neck, expecting an even worse reaction from the beast, but the horse seemed almost relieved. The bucking and thrashing eased slowly, but it finally lay still.

Quinn lay back and took several deep breaths, but the cold was starting to penetrate his clothes. He was lying on ice and pressed into the side of a cold, stone cliff face. He lifted his free leg, bending it at the knee in order to push himself out from the under the horse. He knew that it would be agonizing, but he also knew he needed to get off the ice. Then, to his dread, he realized that the rock behind him made it impossible to push himself free of the horse.

Alright, think! He told himself. He was convinced that there had to be a way out of the awful predicament, but he couldn't see how. In fact, he couldn't see anything at all. The stars did little more than cast deeper shadows into the gloom around him. He was stuck, and there was no way to get free. Instead, he moved as close to the horse as he could. The blood was steaming in the cold, night air, although Quinn couldn't see it. He could feel it, running underneath the horse, whose lingering body heat was softening the ice.

Quinn pushed the horse with his arms, which put a painful pressure on his leg, but did nothing to move the animal. He tried levering his leg free, but there simply wasn't enough room to maneuver. His leg didn't feel broken, but he couldn't be sure. He knew it was cut and smashed by the weight of the horse, which, along with the ice below it, was making it numb.

He decided that he could shout for help. There wasn't much snow above him, so he didn't fear an avalanche, and it was possible that Zollin and Mansel might not be too far away.

"Help," he bellowed. "Can anyone hear me?" He waited for an answer, but the only sound was his echoing voice. "Please, I need help!"

After a while, desperation and pain mingled with lack of sleep, and he grew drowsy. The cold was seeping into his body and making him shiver and shake. He dozed off, only to be woken up by shuttering cold. His muscles were beginning to cramp, but he had no way to relieve the spasms. Just before the sun came up, he passed out. The sun didn't add much warmth, but it was enough to keep him from freezing to death. The smell of blood and decaying flesh did, however, attract other wildlife. The sky was soon full of circling vultures just waiting to glide down and feast on the horse's flesh.

Kelvich had gotten an early start. He hadn't been able to rest well at all, his small fire simply wasn't able to do more than ward off the worst of the cold. He was on the trail by dawn, and as noon approached he could see the carrion eaters circling lower and lower. He was afraid of what he might find on the trail, but conjecture wasn't going to help him. He decided that he could afford to ride as quickly as he could along the slushy trail to see if there was any way of helping whatever was drawing the vultures. He climbed into the saddle and spurred his horse forward.

When Quinn woke up, his clothes were wet. He could move his leg just a little; the snow and ice were melting and had soaked into his clothes. His leg was numb, which turned out to be a good thing since the pain he would have felt while trying to pull his leg free would have been overwhelming. The carrion birds circling overhead were not a good sign, he thought. They were actually quite close, and he was afraid that they might swoop down on him at any minute.

He had been working to free his leg for half an hour or so when he heard the deep throated growl above him. He froze, scarcely daring to breathe. He had heard that sound before, and his mind flashed back to the last time they had come through Telford's Pass. A band of mercenaries had been waiting for them, but they were attacked by the big lions that roamed the mountains. They were large, powerful animals, with huge teeth that curved up from their lower jaws. They were almost as big as horses, and it would take more than his throwing knives to fend one off. His only hope was to get his leg free from the horse and hope that the animal was distracted enough by the ample meat of the dead mount to ignore him while he made his escape.

He turned his attention back to pulling his leg free of the horse. It was maddening to feel the movement, but to not be able to break free. The ice had melted beneath his leg, but it had also melted beneath the horse, allowing the bulk to settle further down on the wounded leg. Quinn pushed on the horse and pulled with his leg as hard as he could. It was difficult, but he felt he was making progress. Then the lion sprang down on the far side of the horse.

Quinn started to scream but clamped his jaw shut so tightly that he tasted blood. He didn't dare move, but he knew it was only a matter of time before the lion pounced on him and ripped into his flesh. He saw the beast's head jerk, and the big fang ripped a long gash in the horse's stomach. The intestines spilled out, filling the air with a sickening smell, which the lion seemed to relish. Then the beast took the horse's hind leg in its mouth and tugged. The bones snapped, as muscles and tendons tore.

The horse had been moved, too, not completely freeing Quinn's leg, but shifting it enough that he was able to squirm out from beneath his fallen mount. He chanced a look down at his leg. His woolen pants were soaked with blood, although how much was his own he couldn't tell. He wanted to roll over and inspect the wounds, but he had to create distance between himself and the lion. He tried desperately to flex the muscles of his leg to speed up the circulation that was just beginning to return to the muscles in his thigh and calf. It was agonizing, both fiery and sharp, stabbing at him and shooting pains all the way up his back and into his neck. He had managed to crawl a few feet when he saw the huge head of the lion rise up above the carcass of the horse and look at him with menacing, yellow eyes. He saw the intelligence of the lion, knew that it recognized him and was thinking about him, trying to decide if he were easy prey or a legitimate threat. The desire to eat him was a given, but Quinn had weapons, and he wasn't going down without a fight.

He had one throwing knife in his hand, and another one at his belt. He drew it slowly and then waved his arm at the animal, but didn't throw his knife. The lion flinched and growled deep in its throat. He pretended to throw the knife again, this time the lion simply roared. The sound was deafening and made Quinn's ears ring. He felt the hot breath that smelled like death roll over him. Then he threw his first knife. It slammed into the side of the lion's head, cutting into the thick jaw muscle, wedging into the bone. The lion screamed in pain, and Quinn didn't hesitate. He threw the other knife, which found the inside jaw of the lion. The beast fell back as blood sprayed from its mouth in a red cloud.

Quinn was scrambling to get away, but his right leg simply wouldn't cooperate. He struggled to his feet and hopped a few paces before stumbling back onto the icy trail. The lion behind him was shaking its head to dislodge the knife. Its tongue, the roof of its mouth, and its cheeks were all cut. Blood was dripping out of its open mouth, and its eyes were now full of rage. It began forward slowly as Quinn struggled back to his feet. He drew his sword, although it felt puny against such a large creature.

Kelvich had heard the roars and had thrown caution to the wind. He had spurred the horse into a gallop. When they came around the bend and the horse saw the lion, it dug its hooves into the slushy icy and came skidding to a halt.

"Hey!" Kelvich screamed, not sure what else to do. "Over here!"

The lion spun around and roared, as if warning them not to interfere. Quinn fought the urge to run away. Even if his leg had been fine, he wouldn't have been able to outrun the lion. And the beast would have pounced immediately. Instead, he braced himself, waving the sword in front of him to ward the beast off.

"Quinn!" Kelvich shouted. "What should I do?"

"What can you do?" Quinn shouted back.

The lion roared, pawing the air between them with a massive, shaggy foreleg.

"I don't know."

"Just keep shouting," Quinn said, trying desperately to come up with an idea.

He leaned over and picked up a loose rock that was resting on the dirty snow at his feet. It wasn't very large, but it might work. The lion was wounded and trapped between them. If they could give it an avenue of escape, it might take it. Quinn had to use the sword like a cane to keep from toppling over, but he managed to hobble back toward the cliff face he'd been pinned against. The trail was open, the lion could run away, if they were lucky. It was swinging its head between the prey it wanted and the noise behind it. Quinn waited until the animal was looking back at Kelvich and then threw the rock, not at the lion's head, but at its rump. The rock found its mark and caused the lion to leap forward, down the trail.

For a moment, Quinn's heart leapt. He thought the clever plan had worked, but just as quickly as the lion had bolted, stung by the rock, it spun around and growled. Now it could keep an eye on both of its antagonists without turning. Quinn started back peddling, using the cliff face to keep his balance and holding the sword in front of him. The lion followed step for step. When Quinn got to the horse, his heart was thundering in his chest. The lion was moving closer and closer. He was convinced it was only moments away from pouncing on him and slashing his throat with its massive fangs.

"Quinn, cut the horse!" Kelvich shouted.

The lion growled louder, making it hard for Quinn to hear the sorcerer.

"Cut the horse, make it bleed."

The logic finally broke through Quinn's terrified mind. He stabbed his horse with his sword several times. Most of the blood had settled, but the open flesh trickled red. He continued the grisly work as he moved back. The lion hesitated over the fallen horse. It was angry and wanted desperately to attack Quinn, but it wanted to protect the feast it had found, as well. The blood welling up on the cuts Quinn had made triggered the lion's instincts to eat. Meals were few and far between in the mountains, requiring a lot of work. Finding an animal as large as a horse, ripe and waiting, was not something to be passed up.

The distance between Quinn and the lion increased. It was hesitant to leave the carcass, and Quinn was beginning to hope that the plan would work. Kelvich had stopped shouting and had climbed down off the horse. Seeing the lion so close to devouring Quinn had frightened him terribly, but he knew that Quinn needed the animal more than he did.

"Get on the horse," he said as Quinn approached.

Kelvich was holding the horse's bridal with one hand and saddle with his other. He never took his eyes off the lion, whose mouth was still dripping blood onto the snow and ice, turning it a dirty, reddish-brown color. Quinn took hold of the saddle and jumped with his one good leg, pulling himself up onto his stomach, then scrambling to get his good leg over the horse's haunches and onto the far side of the saddle.

Kelvich let the horse go, and it turned and immediately trotted back down the trail. Kelvich walked backwards, not wanting to take his eyes off the lion. The beast growled and pawed at the air, but turned its attention to the horse, tearing off a chunk of meat before Kelvich disappeared around the bend.

He turned and ran, huffing and puffing as the cold air burned his lungs. He had been in good shape for a man his age before the attack on Brighton's Gate had injured him. Quinn was working to slow the horse down, but it didn't want to be anywhere near the lion or the smell of Quinn's dead mount. Once he finally got control of the horse, he brought it to a halt and waited on Kelvich.

"How far do you think we should go?" Quinn asked.

"I don't know," Kelvich panted. "But we need to find a place to secure the horse and take a look at that leg of yours."

"Any ideas?"

"I saw a level place not far from here," he panted. "It's about thirty of forty paces up the slope, and I think the horse can probably get you up there."

"That sounds good to me," Quinn said.

His leg was throbbing now that he had time to think about it. When he had been facing the lion, it had been numb, but his mind seemed to block the pain. Now it was on fire, from his thigh to his ankle. Every jolt of the horse sent lancing pain through his leg and up his back. Kelvich used a large rock to stand on, then climbed onto the horse, behind Quinn.

They walked the horse down the trail until they saw the small area Kelvich had mentioned. He slid back off the horse and led it up the incline. Quinn leaned forward and put his arms around the horse's neck. They made it to the little camp area easily enough. There wasn't much scrub brush in the area, and Kelvich knew he would need to find fuel for a fire. They needed fire both to keep them warm and to ward off any wild animals that might smell the blood from Quinn's leg and come investigating.

Kelvich pulled a small knife from his belt after he had lowered Quinn to the ground and hobbled the horse where it couldn't wander off. He used it to cut away the pants leg and then pulled his water skin out to wash off the wounds. The entire right side of Quinn's leg, from mid thigh to his ankle, was cut to ribbons. There were large patches where the skin was completely gone, all the way down to the muscle. It was a ghastly wound, but the bones seemed to be intact, which was good. Kelvich had some medicinal herbs in his saddle bag, but he would have to use one of the blankets to bandage the leg. He used the last of his water to make mud, which he would use to cover the wound before wrapping it with the blanket. The mud wasn't ideal, but it would be better than letting the blanket stick to the wound and reopen it when they removed it.

He pulled out a small mortar and pestle to pulverize the dried herbs. Then he sprinkled them all along the open wounds. Quinn was on his back, his head swimming from fatigue, blood loss, and coming down from the adrenaline rush the lion attack had caused.

"How bad is it?" he asked.

"It's not too bad," Kelvich said. "But it's serious enough that we're going to have to be careful."

"Is it broken?"

"No, I don't think so, just badly cut up. What happened?"

"Exactly what you said would happen," he confessed. "The horse fell, broke his leg, and landed on top of me. I was pinned between the horse and the cliff face. The horse was writhing around, carving my leg up like mince meat."

"That's an apt description."

"I'd be lion food if you hadn't come along when you did," he confessed, more than a little ashamed.

"We still might be," Kelvich said. "We need to get rid of anything that has blood on it. Those lions can smell it from miles away. Odds are there are a lot more of them here about, drawn by your horse."

"I had to put him down," Quinn explained. "He was beating me to death against the rock."

"I'm not chastising you," Kelvich said. "I'm just being honest. Do you have a change of clothes?"

"Sure, in my saddle bag, along with my rations and shield."

"Damn, I didn't think about that. Normally, I'd recommend that we stay off the trail until we get past your fallen mount, but with your leg that's not an option."

"I can make it," Quinn said.

"Don't be foolhardy. If an infection sets in, you'll get blood poisoning and die. Now just lay back and rest while I tend this."

He packed the mud on the leg, then cut his finest blanket into strips to bind up the wounded leg. He had one change of pants in his pack, they were soft leather and too big around the waist for Quinn, but he made them work with Quinn's belt. It had some blood on it, which Kelvich scrubbed off with some snow, after he refilled his water skin and set it out in the sun to melt.

Quinn slept while Kelvich buried the bloody clothes in a patch of slushy snow on the trail. It wasn't perfect, but it was the best they could do. They would need to give the animals time to pick the horse's carcass clean and to let Quinn rest. They would need a fire, more than just a tiny one, that could burn all night long. Kelvich scavenged among the rocks for old wood until the sun went down. He hadn't eaten since he had woken up at day break, but he waited until the very last of the sunlight to start the fire. Then he ate some bread and cheese. Quinn woke up, drank some water, and ate a few bites before falling back asleep.

Kelvich fed the fire through the night, only dozing in short snatches. He heard animals moving around them in the dark, but the fire did its job and was still burning when the sun came up. He woke Quinn, and they shared a light meal before unwrapping Quinn's leg. The mud had done its job and kept the blood from seeping into the bandages. They used water to rinse off as much of the mud as they could. Kelvich added more herbs and then reapplied fresh mud. They wrapped it again and got Kelvich's pants on Quinn. Finally, they made their way slowly down to the trail. Quinn rode, and Kelvich led the horse. The trail was almost impassible now. They had to be careful of every step to keep the horse from stumbling and falling down.

When they got to Quinn's horse, it was little more than bones, although it was covered with vultures, who were picking at the remnants of skin and gristle that clung to the bones. Kelvich shouted and waved his arms, causing the birds to fly away. They recovered the bow and Quinn's supplies, which were mostly intact inside the saddle bags. They spent the remainder of the day traversing the ice and snow on the trail. As the sun sank low, Kelvich's feet ached, as did his legs and back. Quinn had dozed in the saddle, and they had not come to the end of the pass. They found a small camp site, and Kelvich once again scouted for firewood. He had less time and less luck, and they were only able to kindle a small flame that wasn't much help against the cold. They slept the sleep of the exhausted and woke in the early dawn, feeling just as tired as when they went to sleep.

"My leg is as stiff as a board," Quinn said.

"I'm sorry we can't take better care of it."

"It's not your fault. If Zollin were here, he'd mend it up without saying a word."

"That's true," Kelvich said, smiling wistfully.

"I'm sorry for what I said," Quinn said honestly. "You've saved my life, you know. Not just from the lion, but with my leg."

"Well, we're not out of danger yet. We need to get you to Zollin, or to a healer."

"Is there any way we can travel through the night to catch them?" Quinn asked.

"Not with the trail in such poor shape. We'll just have to keep moving as best we can and hope that we get lucky."

"The way things have been going, I wouldn't count on that," Quinn said sourly.

Chapter 22

The dragon flew south again. Its tail was not fully healed, as dragons heal very slowly from their wounds, but although it was painful, it did not hamper the beast. It took a different direction through the mountains this time, not wanting to chance upon the army as it had before. He had taken advantage of the surprise the first time, but there was no guarantee that they wouldn't be prepared now, with scouts watching the skies and Ballistas ready to fire large arrows hundreds of feet into the air. He had no doubt he could destroy the armies, but there was no sense risking a lucky shot that might keep him immobilized for years or, worse, keep him from flying and allow the hoards of humans to swarm over him and kill him.

He soared as high as he could, the air was so cold he was tempted to heat his body with fire, but he didn't want to attract attention. He flew over the Great Valley and crossed the southern range of mountains in less than a day. Then he began his search. He needed an isolated farm or homestead. Ideally one with a large barn that he could take refuge in. He found it shortly after dark. He landed smoothly just outside the home. The cattle in the barn were bellowing in fright, but in the small home, no one seemed to know he was there. He waited, as patiently as any predator. After a while, a man came outside, probably to check on the animals. He didn't see the dragon in the darkness. Normally, he would have devoured the man immediately, but he needed information.

His tail was aching, but he used it anyway, coiling it around the farmer in an instant. The man screamed, but the dragon tightened its tail, snuffing the cry as soon as it happened.

"Are you alone?" hissed the dragon. It had a deep voice that reverberated so low that it was hard to make out. The beast's mouth wasn't created to form human words, but it had adapted and learned the speech of men.

"No, no," said the man when the beast loosened its grip enough to allow the man to breathe.

"How many?"

"Just my wife."

"No parents?"

"N-n-n-no," he said, shaking his head vigorously.

"Good, call her."

"No," he said, his voice a little more resolute.

The dragon squeezed, the man's face turned red, his eyes bulged.

"I'll only tell you once more, call her."

He loosed his grip on the man, who shuttered, taking big, gulping breaths. Then he looked up at the dragon with fearful eyes.

"Do it," the dragon hissed.

"Bev!" he shouted. "Bev, come out here a minute."

The door opened and a girl came out. She had thick, brown hair that hung nearly to her waist. She was plump, but the weight did not detract from her looks. She screamed when she saw the dragon, his eyes reflecting the light from the little home. He'd found what he needed, a woman to be his prophet, his priestess, his slave. She fainted and fell to the ground.

"No," her husband sobbed.

Then the dragon bit his head off. He didn't wait, but instead gobbled the man down and then turned to the barn. It had two doors that were tall for humans and, with both open, he could just squeeze through. He ate everything: both milk cows, the old plow horse, a mule, and the entire flock of sheep and goats. He knocked the stalls down and used his tail like a rake, piling the busted timber, hay, and manure into one corner. He would have the girl carry it all outside eventually, but for now the building would suffice to hide him.

His tail ached, and the pain made him irritable. He squeezed back out of the barn and found the woman just starting to wake up. She was dazed and disoriented. He picked her up with his tail and then carried her back to his new lair. He would make sure she was ready, then send her out to spread his message, to peasants and kings alike.

* * *

It took three days before Zollin and Mansel came to the end of the snow. The ups and downs of the pass were wearisome, but at last they could mount their horses and make better time. When they came out of the mountains, Zollin pulled out the old pathfinder. It was a simple, little device, the needle pointing back the way they had come. Zollin turned it so that the N was lined up with the needle. He knew they needed to turn southwest, but there was nothing to see but trees and deep forest. They would just need to make their way as best they could.

They were about to head out when they heard a gruff sounding voice.

"Ho, highlander! Where are hurrying to?"

Mansel drew his sword, and Zollin raised his staff across his chest. He was holding the reins of his horse, but Mansel was already on his; both animals were stomping nervously away from the hillside.

"Who said that?" Zollin called out.

"Down here, highlander," said the voice.

Zollin and Mansel looked down and saw what appeared to be an old man, but he was the size of a toddler. The man had large hands, they seemed too large for his body. His head was small, but his beard, which was wiry and gray, hung down to his knees. He was wearing thick soled boots that only rose up just above his ankles. His pants and shirt were rough looking fabric that appeared to be woven from the fibrous strands of a tough plant. Around his narrow hips was a thick, leather belt from which hung a mallet-like hammer and a thick, stone chisel. He was only tall enough to come to Zollin's mid-thigh.

"Who are you?" he asked.

"They call me Jute of the Yel clan. And you, highlander?"

"My name is Zollin Quinnson, and this is my friend, Mansel."

"Have you any ale, by chance?" Jute asked.

"No, I'm afraid not."

"Shame, what a shame. I have steel," he said this last as if it should be tempting.

"So do we, little man," Mansel said. "Are you threatening us?" he teased.

"Your friend is soft in the head," Jute replied, speaking directly to Zollin. "I might be willing to trade if you can lay your hands to some ale, but dwarvish steel doesn't come cheap. I'll need several barrels."

"Why would we want your steel?" Zollin asked.

"You're a wizard, aren't you? I don't know what your kind does with it, but its top quality. Make this one," he pointed at Mansel, "a helmet so that what little brains he's got don't get hurt."

"I'm sorry, but we don't have any ale," Zollin said, suppressing an urge to burst out laughing at Mansel's expense.

"What about that bottle of wine?" Jute asked.

Mansel had insisted that they take it, but Zollin had been equally insistent that they not drink it. They traded watches through the night, and he was sure that if Mansel drank he'd be worthless.

"That's my wine," said Mansel. "If you want a taste, you'll have to trade with me."

"Dwarves don't trade with dull witted ogres who don't even have the courtesy to get down off their horses and offer them a cool drink to wet their parched tongues."

"We meant no offense," Zollin said, waving for Mansel to get off of his horse.

"Don't trust him," Mansel said, sounding a little peeved by the continued insults Jute hurled at him. "I wouldn't trust him half as far as I could throw him."

"Highlanders always think they're so powerful. Why, I could tear your arm off, boy. Care to lay a wager on it?"

"You think you could tear my arm off?" Mansel asked in surprise.

"We'll arm wrestle, you and me. The winner keeps the wine."

"Are you serious?" Mansel said. "You want to arm wrestle me?"

"Slow witted and hard of hearing, too, he must have been dropped on his head as a babe. That would certainly explain his looks."

Zollin burst out laughing at this. Mansel felt his face turn scarlet with shame. He jumped off his horse and threw the reins to Zollin, who was trying to compose himself but failing miserably.

"I'll arm wrestle you right now, imp."

"I'm not sure you're using that word correctly. I'm a dwarf, not a devil, child. Didn't your parents teach you to respect your betters?"

"I see nothing to respect, only a foul mouthed, little child who needs to be put in his place. And I'll be the one to do it."

"Oh, we'll see about that, we'll see," said Jute, smiling happily. "Bring the wine, I know just the place for our contest. Just the place, indeed."

Mansel stalked off after Jute, and Zollin, still laughing, followed with the horses. Jute led them into the forest and then to a small clearing right at the foot of the mountains. There were several large boulders in the clearing, and between two of them was a small cave. It looked to be little more than a hole in the ground, but instead of soil, the hole was in rock. It was the root of the mountains, and from the crack in the ground, which was all the hole really was, came the sound of singing that Zollin thought he recognized. It was different from anything he'd heard before, more a deep chanting that a melodious song, but it was music just the same. There were drums and low pitched flutes that gave the music a strong foundation.

"So, you're a dwarf," Zollin said. "As in the people under the mountains?"

"That's right, lad, you may have heard of us. We're quite famous, although, we haven't exactly been social the last few centuries. That's one of the main differences between my kind and yours: we don't feel the need to share our lives with outsiders.

We're more, what you might call, exclusive. Wizards are welcome, all others can bake in the sun, if you take my meaning."

"I think I do," Zollin said.

He couldn't sense magic in the little man, but he sensed it in the cave. He had a strong urge to crawl down into the mountain's roots and see the dwarvish kingdom, but his errand was pressing.

"What do I get when I win?" Mansel said in haughty tone, as if his victory were a foregone conclusion. "Other than the satisfaction of wiping that smug grin off of your puny face."

"Spoken like the ignorant highlander that you are, oaf. I'll bet you anything you want."

"How about the steel you spoke of?" Zollin suggested. He remembered that Kelvich had told him that some metals have magic of their own, and he was beginning to think that perhaps this dwarf might be offering something much more valuable than mere metal.

"It's a bet," Jute said happily.

There was a stump that the dwarf waved to, and Mansel walked slowly to the other side of it before dropping to one knee. Jute walked up to the stump and dropped his little elbow on the stump's surface. Mansel grinned and took Jute's open hand before lowering his own elbow.

"You say go, thick skull," Jute said with an air of superiority.

"Go!" shouted Mansel, rushing his attack just a little.

The dwarf's hand went about halfway down then stopped abruptly, and Zollin saw the surprise in Mansel's eyes. He grunted and then turned his shoulder into the effort, but he couldn't budge the dwarf's arm. Jute, on the other hand, was smiling and looked content. Mansel felt sweat blossom on his skin, and his heart beat faster and faster as he strained to lower the little man's arm. Then, slowly at first, Jute's hand began to rise. Soon it was back at the starting point, and Mansel looked desperate.

"Not as easy as it looks, is it, highlander?" Jute said, his voice straining just a bit and revealing his effort.

"You're cheating," Mansel said through clenched teeth.

Jute only renewed his effort and slowly pulled the warrior's hand down, closer and closer to the surface of the tree stump. Zollin stood wide eyed. He'd been surprised at the dwarf's challenge, but he'd expected that it would be a bigger task than Mansel anticipated. Still, he was truly surprised to see the tiny man overpowering Mansel.

Suddenly it was over, Mansel simply couldn't hang on any longer. The back of his hand pounded the wood, and both man and dwarf moved backward. Jute tottered on his short legs, Mansel rolled first onto his butt and then his back. Sweat was running down his face, which was red with exertion. Both were breathing heavily.

Zollin pulled the large bottle of wine off of Lilly's rump; she had been loaded with most of their supplies on this trip. The wine bottle was still full and almost as wide around as the stump where the arm wrestling contest had taken place. Zollin sat it on the stump and said in a loud voice, "To the winner go the spoils."

"Aye, that's me," said Jute. "It was a good contest, but the best man won."

"You're no man," Mansel panted, "more like mule. You pull like one."

"I'll take that as a compliment, highlander," said Jute. "Now, let's fine some cups and sample this wine. They say that wine won is far sweeter than wine bought."

He disappeared into the cave, and Zollin was left looking at Mansel in surprise and disbelief.

"Can you believe it?" Zollin said. "First a dragon and now dwarves."

"I can't believe that little imp was stronger than me."

Zollin tied the horses to a tree and left them pawing at the pine needles, hoping for some grass. He moved over to the stump and sat down. He was listening to the chanting song from under the mountain. There was a part of him that was restless. He wanted to continue their journey as soon as possible. Brianna was out there, waiting for him to come to her aid. But he had promised his father he would wait, and another part of him was excited about the dwarves. He wondered if more would come out of the small hole and drink the wine.

Mansel got up and brushed the dirt off his back as best as he could before settling in beside Zollin with his back to the stump.

"Is this where we're going to wait for Quinn?" he asked.

"It's as good as any," Zollin replied.

"It's off the trail; they may go right by us."

"Perhaps, but we can build a fire; they'll smell the smoke, even if they don't see it. Surely they'll investigate that."

"You're probably right."

They sat in silence a few more minutes before Jute returned. He was carrying three metal cups, which Zollin thought would make the wine taste even worse. He wasn't a big fan of wine that wasn't mixed with something else. He preferred cider or ale, but he didn't really have an option. Plus, he was anxious to find out more about the dwarves, especially the steel Jute had mentioned.

"Here we go," he said. "Highland wine, that'll be a nice change."

"Change from what?" Mansel asked.

"Oh, we brew spirits, but mostly from roots. You ever try Shochu? It's made from sweet potatoes."

"Never even heard of it," Mansel said, taking a cup from the dwarf, who was eye level with Mansel, who sitting.

"Ah, most highlanders haven't. You prefer the wine, ale, or even mead, but we dwarves are hardier folk. I haven't had wine since I was a youngster," he said with a sparkle in his eye as he pulled the cork from the bottle.

"You live underground?" Zollin asked.

"Not underground," Jute said as he sniffed the opening of the wine. "Under the mountains. We were the first mountain dwellers, and we'll be the last. Some of my kind are as old as these mountains and as stalwart."

"I believe you," said Mansel.

"And so you should, dwarves are honest folk. We do not strive for power or seek to oppress those around us like you highlanders."

"You don't have a very high opinion of humans," Zollin said.

"Well, I don't mean to be offensive," he said, sipping the wine. "Oh, this is well made. But you know, most endeavors highlanders undertake are hasty, and the results are less than desirable. We dwarves know how to take our time. But then again, you have such short lives. It's all a bit mixed up, and philosophy goes over better with a good drink and a good smoke. You don't happen to have any tobacco about, do you?"

"No, I'm sorry," Zollin said.

"All's well, all's well," Jute said amiably. "This wine is a fine treat for an old dwarf like me. Although I was hoping for ale. Perhaps there is a village or farmstead nearby that would trade. Do you know of any?" he asked.

"No," Zollin told him, "I'm afraid we don't, we're not from around here."

"Well, where are you from? Tell me some news from the Five Kingdoms. Are there still five?"

"Yes, of course," Zollin said. "But I don't know much news. We've been on the move quite a bit lately."

"On the move, yet you have no news. Come now, wizard, don't play coy with me. Never try to fool a dwarf, we're much too canny."

"Well," said Mansel, who had already drained his cup of wine and was reaching for more. "There was the dragon."

"Dragon?" Jute said with a note of alarm. "Where did you see the beast?"

"He flew down out of the northern mountains," said Mansel. "There was an attack on a small village in the Great Valley by an army of Skellmarians. While they were attacking, the dragon swooped in and destroyed the village."

"The shaggy men have a dragon?" Jute asked incredulously. "I don't believe that. They couldn't tame a baby goat."

"They didn't tame it," Mansel said. "It was eating Skellmarian and Yelsian alike."

"You don't say? What did it look like?"

"It looked like a dragon," Mansel said in a matter-of-fact tone as he smacked his lips.

"It was red, with darker stripes," Zollin added.

"Big?" Jute asked.

"Huge," Mansel said.

Zollin was nodding in agreement.

"Must have just woken up from hibernation. Their scales turn black from the sun and get harder than steel. Of course, dwarvish steel can still penetrate, but only the finest, and we rarely forge weapons in the sizes highlanders use. What other news?"

"We honestly don't know much," Zollin said. "We were pursued from our village by wizards from the Torr. We spent the winter in the valley and were preparing to leave when the Skellmarians attacked."

"The Torr is still around, huh?" said Jute, not really asking a question. "They're evil meddlers and the worst kind of wizards. Hypocrites, if you ask me."

"Why do you say that?" asked Zollin.

"Because they seek to limit magic. They want to control every magic user, or slay them. They kill the innocent and drive everyone except you highlanders away. Don't you know your purpose, wizard?"

He was talking loudly now, the wine having obviously gone to his head. He had drained several cups and was refilling his again as he spoke.

"You're stewards of the balance," he said, his voice slurring slightly. "You shape the world and have great magical power, but that power is checked by your humanity. Don't you see? The Torr restrain magic for personal gain, even while they sacrifice their humanity. Vile men, they are. Hateful and cruel, you'd do well to steer clear of them."

"One of them has our friend. We've vowed to free her," Zollin said.

"Oh, that's terrible," Jute said. He was swaying on his feet now. "Just terrible. You should send your thick headed friend and save yourself the trouble. They'll have corrupted her by now. And if they get their hooks in you, they'll steal all that's good in the world."

"Hey," Mansel said, he was feeling the effects of the wine as well, but he wasn't as drunk as Jute. "My head's not thick."

"Oh, I meant no offense, highlander. We dwarves all have thick heads. You have to when you're always banging them into stone ceilings."

"Jute, why don't the rest of your people come out and join us?" Zollin said.

"Oh, most dwarves prefer the softer light of the caves. We like a good, thick ceiling of solid stone over our heads. The open sky's a bit too high, and much too bright. It makes you feel like you could go floating away at any moment. I, on the other hand, enjoy getting out and seeing a bit of the world, every now and again. The colors are vivid and the smells are fresh and clear."

He swirled what was left in his cup and picked up the wine bottle. There was only a tiny bit of the wine left, and he poured it into his cup, then frowned and tossed the bottle over his shoulder. It bounced on the soft ground without breaking, but Jute didn't seem to notice.

"I believe I'm ready to turn in," he said loudly.

"But it's the middle of the day," Mansel said, surprised.

"Not where I come from. Down below, there's no sun, no moon, no clocks, and no reason not to trundle off of to bed whenever I feel like it. Right now, I feel like it. My head's a bit light, and I'm afeared that I might float away. Best to get indoors, if you take my meaning."

"Will we see you again?" Zollin asked.

"I should hope so, wizard. And bring back your friend; he's a good sport and all that. Good drinker, too, I might say. But you'll need ale if you want dwarvish steel. Half a dozen small kegs at least, more if you can manage it. Just call down the hole for Jute, and I'll be along directly."

He smiled and hiccupped, then went staggering toward the cave entrance. He was clearly inebriated, but he didn't seem to mind. Once he got to the entrance of his underground home, he took hold of the sides of the opening.

"That's better," he said to himself, but Zollin heard him anyway. "It's good to be home."

And then he was gone, down into the dark. The cave must have dropped down steeply, and the hole was just big enough for Jute to walk through, a little wider and only barely taller than the little dwarf.

"He can't hold his liquor," Mansel said in a superior tone.

"You'd be an expert on that," Zollin said with a sigh. "Let's make camp closer to the trail. Then you can take a nap and sleep off the wine you drank."

"I don't need a nap," Mansel said forcefully, but when he stood up, he swayed unsteadily.

"No, I'm sure you don't," Zollin said.

"Hold on, I'm just a little light headed is all."

"I understand, no hurry."

"Good," Mansel said in a sour tone. "That little imp stole my wine."

"He won it from you and shared it with you, too. There's no reason to be upset."

"You going to drink that?" Mansel said, pointing to Zollin's cup.

Until that moment, Zollin hadn't realized that Jute had left the metal cups with them. They were finely made, but metal cups tend to leave the taste of iron in your mouth. Zollin took another drink of his wine; it tasted fine, or at least as good as any other wine he'd tasted. There was no metallic after taste. He poured out the wine to look inside the cup.

"Oh, now you've gone and wasted it," Mansel said sharply.

"It was mine to waste, leave it be," Zollin said, ignoring Mansel's reproving look.

Inside, the cup looked to be plain metal, but as he probed deeper with his magic he could tell there was something else to the cup, something bright and wholesome. It reminded him of the willow tree where he'd first learned that magic could reside inside other things. That was a time of fun and experimentation, when his magic seemed more like a gift, a key to a whole new world. The metal cup had a touch of similar magic to it. Zollin smiled and took Mansel's cup from the stump where he'd left it. Then he walked over and picked up the wine bottle. He didn't want to leave anything in the clearing that might draw attention to the cave.

Zollin gathered the horses and took Mansel by the arm and led them all back out to the road. There was a little patch of soft looking grass that was as good as any for making their camp. The air was still cold, but the sunlight warmed them all nicely, and the horses could graze while they waited for Quinn and Kelvich to come along. Zollin got them all settled and then retrieved the cups.

"Why are you fiddling with those empty cups?" Mansel asked.

"They aren't empty," Zollin said happily. "They're full of magic."

Chapter 23

They had sailed down the entire length of the Great Valley in just four days. The fisherman, Drogan, and his sons had taken turns steering the ship through the nights. They had whale oil lamps that they hung off the railing of the ship so that they could see what was around them, while the moon and stars offered their light to help them navigate the ever widening stream. Brianna realized that there was no chance of Zollin catching up with them anytime soon, and Branock had made it clear that he meant to sail south from Whistle Bay once they reached it. Her only hope was that they might go ashore to search for passage south, and that she might be able to escape, or, if Branock left her in the care of the fishermen, that she might be able to persuade them to help.

Unfortunately, they sailed straight out to a group of ships that were being loaded with trade goods. Branock bartered passage on the first ship they came to, and Brianna was hauled aboard by rough hands that belonged to rough looking men. They wore mismatched clothing that was tattered and looked to have been mended by the men themselves. They had long hair that they wore in thick braids. Most had beards, but their cheeks were clean shaven, and their mustaches were long and treated with some type of oil that made them glisten and hold fantastic shapes.

"They're from Shuklan," Branock said. "They are not virtuous, so don't go wandering around alone."

"Where are we going?" she asked.

The sailors were staring at her, and she wrapped her overcoat more tightly around her shoulders as if it could protect her from them. The ship smelled of unwashed bodies and food cooked with strange spices.

"That's nothing to worry yourself about," Branock said in a silky tone. "Everything is arranged, and as long as you remain obedient, you have nothing to worry about."

Then he turned and spoke to one of the sailors, handing him a small pouch of coins. He was sending the man to purchase supplies for their trip. He wanted wine and cheese and any fruit the man might be able to obtain. He also wanted news, which would have arrived with the first of the ships that had sailed north with the spring winds.

Brianna understood none of what was said. She looked around the bay, which was bustling with ships. How would Zollin know which one they had taken? The only people who had seen her were the fishermen that had brought them here. She felt an overwhelming despair threatening to rise up and engulf her. It would be no different than if she toppled over the edge of the ship and sunk beneath the bay's frigid, green water.

She took a faltering step toward the ship's railing when a hand grabbed her arm hard enough to bruise. She looked back over her shoulder and saw Branock, his one good eye was trained on her and seemed to burn with a fever of need. He would never let her escape, she knew that now.

"Let's get you down below," he said in an icy tone. "I don't want you to have an accident; that would be of no benefit to anyone."

"You can't keep me," she said in a quiet voice that betrayed her. Tears were stinging her eyes. "Just let me go."

"Oh, don't cry, my dear." Branock's voice mocked her. There was no sympathy in him. "Everything will be well in time. Your young Zollin will come to see that his place is here with me. He'll have everything he's ever dreamed of, including you, if he so desires. Now, come along and stop thinking desperate thoughts. It's unbecoming."

Brianna wanted to scream, but she knew it would do no good. She would get no help from the swarthy sailors, and no one else was coming to her rescue. She was all alone.

* * *

Mansel slept the rest of that day, napping in the afternoon sun. Zollin gathered fallen branches to make a fire. Then he gave both of their horses a good rubdown. Finally, once all the busy work had been done, he set about making their supper—a potato soup with some wild onions he'd discovered and bits of dried meat. It was the last of their vegetables, they would have to rely on dried meat and hard bread until they found a village or farm where they could trade for more food.

With the little pot of soup boiling over the fire, he finally turned his attention back to the cups the dwarf had left with them. There was something bright and hidden just inside the metal. He used his magic to delve into the cups, pushing deeper and deeper until he could sense the space between the elements. The metal was different than that of a weapon. It was, in fact, a mixture of different metals, iron and copper and tin and bronze, but the most compelling thing about it was the magic. The cups almost seemed to shimmer or sing in his hands. He knew the metal could never be used to harm someone, but it could be used to protect. He concentrated on the metal and watched as it swirled into a liquid state. Then he reshaped it, first into a metal breast plate, then into a gauntlet. Finally, he settled on a helmet. It needed a padded, leather lining, but polishing it gave him something to do.

Waiting was hard. He had missed seeing Brianna through the winter, but at least then he'd known she was safe. Now, sitting idle, waiting for his father and Kelvich to catch up to them was more than just difficult, it was painful. He couldn't imagine what she was going though, and the more he thought about it, the firmer his resolve grew to destroy Branock. There would be no escape for the wily wizard this time.

As night fell, and the soup's aroma filled the little glade where they were waiting, Mansel stirred. He moaned and asked for water.

"Why do you always drink so much if it makes you sick?" Zollin asked. "I don't understand the appeal."

"Me, either, it's like I can't help myself. I take a drink and then I can't stop. Maybe it's because my father always drank himself into a stupor every night, but our mother strictly forbid us from drinking anything stronger than cider."

"Do you miss her, your mother, I mean?"

Zollin hoped the pain in his voice wasn't too evident. He'd always been jealous of Mansel, who was bigger and stronger and better with his hands than Zollin was. Quinn had always been fond of Mansel, too, and that didn't help matters. But more than anything, Zollin was jealous that Mansel had a mother. Quinn had taken good care of Zollin growing up, but there were times when he missed his mother so much he felt like he could die.

"Sure, I miss them all, but I will never return for good," Mansel said. "I can never go back to the tannery, and I doubt any of them would understand."

"I suppose," Zollin said.

"You never knew your mother, did you?"

"No, she died giving birth to me."

"That's too bad. At least you had Quinn. He never hit you or treated you like the hired help."

"No, but we had our differences, and it was hard knowing he didn't understand me." Zollin chuckled, "I didn't even understand me. I just knew that I was different, and for a long time that was terrible. Todrek was my only friend, the only one who really understood how I felt."

"I'm sorry that he was killed. I wish that had happened differently."

"Me, too, he didn't deserve that," Zollin said sullenly.

They ate their supper in relative silence, Mansel volunteering to take the first watch. Zollin wasn't tired, but he tried to sleep anyway. He knew he would be exhausted when Mansel woke him halfway through the night, but sleep didn't come for a long time. He tried not to think about Brianna, but it was impossible. He was afraid, he realized, and he hated that as much as he hated Branock. He'd killed Branock's companions, but he couldn't escape the feeling that killing them was exactly what the wizard of the Torr had wanted. Although why Branock had wanted them dead, and why he hadn't done it himself, was another mystery that seemed to gnaw on Zollin's mind whenever he gave it much thought.

The fire was burning low, just dark red embers now, and still Zollin couldn't sleep. The ground was more comfortable than anything he'd slept on since leaving Kelvich's cottage, but still he felt as if it were nothing but rocks and roots digging into his flesh however he lay. The moon was setting when Mansel roused him, but Zollin had only dozed a little. He was tired, but sleep wouldn't come, so getting up was actually a welcome change. He put more wood on the fire for Mansel and then walked away from the little clearing so that the light from the fire wouldn't affect his night vision.

His hand continued to stray to the pocket where he kept the ribbon Brianna had given him. It may have only been an ornament to her, but it was everything to Zollin. It reminded him of his mother's kerchief, and how his father would sit for hours, staring into the fire and pulling the small, delicate fabric his mother had left behind through his fingers. Zollin had not understood so much about his father. Now, with Brianna gone and a deep ache in his heart to get her back, he wondered how his father could have dealt with his wife's death. Zollin kindled the small hope that he could get Brianna back, but death was permanent. Perhaps time dulled the pain, but it would always be there. He realized that he missed his father, and he wished that he could say that he was sorry for the harsh, judgmental words he had said to Quinn before he left Brighton's Gate.

He let his magic roll out of him, and the hot wind inside him felt good. It seemed to strengthen him in some ways, although using it always left him hungry and tired afterward. He could sense the trees and the night creatures as they searched for food. Magic seemed to well up from the cave where Jute had disappeared, but there were no men, no threats that he could see, hear, or feel.

As the night wore on, he decided that waiting for his father was not a good idea. He had done as he'd been told, but with the light, he would push on. He could leave a message, perhaps, but the odds were that Quinn had decided to stay at Brighton's Gate, and perhaps Kelvich with him. He would miss his father, but he felt ready to move on. Even if Mansel decided to stay and wait, Zollin would go. Activity was the only thing that was keeping him from going crazy, and he vowed that he would wait no longer. He would go to Orrock and free Brianna, not matter what the cost.

* * *

The next morning, Kelvich and Quinn pushed on. Quinn's leg was swollen and throbbing now. He couldn't bend it, and every little bump was painful. He had trouble getting up on the horse. He was weak and a little feverish. He longed for a soft bed and a warm fire and some strong wine to dull the pain. Instead, they had settled for a cold camp on a rocky outcropping that had left him just as weary as when he'd lain down.

The trail was even worse than the day before. The temperature was rising, which was a good thing for the most part, but since they were traversing the ice and snow that had built up in the pass, the warmer temperature was causing too much damage. Kelvich considered finding a place to wait out the thaw, but there simply wasn't a good place, nor was there anything to burn to keep them warm. In the spring and summer, the mountains would sprout short, tough, little scrub brush, but it was as if the winter snows had picked the mountains clean.

They moved forward cautiously through the early morning. They had been on the trail a couple of hours, with Kelvich leading the horse and Quinn riding, when they heard the first sound of their pursuer. It sounded at first like a distant roar, but with the way the mountains echoed the sound, it was difficult to tell just how close the lion was. They knew right away that it was a lion, and odds were it was the same lion. They were in its territory, but there was nothing they could do about it. Unlike the mountain rams or the elk that made their homes on the steep slopes, Quinn and Kelvich were forced to use the pass to make their way through the mountains. The horse became more and more agitated, a sure sign that the lion, or lions, was getting close.

"We saw several when we came through last year," said Quinn.

"Mountain lions don't always hunt in packs," Kelvich said hopefully. "The one that attacked you was alone."

"Was it? We didn't see another lion, but I don't think that one lion ate the horse all by itself."

"What should we do?" Kelvich asked.

"What can we do? We're like fish in a barrel. Hiding won't help. We've got to keep moving. Can we go any faster?"

"I wouldn't risk it," the sorcerer said. "We might lose the horse or worse."

"What's worse than being eaten by mountain lions?"

"You have a point."

They increased their pace, but it wasn't easy. Kelvich had trouble traversing the melting snow and ice, the horse did even worse. By noon the roars had stopped, but the horse was as panicky as ever.

"I have an idea," Quinn said. "Let's leave the horse. We'll tie it to the rocks and then push on."

"Do you think you can walk?"

"I'll have to."

"But without the horse, how will we catch up with Zollin and Mansel?"

"We can't worry about that right now," Quinn said. "We'll never catch them if we're eaten by lions."

"Look, I know you're right, but what good will leaving the horse do?"

"It'll buy us some time. The lions aren't out for revenge, they just want to eat. We'll leave them a big meal and hope they leave us alone. At the very least, we'll be able to put some distance between us and them."

"Alright, I don't like it, but I see the wisdom in it. You're hard on your horses," Kelvich said.

"I haven't owned a horse in years," Quinn said. "Everyone I've sat on since this craziness started has been stolen. Now, I'm being forced to walk on a bad leg over a bad road. I suppose it serves me right."

They tied the horse to a rocky outcropping and moved all their necessary gear into a saddle bag which Kelvich laid over one of his stooped shoulders. They tied the remaining blankets to Quinn's back.

"There," Kelvich said. "That's not too heavy, I expect. And if you fall down, it might even offer you some protection."

They walked side by side, with Kelvich taking some of Quinn's weight on his own shoulders. The horse looked at them with wide eyes as they walked away, but the two men didn't look back, even when they heard the horse neighing hysterically. Behind them, the growls continued for a short while, then they abruptly stopped.

"You think it worked?" Kelvich said to Quinn.

He was sweating and grimacing from pain. He had known that walking would be painful, but he hadn't expected it to be this painful. The uneven ice and snow made it even more difficult, his boots slipping on the slick surface as often as not. They were three quarters of the way through the mountains, a half a day's ride to the end of the snow and ice, but they had no way of knowing that. They walked the rest of the day, stopping for short breaks. Kelvich snatched up anything that would burn as they went along. He had a few strips left of the blanket he'd sliced up. He tied these on the ends of the little scrub branches he'd found. The plan was to use them as torches so that they could keep walking. If the lion behind them had been alone, they could be reasonably sure that the horse would easily keep it occupied for a day, and perhaps it would be several more before the beast felt like hunting again after gorging itself on horse flesh. If, on the other hand, the lion was part of a pride, then they could be in danger again very soon.

Just before nightfall they stopped. Kelvich refilled their water skins with snow. It wasn't clean, but it was the only source of water they had, and their exertions through the afternoon had caused them to drink more than normal. Then, with the last of the fading light, Kelvich managed to kindle a small fire. He lit one of the torches, which sputtered and smoked, but it burned just the same. The light it cast was weak, but it allowed them to keep moving, which was good. Just after dark, the roaring started again.

* * *

"I'm setting out," Zollin said as he shook Mansel awake.

"What?" he said, rubbing his eyes and stretching.

"They didn't show, and I'm not waiting."

"Are you sure?" Mansel said.

"Yes, I can't wait anymore. Brianna's out there, and I mean to find her as quickly as I can."

"Okay, I get it. But your dad said to wait for him."

"One day," Zollin said adamantly. "He said to wait one day. He knows where we're going. He'll catch up. You can wait on him if you like. I'm heading southwest, through the forest. It's the quickest route."

Zollin turned to go, he already had his horse packed and ready, along with Lilly, Brianna's mount, who he'd been leading since they left Brighton's Gate.

285

"Wait," Mansel said, grabbing his arm. "I'm not letting you go off alone."

"I can take care of myself," Zollin said.

"I know you can, but I'm still going with you. It's better that we stay together. Give me just a minute, okay?"

It only took Mansel a few moments to get himself ready to leave. Soon they were winding their way through the Peddinggar Forest. Zollin was using the pathfinder Quinn had given him to keep them on course. The trees loomed up, tall and close, their branches weaving a virtual ceiling above their heads. When they'd ridden through the forest last year, the ground had been covered with old, sodden leaves. Now, as the branches above sprouted new, green leaves, the forest floor seemed to be coming alive with flowers.

"This is odd, isn't it?" Mansel said. "How do the flowers grow without sunlight?"

"I don't know," Zollin said. His magic was tingling. It was a new sensation. He felt magic all around him, but it was somehow foreign and strange.

They rode through the morning and late into the afternoon without seeing a soul. There were animals aplenty, though, many of them seemed strangely unafraid. Mansel shot a fat rabbit with his bow, and as the sun faded, they stopped to make camp in a small glade where the sky was at least a little visible through gaps in the branches overhead.

Mansel cleaned the rabbit while Zollin gathered wood for a fire. They cooked the rabbit on a spit and divided the meat. It wasn't much, but it was hot, and they let the fat drip onto their bread to soften it up a little. Zollin was tired, but despite the peaceful surroundings, he had a feeling of dread that he simply couldn't shake. Something about the forest wasn't right. He rolled up in his cloak and fell asleep near the fire, but Mansel woke him not much later.

"Zollin, wake up!" he whispered. There was a note of urgency in his voice.

"What is it?"

"Look," Mansel said, pointing into the darkness.

He had let the fire burn low, and the small glade was shrouded in darkness. In the forest beyond were a set of glowing eyes, watching them.

"What is it?" Zollin asked.

"I'm not sure, but I think it's eyes. I saw them blink."

Zollin noticed that Mansel had his sword out. He closed his eyes and concentrated on his surroundings, letting his magic flow out into the forest.

"It's leaving," said Mansel.

Zollin opened his eyes. The glowing dots were moving further and further away.

"That's strange," said Zollin.

"What is?"

"It's moving backwards."

They watched the eyes until they disappeared. It was an unsettling event, and one that left them both a little shaken. Zollin gripped his staff, more for the familiar feeling it gave him than anything else.

"I don't like this," Mansel said.

"Me either, but what choice do we have?"

"I don't know, but I'm putting more wood on the fire."

"Why? If the fire is bright, we won't be able to see if they come back."

"I don't think I want to see," Mansel said.

"Are you scared?" Zollin teased.

"Not of a man, or even most animals," Mansel admitted. "But there was something about those eyes that didn't look human. My sword isn't much good against your magic. If there's something in these woods that is more magic than man, I don't want to meet in the dark."

Zollin didn't argue, instead he sent a silent spell to stoke the fire, making it dance up and brighten the glade. That's when they noticed the little, winged creatures, hovering all around them.

"What the hell?" Mansel said in a loud voice.

"I don't know, I've never seen them before," Zollin replied. He reached out, and one landed on his open palm.

"Are they bugs?"

"I don't think so."

The creature had a thick, chubby, little body, with brown hair and short, little arms and legs. The head looked almost human, but the eyes were tiny, and there were six of them. The one on Zollin's palm seemed to smile, then it gracefully lifted off and flew up into the dark.

"They're leaving," Mansel said, the relief evident in his voice.

Then the prickly feeling of magic that Zollin had felt all day came back, this time stronger than ever. He spun around and saw the strange creature with glowing eyes step into the firelight.

Chapter 24

The creature was big, easily as tall as a man on a war horse. It had a hump on its back and rounded shoulders. The arms were long and thick with muscle. Its belly matched its hump and sagged over the creature's furry legs, which were as big around as tree trunks. It had no clothes, but most of its body was covered with thick hair; only its arms, feet, and face were smooth. There was no hair on the creature's scalp, the bald head was lined with bright blood vessels and reminded Zollin of the way Branock had looked. It had big eyes that glowed in the firelight.

Mansel didn't wait to find out if the creature had good or evil intentions. He charged forward with his sword held high. The creature held out a hand to fend off its attacker, and Mansel slashed with his sword, which he was holding in a two handed grip. The blade hit the calloused palm and left a small scratch. The creature howled and swatted at Mansel, who dashed back.

"Wait!" Zollin shouted, finally finding his voice.

But it was too late. The creature wasn't waiting any longer. He lumbered forward, causing Mansel to retreat. Zollin held up his hand like the creature had done, but it paid him no heed; instead it stamped its foot on the fire, smothering it the way a man might snuff out a candle between his fingers.

"Heaven help us!" Mansel shouted in the dark.

Zollin could feel the creature, who was full of the strange feeling magic. His own magic seemed to recoil from it, unlike the way it behaved around other wizards and his staff. Zollin produced a ball of fire floating in the air just above his hand. The light the fire cast made the shadows around them dance and caused the creature to stumble back. It was the light it didn't seem to like.

Zollin, all decorum forgotten, shouted, "Brighter!" and the orange ball of flame transformed into an orb of bright yellow fire.

"Noooo," said the creature in a deep voice that Zollin and Mansel felt as much as heard.

"Be gone, vile creature!" Zollin shouted.

The beast stumbled off into the darkness, shielding its eyes from the light. Zollin dropped the fire ball onto their smoldering fire, and it sat there burning until the smoking wood reignited.

"What was that?" Mansel asked.

"I don't know."

"It wasn't a man," he exclaimed. "Much too big for that. And did you see the way it blocked my sword stroke? With its hand—and this sword is sharp, I've seen to that myself."

"I don't think it was a man, either," Zollin agreed.

"But what then?"

"A troll maybe, or an ogre? I don't know."

"Now you're talking about bedtime stories," Mansel said.

"Yeah, I am, sort of like dragons."

Mansel didn't speak, he only stared at Zollin. It took them quite a while to settle back down near the fire, and neither wanted to sleep.

"Kelvich said you would wake up the magical creatures that hadn't been seen in hundreds of years. I thought he was a little soft between the ears, but maybe he was right."

"Jute said something similar. Something about wizards being the balance keepers. All I know is the magic in that creature was different than the magic I know. If I woke it up, I didn't mean to."

"Yeah, I don't think anyone's going to thank you for that big, nasty thing. I've never seen such ugliness."

"I have, every time I look at you."

The two young men laughed, the wizard and the warrior. Both too scared to sleep. They talked of light hearted matters through the long watch of the night. At first light, they set out again, both of them anxious to get out of the forest. They rode all day long, and just before sunset they finally stopped. They were both exhausted. Zollin built a fire while Mansel slept. It was hard for Zollin to stay awake, he'd slept so little. In fact, he'd dozed in the saddle, and he imagined that Mansel had, too. But now he was on watch, and, after their run in with the creature from the night before, he had no desire to be caught off guard.

The moon was bright and full that night, and Zollin kept the fire down to glowing, red coals so that he could see into the dark forest. After a while he heard singing. It was soft at first, and he thought he was imagining it, but it grew louder and louder. It sounded sweet, but it was in a strange and foreign tongue. Zollin couldn't make out the words. He walked quietly around their little camp, trying to distinguish what direction the singing was coming from, but it seemed as if it were coming from all around him.

He closed his eyes and pushed his magic out into the forest. He could feel the beings; they were tall and thin, like saplings. They moved gracefully through the dark, their arms like branches, their feet like tree roots, their hair like willow boughs. They were women, he could tell that, and they seemed to beckon him to come out to them. The temptation was strong. He wanted to leave the camp and dance in the dark. He wanted to touch them, to run his hands over their smooth bodies and feel their embrace.

Then Brianna's face swam up in his mind's eye. She was lovely, her dark hair gleaming, her fair skin soft and inviting. Only, she wasn't beckoning him to run into the darkness, she was crying for him to come to her aid. He felt anger rising up inside of him. Someone had her, he knew that, but he couldn't remember who. The beings in the dark were still calling him, still coaxing him to leave his cares and troubles and join them in their dance through the forest.

"No!" he shouted.

"What?" Mansel said, waking up. "What is it?"

"Don't go to them," Zollin warned. "Don't give in."

"What are you talking about, Zollin?"

Then the attack came. As suddenly as when a candle is blown out, casting a room in darkness, the temptation abruptly ended. And Zollin felt the malice of the forest beings as they rushed forward toward the camp.

"To arms!" Zollin cried.

Mansel, to his credit, still bleary eyed from sleep, was on his feet with his sword in one hand and his shield in the other. Zollin sent a spell to the fire and it erupted with flaming light. The forest creatures faltered as the light blinded them.

"Blast" Zollin shouted, sending electrical energy shooting from his staff.

The creature in his path burst into flames, and the battle truly began. Two of the burning creature's companions went to its aid, but there were almost a dozen more of the creatures. They looked like women carved from living trees. Their hair hung down over their shoulders and breasts, framing their hauntingly beautiful faces, but their arms reached out for Zollin. They didn't seem as intent on Mansel, who swung his sword in arcs, back and forth, to loosen his stiff muscles.

"Who are you?" Zollin shouted. "What do you want?"

"We are the forest dryads," came one haunting voice. It sounded like a throaty, musical instrument to Zollin. "We want you, wizard. Come and take your place with us."

"No," Zollin shouted.

"Then we will kill you."

"Do your worst!" Mansel shouted.

They came at first in twos, from either side of Zollin, who sent energy crackling from his staff in one direction and pulled limbs down from the trees overhead onto the other dryads. The blast of energy sent the two dryads reeling, but the falling branches did little. They covered their heads with their thin arms and advanced.

Mansel leapt forward to intercept them. One tried to bat him aside, but he raised his shield to block the blow, which staggered him, but he managed to stay in the fight, slashing out with his sword in a long arc that severed the nearest creature's thin arm. It wailed in pain, but no blood was drawn. Instead, a thick, sappy substance oozed out and the dryad scooped up its severed limb and held it to the stump. Mansel was surprised to see it not only reattached, but that the creature regained full use of the arm.

Zollin turned and pushed a magical wall out toward the oncoming dryad. It hit the creature and sent it sprawling back. Mansel ducked a second blow and thrust his sword at the dryad's trunk-like midsection. The sword sank into the woody flesh, more dense than a human, but not so dense as a tree. The creature howled again, but Mansel was still moving. He pulled his sword free and spun low, swinging the sword in a level plane so that it cut through the creature's leg. Then he sprinted back toward Zollin. Three more were coming at them, from the front. Zollin sent fireballs shooting out at the creatures, who swatted them away, but not without apprehension. Mansel and Zollin had their back to their campfire, even though the heat was almost unbearable. Two more of the creatures came to flank them.

Zollin swung his staff, hitting the dryad on his side, and it crackled with energy when the wood connected. There was a pop as sparks flew into the air, and the dryad was knocked back as it burst into flames.

Mansel wasn't quite so lucky. The creature on his side feinted one way then lashed out toward the other. It hit Mansel square on the chest and sent him tumbling backward, through the dancing flames of their fire. The blow had knocked the breath from his lungs, and the fire had singed his clothes, but he was uninjured. The dryad then swung a savage punch, with its stumpy hand, at Zollin, who tried to block the blow with his staff. He was only halfway successful, and the punch sent him reeling away from the fire. This was what the remaining dryads were waiting for. They rushed in on him.

Mansel dropped his shield and grabbed a long limb from their fire and rushed forward. He was shouting like mad and waving the firebrand, which caused the dryads to fall back in fear. He stood over Zollin, swinging the branch back and forth, the flame fluttering and sparking in the dark.

Zollin scrambled to his feet. He'd lost his staff, but he didn't need it. He sent waves of fire at the creatures. The flames ignited the flowers on the forest floor and singed the new green leaves. The dryads screamed in fright and rage. One tried to attack them from behind, but Mansel saw it coming and thrust his torch into the creature's face. She bellowed in pain and fled.

"I think fire is what they're afraid of," Mansel said as the dryads sank back into the forest.

"Yes," was all Zollin could manage to say. He was panting; his efforts and lack of sleep seemed to be as heavy as thick iron chains around his arms and legs.

"You think they'll come back?"

"Probably," Zollin said. "I need something to eat."

Mansel seemed to notice his friend for the first time. He grabbed Zollin's arm and dragged him over to the fire. He rummaged in their bags of food and found a loaf of hard bread. He carried it over and tore it open for Zollin, who nodded thankfully.

The bread was dry and tasteless. It was difficult to swallow, but it filled his stomach. He drank some water from one of their canteens and then lay down on the ground.

"You can wake me in an hour or two," he said weakly.

"Don't worry about it," Mansel said. "I may never sleep again. At least as long as we are in the forest."

Zollin slept through the night and into the morning. Mansel had kept watch until the sun lightened the sky, and then he threw more wood on the fire and lay down beside Zollin. They weren't sure what time it was when they woke up, but the fire was down to embers. The small clearing where they had camped was scorched, but there was no other sign of the attack. They had left the horses a few dozen paces away, where a small patch of grass was growing. If they hadn't hobbled them, the horses would have fled, but they were there waiting when they went for them.

"I say we ride due south, out of this forest," said Mansel. "I've had enough nightmarish creatures for a while."

"That sounds good to me, too," Zollin said.

The turned south and rode hard, coming out of the woods and into open plains late in the afternoon. The land was cultivated, but there was no homestead in sight. They turned southwest again, still angling away from the forest. As the daylight faded into twilight, they smelled wood smoke. They rode toward the smell and were rewarded by finding a small farm. There were animals in the yard around a small home. There was no barn, only a hen house and a milk cow that was tied to a post. They dismounted and walked to the small home. Zollin knocked on the door. They heard voices inside, but no one answered.

Zollin knocked again and said, "We're travelers just looking for some supplies. We've silver to trade. We mean you no harm."

"Who's out there?" came a gruff voice.

"My name is Zollin and this is Mansel. We're traveling to Orrock. Do you have any food that you can spare?"

"Perhaps," came the voice. "Show me your silver. Slide it under the door."

Zollin bent down to comply, but Mansel grabbed his arm.

"You aren't going to give him your silver, are you?"

"Yes, why wouldn't I?"

"What if he steals it?"

"Then we'll feast on his chickens tonight," Zollin smiled. He slid the silver under the door and waited.

"Is that enough for a hot meal and a little news?"

"Perhaps. What do you seek?"

"What do you have?"

"We've got bread, cheese, buttermilk. No meat though."

"What about your chickens? We'll share them."

"No, we need the hens."

"Alright, we'll take what you can spare. We don't want to be a burden," Zollin said.

They stepped back from the doorway and waited. It took several minutes, but finally the door opened. The man who stepped out was thin and balding. His skin was dark and leathery from too much sun. He wore short boots, wool breeches, and a shirt that was too big, the sleeves tied at his wrists with leather thongs. He had a bag and small pitcher in one hand. Two wooden cups in the other.

"Leave the pitcher and cups, if you don't mind," the man said. "I appreciate the silver, but I've no room for you to sleep."

"That's okay," Zollin confided. "We're on our way to Orrock. Can you tell us which way is the fastest?"

"If you head south, you'll come to the Weaver's Road that runs from Felson to Orrock. That'd be the fastest way, if you ask me."

"Is there any news?" Mansel asked.

"You mean other than the dragon?"

"Dragon?" Mansel and Zollin both asked at the same time.

"Where've you two been, under a rock?" the man asked. "They say there's a dragon burning people's crops and eating their livestock. I've not seen it myself, but there's enough people claiming it's true to make a man believe it. Lots of folks headed to Orrock, too."

"Well, that's unexpected news, but we appreciate it. We'll leave the cups and pitcher outside the door and push on at first light."

"Good, there's hardly enough for me and the family. If times were different, I'd offer more..." He was embarrassed.

"It's fine, really," Zollin said. "We don't want to be a burden."

The man nodded and hurried back inside. They heard him drop a heavy cross beam into the door slot.

"Not very hospitable," Mansel said. "Who drinks buttermilk anyway?"

"I do," Zollin said. "It'll be a nice change from lukewarm water."

"I suppose some toasted bread and cheese would be good, even if we can't cook a chicken."

"A few more days' hard ride and we'll be in Felson. We can stay at an inn and have a real meal. Until then, we make do."

"Listen to you taking charge," Mansel teased.

"Someone has to."

"What about me?"

"I've got the pathfinder."

"I've got a sword."

"I've got the silver," Zollin taunted. And they both laughed.

* * *

The cabin aboard the ship was nicer than the one on the fishing boat. There were two beds, and Brianna was allowed to sleep on one. The first two days she was sick, as the ship rocked over the waves churned up by strong, spring winds. But the ship traveled quickly, first west around the twin peninsulas of Skattle Point and Peddler's Reach, then turning south and skirting Skayler's Island. They were sailing past Isos City and heading for Tragoon Bay. She'd overheard their destination from some of the ship's crew when she was retching over the side of the ship. She didn't understand their words, but she had understood the name of the seaport and their gestures of what they planned to do when they arrived.

She had no real sense of time or distance. The ship was moving constantly, and the strong winds sped them along faster than any horse, but she had no way of knowing that for sure. She only knew the voyage was rough. After she had vomited all the contents of her stomach, in those first few dreadful hours on board, she'd been confined to her cabin with a bucket. But there was precious little left in her stomach, so the bucket was more of an object to hold on to while she dry heaved until her stomach felt as if it had been ripped open with a dull knife. The third day, she managed to sip some water and nibble some dry bread. On the fourth day, she ventured back out into the sunlight. She saw Isos drifting by. The ships in her harbor like pins on a bobbing pin cushion.

Branock did not speak to her, and the sailors only made crude jests which she did not understand. Loneliness set in like a bad cold, making her miserable. She missed home, missed her father's tender words and even the constant chattering of her sisters. Most of all she missed Zollin. She'd been lonely since their adventure had begun, but through the long winter months, she'd taken comfort in the fact that soon they would be together. That hope had been shattered when Branock kidnapped her, now it was fading. It seemed impossible that Zollin would ever find her, and the evil wizard's promise that they could be together if Zollin joined him rang hollow in her ears. She was sure that Branock would stamp out any goodness in Zollin if he gave in to the wizard's demands. She had thought of flinging herself overboard again, but the beauty of the sea and the sights of the shore as they sailed past gave her a will to live.

If they did stop at Tragoon Bay, they would be at least a day's ride from Orrock. She didn't know for sure that they would be going to the Yelsia capital, but it made sense. The road from Tragoon ran east to Orrock and then Felson, before skirting the Rejee Desert and coming to Eddson Keep. Being back on solid ground was her only hope of escape. If they were transferred to another ship and taken south to Osla, she would have no chance.

"We've another two days in this leaky stink pot," Branock said from behind her.

She whirled around and faced her captor. He was sipping wine from a crystal goblet, just as he had throughout their journey. But she'd never seen him drunk; the strong wine seemed to have no effect on him.

"And then what?"

"Well, I can't give away all our plans, now can I? Besides, all that need concern you is that you won't have to smell the sweat and piss of these Shuklanians any longer."

"I prefer them to you," she said defiantly, but it was half-hearted.

Branock laughed. "That's because you cannot understand what they are saying."

She wanted to fight back, to mock and sting with her words if she couldn't hurt him physically, but it was no use. She simply didn't have the strength. And then, as he stared at her with his one bright eye over the rim of his goblet, she realized what she had to do.

"I'm hungry," she said plainly.

Surprise showed in Branock's eye, which was not shocking to Brianna. She'd hardly eaten since leaving Brighton's Gate, and the lack of nourishment had stripped her of energy. Now she would eat, and regain her strength. Then, when the timing was right, she would strike. She didn't know why she hadn't thought of it before. He had no idea that the ring Zollin had given her, with its white azure stone, was protecting her from his magic. He was stronger than she was physically, but not by much. He relied too much on magic and filled his body with fermented drink all day long. He didn't sleep much, but eventually she would find a chance to kill him. Not on the ship, though, at least not on this one. If she killed him now, the Shuklanians would sell her to the slavers in Norsik, if she lived long enough.

"To what do we owe this change?" Branock asked in a mocking tone, but she knew he was suspicious. He would have to be a fool not to be, she thought.

"I'm feeling better, that's all."

"Well, I suppose I could spare a little, you don't look like you eat too much."

"I want fruit and meat, if you have it," she said in a superior tone.

"Fetch it yourself, girl, I've better things to do than wait on you."

Brianna left Branock on the deck and went down to their cabin. He kept the food in a large, wooden chest. She lifted the lid and saw fruit there, mangos and pineapple from Tooga Land, figs and dark purple grapes from Falxis. There were also olives, bread, cheese, and salted fish. She found a small knife, the kind used for slicing bread, common to any kitchen, but deadly just the same. She didn't take it, although the temptation was strong. He would be expecting that, would probably even check to see if she had taken it. Besides, she wasn't ready to strike, not yet. She needed to get stronger and make sure that once she acted, she had an avenue of escape. But it would happen soon, she thought, very, very soon.

Chapter 25

The roaring got closer as the night wore on. Quinn was in agony. In the back of his mind, he knew what the next step should be. Kelvich should leave him for the lions; he was convinced there was an entire pride, and a large one, considering they were still on the hunt after eating his horse. Kelvich could move on much more quickly without Quinn, and although he was no horse, he might be enough reason for the lions to give up the hunt.

"Only a few more hours till daylight," Kelvich said. "We've got to keep moving."

"I don't think I can," Quinn said. Every step was pure agony.

"Don't talk like that, you've got no choice. I'll drag you if I have to."

"It's no good," Quinn said. "Better one live, than we both die."

"I'll not face Zollin and tell him I left his father behind to be eaten by mountain lions."

"Don't tell him that," Quinn said. "Tell him you woke up and I was gone. He doesn't need to know the truth—that his father was foolish and pigheaded; that he got himself hurt and then eaten by lions. It's one heck of a way to go though, don't you think."

"Stop talking that way, we can make it out of this."

"Who are you kidding? We haven't even gotten to the end of the snows yet. On foot, there's no telling how long it will take us to get out of the pass."

"You're right," Kelvich said, suddenly. "We're going about this all wrong. We can't outrun the beasts."

"If you leave me behind, you'll have a chance," Quinn insisted.

"No I won't. There's hardly any meat on you, and even if there were, I couldn't make it out of the pass before the rest of the pride caught up with me. We need a plan, a way to hold the beasts off until they move on."

"What miracles do you have up your sleeve?" Quinn asked.

"Not me," he said in a serious tone. "You! You've still got your sword, and you know how to use it."

"One sword isn't going to be much good against even one lion, and we're facing a whole pride."

"Yes, in the open that's absolutely true, but in a confined space, where they can't get to us except one at a time..."

"Even then we'd be lucky to survive one attack," Quinn argued. "And that's if we can find that kind of place. But there isn't anywhere to hide."

"Yes, there is, it's right below our feet."

"In the snow?"

"Yes, all we need is to find a spot that's melted," Kelvich argued. "We may have to dig a little to make sure we've enough room to hold them off, but it is possible."

"I suppose it's better than walking," Quinn said.

"Give me your sword," Kelvich said.

He took the weapon and began poking around at the edges of the trail. Quinn leaned back against the cold stone and took deep breaths. He was so glad to be still, his body ached all over, and he was so tired, all he could think about was lying down and closing his eyes.

"Here!" Kelvich shouted. "There's a place over here."

Quinn pushed forward off of his resting place with a grunt and hobbled over to where the sorcerer was hunched over. There was indeed a hole in the ice; Kelvich continued to chip away at it with the sword.

"How big is it?" Quinn asked.

"Not sure," Kelvich replied. He handed Quinn the sword and stuck the sputtering torch into the hole. "It's not small." He leaned forward, sticking his head into the hole. Then he popped back up. "It's big enough to get started," he said. "There's a crack in the ice that we should be able to fit into with a little work."

A lion roared so close they both jumped.

"Take this," Kelvich said, handing Quinn the torch. "I'll go down first and then you hand it down to me, and I'll help you down."

"Okay," Quinn said.

He took the torch, and Kelvich turned over onto his knees and backed into the hole. It was deep enough that he could almost stand up straight. Quinn handed him the sword, then the torch.

"You sure there's enough room for me down there?" Quinn asked.

"Positive, now come on."

Quinn eased himself down onto the ground and slid his legs into the hole. He felt Kelvich take hold of his good leg and support him as he pushed himself further and further into the hole. Then he heard them; the lions were running to catch their prey, their paws thudding across the snow and ice.

"Hurry!" Quinn shouted, his pain and fatigue totally forgotten.

He slipped down into the hole and stumbled, his wounded leg bending under his weight and causing him to scream. Kelvich was struggling not to fall. Then the big, tawny head, with its huge teeth, was straining to reach them. Hot, rancid breath that smelled of rotting meat poured down onto them as the teeth snapped at them. Kelvich didn't hesitate, but thrust the sputtering torch up at the animal, which jumped back, singed. They could smell the burned hair.

"Back!" Kelvich shouted, grabbing Quinn's collar and hauling him backward, further into the hole.

It was really a crack that ran between the side of the mountain and the more solid ice in the center of the trail. The torch that had seemed so pitiful in the dark night was now casting light in the small space. It was barely wide enough for them. On one side was bright, white ice that was reflecting the torch light. On the other side was dirt and stone, the side of the mountain. It was dark with moisture, and the bottom of the trench was running water.

"A little further," Kelvich shouted, his voice overly loud in the small space.

The ground was angling down faster than the ice and snow overhead. As they pulled back into the crack, they could stand up straight and even brace their feet on the ice and rock to keep them out of the water. The lions were back, trying to squeeze into the hole.

"Hand me the torch," Quinn said.

Kelvich passed it over, and Quinn swung the firebrand at the animal, which snarled. It was too far away to be burned, but it shied back anyway. Then there was a pop as the ice near the hole cracked.

"They'll be through in a minute!" Quinn shouted. "Give me the sword."

Almost as soon as Quinn had his sword in hand, he felt stronger—which was good because part of the ice roof fell. The big cat didn't exactly fit in the crack. Half of its body was still above ground, but Quinn didn't wait. He knew this was their best chance to plug the hole and buy themselves some time. He thrust the sword out toward the cat's head. He was aiming for an eye, but he missed and the sharp point of the weapon sliced a furrow in the lion's face, bouncing off the skull. The lion roared in pain, the sound so loud it was like a physical blow. Quinn staggered back, but then lurched forward again. Had he been unwounded, he would have had trouble maneuvering in the small hole; as it was, he could hardly do more than shuffle back and forth. He tried to stab at the lion again, but this time the big cat had one paw free and swatted at the blade. Even in the tiny space, the animal was powerful, and Quinn almost lost his grip on the sword. He raised the torch, which scared the lion and kept it from trying to surge forward, and Quinn swung the sword in a short arc. It hit the lion's paw and blood sprayed out, hissing where it hit the torch. He slashed the beast again, and the lion was frantically trying to get away, its wounded paw hanging unnaturally from its foreleg.

Quinn saw his chance and thrust his sword forward again. This time he found his mark, and the wide sword blade punched through the eye and dug into the cat's brain, but then wedged in the eye socket. The creature jerked wretchedly, and Quinn could not hold his sword. It protruded grotesquely as the lion twitched and spasmed in its death throes. The lion's head slammed into the rock wall so hard the skull cracked, but the animal didn't feel any of it. It was already dead, only its body didn't know it yet.

The lions above them roared and paced, but none came close to the opening. Quinn sagged against the wall. It should

306

have been cold, but he was sweating. The lion's body heat, combined with that of Kelvich and the heat from their little torch, was heating the space up nicely. Only their feet were cold. Kelvich handed Quinn the water skin, and he took a long drink. Even though the water tasted muddy, he thought it was as fine as any wine he'd ever drunk. Then he closed his eyes, and was almost instantly asleep.

When he woke up, Kelvich was still snoring beside him. What he wanted to do was to stretch, but the close confines of the hole wouldn't let him. Sunlight was filtering down, but the torch had long since burned out. The lion was still there, the sword still wedged in its eye. The animal's body drooped in the hole and was beginning to smell. Quinn stepped forward and put his hand on the beast. It was cold and stiff. He judged that there was just enough room to climb out of the hole. He looked for movement above ground but saw nothing. He used his good leg to wedge himself higher, so that his head was just below the crack. He was waiting for something to pounce on him, but nothing did. He levered himself a little higher and saw that the trail was deserted.

He took hold of the side of the hole and put his good foot on the side of the lion's head, right beside the flat edge of the sword that was still in the lion's eye. He slowly tried his weight and found that it held solid. He grunted with the effort but managed to get his body above ground. He kicked and scrambled his way out of the hole. The air was cold, but not freezing. The ice and snow he was lying on was very cold, and even though he wanted to close his eyes and sleep again, he knew he needed to get up before his clothes got wet. His feet ached from cold and pressure. He had slept several hours standing up, and his legs were not happy.

He made his way to a rock where he could sit down, stretch his legs out, and wait.

"Kelvich!" he shouted. "Wake up, Kelvich. We're alive."

He heard the older man grunting and groaning in the hole.

"Kelvich, climb out of that hole, will you!"

"Alright, alright," came the reply, followed by a fit of coughing.

Quinn could tell something was happening down below, but it was several moments before he saw the wispy, white hair of the old sorcerer appear at the mouth of the hole.

"How'd you get out?" Kelvich called.

"Use the sword," Quinn replied.

Kelvich was older and thicker through the middle. He got halfway out of the hole and stalled, until Quinn hobbled over and gave him a hand. They managed to get back to dry ground before they collapsed.

"I don't recommend sleeping in a hole," Kelvich moaned, rubbing his back.

"It's better than being eaten by a mountain lion."

"I whole-heartedly agree," Kelvich said. "You were incredibly brave. I'm afraid I was cowering in fear when that beast broke through the hole."

"Best thing that could have happened," Quinn said. "He took out the weak spot and plugged the hole. I don't know where the other lions went, but I'm glad they're gone."

"You saved us, you can be proud of that," Kelvich said.

"It was your plan, sorcerer," Quinn said the title in a friendly way.

"Speaking of plans, do you have any for the lion?"

"What do you mean?"

"Well, in some cultures it is fitting to eat the vanquished beast."

"Trying to eat me is what got him killed," Quinn said. "I won't make that same mistake."

"Good, so what do we do now?"

"Now, we keep walking. And hope that the lions don't come back."

* * *

It took two more days of walking to reach the end of the ice, and a third day before they reached the end of Telford's Pass and found the remains of Zollin and Mansel's camp. The lions had not reappeared, and although Quinn's leg hurt him, his fever broke and he was able to bend the leg. Kelvich had washed the mud away and wrapped it with another blanket. It made for cold nights, but that was unavoidable in the mountains.

They were still moving slowly, but they were making progress. The road from Telford's Pass ran south, but Quinn was in no shape to navigate the woods. They were several days behind Zollin and Mansel, maybe as much as a week, and the gap would only get wider until they found horses, so they decided to go south on the road through the forest. It was easier to traverse, and Kelvich found a suitable walking stick for Quinn. That night they built a large fire and stayed close to it until they were warm all the way through, then they slept on beds of pine needles and new grass. It wasn't a feather bed, but it might as well have been for the two men, whose ordeal in the mountains had been extremely hard.

Chapter 26

Fire burned bright on the horizon. Another village burned. He had started with small farms and worked his way up to the minor villages. Fear, rumor, mayhem were all part of his plan and he thrived on it. The shouts and pleas of the villagers were music to his ears. The humans had dominated these lands long enough. He would make them bow before him, offer their gold, and then he would move on. This village, like the others before it, had not been willing to pay, so he had destroyed them. Oh, there were a few survivors to be sure, but they were necessary to spread his message of fear.

It hadn't taken Bev long to overcome her grief. Apparently life on the farm did not suit her. She had been afraid of the dragon at first, but once his purpose for her became clear, she relished the role. She would approach villages and towns, preaching that he was a god and she was his priestess. She claimed that he wanted their gold, nothing more, no silver, no children as tribute, just gold, all of their gold. The people scoffed at her and ran her out of their towns. They called her crazy, and laughed at her message, until he came roaring in the night. His scales were hardening, but the wound to his tail seemed to be slowing the process. He had needed more time in the mountains, where he could bask in the sun without fear of being seen. So he slept through the days and attacked at night to minimize the risk of retaliation. Men, it seemed, feared what they could not see, and the night held terrors for most of them. Of course, once he had begun burning their homes, the flames illuminated him in dancing, red light, but that only added to his mystique.

Soon he would be ready to move on to the bigger towns, and eventually the king would throw his crown at the dragon's feet. He would leave them in ruins so that they had to scrape and fight just to survive while he moved on to the next kingdom. He would wage his war of terror and fire until the humans bowed to his every wish. Then perhaps he would search out a mate.

He felt the power of the wizards, and although it was tempting to seek them out, he didn't. He would turn his attention to the magic blossoming through the land soon enough. The magic was like life to him, rejuvenating and strengthening. He needed that magic to wake up throughout the Five Kingdoms, and so, he needed the wizards to keep moving. He would have his revenge, but not until the balance of magic was more in his favor.

He took to the air again. The land here had rolling hills and fat rivers where tall trees grew, but no mountains. The trees could scarcely support his weight, and so he was forced to rest on the ground like an animal. He slept in the barn, which still smelled of dung, but soon it would be lined with gold. Oh, how he loved gold, the way it hummed with power. He would have it all and then turn the humans into a horde of slave laborers to find him more. He would build a tall lair, filled with gold, where he would live for a thousand years.

The thought made him happy as he flew through the night back to the little farm with its stinky barn. The woman would be there. She was enamored with him. It was common for lesser creatures to become infatuated with dragons, although their feelings were not love, but more of an entranced devotion. He did not care, as long as she worked tirelessly for him. The time for change was coming, he could taste it in the air with his forked tongue. He soared high into the air, relishing the freedom of flight and dreaming of golden dominion.

* * *

Zollin and Mansel traveled from dawn to dusk every day. They passed many small farms and one small village. Most of the people seemed withdrawn and suspicious. Zollin felt bad for them, since he knew the rumors were more than likely true. There was a dragon, he'd seen it, even battled it, and if Brianna hadn't been in danger, he'd have felt compelled to help them somehow. But the dragon would have to wait. His heart ached for Brianna. He hoped that she was well, but it seemed impossible. How could she be okay in the clutches of the vile pig Branock, he thought.

Mansel seemed less concerned. He was an amiable traveling companion. He could talk when necessary and could ride for hours without uttering a word. He looked every inch an adventurer; in fact, he could have passed for a knight. He had a strong face and broad shoulders, and he rode with his head held high. Zollin knew that his attitude stemmed from his love of the open road and adventure, but others could easily mistake it for privilege. He kept his shield hanging from his saddle, just behind his leg on the left side, where he could easily reach it. He wore his sword over his shoulder so that it wouldn't be constantly slapping his leg or the horse. He wore leather in place of chainmail on his chest, and he had no helmet or armor, but the weapons were enough to deter outlaws. At least Zollin didn't see any, and they certainly didn't come under attack.

They stopped at farms only long enough to barter for food. Most people were glad for the silver, it was easier to keep than possessions, if a dragon were to fly down and set their homes on fire. Zollin was generous, paying more than most things were worth. It was something he might have enjoyed, had his mind and heart not been constantly tormented with guilt and regret over losing Brianna and not going after her immediately. He argued with himself that he should have ridden after Branock directly instead of waiting and going through the mountain pass. But if he had, Kelvich would probably have died, and his father and Mansel would be prisoners, chained in the mud by the King's army outside of Brighton's Gate. Logic told him he'd made the right choice, but his heart argued that he'd betrayed the woman he loved.

They had not stayed at any of the places they'd seen, not even the village, even though it had an inn and they were welcomed there. They ate, re-provisioned, heard the news, then pushed on. The news was all the same, dragons, the people said. The descriptions were all different, some said one dragon, some said many. Some said the dragons were huge, the others said they were the size of horses. None of the people had actually seen the beast, and even though Zollin feared that there might be more than the one he'd fought at Brighton's Gate, he knew better than to trust hearsay. The attacks came at night, so sightings were rare. There was also a woman, she called herself the Priestess, and rumors abounded about her, too. Some said she was dragon born, others that she had been seduced by the creature. She wore a simple dress and had long, brown hair, but both were singed in many places. Zollin couldn't imagine anyone existing close to the dragon he'd battled. The rumors about the woman had two consistent elements: the first was that she warned of the dragon's coming, and the second was that the beast was demanding gold. So far, no stories of tribute had been reported, but if the rumors persisted, it would only be a matter of time before someone did. There was a slight possibility that it was nothing more than rumors, that the dragon had not come south at all, but Zollin doubted that. It was also possible that a group of outlaws were behind the stories, sending in a woman with a story and then setting the fields, farmhouses, and villages on fire when they weren't paid. Again, Zollin doubted this explanation, but he wasn't sure if that was because he, like Mansel, wanted another adventure or because he was being logical.

Adventure, he thought and scoffed at the word. Fighting the dragon had been no adventure and losing Brianna had not been, either. He had power, and he had grown comfortable with it, but didn't feel that flaunting it for fun was a good thing. It was sacred to him, as if it had been bestowed on him for a purpose, and he wanted to live up to that high calling, even though he had no idea what that meant. The dwarf, Jute, had talked of maintaining the balance, and Kelvich had hinted at waking up the magical world, but he really had no idea what either one of them meant. That was okay for now, all he really wanted was to find Brianna and make sure she was safe.

* * *

Branock must have discovered her fear of water. He never allowed her off the boat, but sent a message for a passenger ship to take them up the Tillamook River to Orrock. He had made sure that she was transferred safely and then had gone back to drinking more wine. The ship that took them up the river was a barge, used mostly for cargo, but it had two small cabins. This time he'd graciously given her one of the cabins for her own use. It was the first bit of privacy she'd had. There was no way to heat water on the barge, but she was able to bath in her cabin and sleep on a bed without someone coming in and rummaging about at all hours.

"We'll be in Orrock before the end of the day tomorrow," he told her when she stepped outside to watch the country pass by and soak up the bright, spring sunlight.

The temperature in the mountains had been bitterly cold, and on their voyage down the coast, the winds had been high and cold off the sea, but the days were warming nicely now, and the breeze was refreshing.

"Is that a good thing? Will King Felix set me free?"

"Of course not. For all I know the old man is dead. His son, Prince Simmeron, will do as I tell him. We will wait for your young friend to join us, but we shall not have to suffer these deplorable conditions. We shall have an apartment in the castle, with servants to wait on us. At least, you will if you can remain civil."

"A plush prison is still a prison. I won't be impressed by your gilded cage, wizard," she said bitterly.

"Ah, such spirit, that is a strength of being young and full of hope," Branock said in a mocking tone. "But it comes with such innocence. Perhaps we shall tour the dungeons and see if you still feel the same way about that gilded cage."

"You don't need me, I have nothing to offer you," she argued.

"It's not what you offer me," he said. "Young Zollin is the prize, and he will come for you."

"How? He has no idea where we are."

"He's coming, I can feel him."

She wasn't sure if she believed him, the thought was almost too good to be true. She was afraid of getting her hopes up and being disappointed, but she couldn't help it. The thought that

Zollin could find her and free her was more intoxicating than any wine.

"Zollin's going to kill you," she said.

"Yes, you've told me that. Although, I don't think he'll risk losing you just to kill me. You should learn to see the possibilities here. Together, Zollin and I can rule Yelsia."

"What about King Felix?"

"When you meet his son, you'll not regret his loss. I can offer Zollin wisdom, control of his power, a future. What other option does he have?"

Branock watched her think. He knew that there was much more to his plans than he was pretending with the girl, but he wanted her on his side. He'd been giving her more freedom, which seemed to have a positive effect on her. Of course, if she knew the danger they were both in from his master, she might have flung herself into the river. She would most certainly be killed if she stayed too close to Zollin, but telling her that didn't help his case.

"Perhaps I want my own life?" she said weakly.

"I doubt that," Branock said. "Besides, what you do after Zollin comes to me is of little concern. Go marry a farmer, have a flock of squalling babies, for all I care. But, until he comes, you can stay with me."

"I could kill you," she threatened, but again, her words were fragile and held no threat.

"You could try, but I wouldn't recommend it."

He turned and strolled away from her, his cloak flapping in the breeze. She turned her attention back onto the landscape, but in her mind, she was plotting. She would take in the lay of her surroundings when they settled at Orrock. She might need help escaping, or if Zollin did find her, she wanted to be ready to help.

* * *

Three days had passed since Kelvich and Quinn had gotten free of the mountain pass. The road through Peddinggar had been much easier to travel. There were still hills, some of them quite large, but the road wound around them. At night they heard strange noises in the forest, once they even saw lights moving, but they had not come close to the two men. Kelvich had found wild flowers and strange weeds with medicinal properties, and he made steaming hot drinks that both helped Quinn sleep and seemed to speed the healing of his leg. It would be scarred the rest of his life, but he could walk. The wounds were stiff, and he had to exercise the leg each morning before they set out and stretch it at night, but the constant ache was gone.

They had finally come to a village the night before and took rooms at the small inn. It was a common stop for traders coming and going from the Great Valley. They ate fresh food for the first time since they had left Brighton's Gate. They slept well on soft beds that were not entirely clean, but were a welcome change from sleeping outdoors.

The next morning they began inquiring about purchasing horses. There were several in the town, but the owners seemed reluctant to let go of them. Word of the dragon had spread through the town, and people were making plans either to flee into the forest or away south, toward one of the larger cities. People with horses would have sold most anything except the horses, which they hoped would carry them to their far away destination in safety. So, after several failed attempts, the two men set out on foot. They had turned southwest, even though the road continued due south. They followed a foot trail through the brambles and stiff weeds. They had been told that the next town was a full day's ride, which meant at least a day and half of walking—probably two at the slow gait Quinn could manage.

"Damn lions," he complained.

"Oh, don't blame animals for doing what they're created to do," Kelvich said. "We've had a run of bad luck, that's all."

"We'll never catch up with Zollin and Mansel at this pace."

"What will they do once they reach the city?" Kelvich asked.

"I don't know. I hope they'll take their time and form a solid plan, but who can say. Zollin has a good head on his shoulders, and so does Mansel, although he's a bit more impulsive and reckless."

"Well, there's nothing we can do about it now, except get there as fast as we can."

They walked on, all that day and even into the night for a while, until they found a stream to camp beside. There were plenty of fallen tree limbs near the stream, and Kelvich started a fire while Quinn nursed his leg. Then the sorcerer slept while Quinn kept watch. They switched positions halfway through the night, and the next morning they set out again. It was midday when they met a man leading a cart drawn by a mule. He had covered his belongs with a large quilt, but his wife and daughter rode in the cart.

"Well met," said Kelvich, holding up a hand to show he meant no harm.

"Where do you think you's is going?" the man asked in a husky voice.

"We're headed to Orrock," said Quinn. "We're hoping to find some horses in Willsby, if we can get there today."

"You can," said the man in a snarky tone, "but you won't find horses. Mostly empty houses and abandoned farms, I'd bet. The Priestess is there, calling for everyone to bring out their gold or her dragon's going to burn the whole town. I'd rather be cooked than give up my gold, and I'm not fool enough to wait around and see everything I've worked for burned up. So we're heading to the forest. You should turn back, if you know what's good for you."

"Who's the Priestess?" said Kelvich.

"Some woman; she's got burned clothes and half her hair's burned off. She looks a fool, if you ask me, but rumors are flying. They say Quasil was burned to the ground day before yesterday. And Tranaugh Shire's next, I imagine."

"What is she doing?" Quinn asks.

"She claims that the dragon is a god, calls him Bartoom, or some such nonsense. Says he demands gold or he'll burn the village. She told them to bring it out to her on the edge of town and pile it at her feet, and their sacrifice would assuage the god's wrath and that he would spare the town. I call it what it is, lies and trickery, but there's no sense in taking a fool's chance. We're going to Peddinggar to wait it out. Half the town's gone by now, the other half'll be gone by nightfall. They'll probably go in and steal what's left."

"Who is 'they'?" Kelvich asked.

"Don't know if there is a they, but odds are it's a group of thieves that concocted a story to make people give away their valuables. That's my theory, but I'm not chancing it. If there is a dragon, I don't know why the beast would want gold."

"Well, thanks for the warning," Kelvich said. "Have a safe journey."

"And you," said the man. He slapped the mule's rump and started off again.

Quinn looked at Kelvich. The older man shook his head just a little, as if to say "not here," and they started walking again. Both men pondered their thoughts for a while and finally Kelvich spoke up.

"The dragon has crossed the mountains."

"We knew that though," Quinn said.

"Yes, but it seems the beast is intelligent and working on something."

"You're giving some crazy rumors a lot of credit. It's more likely the villager was right. Some band of thieves heard about Brighton's Gate, and now they're working a con to steal from people. The simplest possibility is usually the correct one."

"You could be right, but if it is the dragon, then we have a bigger problem on our hands."

"What do you mean?"

"I'm not sure," Kelvich said. "If it is thieves, they can be stopped. An intelligent dragon..." he let the phrase hang in the air. "If that is possible, who could stop him?"

"Zollin stopped it at the Gate," Quinn said proudly. "I don't know what it would take to stop a dragon, but I'm sure there are still courageous people willing to fight rather than let the beast run roughshod over Yelsia."

"I hope you're right," Kelvich said. "I hope none of this is true, but Zollin *is* waking up the magical world. That is his destiny, and a lot of things are going to change."

"You said that before, but you didn't mention dragons. Do you think there are other evil creatures that he might *wake up,* as you put it?"

"I would imagine so, and the changes might take a long time to adapt to. Older people like us are too set in our ways to learn new tricks. We'd rather fight to keep things the same than let the current of change sweep us into a new adventure."

"Why do you keep saying this is Zollin's destiny?"

Kelvich hesitated a moment. It wasn't that he was surprised by the question, but that he wasn't sure Quinn was ready to hear the answer. He'd find out, sooner or later, if they survived that long. But Quinn's anger over the dragon didn't make Kelvich want to open up about the Prophecy of Xan.

"Don't keep me in the dark here, Kelvich. You're a good man; you don't have to hide what you know, good or bad."

"We've been through a lot over the last week or so," Kelvich said. "You may not know this, but I've lived four lifetimes."

Quinn looked at the old sorcerer. He was older than Quinn, who was in his late forties, but Kelvich didn't yet look sixty years old. His hair was grey, but plenty of people went grey at a young age. Quinn had even seen men in their thirties go bald or have a head full of grey hair. Perhaps Kelvich had a few more wrinkles than other men his age, but four lifetimes didn't make any sense.

"I'm not sure I follow you," Quinn said.

"I'm a sorcerer, Quinn, do you know what that means?"

"Well, Zollin told me a little. Said you were a teacher or something. Of course, I've heard the bedtime stories and even a few tales that chilled my blood, but I never believed them. To be honest, I'd never seen real magic before Zollin came into his power. So why don't you tell me what a sorcerer is?"

"A sorcerer is different from a wizard," he explained. "We have some rudimentary powers, but they are mostly in the form of knowledge, not like Zollin's. The skill we are most known for is the ability to control magic in other people."

"What do you mean?"

"Well, you know that Zollin can sense magic in other things, like his staff."

Quinn nodded.

"Alright, I can do that, too. But Zollin can manipulate and use that power. I can see the magic in him, sort of like reading a book. I can't manipulate the power in other objects, but I do have the ability to control the magic in people. I can, in many ways, take over their minds and bodies. That's what sorcerers can do, we control magic users."

"That doesn't sound good," Quinn said, frowning.

"It isn't," Kelvich admitted. "I've done a lot of things in my lifetime that I'm not proud of. For me, magic is intoxicating. When I'm near someone with power, I know that I can take it from them."

Quinn had a dark expression. He'd come to trust Kelvich, but now he was wondering if that trust had been misplaced.

"Look, I know it sounds bad, but sorcerers don't always choose to use their power to manipulate and control people. Sometimes we use it to teach. That's what I've been doing with Zollin."

"And what you were supposed to do to the wizards from the Torr," Quinn said.

"Yes, exactly," Kelvich replied.

"So what happened there?"

"A fluke really, I'll explain it later, but the point is I've used my power in the past to do what wizards do. One of the things a wizard can do is prolong his life through regeneration spells. The wizards we fought, the ones from the Torr that followed you to Brighton's Gate, were hundreds of years old. And so am I."

Kelvich waited while Quinn processed these revelations. They walked a long way before the carpenter spoke up again.

"So you're old. What does that have to do with Zollin and waking up the world?"

"I've been to many foreign lands," Kelvich explained. "The Torr would dominate or destroy anyone with magical power, so the Five Kingdoms have not always been safe for me. I've sailed to distant lands, where the people look different and have knowledge of different things. I spent time in a realm called Bushado. In ancient times, the wizards from the Five Kingdoms traveled the world.

"Magic exists throughout the world, and there are six levels of magic. The first level is an illusionist, a person skilled in trickery. They have very little power and even less control. Then there are herbalists, or apothecaries. People who have a gift for herb lore and healing. Then there are alchemists, people skilled in the art of transmutation. They deal in metals and minerals, bending them to their will. These are the first three levels of magic, even though few people recognize it as such. These levels of magic are called the Amnic and the illusionists, herbalists, and apothecaries are called the Amnicolists. Many still exist all over the world, although very few truly understand their power.

"Then there are the other three levels of magic. Sorcerers can sense and control magic in others, but have very little power of their own. Next is a warlock, who has great power, but very little control; in fact the magic they contain drives most insane. Many sorcerers take control of warlocks and, depending on the sorcerer's personality, both can benefit. Then there are wizards, who vary in the strength of their power, but most have at least some skill in two or more of the other levels. These three upper levels of magic are called Terimanic and the sorcerers, warlocks, and wizards are referred to as Interamians. What I learned is that while magic exists all over the world, it is only in the Five Kingdoms that the Interamians, or three upper levels of magic users, exist."

"What does that mean?" Quinn asked.

"Well I can't be sure, but it makes sense that we are the linchpin, the gate, if you will, through which magic flows out to all the world."

"We are?"

"Well, not us individually, I mean the Five Kingdoms. Magic originates and is most powerful here."

"Okay, so what does that have to do with Zollin?"

"The Torr came to power centuries ago, even before I was born. Their quest to control the Interamians, in essence, closed the gate. Magic stopped flowing into the world. Fewer and fewer people had the gift of power, and those that did were forced into joining the Torr or killed. But Zollin has defied the Torr, and his power is unlocking the gate, so to speak. The longer he roams free through the Five Kingdoms, the more magic will be awakened in this realm and throughout the world."

"And you know this how?" Quinn asked.

Kelvich had hoped that Quinn would just take his word for it, but now he had no choice. Quinn was looking at him the way a father looks at a truculent child.

"I was told by a very wise man named Xan in Bushado that I would mentor a wizard who would wake up the world. He said it would be the Roshee Mozioto, the Magic Awakening."

Chapter 27

Felson was a bustling city spread out around the east to west road that ran from Eddson Keep to Orrock and then to the sea. There was a large, stone tower, and a legion of the King's army was stationed in what amounted to a small fort. The city had grown around the military post, providing services to the soldiers, who were paid monthly in silver. In turn, the presence of the fort provided security to the people of the town and so it had grown. There was also a large equine training field for the cavalry, which could set out for any part of the kingdom from their centralized location.

Like most cities of size, Felson was surrounded by a shanty town of huts and makeshift houses that were little more than hovels. . The people of the shanty town stared up at Zollin and Mansel with blank stares as the two young men passed. The town proper was divided by the east-west road. Inns and shops lined both sides of the thoroughfare, with well built, timber homes surrounding the commerce area. It was just before sundown, and the two travelers needed supplies. Zollin would have preferred to keep moving, but he knew that by the time they had purchased all they needed it would be full dark.

They found an inn and climbed down from their weary horses. A young serving boy came running up to them.

"Looking for rooms, gentlemen?" he called out.

"That's right, lad," Mansel said happily. "One with soft beds, plenty of ale, and the best food in town."

"Inns are full up," said the boy. "The town's full of refugees from villages that were destroyed by the dragon."

"You mean there's no place to stay here?" Zollin asked.

Mansel was speechless.

"Well, there's places for an honest traveler to stay, if he can afford it," said the boy, grinning. "Many of the locals are renting rooms and stables. But it isn't cheap."

"That's fine; can you take us to one such place?" Zollin asked.

"Sure," said the boy excitedly. "I know just the place."

"Zollin..." Mansel began, sounding like a disappointed child.

"Go ahead and drink yourself silly," said Zollin. "I'll get our gear settled and then join you in a bit."

Mansel smiled and slapped Zollin on the back. "You're a good man, I don't care what Quinn says about you," he joked.

Zollin took the reins of Mansel's horse and followed the boy through the busy streets. There were people and animals everywhere. Zollin noticed locals staring at the newcomers with disdain from open windows and doorways. Many of the people were moving quickly, with their heads down, trying not to disturb anyone.

"It doesn't look like the refugees are very welcome here," Zollin said to his guide.

"Yes, some say blessing, others say curse. The inn keepers are growing rich and others are worried about thieves. But there is nothing anyone can do about it. Most of the people lost everything when their villages were destroyed."

"Won't the King's army keep the peace in the town?"

"Normally they would, but they're out dragon hunting, most of them, at any rate. There's a few left in the fort, but there are just too many people to keep track of. They do their best, but they're too busy. Although not too busy to sometimes drink at one of the inns."

The boy led Zollin to a long, low house with a small, stone wall encircling it and a larger building behind. The boy ran into the house and returned with a short woman with a pleasant face. She had a few wrinkles around her eyes and across her forehead, some streaks of grey in her short hair, but she smiled at Zollin. There was none of the animosity he'd seen in many of the other local townspeople. More interesting to Zollin was the spark of magic he sensed in her. She was a healer, he could tell that even before she spoke.

"Hello, I'm Miriam," she said, holding out a gloved hand. "I'm sorry about my appearance, I've been working in the garden."

Zollin shook it. "I'm Zollin. I'm just passing through but looking for a place to spend the night."

"Well, Zollin, you've come to the right place. I'm the animal healer here in Felson," she said. "I don't have room in the house; my spare rooms are already taken. But if you don't mind sleeping in the barn, you're welcome to it."

"That would be fine," Zollin said, thinking of how Mansel would complain about the arrangement, but they didn't seem to have much choice. He held out four silver coins to Miriam.

"Oh, no, I can't take your money for making you sleep in the barn," she said, laughing.

"Believe me, it's much better than sleeping out in the open."

"We'll you let Jax see to your horses. He'll rub them down and make sure they're fed and comfortable for just *one* silver coin."

Zollin wasn't sure if she was emphasizing the price for his sake or for Jax's, who looked a little crestfallen.

"I need supplies," Zollin said. "And if you have the time, I'll pay you to check the horses' hooves and make sure they're well."

"I can do that," Miriam said, smiling. "I'll see to the horses and let Jax show you through town. There's a lot of people taking advantage of travelers right now, but there are still honest folk here about."

"That's good to know," said Zollin.

"You take care of Zollin," Miriam said to Jax. "Honest work deserves an honest reward. You remember that."

"Yes, ma'am," he said, obviously relieved to be showing Zollin around rather than being stuck in the barn looking after the horses.

"And see that he gets back early." She turned her attention back to Zollin. "I'm afraid there have been some fights and unpleasantness in the town. I'm sure you'll want to avoid that sort of thing."

"Yes, I would. Thank you again for your generosity and thoughtfulness."

She took the horses from Zollin, who retrieved his staff and watched as she led the animals around the house. Then Jax led Zollin back out into the street.

"What sort of supplies do you need?" he asked.

"Just food mainly. Bread, cheese, dried meat, and fruit. The sort of things that will keep on the road."

"I know a few places," he said, smiling, and led the way at a quick pace.

"Miriam seems nice," Zollin said. "Is she your mother?"

"No, my parents were arrested and hanged."

Zollin couldn't believe his ears. The boy talked about his parents' deaths as though he were discussing the weather.

"They were trying to con some people out of their belongings, and when things didn't work out they stabbed a man. I don't remember too much about them. I was only five years old at the time."

"I'm sorry," Zollin said earnestly.

"Don't be. I get along just fine on my own. I have a loft in Miriam's barn. She feeds me in exchange for a little work. I have a few other patrons, too. The inn keeper where your friend is drinking pays me to help when he's busy. I help Rothon when his supplies come in. He's a furrier, and I stack his pelts when the trappers come to sell him their furs. Plus a few others, and no one tells me to wash up or go to bed or to be home by supper."

Zollin could understand what Jax was saying, but he also knew what the boy wasn't saying. Zollin's mother had died giving birth to him, and the hole in his heart from not having a mother ached terribly at times.

"I lost my mother," Zollin said. "She died giving birth to me. I'm sorry for your loss."

Jax waved the sentiment away. "We're here," he said. "This is Broton's shop. He's the best smoker and curer in town. He may have some dried fruit, too."

They went inside the store and were met by a large, smiling man. The entire store smelled of smoked meat and spices. There were dried peppers hanging from the ceiling in bunches and crates of cured meat for customers to choose from. Zollin had grown up in a small town and had never been inside a shop like this one. There were jars of spices, with different colors and different sizes.

A row of bins held nuts, all shelled and ready to eat. There were crocks of honey, and whole hams hung from hooks over the counter where the man stood.

"Hello, Jax," the man said happily. "It seems you've brought me another fine customer."

"I have," the boy said.

"My name is Broton," the man said. "How can I help you?"

Zollin felt like a kid in a candy store. He bought a small ham, smoked venison, dried pork, and strips of cured beef. He also bought a small jar of All Spice, some dried peppers, a variety of nuts, and a bag of salt. He paid the man in silver and then they moved on.

He bought a large sack of hearty bread that was freshly baked and guaranteed to stay good for a week—at least that was what the baker said. They stopped at another stall and bought vegetables. There were onions, carrots, potatoes, turnips, and some fresh herbs.

Both Zollin and Jax were laden with the supplies as they returned to Miriam's house. They found her in the barn. The horses had been unsaddled and rubbed down. They were eating oats and seemed extremely pleased. Jax led Zollin to a large, empty stall where they left the food, but Zollin kept his staff. He saw at least three cats, all busy patrolling the barn in search of any mouse or rat foolish enough to enter their domain.

"Your horses are in good shape," Miriam said, but there was a strange look in her eye. "Jax, run to the house and fetch my bag. I need to check on something."

The boy left and the woman squared her shoulders at Zollin. She was smaller than he was, but she projected strength that would have intimidated most people.

"Two of those horses are King's army mounts," she said in a flat tone. "Where did you get them?"

"I got them in Brighton's Gate," Zollin said truthfully. "We traded our own mounts for the soldier's horses."

The woman looked at him even more intently. "You mean you stole them," she said.

"No, they took our horses and we took theirs. It's a long story, and one you probably wouldn't believe if I told you."

"You need to convince me," she said threateningly, "or I'll turn you into the King's army officials."

Zollin sighed in exasperation. He could have avoided all of this if he hadn't been trying to repay Miriam's kindness. Having her check on the horses was his way of paying her, but now it seemed that it had been a mistake.

"Did you know a legion of the King's army marched up the Great Valley in early spring?"

"No," she said.

"Well, they did. They were led by a wizard named Branock. Do you know who he is?"

Miriam frowned. "No and I don't believe in wizards, so I think I've heard enough."

She turned and began walking briskly out of the barn.

"Miriam, wait," Zollin called after her, but she ignored him.

He sighed once again, then reached out to her with his magic. He felt the hot wind inside of him mingling with the magic in his staff. Then he lifted her off the ground. It was only a few inches, but it was enough. She screamed and thrashed as Zollin drew her back to him.

"What's going on?" Jax said as he came running into the barn.

"Run, Jax!" Miriam shouted. "Run!"

The boy dropped the leather satchel he'd brought back to the barn and was just about to escape when Zollin snatched him up and levitated him over to where Miriam was still trying to break Zollin's invisible magic grip.

"As I was saying," he said in a loud voice. "He is a wizard."

Jax froze in midair, and Miriam looked terrified.

"As am I," Zollin said calmly. "Now I'm not going to hurt anyone, and I don't want to do anything against your will. I just want you to hear me out. If you still want me to leave, I will."

Miriam nodded, not trusting herself to speak at that moment. When he set them gently back on the floor, Jax collapsed. Miriam bent over him, but he was okay.

"I've never flown before," he told her in a false bravado. "I stumbled is all."

"It may be better if we all sit," Zollin said. The barn floor was bare, hard packed earth that was swept as clean as any floor and laid with freshly cut rushes. They all sat down.

"I'm a wizard," Zollin said, continuing the story. He told them about the army and the attack by the Skellmarians. He told them about the dragon and about Branock's treachery.

"So the dragon's real?" Jax said.

"I can't say that the one I fought and the one demanding gold are the same. It could just be thieves, but I don't think so."

"Wicked!" said the boy.

"A real dragon," Miriam said. Her fear and anger had been swept away by the wonder of a magical creature that she obviously wanted very much to see. "Tell me more about the dragon."

"There's not much to tell, it was big. Long neck, big head with small horns. The tail was long and reminded me of a snake the way it moved. It had big hind feet, but no forelegs. The wings were long and leathery looking. Sort of like a bat."

"And it really breathed fire?" she asked in wonder.

"Yes."

They sat for a moment in silence.

"What other tricks can you do?" Jax asked.

"I don't do tricks," Zollin said good naturedly. "I cast spells."

He lifted his staff and let the blue energy crackle and pop up and down the wood. It even ran up his arm. Then he held out a palm and a small, orange flame appeared just above it, dancing and swaying. The barn had grown dark as the sun began to set. He let the flame transform into a small, gold sphere of energy. It was like a tiny sun, only about the size of an egg, but it was dazzling to look at. He sent it into the air over their heads.

"Unbelievable!" Jax said in an excited voice. "No one will ever believe me."

"No, I don't suspect they will," Miriam said. "But you didn't tell us about the horses."

"I set out in pursuit of Brianna and was stopped by the army," Zollin said. "They hit me over the head and chained my friends and me in the mud. When I came to, we escaped, but we needed horses. They had taken ours and, rather than try to find our own mounts, we took what we needed."

"The mare doesn't belong to the army," Miriam said.

"No, that is Brianna's horse. I mean to see that she rides Lilly to safety."

"So you think that this wizard, Branock, has taken your friend to Orrock?"

"Yes, at least my father does. If she isn't there, then he's taken her to Osla, and I'll take passage on a ship going south."

Miriam nodded. She was thinking. She wouldn't let a criminal stay on her property, but she was genuinely at a loss. Zollin's story seemed plausible enough, although she had no way to check it. The levitation might have been a trick, and the blue, lightning-like energy could have been an illusion, she supposed, but she was looking around her barn by the light of a ball of fire that was hovering over her head. That was difficult to explain.

"So..." Zollin said. "Would you like me to leave?"

"No," said Jax earnestly.

"I think..." Miriam hesitated again. "You are leaving tomorrow, aren't you?"

"Yes," Zollin confirmed. "At first light."

"Fine," she said. "You can stay, but please, I don't want any trouble."

"You won't have any," Zollin said. "I promise."

She smiled. "I've had enough excitement for one day, I'm afraid."

"Here," Zollin said, rising quickly to his feet. He extended his hand to her. "Let me help you up."

She hesitated and then took his hand. When their skin touched, Zollin felt a pulse of magic rush out and mingle with the obscure power in Miriam. Her eyes widened as he pulled her to her feet. They were standing close, and Zollin felt himself attracted to the older woman. She was probably old enough to be his mother, but she was attractive and charismatic. Still, none of those things were what sparked the desire, it was the magic. Something had been sleeping in Miriam, and now it was awake.

Zollin let go of Miriam's hand and stepped back. She was blushing, her heart beating fast. She had felt the attraction as well; it was like approaching a campfire on a cold night. It felt hot and good at the same time. Part of her wanted to step toward Zollin, even though he was much too young and obviously infatuated with the girl he was pursuing. But the temptation was there, a longing deep inside of her to be closer to him, to his power.

"I better go get my friend," Zollin said. "Jax, can you show me where the inn was?"

"Sure!" the boy said excitedly.

"Good, we'll get supper out, and be gone in the morning."

"Good," Miriam echoed. "That's good." But she knew it wasn't.

Chapter 28

The inn was crowded and hot, despite the chilly night. The day had been beautiful and sunny, but as the sun fell, so did the temperature. Inside the inn, a fire was burning in the hearth and the crowded room smelled of smoke, sweat, ale, and broiled meat. Mansel was busy listening to two very drunk men talk about the dragon attack on one of the small villages. When Zollin stepped inside with Jax, he looked around the room to find Mansel, but then realized he preferred the boy's company to that of drunken men.

There was a small table in the corner, shrouded in shadows, and Zollin retreated to it. He ordered cider for himself and Jax, two meals, and honey cakes to wrap things up. They ate, and it made Zollin feel good to see the orphan boy eating. It was pretty obvious that he didn't get meals regularly. He ate everything that was brought, even though Zollin couldn't finish all of the beef steak and fried potatoes that had been brought out for them. He also encouraged Jax to put the extra honey cakes into his pockets for later.

They, like everyone else, talked about the dragon, and Zollin kept an eye on Mansel, who seemed obvious to Zollin's presence. Mansel sat with his sword propped against the table beside him. He laughed and slapped the table with his hand, roaring with the growing crowd of hard drinking men. The serving girls had trouble keeping up with the constant demand for more ale, but they did their best, always flashing a smile in Mansel's direction. The trouble began when one stopped to talk with Mansel, rather than going to a small group of locals to refill their cups.

"Hey," one of the men shouted. "Leave that boy alone and bring us more ale."

The serving girl glanced over, but just then Mansel made a joke and they both laughed.

"They're laughing at you, Povil," one of the men said.

Zollin was watching the group now as Jax chatted happily between bites of his desert. The men were staring angrily and finally the one named Povil stood up. He was an older man, thick through the chest and with a round belly, but he carried the weight well. He screwed up his courage and approached Mansel.

"I told you to leave this freeloader alone and bring us drinks, girl!" Povil said in a loud voice.

Mansel seemed to notice the man for the first time. In fact, he graciously apologized for distracting the girl from her duties. It should have ended there, but Povil needed to make sure his friends knew that he hadn't backed down.

"Shut up, boy. Finish your drink and get the hell out of here."

Mansel stood up. He was as tall as the other man, broad shouldered and muscled, but leaner than Povil.

"I don't think I like you, old man. Sit back down with your friends and mind your own business, or I'll make you regret it."

Povil hesitated, but only for a second, then he cleared his throat and spit on Mansel's boot.

Zollin's heart sank, and he started to rush over to calm things down somehow, but before he could move, Mansel's fist shot out in a straight punch that snapped the man's head back and toppled him like a tree. The man fell, his body bounced on the wooden plank flooring, his arms and legs stiff and his eyes rolling back in his head until only the whites showed.

Then the other men, there were three of them left, launched themselves at Mansel. Zollin stood up, but Jax grabbed his hand and pulled him toward the door. Mansel threw his cup at one man then punched another, but the third slammed his shoulder into Mansel, who fell back onto another table. The men sitting at that table grabbed the man and slung him into yet another table, and then the fight really began.

The pent up tension in the refugees and locals exploded into flying stools and benches. Bones were broken and blood flew. Mansel was giving as good as he got. His sword was knocked to the floor, and for the most part weapons were not drawn. When a group of soldiers arrived, Zollin and Jax were pressed back into the corner. The soldiers, who also served as de facto peace keepers in the town, drew short swords and the fight subsided. Zollin noticed that Mansel had a bloody nose, and one eye was swelling, but his blood was up, and he had an eager smile on his face.

"Who started this?" demanded the centurion of the small group of soldiers. He was an older man, with short cropped, grey hair; an evocati, which meant he was old enough to retire but had chosen to stay on duty. The other soldiers were wearing chainmail under their jerkins, but the centurion wore no armor and no weapons. All the rest of his cohort had short swords just like the one Quinn had from his days in the King's army, which they held at the ready. Zollin felt fear blow its frigid breath on the back of his neck.

"He did," said one of the men who had attacked Mansel. He was pointing a finger directly at Mansel. "He attacked Povil for no reason."

"That's a damn lie," Mansel said angrily.

"You're under arrest," the centurion said to Mansel. "Take him."

Zollin saw Mansel's face harden. Saw him glance around the floor that was now littered with broken tables and benches for his sword. He imagined peace and tranquility and sent the thought across the room with his magic. He was relieved when Mansel's face relaxed, and he didn't object when two of the soldiers took him by the arms and escorted him from the room.

"There will be no more fighting!" the centurion demanded, and there were murmurs of acknowledgement from around the room. "You newcomers are here only so long as you can keep yourselves under control. One more public disturbance, and I'll make it my mission in life to run each and every one of you out of town and back to the pathetic villages you came from."

The room remained silent, even after the soldiers left, the people spoke in hushed whispers. Zollin found his seat and sat down again. It was one of the few that were still intact from the brawl.

"Where will they take him?" Zollin asked Jax.

"They have a guard house inside the fort," Jax said.

"Can you take me there?"

"Yes, but the soldiers may not let you in. They've been working overtime with all the strangers in town and most of the soldiers gone looking for the dragon."

"Well, we better get going and see what we can do," Zollin said, standing up again. The inn keeper looked distraught. Zollin carried two small, leather pouches, one on his belt that was filled with silver coins. The other was under his shirt and had gold coins inside. He pulled four of the gold coins from the hidden pouch and handed them to owner of the inn.

"I'm sorry things got out of hand," Zollin told him. "I hope this covers the damages."

He dropped the coins into the man's hand. The inn keeper's eyes went wide at the sight of the gold. He looked up in surprise, his despair suddenly turned into hope.

"I hope that if the soldiers need you to press charges against my friend that you can look the other way."

"Of course, of course," said the inn keeper.

Zollin nodded to him then walked out with Jax. The boy was looking at him strangely, but he didn't ask the question that was obviously on his mind. Instead, he led Zollin through the dark streets. Windows were shuttered and gates barred. There were people in the alleys, some huddled around small fires, others sleeping where the townsfolk threw their garbage and emptied chamber pots. Zollin wasn't sure, but he thought he saw groups of children scavenging for food in the shadows.

The barracks used by the army were on the outskirts of the town, but the watch tower was built along the road. The fort was built around the tower and consisted of a low, stone wall, about the height of a man on horseback. Much lower than a city or castle wall, but tall enough to make getting in difficult. There was a large, wooden gate that led into the fort and two metal torch holders on either side that spilled light around the entrance.

"They don't leave guards outside, with most of the garrison away from the fort," Jax said. "I'm not even sure if they'll deal with you until morning."

"I'm sure I can get their attention," Zollin said.

He strode up to the wooden door, expecting that someone would notice him. He heard no one and was not challenged. He banged on the wooden door, but again heard nothing. He reached out with his magic and could feel the sentries on duty. They were certainly close enough to have heard his knock, but they were ignoring him. He sent an urgent desire to open the gates toward the men with a pulse of his magic. The power flowed out in a hot gust and soon he heard the wooden crossbeam being lifted, and as he stepped back the door opened.

"Who is it? Who's out there?" said the first soldier. He was barely older than Zollin and looked almost afraid.

"I'm Zollin and I've come to inquire about my friend. He was taken here by some soldiers after a misunderstanding at one of the inns. I'd like to secure his release so that we can leave town."

"I don't know about that," said the young soldier. "Yoric won't like being bothered with this."

"Our fearless leader is set on making an example of your friend," said the older soldier. He was fat and looked bored. He had a drooping mustache that badly needed trimming and even from several paces away Zollin could smell him.

"I heard him say something about a public whipping, perhaps even flogging him on the town square," said the younger soldier.

"That would be unfortunate," said Zollin, trying to keep his temper in check. "May I see him?"

"No, we couldn't allow that," said the younger soldier.

"We'd have to lock you up. It's the only way you'll see your friend," said the older man. "I doubt you'd like that. Yoric's liable to make an example out of you, too."

"I'd prefer to do this in a way that is beneficial to all of us. I'll pay gold for his release," Zollin explained.

"You might try in the morning," said the fat soldier.

"No, that won't do," Zollin said. "I'm sorry to you both."

Then, without warning, a dazzling, blue light shot from Zollin's hands and hit both of the sentries at the same instant. The blast was only meant to stun them and it worked wonderfully, with the two soldiers falling to the ground in quivering heaps. The pulse of magic had only lasted a second and then it was over, but the results were admirable.

"Whoa," said Jax from behind Zollin.

The young wizard turned and looked at the boy. He had been a good guide and deserved more than to be sent away with a coin. In fact, Zollin and Mansel would need to make their escape from the town tonight, not in the morning. He doubted that the small contingent of guards would bother leaving the city unpoliced just to pursue him. Still, he didn't want to make it easy on them if they did.

"Jax, I need you to go and get our horses," Zollin said. "Be sure and pack the supplies we bought today on them. There's gold in it for you if you do a good job."

"Gold," Jax said, his voice hushed with awe.

"That's right, and silver, so you don't have to use the gold coins if you don't want to. You won't have to worry for a long time, at least about money. Can you do that for me?"

"Yes, of course I can."

"Good, get the horses and wait in the shadows on the far side of the street, okay? Don't come to the fort, even if the gate is still open. Do you understand?"

"Yes, I understand," he said excitedly.

"Good, then run along. I've got work to do."

* * *

They had arrived at Orrock just after dark. Branock had pretended to be disinterested, but Brianna could tell he was

342

relieved to be off the small boat. The docks were crawling with sailors; even though the sun was down, they continued to work, loading cargo into ships and offloading into wagons. There were women in threadbare clothes trying to look alluring. Children whose skin was so filthy only their eyes and teeth showed in the flickering light of the dockworkers' torches. They ran past Branock and Brianna, some playing, some in a desperate search for food.

The city walls loomed high and dark. They were big, and even though they were nothing compared to the towering mountain peaks that had surrounded Brianna in Telford's Pass, these walls were straight up and seemed to grow taller and taller as she approached them.

The smaller of the two city gates was still open. Soldiers were posted high on the city walls, but also in the brilliant light that was cast on both sides of the small gate by rows of torches. The torches were in polished bronze sconces so that their light was reflected out into the night. The guards at the gate looked surprised as Branock approached. They allowed sailors and merchants in through the small gate at night only after their cargo was thoroughly inspected. Visitors were sent to one of the several dilapidated inns that were built along the city wall to service the sailors and wenches. It was a depressing place to be after dark, Brianna thought. It would have been terrifying, but Branock was more terrifying. The women, normally brazen in their trade, fell silent and found something of interest on the ground to stare at. The children gave them a wide berth, and no one came out of the shadows as they approached. She assumed it was the scarred head and ruined eye, but she couldn't be sure. Branock had an air of invincibility that was hard to miss. It was as if he was above everything around him and they had no power to touch him.

They approached the guards, who looked uncertain. They stepped forward with their pikes lowered, but they were obviously afraid. It was the first time Brianna had realized how courageous Zollin had been facing Branock alone, risking his life to save her. He hadn't cowered or seemed frightened. Yet the soldiers, professional fighters fully armed and armored, appeared to be terrified.

"We can't let you in, sir," said one the guards. "That's a standing law."

"You can't allow the King's wizard into the city?" Branock asked in a silky voice. "You would really keep us here, in the dock yard, when we have important news for the King?"

"You're a wizard?" the man asked, obviously not having heard anything else Branock said.

"Here, let me show you," Branock said in soft voice.

Suddenly the pike, which was a long spear with a cutting blade as well as a stabbing point and a metal hook used to pull men off of horses, was turned on his companion.

"What are you doing?" the other soldier said.

"I ain't doin' it!" cried the first.

"No, I am," Branock said, obviously pleased with himself.

"Do your duty, Pran!" ordered the guard, who was now facing the other soldier's weapon.

"I'm trying," the first soldier said in a voice near panic.

Brianna reached out and touched Branock. In that instant, the spell broke and the soldier who had been wrestling with his weapon stumbled back, his pike flipping up and over his head.

"Now," said Branock, acting as if he was still fully in control, although Brianna could hear the edge that was in his voice. "Let us pass or I'll have your heads mounted on these very gates by morning."

The soldier named Pran found his balance and waved them through. The other soldier stepped aside, grimacing, but not courageous enough to resist.

Once they were through the gate, Branock took Brianna's arm in a painful grip. He pulled her along at a hurried pace that she had trouble keeping up with. His skin, normally pale, was now red, and even in the constantly changing light from the shops and homes along the street, she could see veins just under the skin of his head pulsing.

"If you ever touch me again, at any time, for any purpose," Branock said in a low voice, "I shall ruin that perfect face and turn you out into the street."

Brianna said nothing. It was taking all her willpower not to cry out in pain because of the way he was gripping her arm.

"For once you have nothing to say, what a surprise," Branock sneered.

They hurried through the bustling city. It wasn't a long walk from the dockside gates to the castle, which rose up even higher than the city walls. There was a man at the doors, and this one seemed to recognize Branock. He didn't speak, but opened the door for the wizard and his prisoner, then stepped aside.

They went through the door, which was only a portion of the larger gate. Inside was a courtyard, with buildings on either side. The gate had been illuminated by a single torch, but the courtyard was lit with torches all along the castle and on the walls of the other buildings. The castle was built with cut stone. It rose up three stories and had round towers on each corner. Branock led her away from the large, ornate door to a smaller door that was nearer the tower to her right. He knocked briskly on the door, which opened. A soldier, this one dressed in an elegant uniform, allowed them inside then closed the door behind them.

Branock led her up the winding stairs, passing guards on each level. On the third level he moved down the hallway at a brisk pace. The lighting was dim here, with most of the torch sconces empty. A small man stepped out of one doorway and came hurrying toward them.

"Are my quarters ready?" Branock asked.

"Yes, my lord," said the man with a slight bow as he turned and began walking beside the tall wizard. "Just down the hall, beyond the King's private audience chamber."

"Good, what is the Prince up to this fine evening? I doubt he is visiting his father."

"No, lord, he is entertaining in his private quarters."

"Send him to me."

"But lord, he doesn't like to be disturbed."

"He'll want to hear what I have to say."

"Yes, my lord," the man said gravely.

"And I require a guard outside my chamber to ensure my guest doesn't wander unattended."

"As you wish."

"Have water drawn up for a bath, food and wine as well. It's been a long journey, and I'm ready to relax. Time is short, Homan, we must be ready when my compatriot arrives. It will not do to be caught unaware. Bring the Prince then wait outside."

"Yes, my lord."

They were almost to the rooms the man had indicated. Brianna noticed the finely carved wooden doors as they passed them. There were horses marching to war, and she thought the scene both beautiful and frightening at the same time.

"These are your quarters, sir," the man named Homan said.

"Excellent, these will do for now."

The steward hurried away and Branock opened the door. The room was dark, but Branock merely raised the walking stick he carried. It looked like a plain, wooden cane, more like what a wealthy merchant carried than what an elderly man leaned on. Light flowed out from the cane and showed a richly appointed suite. There were thick rugs on the floors and firewood was stacked in a large fireplace. Branock sent a gout of flame flying into the hearth. The logs burst into flame, bringing a dancing, golden light to the room.

There were tall chairs of carved wood, with thick cushions lining the seats and backs of the chairs. There was a desk and two other rooms that led off the main area: one was a large bedchamber with ornate furnishings, the other was a much smaller and simpler bedchamber. Branock went to a plain looking table in the smaller bed chamber and lifted a large pitcher of water. He bent over a porcelain bowl and poured the water over his head. There was a soft towel on the table, which he used to pat his skin dry. Then he turned to Brianna, who was standing against the far wall. She was afraid, even though Branock had not tried to hurt or even mistreat her on their journey. The fact that he had forced her into the bedroom made her feel trapped and defensive. She had secreted away a small knife, probably not big enough to kill the wizard, and she certainly didn't want him to see her with it until she could touch him and nullify his magic, but knowing it was just up her sleeve made her feel better.

"This will be your *gilded cage*" he said, emphasizing the last words to mock her. "Make yourself at home; I don't prefer sleeping in beds as a rule. You may take this one," he waved his hand at the bed. "You are to stay in this room until I call for you. If you comply, you shall have everything you need. If you do not, well..." he paused to let his words sink in, "...there are other types of cages, if you take my meaning."

He spun around and marched from the room. There were candles in tall candlesticks on a table by the bed. One of the candles lit up spontaneously just before he swung the door closed. Brianna could see the light from under the door. Her single candle did little to illuminate the room. The ceiling was high, and there were tall windows that were shuttered for the night. She immediately thought of climbing out the window to escape, but then remembered the cut stone of the castle walls. The stones were fit so tightly together that scaling them without a rope would be impossible.

She went over and lit the other candles, then positioned them around the room. The room had rugs all around the bed, which had thick posts on all four corners and thick drapes to keep out the light. There was another of the fancy chairs near the far window and a small table with an ink and quill. There was also a wooden wardrobe. She opened it but found nothing of value: a few more of the soft towels and a thick robe of soft wool. She sat on the bed and felt tears stinging her eyes. She was surrounded by luxury, but all she wanted was to see Zollin again.

Then she heard the outer door slam back against the wall. A loud voice called out, "What's the meaning of this?" Brianna hurried to her own door and leaned against it to hear what was happening.

"Prince Simmeron, I bring news," Branock said in a haughty tone.

"Good news, I hope. I was entertaining several young ladies, if you take my meaning."

"You have work to do," said Branock. "The Skellmarians invaded the valley in force. The army was nearly wiped out. They may all be dead by now. You must send troops north, to guard the passes."

"Skellmarians? You said nothing about the barbarians when I agreed to your ill fated plan."

"Tread lightly, highness," Branock's tone was icy. "I'm a wizard, not a seer."

"I can't send troops north; they're busy looking for the dragon."

"The dragon has come south already?"

"What do you know of it?" the voice said in a pouty tone, as if he were disappointed that Branock already knew the latest gossip.

"It saved your soldiers lives by attacking just after the Skellmarians."

"The Skellmarians have a dragon?" The pouty tone was gone, replaced by fear.

"Don't be a fool; no one can control a dragon. The beast attacked Yelsian and Skellmarian alike. Had it not been for the foul creature, I would have been successful in my attempt to bring Zollin here."

Brianna had to stifle a scornful laugh at the wizard's lie. It was just more proof that he was human and fallible.

"As it was, I was able to do the next best thing. I have his prized possession in the next room. He will come for her."

"A woman is always the downfall of good men."

"Not all men," Branock said angrily. "Now listen to me. We must double the guard and send spies into the city looking for the boy. He will be here soon. I can feel him approaching. Our voyage took longer than I expected and the snow in the mountain passes didn't slow him down as I had hoped. We must prepare for every possible outcome."

"There can be only one outcome," said the Prince angrily. "Since you've come, there's been nothing but problems. The Skellmarians attack. A dragon plagues my lands. My meddlesome brother is sending messages to my father that the Council of Kings is being assembled."

"You haven't allowed the messages to be passed to King Felix, have you?"

"Of course not."

"Good. This is troubling news, but not wholly unexpected. My former master is attempting to stem the changing tides of power, but he shall fail. Too much is at stake."

"You had better be right, wizard. I've bet my kingdom on this plan of yours."

"Once we have Zollin on our side, we will be unstoppable."

"You're sure of that?"

"Absolutely certain," Branock said calmly.

"What if the other kingdoms send armies against us?"

"And why would they do that?"

"Because of you! Because Yelsia now has a wizard, something no kingdom has had in hundreds of years."

"And the very reason why they won't come against us. They'll be too frightened to even contemplate it. And besides, we haven't done anything to provoke them. You worry about nothing."

"Except for the Council of Kings," the voice argued.

"Let me worry about that, you ready the city. Once we have accomplished our mission, no one can stop us."

Brianna pulled back from the door. She had heard enough. Branock's plans were much bigger than she had thought. He planned to rule Yelsia, perhaps even all of the Five Kingdoms. But he couldn't do it without Zollin and now he was coming to rescue her. She decided then that she couldn't let him risk it. She would have to escape so that Branock couldn't use her as bait to capture Zollin. And she had no time to waste. If Branock was right, Zollin would be here soon.

Chapter 29

They had walked all day, and normally one of them would be sleeping while the other kept watch. This night was different, however. Just before dusk they had topped one of the rolling hills to find a large army camped on the plain below them. This legion had over 500 heavy horse troops and there were over two dozen pennants flying. Quinn had never heard of so many knights leading a single legion before, but he'd never seen a dragon before either.

"What do you think they're doing here?" Kelvich asked, as they lay on the ground watching the soldiers.

"Dragon hunting would be my guess," said Quinn.

"That many?"

"It's a good excuse to get out of the dull sentry duty that occupies most of a soldier's life. Besides, no one's seen a dragon, and the rumors aren't clear on what to expect. It could be our dragon from the battle at the Gate, or it could be a whole flight of dragons. Better to have too many troops than not enough."

"What would they do if they found us here?"

"Probably nothing, we're just travelers, and they've probably met a lot if there are as many people fleeing the smaller villages and towns as we've heard."

They sat watching the army. They had no real reason to be interested in the soldiers, but both men understood the value of knowing as much as possible about any situation. Quinn lay thinking about Zollin, wondering if they had seen the same army. His son would have avoided the group most likely, but it was tempting to go and inquire if Zollin or Mansel had been seen. He doubted that it would do much good; it would most likely be exactly like their search for horses. There wasn't a beast to be found for any amount of money in northern Yelsia. The soldiers were most likely going about their tasks with a numb sort of detachment which Quinn remembered well from his own days as a King's soldier and then as part of the legendary Royal Guard. The knights who led the army were probably drinking wine and arguing over which of them was the most famous or most closely related to the royal family.

Kelvich harbored a secret fear that the dragon would draw the interest of the Torr. Zollin was the ultimate prize, but the Torr had been founded on the idea that by consolidating the magical power of the Five Kingdoms, they could deal with any threat, magical or otherwise, to the safety of the realm. Zollin had been enough to send three wizards in search of him, but a dragon demanded the attention of not only the Torr, but the leaders of the other kingdoms as well.

They were still watching the group, lost in their own private thoughts, when they heard the *Whosh! Whosh!* of giant wings. Kelvich had been mostly senseless when the dragon had attacked them at the Gate, and his memory of the event was hazy at best, but Quinn recognized the sound instantly.

"It's here!" Quinn said, scrambling awkwardly to his feet.

"Stay low," ordered Kelvich. "Let's make for those trees," he said, pointing down the hill toward the soldiers.

It was a risky move. They could have ducked back the way they came and avoided the beast altogether, but neither even considered it. The grove of trees was young, the trees little more than saplings with their new spring leaves bright green, but growing sparsely on the trees' limbs. They hurried down the hill just as the dragon came into view. It was hard to see the beast against the night sky. The dragon's scales were dark red, almost black, but not quite. The army's campfires cast a faint light into the sky, and it reflected dully on the beast's hide.

The dragon was taking no chances. It belched out a fiery blast that engulfed dozens of men and set even more tents ablaze. *Whosh! Whosh! Whosh!* The dragon's wings carried it up, into the darkness and out of sight. It might still have been in range of an excellent spear throw, but there was nothing to aim by except the sound of the mighty wings.

"It will come around for another pass." Kelvich shouted.

"What should we do?" Quinn asked.

"Nothing. We'll just have to wait and see if there is an opportunity to help somehow."

They had made it to the safety of the trees, and both were leaning on the slender trunks and panting hard. Below them men were screaming as they burned alive. Others were rushing to find weapons or to control the horses, which were in a panic.

The knights poured out of their pavilions and called for their pages or servants to bring their armor. It was a mistake to be encumbered by the heavy plate mail against a creature that could roast a man alive in his armor, but the knights seemed not to care. They were standing and shouting at the soldiers, but to little avail. Then the dragon was back, swooping in a long, low dive, incinerating anything in its path.

"Oh God," said Kelvich. "They're doomed."

"They need to find cover," Quinn said.

"There isn't much around here."

"Then they should spread out, stay in small bands, but disperse. Staying all together that way is only making them an easy target."

Horses had broken loose and were running in all directions. Some were headed toward the grove of trees where Quinn and Kelvich were watching. Quinn made a split second decision and then hobbled out of the tree line.

"Quinn!" Kelvich shouted. "What the hell are you doing?"

Quinn didn't answer but waved his arms in a shooing motion to slow the horse. A few slowed and approached him, although it was obvious that they were still skittish. Their eyes were wide enough that the whites were showing all around the irises, which reflected the blazing fires started by the dragon. Quinn stepped forward and took hold of one's bridal. Then he swung up into the saddle.

"You stay here," he ordered Kelvich. "I'll be back."

"But, Quinn, wait! You'll be killed down there!"

The warning fell on deaf ears as Quinn bounded away. His body was pumping adrenaline almost as fast as blood. It felt good to be on a horse again. His leg still ached from the long day's walk, but now, as the wind blew through his hair, he became one with the horse. They were racing back toward the camp, but the horse seemed less frightened with a rider on its back.

"Centuries!" Quinn shouted. "Form up in centuries and spread out. Don't bunch together and give the dragon an easy target."

All around him were flames and men and horses. The scene was terrifying, and yet men were rallying to his cry. The dragon was diving again, but this time men and horses were scattering out of its path, and although the beast was agile in the sky, it had trouble correcting its course in mid-dive.

The soldiers were beginning to assemble, moving farther and farther apart. The knights were still struggling to get into their armor, shouting orders and calling for horses.

"Disperse!" Quinn shouted as he raced through the camp. "Disperse and regroup."

The dragon hadn't gone far this time, but circled back quickly and landed near the edge of the camp. This time it sprayed flames in a wicked arc that engulfed half of the camp site. Most of the knights were burned alive, still struggling into their armor. A few managed to escape, and now they came at the beast with their lances leveled for a charge. Kelvich watched in dread fascination as the knights galloped toward what appeared to be the dragon's exposed side. He felt hope leap up when it appeared that the dragon had not seen them, but then it was dashed as the beast's tail whipped into the knights with such force that most were thrown from their horses to skid across the grass.

Finally a volley of arrows arched down out of the night sky. It was like shooting sewing needles at an armored man, but they got the dragon's attention. He roared and charged into the darkness on the far side of the camp. Kelvich knew he should find a horse, but he didn't have the skill with animals that Quinn had. He focused instead on the magic he felt in the dragon. It was strange and illusive. He grasped for it with his mind, but it was like trying to grip water in your hand. The dragon reacted to his probing, though, as if it felt the stab at magical control. The beast flew up into the night again.

The campsite was a fiery mess. The tents and supply wagons were burning. Weapons and armor lay scattered about the field, and the grass was burned black in many spots. Kelvich wondered if the dragon was gone for good, but he had no way of knowing. Quinn was not in sight, either. In fact, most of the soldiers had followed Quinn's advice and scattered. They would stay hidden until they were certain that the dragon was gone, then reconnoiter at the camp site. They didn't need orders; each would follow the standard operating procedures.

Kelvich, on the other hand, was anxious to find his friend. It was possible that Quinn lay slain on the grass somewhere, his body a smoldering corpse. He dreaded sharing that type of information with Zollin and determined to remain positive. For the time being, he just needed to find Quinn, and that meant leaving the safety of the grove of trees. Not that the trees offered any real safety, but stepping out into the open was difficult just the same. The moon was setting when the sorcerer decided it was safe enough to come out of the trees and go in search of his friend.

* * *

The fort was not well fortified. There were several buildings, a well, a storeroom, and an armory. It only took a little time to identify the small barracks building that was probably only used on a temporary basis by the soldiers on duty in the fort or the tower, but was now a semi-permanent home for the troops left to guard the town. There was an office where the grand leader of the army gave orders and saw to the logistics of the legion that was stationed there. And finally, there was a small guard house with bars over the windows. There were only so many ways to make a holding cell, and Zollin was glad he'd been able to find this one so easily. He eased into the slightly darker shadows of the building.

The fort was not well lit, there were only torches burning near the entrance. Zollin reached out with his magic and identified Mansel. He's spent enough time with his formal rival to know him by touch, even if that touch was magic. There were two guards on duty inside the building, guarding their prisoner, Zollin supposed. He sent a strong urge to sleep to the two soldiers. It didn't take long before he could hear their snores and he decided it was time to act. He put his hand on the sides of the building and began to work. The stone used to construct the building was made of sandstone, and it only took a few moments for Zollin to begin turning the stone back into water and sand. The minerals had calcified and cemented themselves together but could be separated with a little magical effort.

It took almost half an hour before he had created an opening large enough for a person to crawl out of. Zollin was sweating and his stomach burned with hunger. His eyes felt hot and he badly wanted to lie down and sleep. The sounds of the snoring soldiers didn't help, but Zollin shook his fatigue off. He stuck his head into the hole he'd made and lit a tiny flame that hovered in the air over his head and cast a soft light around the room. Mansel was asleep on a cot against the wall. There were metal bars separating him from the soldiers, who were sitting in chairs they had leaned back against the wall.

"Mansel," Zollin whispered.

He did not stir, so Zollin levitated a pebble across the room and dropped it on his friend's head. Mansel still did not stir. Zollin knew that Mansel was a heavy sleeper after a night spent drinking, but he should have at least stirred when the rock hit him. Zollin crawled through the opening and moved silently over to his friend. From the small light he was using, he could see swelling and bruising. At the inn, Mansel had sported a black eye and a busted lip. Now the eye was swollen shut, the lid purple and the slit that should have been his eyelid was crusted over. His nose was broken and there was dried blood on his face, chin, and neck.

His jaw was broken as well, the swelling making the odd angle of the fracture harder to spot, but it was obvious as Zollin studied his friend. There was a long gash on the side of Mansel's face opposite the swollen eye and his lips looked like raw meat.

"Oh, Mansel," Zollin said compassionately.

He let the little flame wink out as he put his hands on his friend's shoulder and arm. He let his magic delve into his friend. There were broken ribs and blood was seeping into one lung. His left hand had several broken bones, as if someone had stomped on it with the heel of their boot. His breathing was shallow and, if left unattended, he would probably not have ever woken up, but Zollin set to work immediately. He mended bones and stopped the internal bleeding. It took time to patch the tear in his lung and slowly remove the blood that had built up there. The broken jaw was set and healed, the gash on his check repaired, but the eye took more time. Zollin had no idea how much time he'd spent, only that he was exhausted and he still hadn't seen to his friend's hand. He heard movement outside, but he blocked the thoughts out of his mind. He couldn't worry about the soldiers now, he needed to be careful as he drained the blood that had filled the tissue around the eyeball and was causing the painful swelling.

Mansel was breathing better and his eye was almost healed, when the door opened and light poured into the room.

"Wake up, you lollies, your prisoner is about to escape!" shouted the centurion.

Zollin ignored him as he finished helping Mansel, although the fighter's hand was still a mess, the other wounds were all mended. Given a few days rest, Mansel would be fine, but they didn't have a few days. Zollin stood up and almost swooned. He was exhausted, his head dizzy, and he had to hold the wall to stay on his feet.

"Who the hell are you?" the soldier demanded.

"I'm his friend."

"I guess you're to blame for attacking my sentries?"

"I guess you're to blame for beating my friend almost to death," Zollin said angrily.

"He was in a brawl at the tavern, we had nothing to do with it," the soldier said with a smirk.

"You will regret that," Zollin said.

"That's interesting, because I was just thinking how much you are going to regret crawling into my cage, outsider," the soldier's voice was cold. "I was planning to make an example of your friend, but now it looks like I'll put you on display instead. Open the cage!" he ordered the soldiers who Zollin had lulled to sleep.

"You'll need more than that stick against me," the centurion said.

He stepped into the cage and threw a quick jab into Zollin's face. It wasn't hard enough to do anything but stun Zollin, but that's all it was meant to do. The brutal soldier was an expert at inflicting pain. He stepped forward, throwing powerful uppercuts into Zollin's midsection. The jab had hurt, but the uppercuts knocked the wind out of his lungs and felt liked he was being kicked by a horse. The only thing his mind registered for the moment was the cruel smile on his tormentor's face.

Then, even though he couldn't breathe and his body was screaming in agony as his ribs snapped from the brutal body blows, he lashed out with his magic. He'd dropped his staff and the magic erupted in the form of a slap of energy that was invisible, yet it shook the very walls of the holding cell. The centurion flew back through the open door of the cell and into the stone wall with a sickening crunch that was made from crushed bone and pulverized flesh. He slid down the rough wall, leaving bloody gore in his wake. Zollin was on the ground, and the other two soldiers weren't sure what had happened. They hesitated for a moment, then they slammed the cell door shut, which locked automatically, and ran outside, calling for help.

The spell had roused Mansel, who was now cradling his hand. He stood up and looked at the dead centurion and smiled. Then he turned to Zollin, who was gasping for breath on the floor of the cell.

"That bastard got what he deserved," Mansel said. "You must have done something to me; I thought he was beating me to death."

"He...almost...did..." Zollin managed to say as he tried to coax air back into his lungs.

"Well, he won't do that to anyone else. I got in one good shot and after he had beaten me down he stomped on my hand. I guess it's too mangled even for you to fix."

"Get me...out of here," Zollin gasped.

"Uh, I don't think I can. The cell is still locked, and I don't think you'd want me pulling you through that hole you must have come in through. Besides, if I stick my head through there someone might cut it off."

Zollin waved his hand and the cell door swung open.

"That's a handy trick," Mansel said, smiling.

"We've got horses outside in the street," Zollin said, wincing as he stood up. "I need a little time to heal my ribs. Try not to get us killed."

"Hey, trust me," Mansel joked.

He supported Zollin on one side, and the young wizard used his staff to support the other side. When they peeked out the door of the guardhouse they saw soldiers running to the tower. The sky was slate grey, which meant the sun would be rising soon. Zollin had his attention focused inward, trying to knit the broken ribs. There were three, and every step made the fractures grind together, sending waves of agony through Zollin's entire body.

It was still dark enough that, by staying close to the side of the building, they were able to avoid detection. They moved away from the tower where the soldiers gathered and also away from the gate, which was their only way out of the fort. The closest building to the guardhouse was the armory.

"The door's locked," Mansel whispered.

Zollin sent a spell through into the lock and flipped the tumblers so that the door swung open. They moved quickly into the darkness of the room and locked the door behind them. Zollin leaned against the wall and worked on healing his body. He was weak, both from the fight and from working so much magic. He hadn't slept, and it had been hours since he ate. He was trembling all over and fighting the urge to pass out.

Mansel was waiting by the door. There were no windows in the armory, and it was pitch black inside. He wanted a small light so that he could at least arm himself, but he knew that fighting his way out of the fort simply wasn't an option. He needed to keep the soldiers out until Zollin could finish healing himself. His magic was their only hope of escape.

It didn't take the soldiers long to get organized. One cohort was sent to guard the gatehouse. The rest went straight to the guardhouse. Once they realized that Mansel and Zollin had escaped, they spread out to search for them. Mansel held the door shut, hoping that if the soldiers sent to search the armory had keys, he could hold them off long enough for Zollin to come back around. His broken hand was throbbing with pain, but the adrenaline from making their escape was keeping his mind focused on the task. He held the door handle with his left hand and braced himself in hopes of being able to hold the door shut.

The soldiers didn't have a key, or if they did, they didn't use it. They checked the door, but it was locked and they must have assumed that Mansel and Zollin couldn't have gotten into the armory. If they had thought about the fact that they had somehow escaped the guardhouse, they might have investigated the armory more thoroughly, but they didn't.

"That was close," Mansel whispered.

Zollin didn't respond. He was working on the third rib and, although the pain was easing, the fatigue was growing. He needed food, but he had to stay focused on the job at hand. Thinking about food, or the soldiers that were looking for them, only made the job at hand more difficult.

It only took about five minutes for the soldiers to sweep through the fort. Mansel could hear them talking about the possibilities. They would be back soon, and he couldn't shake the feeling that they were about to get caught. Suddenly a dim light illuminated the armory. Mansel turned and saw that Zollin had conjured up another small flame. His face was pale and damp with sweat, but he was moving without pain.

"You okay now?" Mansel asked.

"Yes, just incredibly tired and hungry."

"How can you think of food at a time like this?" Mansel joked. "I can see wanting a horn of ale, but food?"

"Let's just get out of here."

"I'm with you. What's the plan?"

"We walk out."

"That's it? Just walk right out?"

"Yes," Zollin said. "And the quicker, the better."

Chapter 30

Once Mansel had recovered his sword, they swung open the armory door. The soldiers began shouting and running toward them. Zollin didn't wait, but sent bursts of energy from his staff that stunned the soldiers. The bursts knocked them off their feet and left most of them unconscious. There were over a hundred men, but Zollin subdued them all in a matter of minutes, just from the door of the armory. At one point someone shot an arrow at him, but he deflected it easily enough. The heat of the magic inside of him was so intense it felt like he was reaching into a hot oven with his whole body. He remembered the way the wizard Cassis from the Torr had died. Zollin hadn't killed him; he'd died because he couldn't sustain the magic he was using. It was the first time Zollin had really understood his own limits. He didn't feel that he was in danger of overdoing anything at the moment, but he could see that there was a line that he could not cross; his physical body just couldn't survive it.

They walked toward the gate and were confronted by the soldiers assigned to guard it.

"Watch him, he's some kind of a sorcerer," said one of the men.

"He's a wizard, actually," Mansel said in a superior tone.

"You're both under arrest," said another of the soldiers. "Throw down your weapons, and you won't be hurt."

"That's good advice," Zollin said. "We are leaving this fort and this town. Stand aside, and we won't hurt anyone."

"You lay your weapons down," shouted the first soldier.

Zollin didn't wait, he sent a burst of energy that shook the soldier violently for a moment before he fell to the ground unconscious.

"Now move away from the gate!" Mansel shouted.

The soldiers scrambled away.

"None of your men are dead, just stunned," Zollin explained. "The only exception was your centurion. I killed him in self defense, but ultimately it was his cruelty that killed him."

The soldiers didn't respond, so Mansel opened the smaller gate door. Just as dawn was breaking over the horizon, they stepped out into the street. Jax was waiting just where Zollin had told him to. The boy looked tired, but he was awake and alert. He met them in the road and he wasn't alone.

"Who's this?" Mansel asked.

"I'm Miriam. Jax and I are coming with you."

"Oh no you're not," Zollin said.

"Yes, we are. Neither of you looks strong enough to ride very long, and I can stand watch while you rest. Once you've done that, we'll discuss what we do next."

Zollin was too tired to argue. They had loaded Lilly with the new provisions. Miriam had a horse for herself and Jax to ride, so Zollin climbed into his own saddle. Mansel looked confused, but he didn't argue. Instead, he mounted his own horse, carefully cradling his broken hand, and followed Zollin.

* * *

Kelvich wandered through the obliterated camp. There were smoldering tents and patches of burning grass. And bodies, most were burned beyond recognition. The stench was overwhelming. Kelvich gagged as he searched for Quinn. He had no idea how many of the soldiers had survived, and none had yet returned to camp.

"Quinn!" the old sorcerer called out. "Quinn, are you here?"

The only sound was the crackle of the fires. Some men had been wounded by the dragon attack, but they were all silent now. Kelvich had heard them crying out in pain when he was hidden in the grove of trees, but now they were all gone, either deeply in shock or dead.

The ruined camp was hard to accept. Tears filled Kelvich's eyes as he wandered through the remains. He had never understood such wanton destruction. He was angry and afraid at the same time. The dragon could return, he thought, and roast him just as easily as it had the soldiers.

Then he heard hoof beats. Horses were approaching, and he turned and waved his hands.

"Here, over here!" he called out.

There were several riders, but Kelvich only cared about one. The lead rider was unmistakable. He had no armor and his compact build seemed even smaller on top of the horse, but it was obviously Quinn.

"Kelvich!" he called out as he approached. "Has the beast returned?"

"No," Kelvich answered. "Are you alright?"

"Fine, thanks. Has anyone else returned yet?"

"No, not yet."

"Any survivors?"

"None that I've found," Kelvich said sadly.

"Well, that's unfortunate, but we must turn our attention to the living. Let's see what condition the supply train is in."

He swung down from his horse and limped along beside his friend. He realized then that he and the old sorcerer had truly become friends. He was more than Zollin's mentor, he was Quinn's friend, a brother who had rescued him from mortal danger and helped him survive the terrible flight through Telford's Pass. Quinn had seen his share of fighting and death, but he realized that Kelvich had not. The older man was wise, but the horrors of the dragon attack were almost too much for him. He felt sorry for the older man.

"What did you see?" Quinn asked gently.

"I saw you acting like a fool," he said. "What in the world possessed you to go riding into that camp?"

"I don't know," Quinn said. "When I was in the army, I was content to take orders, but having a child and raising that child on my own changed me. I can't just sit back and watch people destroy themselves."

"All I could think of was what I was going to tell Zollin about how you died."

"I doubt he would care overmuch," Quinn said sadly. "He feels that I have treated him unfairly."

"The young man I know cares for you deeply," Kelvich assured Quinn.

"Thank you, but he told me how he really felt before he left the valley. He feels that I pushed him to be something he's not, and I can't say that he's wrong. After his mother died, all I wanted was for him to be safe and to have the life that I didn't have. To be honest, I never even considered remarrying. Perhaps I should have, if only for Zollin's sake."

"I can't speak to what should or shouldn't have been," Kelvich said, appreciative for something to talk about besides the carnage of the army camp they were walking through. "What I do know is that Zollin is a strong, bright, and honorable young man. Perhaps his path to becoming that man was difficult. I can't imagine growing up without a mother, but you did something right. He has power, but he is as humble as anyone I've ever met. He could have anything he wants and do whatever he wants, yet he never takes advantage of his power or the people around him. You have a lot to be proud of."

"Oh, I'm proud of him, more than he will ever know. I just hope I haven't pushed him so hard that I've destroyed any hope of having a relationship with him as a man."

"I doubt that," Kelvich said. "He is quick to forgive."

"Others, but family wounds often linger and fester. I can only hope that you are right."

They found the supply wagons. Most were destroyed, but there were a few that had little or no damage. They set about moving the good wagons away from the others. The camp had now become a graveyard. Other troops were starting to return, each man searching the bodies, looking for friends they hoped not to find. Some had begun digging graves, while others stood watch with longbows and crossbows. As light began to fill the eastern sky, the remaining legionaries finally filtered back to camp. There were several senior officers, but the knights were all dead. Quinn spoke to the men who would now be left with the responsibility of leading their troops.

"You can do what you want," Quinn said. "You've got your orders, but I don't think marching out into the open is the best way to defeat a dragon. I am going to Orrock with all haste. You can follow me, perhaps send one or two men with Kelvich and I to report to the King. He must know what he's up against."

The soldiers looked at one another, uncertain what to do. They were line officers, charged with training and leading their squads and regiments into battle, but strategy was always someone else's decision.

"Perhaps we should take our troops back to Felson," said one of the officers. "We can send a few men with you and wait for orders at our base."

"That sounds like good sense," Quinn said. "You might also send riders to warn the villages. Let them know the threat is real. They can either accompany your troops back to Felson or try paying the tribute."

"Do you really think a dragon cares about gold?" someone asked.

"I have no idea," Quinn said. "It doesn't make much sense, does it? But if it means the difference between my village and home being destroyed or not, I say it's worth a shot."

The officers took half an hour composing a message for the King, then sent two riders with Quinn and Kelvich. They also allowed Quinn to borrow two horses for himself and Kelvich, with the promise that they would allow the soldiers riding with them to Orrock to return with the horses once they had delivered their message to the king.

"Well," said Kelvich, "I had no idea we'd have a military escort into the capital."

Quinn smiled grimly. "Let's just hope we get there before Zollin and Mansel tear the castle down."

* * *

When she woke up, it took her a moment to remember where she was. It had been so long since she had slept in a proper bed that she thought at first that she was back in her father's house.

Then the realization hit her that she was a captive, locked in the royal castle at Orrock. It seemed impossible. She thought of all the times she had dreamed of being a princess as a child. She had imagined being whisked away by a handsome prince in shining armor to a grand life in the royal castle. Instead, she had been kidnapped by an arrogant and evil wizard, sailing down the coast in a boat full of foreigners who looked more like pirates than merchant sailors. Now she was being held captive in the very place she had once dreamed of living, only now her dreams were different. Her dream now was of exploring the Five Kingdoms with Zollin.

She held on tightly to the memory of the man she loved. He was coming for her and Branock was afraid. That thought gave her strength and the resolve to do whatever it took to escape the evil wizard's clutches. Her first challenge was to find out as much as she possibly could about the castle and how things worked. Branock had promised her servants to provide for her every need, and he had even given her an idea of how she could spend time alone with those servants.

She rose shortly after dawn and went to the door of her room. It was locked, although she couldn't understand why anyone would put a lock on the outside of a door. Still, she was forced to knock on the door. It was several minutes before her captor answered her insistent plea.

"What do you want?" he asked as he opened the door wide.

"May I have a bath?" she asked.

"Yes, you could use one, eh? Well, I'll have someone bring you up some water and fresh clothes, too. It won't do to have our prize looking tarnished. Stay here and I'll see that you have all that you need."

"Alright," Brianna said, feigning obedience.

He closed the door, and although she didn't hear a lock, she was sure that he had secured the door somehow. She waited and before long a servant arrived with a tray of food. She hadn't eaten much on the voyage south. She had overcome sea sickness, but the constant motion of the ship had left her without much of an appetite. Now she recognized the need to eat and regain as much strength as possible. The servant had brought boiled eggs, toasted bread, fruit, and a small bowl of porridge sweetened with honey. There was also a small decanter of apple cider and a crystal goblet to drink it from. She ate everything and afterward her stomach was beyond full, but she felt good.

Soon more servants arrived. The first ones, there were four altogether, carried a large porcelain tub. Then came more servants with large, clay pots full of steaming water. They poured the pots of water into the tub until it was brimming with hot water. Brianna stripped down and climbed into the water, which felt heavenly. With a full stomach and the warm soaking bath, she was soon dozing. Another servant arrived with soap and brushes. She was a small woman, older than Brianna's mother, and she wore a long dress that was very utilitarian. She smiled as she offered to scrub Brianna.

"If my lady would like, I'll wash," she offered.

It was exactly what Brianna had been hoping for. She was perfectly capable of taking a bath without any assistance, but she was hoping for some time to talk to one of the servants. She needed information, and she was betting the serving folk had answers and would be more inclined to share them.

"I would like that very much," Brianna said. "What's your name?"

"They call me Edina, my lady," she said.

"That's a beautiful name."

"Thank you."

"I'm Brianna."

"Yes, my lady."

The bath was efficiently given without too much idle chit-chat. Once the scrubbing was over and Edina was helping her dry off, Brianna asked the question that was on her mind.

"Can you tell me about the King?"

"King Felix is very sick," Edina said simply. "It will be his time to pass over soon."

"How long have you served the royal family?"

"All my life, my lady."

"Oh, you must know so much about castle life. How do you ever get used to it all?"

"It's not as difficult as you might think. Life in a castle is just like life anywhere else, only the lord has a little more influence and a lot more worry."

"With the King so ill, who is in charge of the kingdom?"

"The Prince has taken up his father's duties," she said, but there was a hint of disapproval in her tone.

"Prince Wilam?" Brianna asked.

"No, the First Prince is the diplomat in Osla," Edina said. "Prince Simmeron has taken control of the castle, and if the King does not improve, he'll find a way to become King."

"But what about his brother?"

"Being a member of the royal family is a dangerous proposition," Edina said in a matter-of-fact tone. "If you're going to survive around here, you'll need to keep your guard up."

Brianna considered that fact as Edina helped her into a long, flowing, blue dress. She didn't want to survive, she wanted to escape the castle and get out of the city as quickly as possible.

"So, you're with the wizard?" Edina asked.

"I'm bait," Brianna explained. "Branock is using me to lure my friend here so that he can convince him to join forces with Branock."

"Hum," Edina said as she pondered this new information. "What will happen when this friend shows up?" she asked, emphasizing the word friend.

"I don't know. Zollin doesn't want to join Branock, but what choice does he have. Unless..." She was afraid to trust Edina, but what choice did she have? She needed help and the castle servant was her only choice. She could be a spy for Branock, but would finding out that she planned to escape really be a surprise? She decided she had very little to lose and everything to gain. "...Unless I can somehow get out of the castle."

"Is your friend a wizard, too?" she asked.

"Yes."

"Can he heal people?"

"Yes, I've seen him work miracles," Brianna said, trying to hide her excitement.

"Do you think he could heal the king?"

"I think it's possible," Brianna said. "I can't say for sure, though."

Edina looked at Brianna for a long moment, her small eyes seemed to penetrate deep into the young captive's soul. Then she pulled Brianna to the far side of the room and spoke in a whisper.

"If I get you out, could your friend get past the guards and into the King's private quarters?"

374

"I don't know, I think so. He's very powerful."

"He might have to fight the king's Royal Guard."

"I know he could do it."

"I've been around this castle a long time, and I've seen things I wish I could forget. I've seen men live and die, but the lingering sickness King Felix is suffering from isn't natural. As soon as Prince Wilam was sent to Osla, King Felix fell ill. Prince Simmeron blamed the King's surgeon and accused him of incompetence, then had him locked up in the dungeon. Of course the Prince brought in another healer, who hasn't made a wit of difference, but Simmeron doesn't seem to care as long as the King stays sick."

"You mean...?"

"Yes, I mean the Prince is killing his father. There, I've said it. If you're a spy, just go ahead and report me. I don't care anymore. What Simmeron is doing isn't right. King Felix is a good man, and he doesn't deserve to die this way. Prince Wilam wouldn't stand for it, but something is keeping him in Osla."

"I'm no spy," Brianna said. "I just want to get out of the castle and away from Branock."

"I can get you out, but it will take a few days. I don't know the bald wizard's habits yet. But if you can wait that long, and if you promise to convince your friend to help the king, I'll get you out."

"It's a deal," Brianna said, throwing her arms around the servant's shoulders and pulling her close.

At first Edina hesitated, but she embraced Brianna, then pulled away.

"I better go now," she said. "I'll make sure I see you at least once a day."

"Thank you so much," Brianna said.

Finally, hope seemed to break through the clouds of darkness surrounding her. She had an ally now, and together they would find a way to break free of the evil wizard Branock's grasping plan.

Chapter 31

They had ridden along the dark road out of town as the sun peeked over the eastern horizon. Then they rode for another hour across the countryside. Miriam assured Zollin that she knew where she was and where she was going. Mansel rode in silence, sipping water and wine from two separate skins that he had slung across his saddle. His hand was throbbing, and he was light headed from the pain and lack of sleep, but he stayed in the saddle and didn't complain. Growing up in a busy house with older brothers had taught him that showing weakness of any kind was an invitation for torment. So he dealt with the pain in silence.

Jax, on the other hand, was a virtual chatterbox. He talked about everything he saw, and it was obvious that he had never left the city. He rode behind Miriam on a sturdy looking, brown horse that was smaller than the cavalry horses that Zollin and Mansel rode. But the horse didn't seem bothered by the extra weight. Miriam led the small group, and although she didn't talk much, she was bright eyed and seemed excited.

Zollin had not stopped eating. He had cut off a portion of the smoked ham for Mansel as soon as they left the city, but he had steadily eaten the rest. He drank water and saved the other rations, but the ham was fair game. He only stopped eating long enough to ask a question, or to answer one of Jax's many questions. When they reached a small grove of trees near a swiftly flowing stream, Zollin finally stopped eating. There wasn't much left of the ham, but Zollin wrapped it up anyway. He wiped his greasy hands on his pants then helped Mansel down from his horse. The wounded swordsman found a soft place to lie down and fell almost instantly asleep.

Jax was charged with looking after the horses. There was plenty of fresh, spring grass for the horses to eat, so he loosened their girth straps and led them down to the stream for a drink. Zollin followed them and washed his face and hands in the cold water. Then he returned to their new camp. Miriam had found a comfortable spot to sit and watch for anyone approaching from Felson. Zollin approached her.

"So, will you tell me why you insisted on coming with us?" Zollin asked.

"I think you know," she responded.

Zollin's mind flashed to that moment in her barn when their hands had touched. He remembered the flash of desire that had heated his blood, but he was determined not to give into the temptation. He had made no commitment to Brianna, but he loved her just the same and he was determined to stay faithful to her.

"That can never happen," he said. "I'm in love with another."

Miriam laughed; it was a full throated, belly laugh that made Zollin smile, despite the fact that he was both embarrassed and a little offended by her response.

"What is so funny?" he demanded.

"I'm not here because I'm infatuated with you. What kind of a woman do you take me for? I'm old enough to be your mother."

"I didn't mean any offense," he said sullenly.

"Oh, I'm not offended. I'm flattered. And I'll admit, you're a handsome young man and the thought of taking advantage of you crossed my mind, but that's not why I came. You're a wizard, and I don't know much about wizards or magic, but when you touched me something changed. It was like a part of me that

I've always known about, but could never really connect with, suddenly woke up. I'm seeing things differently and I don't want that to end. I want to learn."

"Learn what?"

"About healing," she replied with a straight face, all traces of her humor gone. "When we touched, I think you passed something on to me. Some bit of magic or hidden knowledge."

"I didn't," Zollin said.

"Well, something is different. I know that much, and until I figure it all out, I'm tagging along."

"We aren't out for a joyride," Zollin said. "We're going to Orrock to free our friend."

"Is your friend a criminal?" she asked seriously.

"No, she was taken because the wizards of the Torr want me, dead or alive. One of them, a vile man named Branock, kidnapped her and is using her to lure me into the city."

"And you're going, even though you know it's a trap?"

"I have to," Zollin said, swallowing the lump in his throat as he realized what he was going to say next. "I love her."

"Well, that's a good reason to try and rescue someone, but love has a way of blinding people to danger. Let me come with you, I'll help if I can."

"I can't guarantee your safety," Zollin said. "And after we get a little rest, we will be moving as fast as possible."

"I can keep up and I'll pull my weight. Jax and I don't eat much, and you might be surprised how useful Jax can be."

"Alright," Zollin said. "Don't let us sleep past sunset. And if you see soldiers, or anyone approaching for that matter, wake me up immediately."

"Okay," she said.

Zollin turned back to where Mansel was asleep. He was cradling his broken hand. It was the only thing Zollin hadn't had a chance to heal before they broke out of the guard house in the fort. All he wanted was to lie down and sleep, but he knew he needed to help Mansel. It might be better if his friend were asleep anyway. He sat down on the soft grass beside Mansel and reached out with his magic. There were dozens of small bones in the hand, and it took a full hour to check each one and heal the six that had been broken or fractured. The hand was swollen, too, so Zollin made sure that the swelling was taken care of. By the time he was finished, Jax was curled up behind him, sleeping blissfully. Zollin walked back down to the stream and filled his stomach with cold water. He was hungry, too, but food would have to wait until he got some sleep.

The sun was just starting to set when Miriam shook Zollin awake. He opened his eyes and stretched. No one had approached the camp, and Miriam had gotten the horses ready before waking anyone up. She had also prepared a cold meal of bread, cheese, and fruit.

"Hey," Mansel said, flexing his hand. "My hand is better."

"Your mind is still a bit slow though," Zollin teased.

"Hey, you may be a wizard, but when I lop off your head, I'll be the one laughing."

They mounted their horses and Zollin checked their direction with his pathfinder in the last of the fading daylight. They were moving steadily southwest. He didn't know how long it would take them to reach Orrock, but he was glad that he was moving again. He rubbed Brianna's ribbon between his fingers. He didn't like to bring it out where people might see it, but, riding along in the dark, he wasn't too worried. There was just enough

380

starlight to see the shadowy forms of the other riders. They rode in silence, everyone pondering his or her own thoughts. It was close to midnight when they passed through a small village, but there were no signs of life; even in the small inn, the windows were all dark.

Not long after they had passed the village they came back to Weaver's Road, which ran from Eddson Keep to Orrock. They saw no sign of other travelers, so they resumed their journey, able to move much more quickly on the open road than through the less traveled country lanes. They decided to stop just long enough to get food out of their provisions. The plan was to keep riding through the night and as long as they could the next day before stopping for rest. Even though Zollin, Mansel, and Jax had slept all day, they were still tired, and Miriam, who had rested very little the night before and kept watch over the camp all day, was exhausted. They needed to walk the horses for a while, which they did while they ate dried meat and crusty bread. It was not a savory meal, but it was food and they were all hungry.

They had just remounted their horses when they saw a shadow approaching. The figure was riding a horse and carrying a lamp of some sort. The light was pitched low, revealing the horse and the ground around it, but not the rider.

"Who would that be?" Miriam asked.

"Probably just another traveler," said Zollin.

"Maybe, maybe not," Mansel said. "You care if I check it out?"

"Not at all," Zollin said.

Mansel loosened the sword in his sheath as he spurred his horse forward. The moon was just a sliver and, although the stars were shining brightly, the night was still very dark. Zollin, Jax, and Miriam strained to see what would happen.

Mansel stopped in the road, just ahead of the rider. Mansel was restless, perhaps looking for a fight, but something seemed odd about the man. He raised a hand and called out.

"Hello, traveler," he said. "Where are you headed this night?"

The shadowy figure manipulated the lamp so that the light illuminated Mansel while still shrouding the stranger in darkness. Mansel squinted in the light.

"I don't want trouble," the stranger said in a croaking voice.

"Nor do we," Mansel replied. "So, where are you headed?"

"Felson," he croaked. "I have business there."

"Alright," Mansel said, a little disappointed. The truth was he had hoped that meeting a stranger on the road in the middle of the night would allow him to work out some of his pent up frustrations. He had enjoyed the fight in the inn the previous night, but his rough treatment at the hands of the soldiers had left him frustrated and on edge. But the stranger seemed like a simple traveler, so he shouted to Zollin and the others.

"It's okay, he's harmless."

Zollin and Miriam urged their horses forward. The stranger watched them come, keeping the light between them and himself so that they never saw the man's face. They rode around the stranger and down the road, perhaps a hundred paces. Then the attack came. It was swift and well rehearsed. Even in the dark, their attackers knew exactly what they needed to do. There were two brigands on either side of the road. They rushed at the group, shouting as they came. The startled horses reared, causing Jax and

Miriam to fall off the back of their brown horse. Zollin and Mansel were struggling to get their animals under control, so they wouldn't fall as well, when the brigands took hold of the horses' bridles. Another grabbed Miriam's horse while holding a sword pointed at the healer. The fourth put his boot on the middle of Jax's back, effectively pinning him to the ground, while he kept an eye on Zollin and Mansel.

Mansel started to draw his sword, but the man holding Jax told him to stop.

"I wouldn't if I were you," said the outlaw. "This boy's the first to die and your lady friend will be next."

"Bastards!" Mansel shouted in frustration.

"That's right, we are bastards," said the man with his foot on Jax. "We're murdering thieves, too, so don't try anything stupid."

"What do you want?" Zollin said.

"Everything, of course, but we'll start with your gold."

"Zollin," Mansel said angrily. "Can you keep them safe?"

"Yes," said Zollin in a calm voice.

"Don't be so certain," said the outlaw with grim determination.

But Zollin wasn't listening. It took a lot of concentration to identify the four bandits since they were in different places, but he managed it. He gave them all a hard push with his magic, which knocked them back all at once.

"Jax! Run to me!" Zollin shouted.

The boy scrambled up quickly as Mansel drew his sword. Zollin raised his staff in the air, and the end of it glowed so brightly it cast light all around them. They could see the brigands with shock on their faces. Mansel didn't hesitated but spurred his horse forward, toward the outlaw who had seemed to be the leader. That's when Zollin noticed the arrow racing toward his friend. The man they had passed on the road was now shooting at them from the darkness ahead. Zollin deflected the arrow and reached out with his magic. The man was at least a hundred feet from them, but he was the only living thing in that direction. Zollin levitated the man high into the air. The man was screaming in terror as Mansel cut down the first outlaw. The man had managed to get back to his feet and draw a heavy looking, short sword, but he was not prepared for the force of Mansel's blow. It had all the momentum of the charging horse, as well as Mansel's own strength. The outlaw's sword was batted aside, and Mansel's weapon sliced cleanly into the man's neck and through the collar bone. Blood flashed out into the air, but Mansel was already past the man and wheeling his horse. The other outlaws were trying to flee, but they were on foot. Mansel guided his horse around Miriam, who was trying to calm her own horse back down from all the excitement.

Zollin levitated the man through the air back to where he and the others were waiting. Jax had just scrambled up behind Zollin when the man came crashing down. The stranger's light had been dropped when Zollin lifted him. Now he lay in the dirt, one leg twisted at an odd angle. He was still screaming.

Mansel let his horse charge down the outlaw who had been holding Miriam's horse. The other two bandits had fled in different directions, so Mansel let them go. He would have liked a fight, but riding down cowards didn't interest him.

"That was amazing," Jax said exuberantly.

"Are you okay?" Zollin asked.

"Sure," the boy said. "I'm fine."

"Miriam?" Zollin asked.

She hadn't gotten back on her horse yet. She was staring at the man lying crumpled in the road. A look of terror, loathing, and compassion mingled on her face.

"Miriam? Are you okay?" Zollin asked.

"I'll be pretty sore for a few days, but nothing is broken."

"Mansel, watch this creature," Zollin said as he climbed down off his horse. "Jax, take the reins."

He walked over to Miriam and put his hands on her shoulders. There was the sting of electricity, and then his mind sought out the problems that had been caused by her fall. She had several sections of her spine that were out of alignment and bruises were forming on her back and bottom. He straightened her spine with several sharp movements of magic. Her back popped with each one, but the relief she felt was immediate. Healing the bruises took several minutes, but it was fairly easy work. When he was done, he went back to his horse and retrieved the bottle of wine from one of the saddle bags.

"Don't drink all of that," Mansel said. "I'll want some when I'm done with this one."

"What are you going to do to him?" Miriam asked, the worry in her voice evident.

"Find out who he is for starters," said Zollin. "Learn why his companions were trying to rob us."

"Are you going to hurt him?"

"That depends on how cooperative he is," Zollin said.

The man was moaning in pain and quickly growing weaker.

"Who are you?" Mansel demanded.

"Help me, my leg's broken," the man moaned.

"That's not all that will be broken if you don't start talking," Mansel threatened.

"I'm, I'm Brayford. Please help me."

"I will help you," Zollin said.

He reached out with his mind and felt the shattered bones around the outlaw's left leg. The damage was extensive and healing it would have taken hours. Instead he blocked the nerves around the wound. It felt like he was sticking his finger into a crack in a large water reservoir. He had stopped the pain for the moment, but his efforts would only last a short while.

"Oh," said Brayford, the relief evident in his voice. "That's better."

"Why did you attack us?" Mansel asked.

"We didn't attack you. We just wanted your valuables, that's all. We have families to feed."

"This is not the way to do it," Zollin said.

"Were there any more of your band? Mansel asked. "Will they be waiting for us along the road ahead?"

"No," the man said, shaking his head. "It was just the five of us."

"There's only three of you now, your companions fled, but two of them will never bother another living soul."

"I'm sorry," said the outlaw as tears coursed down his cheeks. "We shouldn't have done this. I'm so sorry."

"You're a thief and a liar," Mansel spat at the man, then turned to Zollin. "What should we do?"

"The King's law is clear," Zollin said. "Outlaws who raise arms against their countrymen should be hanged."

"There's no good trees," Mansel said.

"You aren't going to kill him," Miriam said.

"He's an outlaw."

"And you've never done anything wrong?" she questioned.

"Sure we have, but we've never attacked innocent people along the highway. We don't have the time or the resources to take care of the man. Leaving him alone here would be crueler than a quick death."

"No, no, no, please," Brayford begged. "Don't kill me."

"What other choices do we have?" Zollin asked her.

It was obvious that Miriam was torn. She knew that what Zollin said was true, but it went against every instinct she had to kill the man. Just knowing that Mansel had killed two others made her stomach twist in knots and threaten to make her vomit.

"These men would have robbed and beaten us, then left us for dead. They would have done worse to you," Mansel argued. "They don't deserve to live, any of them."

"But who are we to pass judgment on them?"

"We were the victims they intended to abuse and steal from," Mansel said hotly.

"They were caught in the act," Zollin said. "This man was part of them. In fact, he tried to kill Mansel with a longbow."

He understood Miriam's compassion. Now that the danger had passed, the idea of killing the outlaw seemed repugnant, but so did allowing the man to live and hurt others.

"Can't you heal him?" Miriam asked.

"No, it would take too long."

"But we can't keep riding all night," she argued. "We could make camp and rest while you healed him."

"I told you we would be pushing hard for Orrock. I won't waste time healing this man while Brianna suffers at the hands of her captors."

"Well, then I'll stay with him. I don't normally work on humans, but a broken leg is a broken leg."

"His knee is shattered. He'll never walk without a crutch, and he might even lose the leg. There is very little you can do for him."

"I can ease his pain," she argued. "I can help get him to a town or village where he can recover."

"And how will he pay for his recovery? How will he earn a living? He's already turned to crime and that was when he was perfectly healthy."

"I can change. I swear it," begged Brayford.

"If he were a horse, what would you diagnose?" Zollin asked.

Miriam's face fell. She saw the logic in his argument, even though she hated the outcome. Still, she wasn't so stubborn that she would argue anymore.

"I'm sorry," she said.

Zollin didn't know if she were saying it to him or to the outlaw. He looked at Mansel who nodded and said, "I'll catch up with you."

"Alright," Zollin said. "Come on, Miriam, let's go."

Mansel had taken a torch from the supplies behind his saddle. Zollin waved his hand and the torch crackled to life, while at the same time the light from his staff faded. He felt his energy flagging as well. The man on the ground was crying, so he cast one last spell, and the man fell asleep. He didn't want Jax to hear the outlaw screaming for mercy before Mansel killed him.

They rode on, into the darkness. Zollin felt Jax leaning against him, his breathing slow and steady. The excitement had passed and Jax was able to sleep easily. He wondered if his own dreams would be as gentle, or if he would see the outlaw begging for mercy that he would not receive. He tried to tell himself that it wasn't his fault, but he didn't have to drop the man. He could have lowered him to the ground just as easily. He tried to shake off the feelings of guilt and fear, but they were relentless.

A few minutes later, Mansel came riding up behind them, his torch illuminating the small group. They rode through the night in silence, hoping that the light of a new day would ease the awkwardness between them.

Chapter 32

It was the next morning before Brianna saw Edina again. The petite servant brought her breakfast. The day was bright and the air through the windows was fresh. Still, Brianna felt like a prisoner. She had not seen or heard from Branock since the morning before. Edina had a tray of food, much like the day before, only this time she was accompanied by a large man in light armor, armed with a short, two edged sword that reminded Brianna of Quinn's weapon. He wore the uniform of the King's Royal Guard and waited just inside the doorway.

Brianna was worried that the guard was there to monitor their conversation, but Edina did not seem bothered.

"This is Helston," she informed Brianna. "He will accompany you wherever you go today."

"I can leave the room?" Brianna asked.

"That was what I was instructed to tell you. If you try to escape, he will bring you back and you will be confined to your room. Do you understand?"

"Yes."

"Good, eat your breakfast. It is a beautiful day, and you need your strength."

Edina tidied up the room while Brianna ate, then combed her hair and made sure she was presentable.

"You know you don't have to do this," Brianna said.

"It is my duty, my lady," Edina said, winking at the young captive.

Brianna didn't argue anymore. She wanted so badly to ask questions, but she knew better than to say anything in front of Helston.

When Edina left, Brianna waited for the bulky soldier to order her out of the room. Instead, he stood as still as a statue, neither speaking nor even looking at her. Finally, after waiting for over an hour, she asked what was on her mind.

"Aren't you supposed to take me somewhere?"

"My orders are to make sure you don't leave the castle grounds," the big man said gruffly.

"So I can just go wherever I want as long as I stay inside the castle?"

The soldier ignored her. Brianna frowned in frustration. She chided herself silently for wasting an hour. She needed to explore the castle and make sure she knew her way around. She would need to know the layout if she was going to escape, and she also needed to be able to show Zollin the way back inside so that he could help King Felix.

She walked to the door and waited for a moment, but Helston still did not look at her. She opened the door, which was no longer locked. It swung open easily and she stepped through into the room, which she saw Branock had now lined with books. There were tall, sturdy looking book cases on every wall, most of them already filled with books.

"Where did all this come from?" she asked her guard, but Helston did not speak.

"Were you ordered not to talk to me, or are you always this quiet?"

Still no answer came, so she pushed on. She tried the outer door and it, too, swung open. She turned up the hallway and found the finely carved doors again. She traced her hand over the images but didn't try to open the doors. She wanted to find Edina or another of the servants to give her a guided tour, but she doubted that they would be allowed to do that. She found the stairs and wound her way down to the second level. There she found a large, rectangular hallway lined with rooms on either side. She circled the hallway, seeing that some rooms were open and empty. Others were closed, but voices could be heard talking inside. Still other rooms were occupied by people doing work or lounging on the rich furnishings. They looked up and stared at her, but none spoke.

On the lower level she found the servants busy at work. Most were cleaning or cooking, but others seemed to be hurrying from one place to the next. Most were talking and laughing, but they fell silent when she approached. At first she thought it was because she was Branock's prisoner, but then she realized that they treated all of the castle's inhabitants that way. She wandered into the grand audience chamber, which was also the feasting hall. There were ornate tapestries depicting the Kings of Yelsia leading armies or slaying ferocious beasts. She was looking at them when she heard giggling from one of the anterooms. She knew instinctively that the smart thing was to move in the other direction, but she was curious. She gave Helston a look to see what he thought of the sound, but his face was as impassive as ever.

She continued to study the tapestries, but she was no longer paying attention to what she was seeing. Instead she heard the unmistakable sounds of flirting. It reminded her of being in essentials school. She had often flirted with the boys who were constantly performing for her attention. Then she thought of Zollin, shy and reclusive. He had never really attracted her attention, and she wondered how she could have missed him. Of course, he had been older, but plenty of the older boys had flirted with her. Many had even made offers to her father for her hand in marriage, but luckily he had turned them all down. She wondered if Quinn had made an offer for her. She didn't know, but she made a mental note to ask him about it when she escaped.

"Don't make me beg," said a pouty feminine voice.

"I grow tired of these games," said a familiar voice.

Brianna tried hard to place it. It took her longer than she expected.

"Don't I please you anymore?" said the woman.

"No, I am not pleased. Send her away," said the man. "Send them all away, steward."

The giggling stopped and Brianna pretended to be fascinated with a small bit of stitching on one of the tapestries.

"You are to blame for this, wizard," accused the voice.

Then it hit her, it was Prince Simmeron's voice. She ignored the scantily clad women who were hurried out of the room by the small statured steward that she remembered from the night she and Branock arrived at the castle.

"Soon you will have the world at your feet, highness," said Branock, his silky voice making Brianna's blood run cold.

"It's your constant worrying and scheming. I prefer a peaceful palace. More fun and less strategy."

"I apologize, my lord," said Branock. "I shall not bother you again with these paltry affairs."

"Good, I'm glad of it. I have enough on my mind, with an ailing father and a kingdom to rule."

Then came another voice, this one different than the others.

"My lord Prince," it said. "May I introduce Owant of Osla."

There was a pause and Brianna wasn't trying to hide her interest anymore. She was still in the grand hall, but close to the double outer doors, which were towering, wooden carvings that swung easily on brass hinges. One was closed, but the other was propped open. Beyond was another chamber, but Brianna couldn't see into it. The sound, however, carried easily over the polished stone floor.

"Prince Simmeron, it is always good to be summoned by royalty," said a voice that Brianna thought was smug, considering the company.

"The good Prince did not summon you," said Branock in a lofty tone. "I did. We have work for you and your minions."

"The Mezzlyn are always at your service, Branock," Owant said, but he said the wizard's name with disdain.

"You were wise to heed my warning not to return to Osla."

"You promised gold," Owant reminded him.

"I promised you work," said Branock. "Work for which you will be handsomely rewarded."

"I await your command."

"This has to be kept quiet," said Simmeron. "And I don't want to know the details."

Brianna heard his boots slapping on the stone floor, and she again turned her attention to the tapestry. The voices had waited as the Prince exited the room, and Brianna's heart was beating like mad as she feigned interest in the stitching once again. The footsteps grew louder as the Prince made his way into the great hall, then suddenly they stopped.

"Who are you?" he asked.

Brianna turned around, trying to look surprised. The Prince looked angry at first, but then his face changed. His eyes roamed her body in a way that made her extremely uncomfortable.

"We haven't had the pleasure," he said in a haughty tone. "I am Prince Simmeron," he said.

"Hello," Brianna said, not sure what to say.

"Most people bow to the King," he prompted.

"Oh, yes, I'm sorry," she said, giving a slight curtsey that her mother would have scolded her for.

"You are new to the castle?" he asked.

"Yes, I am Brianna, from Tranaugh Shire."

"Oh, you're Branock's captive. How exciting. You don't seem like a fugitive. Shouldn't you be in the dungeons?"

Brianna realized that the prince was trying to tease or make a joke. It was awkward and not funny at all, but she smiled anyway, not wanting to make him angry.

"Helston is my guard," she said in a small voice.

"Oh, and a good one, too, I suppose. Who did you have to bribe to get this choice assignment, Helston?"

The guard didn't respond to the prince's poor attempt at humor and Simmeron grimaced. He walked up to the soldier, who towered over him. Simmeron was of average height, with stringy hair that fell around his shoulders, which were slumped. He wasn't grossly overweight, but he had a round belly and plump arms that were crammed into his silky shirt like sausages.

"Answer your King, soldier, or you'll find yourself posted to the highlands for the rest of your career," Simmeron ordered.

"I was assigned by the captain of the guard," Helston said. "I didn't bribe anyone for anything."

"I'm sure you didn't. You are relieved, sir," the prince said.

"But my liege, the captain gave specific orders-"

Simmeron cut him off mid-sentence. "And I give the captain orders. You are relieved, now be gone!"

"Yes, my lord," Helston said, looking agitated.

Simmeron and Brianna watched the soldier stalk away. Brianna felt a new sense of dread rising up in her stomach. She wasn't sure what was happening, but she was sure it wasn't going to be good.

"Now, that's better. I prefer to spend time with my friends alone," Simmeron said.

"Are we friends, my lord?" Brianna said uneasily.

"Of course we are. Let me show you around the castle."

He took her hand and pulled her across the grand hall. There were large, stone pillars supporting the towering roof and floors above them. He moved out to the center of the room and pointed at the throne. It was made of polished mahogany inlaid with designs of pure gold. There was a smaller throne made of ivory and inlaid with silver that sat back a little from the larger throne.

"My mother's throne has sat empty for a long time," Simmeron said. "Would you be so kind as to try it out?"

"Do you think that's wise?" Brianna asked. She was very uncomfortable and the prince was only making matters worse.

"Oh, I think it is very wise," he said in an attempt to sound convincing, but failed. "I'd very much like to see you there, perhaps on a permanent basis."

"No," Brianna said a little too forcefully. "That wouldn't be proper," she added, trying not to let her disdain for the Prince show.

"I insist, I insist," he said playfully, pulling her toward the dais where the thrones sat.

He practically dragged her up the steps and led her to the chair. She sat down and he applauded. He sat on the edge of the larger throne, the king's throne, and turned toward her.

"You know, you are the first girl I've ever seen sit there, other than my mother. How old are you, Brianna?"

"Fifteen," she said.

"Ah, just perfect for marriage. Are you pure?"

"I'm not sure I understand what you are asking," she said, trying desperately to find a way to escape the Prince.

"It doesn't matter; I don't hold with the traditional ways myself. You are beautiful, Brianna, but of course you know that, don't you. I would very much like to have dinner with you tonight. Yes, I'll arrange everything."

"Oh, my lord, I'm sure you're much too busy to entertain me."

"Nonsense," the Prince said. "I want to get to know you. I'm quite smitten, you know. I'll have a special meal prepared and a singer, one with a beautiful voice, to entertain us with songs of romance and glory."

Brianna was desperately trying to think of a way to escape the Prince's invitation, and then she had an idea. It was risky, to say the least, but her father had always said, *Fortune favors the brave.* She needed to be daring and there was no time like the present.

"If I'm to dine with my lord, I'll need time to prepare. Would you please excuse me?"

"Oh, no, you look stunning just as you are. Please, stay with me. I must confess, I get lonely in the castle. People tend to give you whatever you want when you're about to become King."

She wasn't sure if he was actually complaining, or trying to send her a subtle hint about refusing him. She needed to get free from him and escape from the castle. If she could get away and find a good hiding place, even for just a few days, Zollin would rescue her. She couldn't give up.

"My lord, I want to look my very best for you tonight. It won't take me long. Edina can help me. Please, my liege," she added, trying not to let the words catch in her throat.

"Oh, if you insist."

He clapped his hands. Servants came quickly to the Prince and he ordered them to find Edina. Then he began making preparations for their meal. He was ordering the servants to roast quail and prepare his favorite dishes when Edina arrived. When she saw Brianna, her eyes grew round. Brianna willed her to be strong.

"Ah, my lord," Brianna said. "Here is my maid servant. May I have your leave to go and prepare for our dinner?"

"Oh, it is hard to let you go, my love. I'm afraid you'll be taking my heart with you. Please hurry, I don't think I can stand another minute away from you than necessary."

"We shall be as fast as the wind, my lord. I only need to get a special perfume so that I am ready for our special night," she said. "Edina will escort me, and we will return as quickly as possible."

"Very well, my love. And know this: you shall look heavenly on my mother's throne, my angel."

Brianna tried not to laugh as she nodded. She was afraid to speak and instead hurried away with Edina. They started for the main entrance, but Brianna remembered that Branock was in a room just beyond the main doors. She angled back toward the servants' quarters where she had entered the grand hall.

"What are you doing?" Edina said.

"I'm taking advantage of the situation."

"But where is Helston?"

"The Prince sent him away. This is the perfect opportunity to escape."

"But I cannot leave," Edina said. "My family is here. If I leave or if you disappear under my care, they'll be in danger. The Prince has a volatile temper, and there is no telling what he will do when you do not return."

Brianna looked at the woman who had become her only friend. She realized she knew nothing about Edina, but the last thing she wanted was for the woman or her friends to be in danger.

"I'm sorry," Brianna said.

Then, just as Edina was about to speak again, Brianna hit her flush on the jaw. Edina's head snapped back violently, and she dropped hard to the floor. Brianna had meant to try and catch her as she fell, but the punch had caused something to pop in her hand and the pain was all she could think about. She clutched it close to her chest and hopped up and down. She knew she needed to make good her escape, but it took a moment to master the pain.

When she was finally able, she realized that she was in a long corridor. It made little sense to try to find a hiding place for Edina; instead she hurried along, leaving the little servant where she was. She felt guilty for hitting the woman, and for leaving her without any idea of what she was doing, but the window of opportunity would not stay open long. She had to get out of the castle as fast as possible. What she would do when she was free was anyone's guess. She had no money and no friends in the city, but she had a chance to escape and she would not squander it. Besides, she had an idea of what Prince Simmeron was planning for later that evening, and she would die before she gave herself to the pompous Prince.

At the end of the hallway, she could either go out through the castle's main entrance, or enter the kitchens. She opted for the kitchens, hoping to avoid Branock. The kitchens were bustling with people, all busy with specific jobs that they were intent on completing. Brianna had never thought of all the work it took to keep the castle functioning. She had hated the chores she was forced to do for her mother, who never seemed to do anything but give her daughters more work, but Brianna realized that the castle servants worked much harder than she ever had.

She looked desperately for a door, although what she would do to get out of the castle grounds and past the guards was a mystery that she would have to solve later. For now, she needed to get out of the castle before someone found her or found Edina and raised the alarm.

After several twists and turns, past ovens and long tables where meat and vegetables were being prepared for various meals, she finally saw a door that led out into the afternoon sunlight. She hurried toward the door and her heart almost stopped when a large soldier stepped into the doorway. At first she thought it was Helston, but it was just a hungry man looking for food. He squeezed past her in the tight space without a word.

At last she was outside, but she was also turned around. She had entered the castle courtyard at night and from a different direction. She was now on the far side of the castle, but she had no idea how to get back to the main gate, or how to get out of the gate without being seen. Then she spotted a wagon that had just been emptied of wine casks. She hurried toward it as the driver climbed up onto the seat and took hold of the reins.

"Are you leaving the castle?" she asked the man.

"Aye, I've got to get back to the warehouse and fetch some more ale," the man replied.

"May I ride with you?" she asked.

"A sweet little thing like you? Absolutely."

"I just need a ride," she said.

"Well come on, then, I haven't got all day."

She climbed up onto the bench seat at the front of the wagon. He flicked the reins and the horses lumbered forward. He turned the wagon into the main yard at the front of the castle. It was full of people going to and from various buildings in the castle complex. She had to fight the urge to hide her face. She tried to look bored but doubted that she pulled it off.

At the gate one of the guards hailed the wagon driver, but didn't stop him. The wagon lumbered out of the gate, the big, wooden wheels creaking as they rolled over the wooden threshold. Once they were out of the castle, Brianna's nerves grew. She had never been in a city even close to the size of Orrock. She had no idea where to go or how to find Zollin.

"You must be new," the man driving the wagon said. "How long you been serving at the castle?"

"I just started," Brianna lied.

"I figured, I know most of the kitchen girls."

"Oh, I don't work in the kitchen. I help nurse the King."

The man's tone changed. He seemed almost angry.

"He's pretty sick, 'eh, that sure seems odd to me. He was always as healthy as a horse."

Brianna didn't know what to say. "We're doing everything we can for him."

"Not enough in my opinion," he grumbled. "That silly kid of his is going to ruin this country."

"That's a bit harsh, don't you think?"

"No, I don't think it's harsh enough. He's a spoiled brat who doesn't know and doesn't care about anything. When the First Prince returns, things will be different."

"I hope you're right," she said. "I can get off here."

"Alright," he said. "I'm sorry if I let my fool mouth get the best of me. Sometimes I don't think before I speak."

"Don't worry, I promise I'll never tell a soul."

The man frowned as he looked at her, but she didn't explain anything, she simply jumped off the wagon and ran into the city alone.

Chapter 33

They rode through the morning and into the afternoon. Everyone, except for Jax, was lost in his or her own thoughts. The young boy seemed to be energized by the excitement of the adventure. He kept up a running commentary on everything they saw along the road. They came to an inn as the day began to wane. They stopped and stabled the horses. Inside the inn they got two rooms, and everyone ate their fill of a hearty stew that wasn't very good, but was hot and spicy enough to make their noses run. Then they retired for the night, even Mansel, whose habit was to drink himself into a stupor at every inn he visited. They slept straight through the evening and into the early morning. Just before sun up, Zollin roused himself from bed and went out to the stables to check on the horses. He had paid extra for a double portion of oats and a good rubdown for each horse. It had been worth the money. The horses seemed rested and ready to continue the journey. Zollin saddled them and led them out in front of the inn.

Inside, the others were up and eating a hearty breakfast of fried ham, eggs, and bread with a salty gravy ladled over it. Zollin ate a plate full of the rich food, and they had coffee as well. To Zollin, it tasted a lot like burned toast, but with fresh cream and honey, it was a nice change from water or cider. Then they set out, everyone feeling better it seemed, except for Miriam. She was quiet, her forehead furrowed in lines as she pondered weighty matters that Zollin didn't understand and frankly didn't care to dive into.

The weather was beautiful, sunny but not hot. A cool, invigorating breeze was blowing, and the horses were spirited. It was a wonderful day, but early in the afternoon, Miriam was simply unable to contain her grief.

"How could we do it?" she asked. "We killed a defenseless man."

"We carried out the King's justice," Mansel said.

"Oh, don't drag the King into this. It was our decision and we made it."

"That's right," Zollin said. "We made a decision that was difficult, but just."

"How can we call slaying a defenseless man justice?"

"Because he was an outlaw," Zollin said in exasperation. "He tried to kill Mansel."

"Only because Mansel was attacking his companion."

"Did you forget that they held a sword to your throat?" Mansel asked.

"No, I didn't, but what makes me different from brigands and outlaws is that I can have mercy."

"Yes, mercy is good, and in the right circumstances, we might have opted for mercy. But in this case, the best course of action was the one we took."

"I'm not sure I agree," Miriam said.

"You have a right to your own opinion, but what's done is done. Looking back and second guessing ourselves won't change anything."

"I know you're right, but I just can't get over what happened."

"If Zollin hadn't been there, you wouldn't have gotten over what they did to you—that's if you had been lucky enough to live through the ordeal."

"I don't understand," Jax said. "We fought and won, what's the big deal?"

"It's nothing, Jax, just ignore me," Miriam said.

They rode on in silence after that. In some ways, Zollin wished that Miriam and Jax had stayed in Felson, but he knew he was further along the road than he could have been if they had stayed behind. Perhaps Miriam's guilt was the price they had to pay for her help, but at times it seemed too high.

When they reached the next town, late that afternoon, Miriam said she wanted to stay, but Zollin insisted on continuing. After a bit of debate, Miriam agreed that turning back was best for her. She longed to stay with Zollin and learn from him, but her heart simply wasn't in the task. Jax, of course, begged to be brought along, but Zollin and Mansel knew they were headed for a fight. There was just no way of protecting the boy, and so they left him with Miriam at the inn, with enough money to stay a few days before turning back to Felson.

They rode hard, late into the night, and as the moon began to set, they settled down for a few hours' sleep. Zollin took the first watch. It would be short, he knew, and although he was very tired, he was looking forward to some time alone. He needed to make sure that the decision he'd made had been the right one. Before, when others had been killed, he'd had no time to ponder the right or wrong of his actions. And, had Miriam not been with them, he probably wouldn't have pondered his actions this time. But her insistence that some other choice existed gave him pause and made him think. When he was on the road, he pushed the grave thoughts away, but now, as the night grew colder and Mansel's snores joined with the nocturnal insect chorus around them, Zollin opened himself up to a critical assessment of his behavior.

He had the power to kill anyone, at any time, but that power was no different than a strong man with a sword, or a marksman with a bow. The question he struggled with was that his greater power not only gave him the power of death, but also of life. He was a wizard, not just a healer, but someone who had great magical power in all the disciplines. This power should be paired, he thought, with greater mercy and wisdom. But how was he, only seventeen years old, supposed to come by mercy and wisdom when all he'd know was death, hardship, and disappointment?

He pondered these thoughts through his watch, not really coming any closer to understanding them, but feeling better for having the courage to face them. When he slept that night, he clutched Brianna's ribbon in his hand and dreamed of seeing her again.

* * *

"You fool," Branock shouted. "You sent her guard away?"

"I am Prince in this castle," Simmeron shouted back. "I'll do as I please."

"Damn your idiocy, you may have killed us all."

"I don't see how losing one wench will get anyone killed; besides, the wizard doesn't know she's not here."

"I'm not worried about Zollin, it's Offendorl that you should be worried about."

"Why must I worry about an old man in a castle far away?"

"Because that old man is the most powerful wizard in the Five Kingdoms!" Branock shouted. "He will tolerate no rebellion to his rule, and he shows no mercy to those that challenge him."

"I haven't challenged him," Simmeron said. "Whatever issues you have with the Torr are not my concern."

"You have brought a wizard into your service," Branock said. "You have broken a treaty that is over a century old. If we do not persuade Zollin to join us, we stand no hope of resisting the Torr. I cannot defeat them alone."

"Then I suggest we find the girl. She can't have gone far."

"Yes, well she wouldn't have gone anywhere if you hadn't sent her guard away and then given her permission to leave."

"I thought she was going to get perfume for our night together!" Simmeron shouted.

"You fool, she was a prisoner."

"Your prisoner, not mine. All I saw was a beautiful girl. I think I'll marry her when the soldiers bring her back. She can't possibly say no to that, and I'll need a good queen when my father dies."

"Fool! The only way this ploy works is if we give the girl to Zollin. She's the bait and the whole reason he's coming here. If she's married to you when he arrives, we'll have to kill him and then where will we be?"

"I don't care, I want her."

"You can have any woman in the realm, your highness," Branock said the title with obvious disdain.

"I don't want just any woman, I want Brianna."

"You only want her because she had the courage to resist you."

"Shut up, wizard, I do not want or need your counsel."

"You're a fool," Branock said again.

"Say that one more time and I'll have your tongue cut out," he said, but his voice cracked as he said it.

Branock laughed, then he turned to the Prince, his eyes glowing with magical power. He waved a hand and the door to the Prince's private audience chamber slammed shut. Simmeron jumped at the sound. Branock lifted his small staff and pointed it at the man.

"Your whole army could not defeat me," he said, his voice brimming with magical power that made it deep and resonant. "I am Branock, wizard of the Torr, and now of Yelsia. I shall not be threatened."

"I am Prince Simmeron, soon to be King-"

"Only if I provide the throne," Branock said.

"I want the girl," the Prince whispered.

Branock realized the only way to mend the potentially devastating situation was to play along with the spoiled Prince and then deal with him at a more convenient time.

"Fine, but not until after we secure the boy."

"But I can see her, once we bring her back to the castle?"

"Yes, you can see her, but no touching her, do you understand?"

The Prince nodded and Branock stormed from the room.

* * *

That same night, Brianna didn't sleep at all. She had no money and nowhere to go. She was afraid to go too far from the city, knowing that troops would soon be dispatched to search for her. A young girl obviously leaving the city would be a dead giveaway. Her best option was to blend in with the people of the city. She didn't want to be locked inside the city walls, so she wandered through the markets on the outskirts of the city until the sun went down, then she found an empty vendor's stall to hide in. It was small enough that she could sit, but not big enough to stretch out in. Several times soldiers passed the empty stall, but none stopped to look for her there. By the next morning she was frigid with cold and exhausted. She found a tailor and traded her finely made dress for simple, homespun clothes and a few coppers. It wasn't enough money to survive on for more than a day, but it was enough to get her a room in one of the run down inns near the river.

She hoped, after hiding out all day, that the search for her might lessen, but she was wrong. The room she had been shown to was small; the only furnishings were a hook on the wall and the narrow bed. She opted to pull the rough blanket off of the filthy bed, which she was certain was infested with lice or other vermin, and slept on the floor. She locked the door and made sure that, if she had to escape out the window, there was a safe place to land. Below the window was a pile of garbage. It wasn't an ideal place to land, but the refuse heap was better than landing on the hard packed street, and even though she was on the second floor of the inn, the building was built low and the drop was not far. She was certain that if she had to jump from the window, she could do so without being hurt.

The inn keeper had served ale to some of the soldiers searching for Brianna the night before. He knew as soon as Brianna showed up in the morning requesting a room that she was the girl the soldiers were looking for. He took her money, fed her stale bread and goat's milk, then went in search of the nearest soldier in the King's army. They didn't check to see if the door was locked, they simply kicked the door in with one hard blow and fell on her before she could even cast off the blanket.

Brianna screamed in terror, but it made no difference. She kicked and squirmed, but the soldiers were too strong to escape from. They took hold of her arms above the elbows and jerked her to her feet. She felt helpless as they pushed her along, her feet barely touching the ground. She could feel the bruises forming from their unrelenting grip on her arms, and her shoulders felt as if they were going to pop out of their sockets.

"Let me go," she screamed at the soldiers. "Let me go, you're hurting me."

But the men didn't speak. They forced her out of the inn and back into the city. People stared, but no one tried to help her. Brianna was sobbing, she was terrified of what Branock would do to her now and devastated that she hadn't gotten away. They carried her through the castle gate and received cheers of congratulations from the other soldiers. Brianna noticed that the King's Royal Guard didn't cheer, or even speak. They just watched the spectacle with silent disdain. The main doors to the castle were open, and Brianna was flung inside. Branock was there, meeting with military officers who had pulled their troops from defensive positions around the city to look for Brianna.

She sprawled onto the stone floor of the castle entry, hitting her head and seeing stars, as well as bruising one knee. Branock left the officer he was talking with and came over to where Brianna lay on the floor.

"I warned you, didn't I?" he said, his voice even and tight, hiding his anger. "I see your night of freedom didn't sit well with you."

He started to levitate her to her feet, but she still had the white azure stone ring that Zollin had given her and his spell did nothing. He cursed silently and turned to one of the officers he had been speaking with.

"I will return momentarily to finish this conversation," he said. Then he turned to the two soldiers who had brought Brianna to the castle. "Where did you find her?"

"She was hiding in one of the inns on the outskirts," said one of the men.

They conveniently forgot to mention that the inn keeper had tipped them off. Branock sent them away with coins for their reward, then marched Brianna back to her room on the third floor.

"You are confined to this room," he growled at her. "And if you try anything else, you will find yourself in a cell in the dungeons."

He slammed the door and sealed it magically with a wave of his hand. He was just turning to leave when Prince Simmeron came sweeping into the room. His retinue, which included his steward, two guards, and several personal servants, waited outside.

"You see," Simmeron crowed. "I told you they would find her."

"You were right," Branock said, pacifying the Prince.

"Now, let me see her. You promised me."

"I did, but she needs a bit of cleaning up."

"I don't care about a little dirt, I want to see her."

Branock decided that perhaps letting the Prince see her in homespun clothes, with tangled, matted hair and dirt on her face, might change his opinion of her, but he was wrong. He opened the door, and Brianna, who had been inspecting the bruises on her upper arms, pulled the collar of her shirt back up over her shoulder and glared at the Prince.

"Ah, my love," he said when he saw her. "You poor thing. Quickly Branock, fetch the servants. My fair Brianna needs care."

"She should stew in her own juices for a while, your highness."

"Nonsense. Send for a bath and fresh clothes."

Brianna was furious. Her plan had been bold, but not well thought out. She had made good her escape, but lack of funds and poor knowledge of the city had kept her from having a safe haven. She was so tired that she couldn't keep the tears from streaking down her cheeks. Now the arrogant Prince was fawning over her, and hope that she would ever be with Zollin again was like a fading spark.

"I shall," Branock said, "but let her rest for now, we have business to attend to."

"Business can wait," the Prince said.

"As you wish, but remember your promise. Not until Zollin joins us."

"Hope deferred makes the heart sick."

"You gave me your word, Simmeron. Don't make me regret this."

"What's to regret?" he said, smiling at Brianna. "Your young wizard should be honored to give his love to the King."

"Don't be a fool," Branock said.

"I will die before I let you touch me," Brianna said.

"You see, she is strong. She is not like the other wenches my steward brings to the castle. They are all either milksops or whores. Brianna speaks her mind. Do not worry, my love, you will come to see how great I am. Soon I will be King of Yelsia and then we shall be married. You will live in luxury and bear my children. Every desire you have will be fulfilled."

"I desire to leave this place and never look back," Brianna said.

"I shall build you a palace wherever your heart desires."

The servants finally arrived, and Branock convinced the Prince to see to their business. When the doors finally closed, Brianna sobbed uncontrollably. She sat in the hot water, letting the servants scrub the filth from her body, but it was the loss of hope that haunted her. When they dressed her and combed her hair, she complied easily enough, but her mind was far away, on a snowy mountain with Zollin. She remembered the morning they had spent together, kindling the fire and warming themselves by it.

Oh Zollin, she thought to herself. *Where are you?*

* * *

At that moment, Zollin and Mansel were riding swiftly toward Orrock. They had passed through a small village and learned that they were a hard day's ride from the city. They planned to ride until they reached Orrock, even if they didn't reach it until late in the night. Zollin and Mansel had only gotten a couple hours of sleep, but the proximity to their goal at long last spurred them on.

"What do we do once we reach the city?" Mansel asked.

"We need to get a lay of the land," Zollin replied. "I've never been to Orrock, have you?"

Mansel shook his head.

"Quinn made me promise we would wait two days if he hadn't caught back up with us by the time we reached the city, but I doubt he is coming."

"Why wouldn't he come?"

"Because I told him not to."

"Why would you do that?" Mansel asked in surprised.

"Father-son stuff," Zollin replied.

This seemed to pacify Mansel, and they continued in silence for a while.

"It seems to me, if this wizard really has sway in the capital, then surely he'll be ensconced in the castle. Do you think you can deal with an entire army and the castle defenses as well?"

"I don't know, I've never tried."

"Well, give me an idea of what we'll be doing. I mean, I'm as keen on rescuing Brianna as you are, but I just don't know how we're going to do it."

"Me either! You think I have a plan all worked out in my head or something? I'm just hoping that we can figure something out when we get there."

"If Quinn were here, he would know what to do," Mansel said.

"Maybe, but he isn't here. This is up to you and me, unless you want out."

"I'm not backing down, I'm no coward."

"I didn't say you were," Zollin argued.

"I'm just saying we need a plan. If you go riding in there and start striking people down with lightning bolts, we're going to be wanted men for the rest of our lives."

"Well then maybe you'll understand how I feel."

"Don't act like we haven't been with you every step of the way since Tranaugh Shire, Zollin. People have tried to kill me, too."

"All I care about is getting Brianna back."

"All I'm trying to say is that we should wait for Quinn."

"We don't even know if he's coming."

"You promised you'd give him two days."

Zollin wanted to rail at the thought of leaving Brianna in Branock's vile clutches for even one minute more than he had to. But still, he knew he couldn't simply ride into the castle without a plan. And forming a plan meant getting to know the city, making friends, having a way to leave the city safely and a back plan if something went wrong. Mansel was right, Quinn was certainly much better at forming plans than Zollin was. He tended to act on his emotions or react to what was happening, rather than thinking through the consequences of his actions.

"Alright, two days, but if he doesn't show up in two days, we figure something out ourselves."

Mansel nodded and they rode on.

Chapter 34

Kelvich was exhausted by Quinn's unrelenting pace. They rode all day long and late into the night. When they reached Felson, he was forced to take a room at the inn and stay behind. Quinn rode on, leaving his friend felt wrong but he was anxious to catch up to Zollin and Mansel. The messengers did their best to keep up with him, but their duty only pushed them so hard. Quinn had no idea what his son was facing or if he would ever see him again, so it came as no surprise that after a full day's ride from Felson, he left the soldiers making camp and rode on through the night.

His mount was tired and it was hard to see in the darkness, so he walked his mount through the long hours of the night. When he came to an inn the next morning, he paid the inn keeper to feed, water, and rub down his mount while Quinn slept for two hours. Then, shortly before noon, he set out again. In his mind, he kept seeing Zollin's face as he accused Quinn of caring more about his work than about his family. It didn't surprise him really, he had thought similar things about his father, but the remarks still cut him deeply. Zollin had no idea how much Quinn cared about his son, but perhaps one day he would have a son of his own and then he might understand.

Just before sundown he came to a small village. There was no inn, but one farmer had room in his barn. He was already sheltering a woman and a young boy, so he invited Quinn to stay with them as well. Quinn refused to stay the night, but he did accept care for his horse and a hot meal. He was so tired that every bone, muscle, and joint ached, but he refused to stop. He would walk his horse until he couldn't take another step, then sleep for a few more hours. But first, his horse needed food, water, and rest. And, if truth be told, Quinn needed the same.

The farmer's name was Olin, and he was preparing a vegetable stew that was mostly potatoes and there was some freshly baked bread and soft cheese. Quinn had very little money left, but he gave the man a silver coin and found a place to sit and wait for the food to finish cooking.

"You look familiar," said an inquisitive voice.

Quinn had begun to doze, and at the sound, he opened his eyes to find a young boy of eleven or twelve years. He had shaggy hair and bright eyes that were studying Quinn intently.

"I do, eh? Well, you're completely new to me."

"Where are you traveling to?" the boy asked.

"Orrock. You?"

"Back to Felson. We were going to Orrock, but we decided to turn back."

"Oh really? Any particular reason?"

"Too dangerous, I guess. I'm Jax."

"Quinn," he said as they shook hands. "So what's so dangerous about Orrock? Has something happened there?"

"No, not yet. But I have a friend who is going to face an evil wizard."

"You do!" Quinn said, sitting up suddenly, his fatigue completely forgotten. "What's his name? Do you remember his name?"

"Of course I do. His name is Zollin."

"And is Mansel still with him? Are they well?"

"They were fine when we left them. That was two days ago."

"He's my son," Quinn said, tears filling his eyes. "I'm trying to catch up to them."

"You better ride fast then, they are pushing hard for Orrock."

"I will," Quinn said, climbing to his feet. His body still hurt, but the news of Zollin and Mansel had been just the encouragement he needed to push on.

He thanked the farmer as he wolfed down the stew. It wasn't quite ready, the potatoes were still a bit raw, but he ate it anyway.

"You're welcome to stay the night," Olin said. "That silver coin is more than enough payment."

"No, it isn't about payment. I'm trying to catch up with my son. He's a few days ahead of me, so I'll keep moving. Thank you so much."

"Watch out for brigands," Miriam said. "Jax told me that you were leaving to find Zollin."

Quinn turned around, but he was unprepared for what he saw. The woman before him was thin, about his own age, with traces of silver in her hair and fine lines around her eyes and at the corners of her mouth. Quinn had seen many women since his wife died, some even more beautiful than Miriam, but none had stirred his blood or made him feel the longing for a woman's touch. Miriam made him feel things he didn't know he was capable of anymore and all at just a glance.

"He's my son," Quinn managed to say.

"He's a fine young man. Very talented," she said, hinting that she knew him well enough to know that he was a wizard.

"May I ask why you rode with him?"

"It was a whim really," she said. "I'm an animal healer and I was hoping to learn some things."

"Oh, okay. So you're from Felson?"

"Yes, I have a home there."

"And you're going back?"

"Yes."

"Would you do me a favor? I have a friend who is staying at one of the inns. He's an older man named Kelvich. Would you pass on the information that you met me, and what you know about Zollin, as well?"

"Sure, I guess I could do that."

"Thank you so much. I can't stay, but your news has meant so much to me. I wish I could repay you somehow," he said, suddenly wishing that he didn't have to leave so abruptly.

"Well, perhaps when you find Zollin and his friend in Orrock, you could come back and visit us in Felson."

"That would be welcome, thank you."

She smiled then turned away. He was glad that she had ended the conversation, he wasn't sure that he could have done that, and he was more anxious than ever to find Zollin.

"Oh, by the way. Kelvich can teach you a thing or two. He's Zollin's mentor."

Miriam had turned back with a smile and she nodded then hurried away. Quinn felt as giddy as a child at festival time. It was an emotion he didn't think was possible to feel at his age and with the wounds in his past. Yet here he was, waiting as Olin brought his horse back out of the barn, thinking about a woman. He hadn't had serious thoughts about a woman since his wife had passed away seventeen years ago. But he was glad that it was possible. He did feel a little guilty, as if having feelings for another woman was somehow betraying Zollin's mother, but he was wise enough to push those thoughts away and focus on the truth.   He was a man, Miriam was a woman, that was a combination that opened all kinds of possibilities.

* * *

Brianna slept through most of the day.   Just as the sun began to set, servants appeared again.   This time they set up a small table in her little room, covering it with a linen cloth and setting out dishes for two.

Edina came into the room. She had a bruise on her jaw and flowers in her arms. She glanced at Brianna, but her gaze did not linger.

"What's going on here?" Brianna asked.

"You'll be dinning with the Prince this evening," said one of the other servants.

"Here?"

"Yes," Edina said as she turned to go out of the room.

Brianna felt horrible that she had hurt the woman and now Edina was forced to wait on her. The thought crossed her mind that perhaps Edina had been mistreated by the people of the castle for many years. That may have been the case, but it was not the way Brianna wanted to treat her.

The servants left, but two returned. One was Edina and the other was a woman Brianna had never seen before. They were carrying a dress between them. It was scarlet, and even though the thought of who she would be wearing it for made her skin crawl, she couldn't help but be impressed by the garment. They laid it on the bed and closed the door. Then both women hurried over to Brianna.

"We have a plan," Edina said.

420

Brianna couldn't hold back the tears.

"I'm so sorry I hit you," she said.

"There's no time for that," Edina said.

"Don't cry, the Prince won't like it," the other woman said.

"This is Wilamet, she's going to help us," Edina explained.

"You promise your man can heal King Felix?" Wilamet asked.

"Yes, I'm sure of it," Brianna said.

She wasn't sure, but it was as if hope had suddenly glowed to life again. She had help and they had a plan. She didn't care what it took; she wouldn't come back to this castle and the vain Prince Simmeron again.

"Alright," Edina said, "after your dinner with the Prince, chances are he'll fall into a drunken stupor. In the night, the wizard sometimes paces the halls, but he sleeps for at least a few hours. When we come to clean up from your dinner with the Prince, we will bring you a rope. You'll have to climb out of the window. Can you do that?"

"I'll do anything to get out of here," Brianna said.

"Remember you said that when Simmeron is pawing all over you like he's a cat and you're a ball of yarn. This plan only works if he's too drunk to countermand the order to clean the room up, so you need to play along so he'll keep drinking."

"What do you mean, play along?" Brianna asked, her heart suddenly in her throat.

"You do what a woman does," Wilamet said.

"The rumor around the castle is that Branock has forbidden Simmeron from taking you to his bed for now, but Simmeron has no concept of self denial. He'll want what every man wants, and you need to tease him with just enough that he has hope of getting what he wants."

"But I've never been with a man," Brianna said.

"And hopefully you still won't after tonight," Edina said. "But remember your resolve. This is the only way we can get you out of the castle now. And unless your friend can help King Felix, Prince Simmeron will be the next king of Yelsia."

"And then none of us are safe," said Wilamet.

"You're our last chance," Edina said. "Branock has met with the leader of the Mezzlyn and that can only mean one thing."

"They're going to try and kill Zollin again?" Brianna asked in horror.

"No, they want him alive," Wilamet said. "The wizard must have sent assassins to kill Prince Wilam."

"If he dies and the King dies," Edina said, pausing slightly to let the impact of her words sink in, "there is no one to stop Simmeron from taking the throne. It's royal law."

"Then we must stop him," Brianna said.

She was so scared that she was shaking, but she knew she had to be strong, now more than ever. Zollin needed her to be free, and the people, especially the friends who were willing to help her now, needed her to help thwart Simmeron. This was why she had left Tranaugh Shire with Zollin; why she refused to be left behind. She had a role to play in the events taking place and she would face them bravely.

"Get me ready," she told them.

They spent an hour dressing her and applying perfumes. They combed her hair until it was gleaming in the last few rays of daylight. Then they wound it in a complicated braid that was lovely, but would also be out of her way when the time came to make her escape.

"Remember, keep him drinking," Wilamet said. "He can't hold his liquor."

"You'll have to drink some, too," Edina warned her. "But if you simply pretend to drink and pretend to refill you cup, he won't notice. He only sees what he wants to see."

"Keep him drinking and don't forget to refill my cup. I've got it," Brianna assured them.

"And show him just enough to keep him interested," Wilamet said. "Play hard to get, but not too hard. He has to believe that he'll get what he wants eventually."

"I'll do my best," Brianna said.

"Just flirt, you can do that," Edina said.

"Okay, I'll be fine. Thank you both so much."

"Don't forget your promise," Wilamet said.

"I won't."

They left the room, and Brianna spent the next hour alone with her nerves. Her emotions swung from one extreme to the other. She couldn't help but look out the window. It was a long way down, and if something happened, she would probably not survive the fall. Still, if she died trying to escape, at least Zollin wouldn't be drawn into Branock's trap. Not that she wanted to die, she wanted to live. She wanted to escape the castle and be reunited with Zollin and Mansel and Quinn. She wanted them to ride away from all the strife and be safe.

She shook away the wishful thinking. That was not the life of a wizard, she knew that much at least. Zollin had been given incredible power and there was surely a reason why. She doubted very much that it had to do with living a peaceful life. Still, she couldn't help but wonder what life would have been like in Tranaugh Shire with Zollin. Would he have been a carpenter? Would they have a child on the way now? Could she love him without his power? That thought, more than anything else, frightened her. She had to ask herself if she honestly loved Zollin, or if it was an infatuation sparked by his amazing power? She didn't know. She had not been able to spend much time with him, and her desire for him was obviously magnified by the danger she found herself in. She wanted to say that she honestly loved him and that his magic didn't matter, but she was just too honest with herself. Before that fateful day when he had taken her to look at the cabin he had built for Todrek and then showed her his abilities, she had been nothing more than a spoiled girl. He had known that and called her on it. She had flatly denied it, and then his power had captivated her mind and heart so much that when he fled Tranaugh Shire she had followed him. If Quinn had convinced her father to give her to Zollin, she would have resented him. She would have been dutiful, and perhaps in time would have grown to love him, but his magic had been the spark that kindled her love for him.

She felt tears starting to sting her eyes. She still longed for Zollin, but she was confused. She didn't know if what she felt was genuine, and she didn't know how to find out.

She was still lost in thought when there was a knock at the door. More servants came in. The first was carrying a large candelabra made of polished bronze, with scented beeswax tapers that were lit once the ornate candle holder was placed on a table in the corner of the room. Another servant carried in a large decanter of dark red wine. He set the decanter on the table and then a man with a lyre and stool entered the room. He had a black strip of

424

cloth tied around his head and was led into the room by another servant.

"He's blind, that's how the good Prince prefers it," the servant leading the musician said.

Brianna nodded, not trusting herself to speak at the moment. Another servant came in and spread flower petals around the room. A fire was kindled in the fireplace. Then she was left alone again. The musician played his instrument and sang softly. It was very strange, Brianna thought, to be in a room alone with a blind musician who was singing to her softly.

Then Prince Simmeron arrived. He was wearing a purple robe and his hair had been combed. He smiled, but it sent chills of disgust through Brianna.

"You look lovely, my angel," he said.

"Thank you, my lord."

"Isn't it romantic?" he said as he waved his hand around the room.

She wanted to say that he had no part in preparing the room, and how dare he brag as if he had done it himself. Not to mention the fact that she was a prisoner, confined to the room, but she held herself in check.

"It is lovely, my lord."

"I like it when you call me that," he said, and there was a hungry look in his eye that had nothing to do with food. "Say it again."

"I'm sorry, I don't understand, highness."

"Call me your lord again," he said smugly.

"Yes, my lord."

He laughed a high pitched, irritating laugh that grated on her nerves. She was standing with the table between them. The dress he'd sent to her was low cut across her chest and she felt extremely self conscious about it, especially when his gaze continued to drop from her eyes.

"What are we dining on?" she asked.

"Ah, well..." he hesitated, annoyance crossing his features. "The last time I prepared a special meal, you ran out on me."

She pouted a little, it was something she had done often enough growing up, when she had wanted a boy's attention. She only hoped it would work now.

"I was afraid," she said. "You're so powerful, and I'm just not sure if I will please you."

"Don't be foolish," he chided, but he was obviously impressed with her reply. "I have great plans for you, my darling."

"You must say that to every girl you meet," she teased.

"That isn't true. I swear it. In fact, I meet very few women, and none have ever captured my heart the way you have."

"I'm flattered, my lord," she said, emphasizing the courtesy title.

He giggled and started around the table, but then the doors opened again and servants came in with trays of steaming food. There was a large rack of lamb, vegetables, freshly baked bread, cream butter, smoked cheese, and a cherry jelly. Servants stayed, one for each of them, and one to carve the lamb. Seats were pulled out, napkins neatly arranged, and plates prepared.

Prince Simmeron held up his goblet and his servant filled it from the decanter. Brianna remembered what her mother had taught her about mimicking when she wasn't sure what else to do. So Brianna held up her cup, just as Simmeron had. They ate in relative silence. Brianna found that while the food was excellent, she spent more time arranging the food on her plate than actually eating it. If being with the Prince wasn't enough to ruin her appetite, having a servant continually looking over her shoulder while she ate made her even more nervous and less inclined to eat.

The Prince did eat; in fact, he gorged himself on both food and wine. Brianna hoped that the food would not keep him from getting too drunk. Luckily the rich food sat heavily, and once the meal was over he wanted to lie down. The servants arranged pillows on the bed, and he stretched out, requesting a song. Brianna sat stiffly on the bed beside the Prince, who continued to drink. Another decanter of dark red wine was brought up and he continually filled his glass. After a while he began to paw at Brianna. It was clumsy and not at all flattering. It was obvious that he knew nothing about women and had been catered to his whole life. Why he was trying to woo her, she had no idea, but she was able to fend him off easily enough. After an hour or so, she saw his eyelids drooping. That gave her hope, at least until he sat up and decided he wanted to kiss her.

More than anything, she had hoped to avoid this, but it seemed inevitable. He leaned in and she turned her head playfully. His wet lips smacked on her cheek, and she had to fight with all her strength not to wipe her face.

"Kiss me," he slurred. "We can kiss, that isn't forbidden."

"I don't know," Brianna teased. "I'm a lady; I mustn't give my lord too much too soon. What will you think of me if I do?"

"I will think that you are the most beautiful woman in the kingdom," he said, his words running together as he tried to pull her closer.

His breath reeked of wine and she resisted instinctually. Kissing the Prince should have been a wonderful, exciting delight, she thought. Her sisters would all be so jealous and her mother would scold her for resisting, but Brianna hated every second of this. She needed a distraction, something to kill some time until he fell asleep.

"What if I rub your shoulders, my lord, you look so tense. Is something bothering you?"

She didn't wait for the prince to respond, but moved swiftly to the other side of the bed and began rubbing his shoulders. He rolled onto his stomach and sighed.

"This is exactly what I needed, my love," he said. "You are the only one that understands the strain of running a kingdom. I knew that you were the one for me the moment I laid my eyes on you."

"What has you so tense, my lord?" she asked. It seemed like a logical question, and she didn't know what she might learn from the Prince in his inebriated state.

"It's my wizard, all he does is scheme. He is very clever, but he worries me day and night with details and tasks that require my attention."

"Why don't you send him away?"

"Because he's a wizard. He's my wizard. I'm the first King to have one in over a century. My brother doesn't have a wizard. My father never had one, but I do. I will be the great King they could never be. They think me weak, but I am not weak. I am not held back by the senseless rules they hold to so dearly. I will raise Yelsia until it is first of the Five Kingdoms and reclaim the glory that is rightfully ours."

"You are so strong," she said softly.

"I am strong."

"And so wise."

"Yes," he mumbled sleepily.

"You will be a great King," she lied.

"I...already...am," he said, then began snoring.

Brianna started shaking all over and the urge to burst into tears was overwhelming. She realized then that she'd been afraid, and her pent-up emotions were suddenly released. She dropped down to the floor, cradled her knees to her chest, and cried. It felt good to release the tension she felt, to be honest with herself and feel all the things that she had for so long bottled up and denied. Then, once the tears and emotion had spent themselves, she stood. Her legs felt shaky at first, but her strength and resolve were returning.

She went to the small basin and washed her face. Her eyes were puffy and red, but that couldn't be helped now, as long as it didn't interfere with her escape attempt. There was a small bell that had been set out to summon servants who were waiting to care for Simmeron's every need. She was afraid at first that ringing the bell might wake the Prince but she didn't know what else to do. She gave the bell a small shake and it rang clear and pure.

The Prince didn't stir, but the door opened and Wilamet appeared. She nodded and approached the table where Brianna and Simmeron had been served their supper. She bent low and pulled a small bundle from under the table. She handed it to Brianna and mouthed the words, *hide this,* without making a sound. Brianna took the bundle and turned to face the room. She realized for the first time that the blind singer was still in the room. His presence had been forgotten, and if Wilamet had said anything, Brianna was certain the man would have reported it. She needed to be careful, she realized, and that thought brought the reality of her dangerous position even closer to her.

She spoke to Wilamet as she bent over to slide the bundle under the bed.

"I'm afraid the Prince had too much wine this evening," she said out loud.

"Yes, my lady, I'll make sure everything is taken care of," Wilamet said.

The servants began gathering plates and cups, then hurried from the room. Brianna went to the door, which was still open, and saw that Branock was sitting on the far side of the main room her bedchamber was attached to. He was drinking wine and reading by candlelight, his eyes flicking up to meet hers, before dropping back to the book he was reading.

"My lady," the singer said without turning around. "Would you like me to continue playing?"

"No," Brianna said. "That's enough for this evening, thank you. You did a lovely job."

"You are too kind, my lady," he said, but he did not move.

At first Brianna wondered why he simply sat on his stool now that she had dismissed him, but then she realized that he was waiting for someone to lead him from the room. Brianna dropped into a chair. Her curiosity about the bundle she had hidden under the bed was hard to master, but she knew she couldn't look into it until the servants were all gone. She also had no idea if Branock was somehow keeping a watch on her. She would need to be careful.

Servants arrived and efficiently removed the table, chairs, dishes, and most of the flower petals that had been scattered around the room. Brianna felt bad just sitting and watching, so she helped pick up the flower petals. A man came and escorted the blind singer from the room. Four men of the Royal Guard came in with a stretcher made from two long ash poles with a sturdy fabric sewn around them. They rolled Simmeron onto the stretcher and then carried him out of the room.

When Brianna looked up, as the servants left, she found Branock standing in her doorway. His face was impassive and she wondered what he was thinking. She hoped he could not see the anxiety that she felt must surely be plain on her own features.

"I had to have him removed," Branock explained. "It wouldn't do to have rumors flying around the city about the two of you. Although, I would get used to coddling the soft witted Prince. You may have to become his bride once Zollin joins us."

"Never," Brianna said defiantly. She hadn't meant to say or do anything that might show how determined she was to escape, but the thought of being forced to marry the spoiled Prince had simply been too repugnant.

"You should never say never, my dear."

"I'll die first," she threatened.

"What a shame, but then there are plenty of other pretty girls to entertain the Prince, and Zollin, for that matter."

He spun away, the door slammed shut, and Brianna felt as if she had been punched in the stomach. She had never thought of Zollin with another girl, not since the inn keeper's daughter in Brighton's Gate had fawned over him so blatantly. Even then she had not taken it seriously. She had been jealous, but not worried. Now, the realization that some other woman might take her place was painful to think about. She wanted Zollin to be happy—she had just never considered that he might be happy with someone else.

She went to the door and listened. There was no sound in the outer room. Still, she waited. After a while it seemed silly to be so cautious. She went to the bed and retrieved the bundle. It was mostly clothes. There were wool pants and a matching shirt, a thick cloak, and, of course, the rope. There was also a small pouch of coins, mostly coppers, but there were a few silver coins as well. Folded up neatly in the middle of the bundle was a note. Brianna unfolded and read it.

Wait until well past midnight, then climb out of the window. Make sure there are no candles burning in your room, so you won't be seen. Make your way to the side door of the castle gate, the guard there will let you through. I'll be waiting for you.

There was no signature on the note, but Brianna guessed it was from Wilamet. The money had probably been gathered from several sources, but it amounted to a major sacrifice by the servants who were helping her. She made up her mind not to let them down.

It took a while to work herself free of the gown she was wearing. She hung it neatly on the wardrobe, then pulled on the new clothes. She tucked the cloak, rope, and small purse of coins under the covers, then climbed into bed. She had no intention of sleeping, but she needed to wait a few hours before trying to make her escape.

As she lay there, in the dark, she wondered where Zollin was and what he was doing.

Chapter 35

Zollin was at that very moment standing on a hilltop looking at the sprawl of Orrock. The city was enclosed with a high wall, and the castle rose up from the center of the city. Around the wall were more houses and shops. It was as if the city began at the castle and then spread out in an unorganized mass.

"Wow," said Mansel, who was standing beside Zollin.

"Yeah, I've never seen anything like it."

"They say there are cities in the south that are even bigger."

"It's hard to imagine," Zollin said. "Why would people want to live like this?"

"I don't know, it might be alright. Lots of women in a city this big," Mansel said, smiling.

"That's beside the point. It looks like some of those homes are nothing more than mud huts."

"Well, the poor have to live somewhere," Mansel said. "What do we do now?"

"We need to find an inn," Zollin said.

"If the wizard wanted you to follow him, wouldn't the inns be guarded?"

"Maybe," Zollin said. He hadn't really thought of that. "Perhaps it would be better to make camp here, and then ride into the city separately tomorrow. Find out as much as we can, then meet back here."

"Sounds like a good plan to me."

"I'll take first watch," Zollin said.

They moved back down the hill and hobbled the horses. They built a small fire, and Mansel was soon snoring away. Zollin moved outside the circle of light cast by the fire and made his way, on foot, back up the hill so that he could see the city. There were still lights burning in windows, but very little movement. The river beyond the city was like a black ribbon that lay across the land as far as Zollin could see. Not that he could see much by starlight. There was no moon that night, and the darkness felt oppressive. Zollin wondered what Brianna was doing at that moment. He felt anxious to free her and afraid of what he might find. He was not so naive as to think she might not be abused by her captor. Brianna was beautiful, her dark hair and brown eyes were captivating, and just the memory of her long, willowy body stirred Zollin's blood.

"Soon," he whispered in the darkness. "I'll be there to get you soon," he promised her.

* * *

Brianna was still awake three hours later when she judged that it was late enough to make her escape. She rose silently from the bed and went to the door to listen for movement or voices. There was nothing to be heard. She had no idea what Branock was doing, but she couldn't worry about him now. She tucked the small pouch of coins into the top of her woolen pants. The garment was tightened around her narrow hips by a leather thong that was threaded through small holes around the waistline. She made sure the pants were secure, then pulled the cloak over her head. It had a hood, but she left it back for the climb down the castle. She tied the rope to the foot of the heavy bed. She gave it a strong tug, but the bed didn't budge. She doubted that her weight would be enough to move the massive piece of furniture.

Next, she opened the window and peered down. There was no light below her, and no movement could be detected. She was nervous, her heart beating loudly in her ears. She would have to climb down blind, but it couldn't be helped. She flung the end of the rope out the window and waited for someone to raise the alarm, but nothing happened. It was now or never, she knew that, but fear still held her back for a long moment.

She had never considered that she might be afraid of heights, but then, she'd never been in a building this tall before, either, much less considered crawling out the window. Then she thought of Simmeron, with his leering gaze at her chest and groping, clumsy hands. Death was better, she reminded herself, and then she threw one leg over the windowsill. She didn't have a lot of time to waste, and she wasn't sure how long the climb down would take her. She took several deep breaths and then put her hands on the rope that was inside the room. She needed to get her other leg up and out, then somehow turn so that she was facing the castle. It was not a natural thing to do, but after sitting on the windowsill for a moment, she used one hand to lift herself slightly up and turned so that she was lying across the window with her feet hanging out over midair.

She shimmied backwards, her feet slowly getting closer to the wall and her hands in a death grip on the rope. It wasn't thick and she felt weak grasping it, but she knew she had to keep going. If she went back inside now, she would never have the courage to climb back out of the window. She kept moving until only her arms were holding her to the window, her hands still on the rope and her upper arms hooked over the sill. Her feet could touch the wall and she scrambled on the rough, stone surface. Her shoes were too smooth on the bottom and she slipped, almost giving herself a heart attack. She kicked off her shoes and found that her bare feet had much more traction on the wall. She slowly let her shoulders move back until she was holding onto the windowsill with one hand while the other slid over the sill and clutched the rope just beyond it. Then, in a monumental act of will, she took her hand off the windowsill and grabbed the rope. There was a tense moment as her body rocked from side to side, then she had her balance again. She started her decent. It was nerve wracking, but not as difficult as she had feared at first. Her muscles trembled under the strain, but she was moving slowly and steadily down the side of the castle wall. She could feel the rope rubbing her hands raw, but the pain was a small price to pay for her freedom.

She came to another window and managed to angle herself to the side of it. Then there was a long stretch of wall and all around her was blackness. She couldn't see the surface of the wall, or the rope, and certainly not the ground, but she kept moving. Eventually her foot touched a flat surface below her. In the dark, she was too scared to believe that she had actually made it to the ground. She explored with one foot and then two. Finally, she lowered herself enough that she was standing and could relax her arms and back. The muscles burned and her legs were shaking. Her hands felt like they were made of stone, but she didn't try to let go of the rope. First she used her feet to explore the ground in the darkness. She felt the tangled end of the rope and her shoes. She sat down and slipped them back on her feet. When she stood up, she felt better, but was still afraid to let go of the rope. She stayed close to the castle wall, with one hand on the rope and one stretched in front of her. When she got to the round, corner tower of the castle, she let go of the rope. Then she carefully made her way around the tower. She could see light in the distance now, and she realized that she must have come down on the back side of the castle. She remembered that from her room she could see the river, so it all made sense to her now. She had descended between the castle and the tall castle wall, which explained the oppressive darkness. Now she moved more quickly. She was still in the dark, but just seeing the evidence of light ahead gave her courage, as well as an overwhelming desire to move toward the light.

She peeked around the corner of the next tower with a little more caution. The expanse of the castle courtyard lay before her. She could see the massive gate, which was now closed and barred. The smaller side door was also closed, but there was a guard in front of it. He was scanning the courtyard, and Brianna wasn't sure if he was looking for her or simply just staying alert. She knew that if the guard didn't help her, there was no way she could escape, and Branock's threat of throwing her into the dungeon echoed in her mind. She felt fear, like a giant fist squeezing her chest. She was trembling all over when she stepped out of the shadows and into the dim light that was cast by a row of torches set in polished, bronze sconces along the front of the castle and on either side of the main gate.

She tried to walk with confidence, as if being out of the castle in the middle of the night was absolutely normal. The guard caught sight of her and waved her over. He was looking to see if anyone else was around as she approached.

"You Brianna?" he asked.

"Yes."

"I ought to knock you silly and let the wizard have you, for hitting Edina the way you did," he growled at here. "She's a good woman."

"Yes, she is, and I'm very sorry I did that. I was desperate."

"Yeah, well, I can't say I blame you for that. I don't even want to think about what a wizard does to a fine young lady like yourself. Wilamet's waiting, but anything happens to her, I'm coming after you and I don't care who's got you. I'll find you and I'll kill you, got it?"

"Yes," Brianna whispered.

"Here," he handed Brianna a thick leather strap that had something heavy inside at one end. "You know how to use that?"

"No," she said.

"It's called a black jack and you're going to hit me on the back of the head with it. It'll knock me out without making much noise."

He bent over and laid his pike down on the ground. Then he turned to one side and gritted his teeth.

"As soon as you're done, get out of here and leave the door open," he said.

Brianna took a deep breath and then swung the black jack hard. The guard dropped like a stone, and Brianna didn't bother to inspect her handiwork. Instead, she unlatched the gate door and hurried through it. Wilamet was waiting in the shadows. She took Brianna by the hand and hurried with her through side streets and into a small shop that was built against the castle wall. Inside the shop, a large man with a huge stomach and a drooping mustache was waiting. He had a single candle lit, and when Wilamet opened the door without knocking, he stood up. The big man led them to a room in the rear of the shop and then pulled back a thick rug that was on the floor, revealing a hidden door in the floor's wooden planking. Without ever saying a word, the man opened the door and Wilamet hurried down the stone steps underneath.

Brianna followed her and the man closed the door, blocking off all the light so that it was as dark as a tomb and just as musty.

Brianna could smell earth and dust. She guessed the hidden room wasn't used often.

"This way," Wilamet whispered.

Brianna felt the servant take her hand and lead her through the darkness. They came to a stop as Wilamet felt on the wall for the latch to another room. Brianna felt a puff of air as the door swung open and then they were moving again, this time in a different direction. They heard scrabbling noises that Brianna was sure were nothing more than vermin scouring the dark passage for food, but her blood ran cold just the same. Finally, a light became visible ahead. As they moved toward it, Brianna began to see the dark silhouette of her companion.

The light came from another single candle; this one was burning in a small room with three tiny cots, a table, and four chairs. The candle was sitting in the middle of the table, with wax running down and securing it to the rough, wooden surface. There was bread wrapped in cloth on the table and a large pitcher of water.

"We'll stay here until your friend arrives in the city," Wilamet said.

"How will we know he's here?" Brianna asked.

"We have friends. They'll pass on the information to Bron upstairs. He'll pass it along to us, with food and anything else we need."

Brianna felt as if a huge weight had been lifted off her shoulders. The pain in her hands from the climb down the castle wall flared to life as the first hint of safety washed over her. It wasn't as if she was safe with Zollin, hundreds of miles away, but at least she had a good hiding place and she was away from Branock and Simmeron.

She dropped into one of the chairs, exhausted and hurting. She examined her hands. They would be stiff and sore for weeks, she thought. The skin was almost all rubbed off by the rough surface of the rope, and her palms were an angry, red color.

"Tomorrow we will get a healing salve for your hands," Wilamet said in a quiet voice.

"You've already done so much," Brianna whispered. "Why would you risk so much for me?"

"I'm not doing it for you," she said. "I have many friends who serve the King. Our future shouldn't be in the hands of that spoiled bully of a Prince."

"But you could lose everything. You could even be killed for helping me escape."

"Sometimes you have to take a chance to get what you want. You were my chance."

"I wish I had your courage," Brianna said.

"You have plenty of courage," Wilamet said. "You showed that by having dinner with Simmeron. And then you climbed down the castle wall," she said, waving a hand in a dismissive gesture. "I could never have done that."

Wilamet wrapped her cloak around her shoulders and sat down on one of the cots. "We better get some sleep. That's the only candle we've got."

Brianna stood up and moved the chair she had been sitting in. Then she blew out the candle and stepped back until her legs brushed the edge of her own cot. She wasn't cold, the room was warm enough, but the darkness felt overwhelming, so she pulled her own cloak around her and lay down. She was tired, and sleep came mercifully swift, but her dreams were as torturous as the rope had been on her hands. She dreamed that Zollin fell and the city of

Orrock burned to the ground while the sound of thousands of marching soldiers shook the ground.

Chapter 36

Mansel woke Zollin shortly after dawn. They took the time to eat a big breakfast. Then they each set out in a different direction. Their plan was to enter the city from different directions, learn as much as they could, then rendezvous back on the little hilltop they had camped near, late in the afternoon. Zollin walked his horse and Lilly. He could have ridden into the city, but he wanted not only distance, but an interval of time between his arrival and Mansel's.

It was difficult not to be awed by everything he saw in the communities around the city. Venders called out to him as he passed through the muddy lanes. Children ran and played while parents worked. The sound alone was so unusual to Zollin that he had trouble concentrating. Then there were the blank stares and vacant expression on the faces of the poor. They sat in hovels, either alone or in pairs, never speaking, just staring. Zollin was sure that they saw him, although they showed no interest. They didn't turn their heads or even follow him with their eyes. They seemed like lifeless hulls just waiting to die. Seeing them was both depressing and sad. He felt sorry for them, but Quinn had taught him that happiness in life lay on the far side of hard work, without it there would be no joy.

Thinking of his father made him even more melancholy. He wished that he could go back in time and handle things differently with Quinn. He didn't mean to leave his father angry, his parting words an indictment of the perceived failures Quinn had made as a parent. Zollin loved his father, and he was fairly certain that Quinn loved him, too. He just had never really shown Zollin love, not the way that Zollin needed him to. Sometime in the future, once he was no longer hounded by the Torr or busy rescuing Brianna, he would return the Great Valley and make things right with his father.

He focused his mind on the task at hand as a group of soldiers came marching past. He realized then that if Branock was here and waiting for him, a young man with a staff and two horses probably fit his description perfectly—at the very least they made him stand out. He needed to find a livery stable or an inn where he could leave the horses and hide his staff. He stopped a young boy who was hurrying past.

"Can you point me to a place where I can leave my horses?" Zollin asked the boy, who had wide eyes and an eager expression.

"This way, sir," he called. "I know just the place."

The boy led him down a side path, between mud huts and shacks that looked like they were made from scrap wood. Finally they came to a rather sturdy looking building; it was old, but well kept. There were goats in a pen out front and a chicken coop to one side. A man was cleaning the hoof of a horse as they approached.

"Soll," the boy cried. "This man needs a place to stable his horse."

The man looked up. He had a patch over one eye, and his shaggy hair was tied back with a leather strip that ran around and around the hair, finally ending in a tassel that Zollin recognized as some sort of religious garment.

"Is that so, Nalan? Well I might have room. Are we trading or do you have payment?"

"I can pay," Zollin said. "I've got a silver coin if you'll check the horses' hooves and give them a good rubdown, perhaps some oats."

"For silver, I'll make sure they get oats," Soll said. "Come with me."

He led Zollin into the dark interior of the building. There was a small room to one side which Zollin guessed was the man's home. There was a stove pipe running up from the room and into a loft that was accessible by a wooden ladder. There were several stalls in the building, but most of them were empty.

"This is a fine place," Zollin said.

"Aye, this was part of the original garrison when Orrock was nothing more than a fort. My father renovated it and now I run it."

"Is it a livery?"

"It's whatever you need it to be. There are some beds upstairs in the loft, plenty of space and no questions asked."

It struck Zollin this that this was the kind of place outlaws stayed in after a big score. He pulled Soll aside and asked him a private question.

"Is there a back door for hasty exits?"

"Out of the hayloft," Soll explained. "Across the roof tops and away you go. It will buy you some time if you need it. Plus the ladder is the only way up."

"How much would it take for you to hold this place for me and few friends?" Zollin asked.

The man looked at him shrewdly, then held up five fingers. Zollin dropped five more silver coins in the man's hand and led his horse to one of the stalls.

"I assume that buys your silence, too," Zollin said.

"I don't know you, and I've never seen you," Soll said with a smile. Zollin bent down to the boy who had brought him to the building. He fished another silver coin out of his purse, which was starting to sag a bit. He hadn't refilled the pouch since leaving the Great Valley. Still, the boy had brought Zollin to the perfect place. There were large windows in the loft that would allow him to keep watch at night and make a fast getaway if that became necessary. The boy had earned his reward.

"I'm going to give you this, but you have to promise you won't tell anyone where you got it."

"I can do that," the boy said, his eyes glued to the coin.

"Good, don't spend it all in one place," Zollin warned him in a light hearted manner. He grinned as he remembered how often he'd heard his father say the same thing to him.

The boy took the coin and tucked it safely away before running back out into the bright, spring morning. Zollin turned back to Soll, who was unsaddling Zollin's horse. He set his staff just inside the stall and asked a question.

"Does my money buy me any information about the city?"

"Depends on what you want to know," Soll said without looking up from the saddle straps.

"I need to know if a girl has been brought to the castle," Zollin said.

"Could be, there's lots going on at the castle with the King ill and all."

"Have you heard anything?"

"Just rumors. They say that Prince Simmeron has a wizard in his service now. The city guard is on alert, and there are troops from the King's army making passes through the outskirts. There's lots of speculation as to what is going on, but no one knows for sure."

"That's good enough. I need to know the best way in and out of the city from here," Zollin said.

Soll supplied the information as he began to rub down the horse.

"And who should I talk to about what goes on in the castle," Zollin asked.

"That's a tough question. There are folks that know, but I don't run in those circles. I rarely get inside the walls of the city. I do most of my business with people who prefer to keep a low profile, if you take my meaning."

"I do; can you point me in the right direction?"

Soll recommended starting his search with a vender close to the city walls. Zollin felt strangely alone without his staff. It was a powerful tool, but it had also become part of how he saw himself. He was wearing wool riding pants with a leather backside and the shirt and vest that Brianna had made for him. His hair was getting longer, but he had no beard, no robes, nor a long, pointy hat. Yet the staff was both a weapon and a fashion statement. You might occasionally see a traveler on foot carrying a staff, but even that was rare. For Zollin, the staff was a badge of office that he wore proudly.

He made his way through the muddy streets. The closer he got to city, the more crowded the communities became. Near the city wall he found a row of shops. One was a tavern. It had a sign above the door with a painting of a bloody sword. Soll had said it was a favorite of the King's army, and the tavern's owner was a man named Rawlings. It was still early in the day and the tavern was deserted. When Zollin entered the shop was quiet, but soon a short man with a bald head and thick arms appeared carrying a keg of ale.

"Hello, sir, may I be of service?" the man said.

"Are you Rawlings?"

"Aye, that's my name. And what is yours?"

"My name is Zollin, and Soll said that you might be able to help me."

"Soll is a good man and an old friend. I'll help you if I can."

The tavern had a long counter where drinks were served and several round tables with stools set up neatly around them. Zollin approached the bar and laid two silver coins on the counter. Rawlings poured two mugs of ale and handed one to Zollin, who took a sip of the frothy head.

"I was hoping for news of the castle," Zollin said.

"Thought you might be," said Rawlings. "There's little else happening in the city just now. You the wizard?"

Zollin was caught completely off guard, and although he shook his head it was hardly believable.

"I know," said Rawlings. "First there's dragons come down from the highlands, and now there's a wizard in the King's service. We've got nothing but bedtime stories to tell," he said laughing.

Zollin was relieved. He had been afraid that the tavern master had discovered him, but the man obviously didn't believe the talk.

"What about a wizard?" Zollin asked, taking another sip of the ale.

"Rumor has it that the Prince has found a wizard, but most likely it's a charlatan taking advantage of the King's foolish son.

Anyhow, the wizard's calling the shots, from what I hear, and prepping the army for some kind of attack on the castle."

"That is odd," said Zollin, his fears confirmed.

"Aye, it is. And there's a maiden in distress, just waiting on her lover to come rescue her, to hear the army boys tell it. Like I said, just bedtime stories."

Zollin took a drink and tried to collect his thoughts for another question, but the tavern man didn't need any help carrying on a conversation.

"The girl escaped though, at least that's what I heard. Some of the troopers stopped in for a moment this morning and let me know. The wizard's got everyone out looking for her."

"She's escaped?" Zollin said, trying to sound interested and not give away just how excited he was.

"That's what I heard, but she couldn't have gotten far. She climbed out the window using a rope. That's no mean trick. Then clubbed a guard over the head and got clean away. She tried that trick once before, but she was found on the riverside. I hope she has better luck this time."

Zollin thanked the man and finished his ale. It made him a little light headed, but it was worth the information. He went out of the tavern and pretended to browse through the other shops while he processed the information. He needed a way to let Brianna know he was here, in the city, but he wasn't sure how he could do that. He had no idea where to look for her, but if he could somehow find her, they could escape without a confrontation. It was worth a try. He also needed to find Mansel and let him know what he had learned.

* * *

Mansel rode swiftly around the city sprawl in the opposite direct from Zollin. He was excited to explore the city. He rode through the muddy streets that led up to the city walls. He was impressed by the sheer number of vendors hawking their wares as he rode past them. They called for him to stop and see their goods. They had everything from weapons to jewelry, but he had no time to look through the exotic wares of the many merchants. He was convinced that the best information would come from close to the castle. If Brianna was being held captive in the royal castle, the people of the city would know it. His mother had always said that tavern maids know everything about a village, so why not a town, even a large town like Orrock.

He was challenged at the gate, but the guards only asked his businesses and then let him pass. He rode through the cobblestone streets and found an inn that looked like the kind of place he would enjoy. He went in and ordered a mug of ale from a plump maid, who flashed him a knowing smile. When she brought the drink, he laid a silver on the table and asked her to join him.

"You look like you could use a break," he said. "Have a seat and I'll buy you a drink as well."

"It's a bit early in the day for ale," she said teasingly.

"Oh, it's never too early for ale," Mansel said, grinning. "Will you sit with me?"

She looked around and lowered her serving tray.

"Alright, but only for a short time. I've still work to do."

"I'm sure you do. But first, tell me the news of the city."

"What news?" she said.

"The best kind..." he said pausing for effect. "The castle gossip."

She giggled and he chuckled, then they both took a long drink of ale.

"Well..." she said, wiping her mouth with her sleeve. "I hear tales of a wizard."

"A wizard?" Mansel said, feigning surprise. He leaned forward and conspiratorially whispered, "Tell me more."

"They say he has a young maiden held captive in the castle, and that she is as beautiful as any highborn lady. Some say that Prince Simmeron is smitten with her, others that she serves the wizard. The army's all on patrols looking for her. I heard she ran off with one of the soldiers."

"Now why would she do that?" he asked.

"Because she's in love, silly."

"Oh, love..." he said. "I don't believe in it myself," he said with a wink.

"The right woman could make you change your mind," she said.

Mansel felt her hand brushing his knee under the table and had a difficult time remembering what he was at the inn for.

"My name's Reena," she said. "I've a room in back. Would you care to see it?"

Mansel smiled and thought to himself how much he liked Orrock, as she led him away.

* * *

Zollin bought himself a flaky-crusted meat pie for lunch. He wasn't sure exactly what type of meat was in the savory pie, but there were onions and peppers and spices that made his mouth burn. He drank a sweetened fruit juice that a different vendor kept cold with big blocks of ice brought down from the highlands and insulated with sawdust in a cellar under his shop. The juice was delicious, and Zollin had three cups of the sweet drink before needing to find a quiet place to relieve his bladder.

Outside the city, most people did their business behind their shops or homes. Privacy was in short supply but so was modesty. Zollin wandered around for a while until his need overcame his desire for privacy. He saw two other men in an alley relieving themselves, and he decided to join them. He tried to ignore what was going on around him, and when he finished he found that the first two men had been joined by three others. They wore threadbare clothes that were in desperate need of washing. Their faces were streaked with grime and their hair hung in greasy cords.

"Well, well," said one of the men. "Haven't seen you before. Think you can just come do your business in our alley, do you?"

"I didn't mean to trespass. I'm from out of town, and I didn't mean to intrude," Zollin explained.

"But you did intrude, didn't ya? And now, I'm thinking that I need satisfaction. Perhaps a pound of your flesh would make me feel better about you walking in here and doing your business in my alley."

"I didn't realize this was your area. I apologize."

"Yeah? Well I don't accept. Now, if you were to offer to pay for your privileges, I might decide to look the other way, so to speak."

"I can pay," Zollin said. "How does a silver sound?"

"It sounds light," said the man. "I think I'll just kill you and take your whole purse. That might satisfy me."

Zollin felt his face flush with anger. He had meant to apologize to the men sincerely. The last thing he wanted was to start a brawl that would attract the soldiers who were looking for

Brianna, but he was sick of dealing with arrogant men who tried to bully him. He felt the wind of his magic stirring inside him, hot and volatile.

"You can try," Zollin said, holding his hands up.

"You're a cool cucumber, that's for sure," said the man. "But I ain't the kind to bluff with, sonny. You give us that purse and we might let you crawl out of here alive."

Zollin had heard enough. He clapped his hands together and slammed an invisible wall of magic into the ruffians. Four of the men were knocked off their feet, but at the first sign of movement, the talker lunged forward, producing a knife from somewhere in his filthy clothing. It was longer than his hand from palm to fingertips. A narrow, curving blade, intended for close quarters. He slashed at Zollin with the knife. Zollin tried to dodge to the side and escape the blade, but he was only partially successful. The blade's tip sliced through his vest and shirt and carved a fiery line across his ribs. Zollin reacted to the pain without any conscious thought. Energy, so brilliant it caused Zollin to close his eyes, flashed from his hand and hit the man in the chest. It lasted only a second, but the crack of the energy splitting the air was as loud as thunder from a storm. The man was knocked backwards by the force of the strike, and he landed in the mud with a blackened hole where his chest once was. His face was frozen in look of pure horror, and every hair on his body stood out straight.

The other men were just getting back to their feet, and it took all of Zollin's self control not to blast them with the same intense spell that had slain their leader. They looked at their friend in horror then looked back at Zollin, who was holding his side.

Blood was seeping out of the wound, hot and slick. He grimaced in pain as the other men fled the alley.

Zollin knew he needed to get as far away from the dead man as possible, but he also knew wandering through the streets bleeding was no way to blend in. He sent his mind magically into the wound. It was dirty; he could feel the foreign matter, so tiny yet absolutely deadly, clinging to his flesh. He pushed the filth out of the wound then, as quickly as he could, he knit the flesh back together. He was just moving out of the alley when a squad of soldiers arrived and blocked his escape.

Chapter 37

Zollin froze, just looking at the soldiers. They had pikes, long spears with a blade on one side and a spike on the other. They were used for pulling riders off of horses, but were just as effective for killing a man on foot. Zollin was just about to try his luck pretending the killer had run from the scene when one of the ruffians appeared and pointed at Zollin.

"That's him there, a sorcerer by the looks of him," the man said.

Zollin felt panic begin to sink in. The last thing he wanted was a pitched battle that would give away his position, but it was too late for that. He had been careless, and now he had to deal with the consequences.

"I don't know what he's talking about," Zollin said. "I just came back here to relieve myself and I saw that man's body." He pointed to the dead man in the mud, whose chest was still smoking from Zollin's spell.

"What's your name?" one of the soldiers asked.

"Hans," Zollin said.

"Where are you from?"

"Felson," Zollin lied again. "I'm here looking for work."

"Take him," the soldier said.

Three of the men raised their weapons and moved forward. Two took hold of Zollin's arms, the third took a position behind him. They followed the other soldiers out of the alley and turned toward the city. Zollin wasn't sure what to do. He knew he could free himself, but that would result in a pitched battle and the need to flee. He wouldn't be able to find Brianna by hiding. On the other hand, revealing himself publicly might allow her to find him, but then what? He would have to fight the King's army, and most likely Branock, to escape. Neither option seemed profitable. So, for now, he just followed the soldiers.

They went through the city gate and then down the cobblestone streets toward the castle. Normally people who were arrested were carried out of the city, but with everyone looking for the missing girl and on guard in case a wizard showed up in the city, everyone was being brought to the guardhouse in the castle complex.

Zollin used the time he was being moved to look around the city. He was looking frantically for Brianna but saw no sign of her. At the castle gates they were stopped and then Zollin was pushed forward. He didn't resist. The guard at the gate looked him over and then nodded. It was obvious that the guard thought the he was just a grifter or con man, but he was taken into the castle courtyard. Outside the guardhouse, he was placed in chains and then taken inside and locked in a cell. He guessed that no one believed he was a wizard. In the guard house, he sat on a plain, wooden bench in a small cell and looked around. There were a few other prisoners, all chained and sitting on their own benches inside cells of barred steel. Zollin pondered his situation. He wasn't sure what to do. He could escape, but he thought that if he waited, he might be able to slip out after dark and no one would be any wiser. He tried to imagine what his father would tell him to do. If Quinn had been with him, he wouldn't be in this mess, he thought. He couldn't decide if he was angry at his father or just lonely.

* * *

Mansel came out of the inn with a half a dozen sweet barley cakes. He munched on them merrily as he climbed back into his saddle. It was early afternoon, and he felt that he had accomplished what he came for. He'd left the serving maid with promises that he would return, although he had no idea when he would or even if he would be able to. For now, he needed to get out of the city and find Zollin again. The news that Brianna had escaped was the best he had heard since leaving Tranaugh Shire. He was sure that Zollin would be thrilled, but uncertain what they needed to do to find her. He thought, perhaps, that Zollin could find her using magic.

He was lost in his own thoughts, eating the last of the sweet cakes, when three guards stepped out in front of his horse. They had pikes and wore the jerkins of the King's army. They lowered their weapons menacingly.

"State your business," said one of the soldiers.

"I'm here on pleasure," Mansel said.

"From where?"

"Uh," Mansel wasn't sure what to say. He was quick with a sword, but not with words. "Tran, I mean Brighton's Gate."

The soldiers looked suspicious and didn't move aside.

"You need to dismount," said the soldier.

Mansel wanted to argue, but he decided, that in this case, that would be a mistake.

"Is something wrong?"

"Where'd you get that horse?"

"He's mine. I bought him when he was just a colt," Mansel lied again.

He wasn't sure what to say, but he wasn't going to admit he had taken the horse from the King's army in the Great Valley.

"This is a cavalry horse and gear," said the soldier. "You'll be detained for horse theft and crimes against the crown."

Mansel didn't want to hurt the soldiers, but he wasn't sure what to do. He could make a run for it, but he had no idea how he would get out of the city. And if he fought them, most likely someone would get killed, perhaps even himself. He raised his hands and watched with anguish as they took his sword. Of all his possessions, he loved the sword that Zollin had made for him, not just because it seemed like such a fine weapon, but because it had been made before his eyes from the links of a chain the army had used to confine him to the mud. One soldier led his horse away, while two more took hold of his arms.

The long walk through the city was humiliating, even though it seemed to hold very little interest to the citizens of Orrock. They went about their business after only a single glance at Mansel. When they reached the castle, he was once again chained and led into the guard house. He was surprised to see Zollin sitting there, his face a mask that hid his own surprise quite well. Mansel was locked in the cell adjacent to Zollin's, and the guards seemed to have no interest in either of them.

Both the wizard and the warrior tried to stay nonchalant as they slowly slid toward each other on their benches. After a while, Zollin guessed that it was okay to talk; the other prisoners certainly were, and the guards paid no attention to any of them. Still, he kept his voice pitched low.

"Fancy meeting you here," he said.

"I got nailed for horse theft," Mansel said. "I'm getting tired of being chained up and thrown in jail. I'm not sure if hanging out with you is good for me. I think you're a bad influence."

"Very funny," Zollin said, but he was smiling.

"So what's the plan?"

"I don't know. I found out that Brianna has escaped."

"I heard that, too."

"Any luck finding her?"

"No, I was busy getting information."

"I found out about Brianna in less than two hours, what have you been doing all this time?"

"I was building a relationship with a key person in the city."

"You were with another tavern maid, weren't you," Zollin accused.

"No, she was a serving maid at a very reputable inn here in the city. It's not my fault that women don't want my silver."

"Silver doesn't take as long as the payment you provide."

"True, but I'm saving you money."

"What else did you learn?"

"That this isn't Brianna's first escape attempt. No one really knows what happened, but somehow she climbed out of the castle using a rope, cold cocked a guard, and hasn't been seen since."

"I wish we knew what she was planning," Zollin said.

"Well, she must be here in the city," Mansel explained. "She was found in an inn on the riverside the first time. Patrols were sent out of the city to search for her. The fact that they haven't found her yet is a good indication she went to ground here. She had help, that's obvious. They're probably still hiding together, waiting for things to cool down before they make their next move."

Zollin felt his heart rise up in his throat. He couldn't imagine how Brianna must have felt. Trapped, alone, and abandoned by him, she probably turned to the first man who gave her hope. Now she was hiding with that person, and the jealousy he felt was like an itch he couldn't reach. He knew he should just be happy that she was out of Branock's clutches, but instead he was angry. He shouldn't have waited so long. He should have ridden after her from the start. He should have blasted the army soldiers in the Great Valley and ridden Branock down.

"Speaking of next moves, what's ours?" Mansel asked.

"Well, apparently the search for Brianna has distracted everyone from their search for me. I was told that the army and city guard had been preparing for us to storm the castle. I got picked up after being attacked by brigands outside the city walls."

He lifted his arm and showed Mansel where the knife had sliced through the vest and shirt underneath.

"I would have escaped, but I had to heal the wound first."

"Well, how are we going to get out of this one?"

"I was thinking we wait until nightfall, and then we can make a break for it."

"It worked for Brianna," Mansel said with a smile.

"Then we need to find her," Zollin said. "I'm not sure how to do that."

"You may not have to. Word will get out the *wizard* everyone was waiting for escaped, and she'll know you're here. We can start a few rumors ourselves, and she can come to us."

"That might work," Zollin said, but the thought of waiting while Brianna was with another man was a painful thought.

"Well, if something changes wake me up; otherwise I'm getting some sleep. I'm exhausted."

"You should be, after spending all the day gathering information," Zollin said.

"You're welcome by the way."

"Shut up," Zollin said, but he couldn't keep from smiling when he said it.

* * *

Branock was pacing. He would have to find more competent help once he was King. The castle was filled with disloyal servants, and the officers of the King's army appeared to be useless at doing anything other than marching and polishing their armor. He had sent out the very guards who should be preparing for Zollin's arrival to find Brianna. He could feel the boy; his bright spark of magic was so close it was a distraction. Until he had Zollin under his thumb, he wouldn't feel safe, he thought to himself.

Then he felt the pulse of magic as Zollin blasted the ruffian in the alley outside the city. The raw power had been like a thunder clap that shakes an entire house and leaves you feeling unsettled. It was in that moment that he knew he had to prepare. He would have no help from the army, no better chance to bring Zollin under his control. If the boy didn't know that Brianna had escaped, he could still use her to convince Zollin to join him. His mission was to win the powerful young wizard over, but he had to be prepared for battle. He spent over an hour, thinking though the list of spells he had prepared in case he had to fight. It was always a temptation when fighting another wizard to simply throw raw power at one another until someone's defenses broke, but that was not wise. Zollin was stronger than Branock, but he still did not have the knowledge that made his power efficient. Still, Zollin had shown that he could think on his feet. When he had battled Whytlethane, he had shown initiative and awareness of his surroundings. The boy was smart, but Branock had years of experience to rely on. He would not make the same mistakes he had made in the forest, when his fire spell had rebounded and almost consumed him. He would be prepared this time.

"My lord," said a guard coming in to make his daily report. "We have two men who match the descriptions you gave us. One was picked up after allegedly killing a vagrant outside the city. The other was detained for being in possession of a cavalry horse and gear. Both have been placed in the guard house."

Branock's pace quickened, but he did not speak. His mind was turning. This was his chance and he knew it, but it might be his only chance and he needed it to be perfect.

"Assemble the Royal Guard," Branock said. "I want them here, all of them."

"But, sir, they're guarding the King and the Prince. They're stationed all around the castle."

"Do it!" Branock spat. "Or I'll have your head for a piss pot."

The guard hurried away, but Branock knew that his order would come with strings attached. The Prince would want to know what was happening. He still needed the greedy royal heir; unfortunately, Simmeron had proved to be a self-absorbed puppet. He served a purpose, but his constant demands and inflated sense of self importance were a burden.

It took the Prince twenty minutes to finally arrive, by that time most of the Royal Guard had assembled. They were talented fighters, each trained not only with sword and shield, but with an array of weapons, as well as tactics, strategy, horsemanship, and stealth.

"What is it?" Simmeron asked. "Have you found my wandering flower?"

"No, she is still missing. What I have found, or rather the city guard has found, is Zollin."

"The other wizard?"

"Yes, he will not be easily overcome."

"Where is he?" asked the Prince, his excitement both obvious and annoying.

"He's in the guardhouse," Branock said.

"Then victory is ours. We have him in our custody. We shall be unstoppable!" he shouted.

"Don't be a fool," Branock said. "Your guards cannot hold him. He is submitting because he does not want to reveal himself. We must be ready for anything. If he learns that Brianna is not here, he will not hesitate to kill us all."

The Prince turned white, and Branock now had the Royal Guard's attention.

"Here is what I propose. We have one of his companions as well. I want the castle gates closed and men watching for anyone else who might try to gain entrance. I need two of the Royal Guard to detain his companion, here at the entrance to the castle. No one is to be in the courtyard except for me. If I cannot convince Zollin to join us, then the Royal Guard must slay him. Captain," Branock said, turning to the man in charge of the Royal Guard, "I want your men in the front two towers, armed with cross bows. If battle is joined, fire your bolts at him until he is dead. Do not be fooled gentlemen, Zollin is a powerful wizard and we must not underestimate him."

"What if you are slain?" Simmeron asked.

"Then you should do all you can to destroy the boy. If not, he will kill you all."

Branock knew that was a lie. In fact, it was hard to believe the guard's report that Zollin had even killed a vagrant outside of the city. It could have been a ruse to get him inside the castle, but it was always better to face your opponent head on than to wait and allow them to foment plans for your demise.

"Move," Branock said.

"Where should I wait?" Simmeron asked.

"I don't care," said Branock.

"I think the castle turret," the Prince said. "It should give me the best view of the battle."

"Pray there is not a battle," Branock said, lowering his voice. "If Zollin does not join us, we are doomed."

Chapter 38

Once the order was given to have Mansel brought to the castle, two things happened at once. One guard went to the guardhouse, while a servant, who had been eavesdropping on Branock, went quickly from the castle and through the town. He spoke to Bron and then hurried down into the secret room where Brianna and Wilamet waited. There was no time to get either one back into the castle before the gates were locked, but Brianna wanted to know what was happening. She and Wilamet had slept late into the day in the dark room, but now they were awake and they made their way out into the bright sunlight. They raised their hoods and moved toward the castle, despite the danger of being seen or recognized.

Brianna's heart was racing; behind the towering walls, her beloved Zollin was about to face Branock. She knew he could defeat the wizard one on one, but the Royal Guard had been involved, and that changed everything.

In the guardhouse, three men approached Zollin's cell. He had been hoping to avoid any attention, but now it seemed he was going to be forced into action. But they didn't stop at his cell; instead the soldiers went to Mansel's cell.

"You, boy," said one of the men. "Stand up, you're coming with us."

"Coming where?" Mansel asked.

"You'll find out," the soldier replied. "Now shut your mouth and do as you're told."

Zollin stood up. "I'm the wizard," he said. "I've come for the girl."

"Sure you are," said the soldier, shaking his head and laughing. "And I'm the King."

"It's okay, Zollin," said Mansel. "Just another day and another false accusation."

"Move!" shouted the soldier, pushing Mansel from behind.

"Don't touch him!" Zollin shouted.

"Shut your hole, or I'll shut it for you."

Zollin was struggling to keep from blasting the arrogant soldier. He strained to see what was happening outside the guardhouse, and Mansel was led out. There was a lot of activity, but it was impossible to see exactly what was going on. Zollin slumped down, clamping down on the furious energy writhing within him. He didn't want to lose control the way he had in the alley. It wouldn't help matters, he told himself.

Outside, Mansel was led across to the castle's main entrance. It was much darker inside the building than out in the bright afternoon sunshine. Mansel had to blink and wait for his eyes to adjust before he could clearly see the man in front of him. He was completely unfamiliar to Mansel, but the bald head and scarred skin gave the man an intimidating persona. The milk white eye didn't help matters, and when the man smiled it sent a chill down Mansel's spine.

"Mansel, I believe, is that right? I remember you from the forest. You may not recognize me; a lot has changed since I healed your broken ribs."

"I remember that you attacked us," Mansel said when he realized who he was talking to. He had known that Branock had attacked Zollin and kidnapped Brianna at Brighton's Gate, but he had not personally seen the wizard. He had been busy fighting the Skellmarians.

"It looks like the beating you took that day left an impression on you," Mansel said.

"Ah, you mean my new look," Branock said, waving to his face, which was mostly healed from the burn, but there was still scar tissue underneath the surface that gave his face an unnatural look. "Yes, it is a change, but not a bad one. In fact, I feel that our previous encounter changed my life. I'm not the man I used to be."

"Still a murderous coward who hides behind women," Mansel said through clenched teeth.

"Oh, don't be so dramatic. I did what I had to do to ensure the future of our fair realm. What's one life weighed against the balance of an entire nation?"

"Don't try to win me over; I know evil when I see it."

"I am not evil," said Branock. "I do sometimes take drastic actions, but my motives are pure, I assure you. You do not understand the power of the Torr or the master's evil intent. We must not let Zollin be seduced by them and coerced into joining them."

"Didn't you come to Tranaugh Shire to recruit him for the Torr? You call those thugs at the Torr master for a reason," Mansel said, flexing his hands and wishing he had a sword to use on the man before him.

"No, he is not my master. Not anymore, and I came to save Zollin from the Torr."

"Or to kill him if he wouldn't join you?"

"I was wrong, I see that now. I was desperate and afraid. I have burned my bridges to the Torr, but Offendorl will not forget. He will gather armies and march against Yelsia to find Zollin."

"Sort of the way you did in the Great Valley."

"No, you twist the facts. I was escorted up the valley by the army because there were rumors of a Skellmarian invasion. Rumors that turned out to be true. I wanted to reason with Zollin, but he attacked me. I don't know why. I only took Brianna because it was the only way to safely get the chance to talk with Zollin. I have treated her as an honored guest. She has not suffered in any way."

"I doubt that she would agree."

"You can ask her yourself, just as soon as Zollin agrees to speak peacefully."

"So what are doing talking to me if it's Zollin you want to speak with?"

"I was hoping that you might consent to go to him and assure him I mean him no harm. Tell him that I only want to talk and that I have the full authority of the crown to grant you and Zollin a full pardon for any crimes. Please, Mansel, I only want to talk with him. Won't you help me?"

"Yes," Mansel said. "As soon as I speak with Brianna."

* * *

"We have to find a way into the castle," Brianna said.

"You can't," said Jorkin, the castle servant who had warned them of Branock's plan. "The gates are locked and the guards have orders not to allow anyone into the castle."

"There is one way," said Wilamet. "But we must hurry."

She led them through the crowded streets. They moved as swiftly as they dared without drawing attention to themselves. They circled the castle complex and went to the riverside city gate. They were not challenged as they passed through, and then Wilamet led them to the garrison house next to the docks. A small contingent of the King's army was posted there to keep a watch over the river traffic and to help keep the peace along the harbor. Most of the troops were spread out through the harbor itself, most probably had orders to find Brianna. Wilamet went straight to the garrison house and went inside. Brianna followed while Jorkin watched from outside.

"We are here on King's business," said Wilamet. "King Felix ordered that the tunnel be inspected every year."

"That's strange," said the soldier, who had been sitting in a wooden chair that was leaning back against the wall. He had been half asleep when Wilamet rushed into the small building. It consisted of a small room with cots for the soldiers to sleep on. There were around two dozen beds lined up in neat rows. There was a small guard's cell in one corner and a thick, wooden door with an iron lock at the far end of the room.

"I've never heard of any such order," he said.

"Would you like to return to Steward Homan and tell him that you refused to allow the King's servants access and that is why the King's edict had not been carried out?"

Brianna doubted if all the words Wilamet was using really applied to the situation, but the soldier didn't seem to notice. He did, however, pick up on the official sounding language and titles. He thought about what he should do, his forehead wrinkled in thought. Finally he nodded and pulled a strange looking key from the drawer of a small desk in the garrison's entry room, where they stood. He led them back through the barracks and unlocked the door. A dark set of stone steps led down into what reminded Brianna of the secret passage under the city wall.

Wilamet snatched up a torched from a wall sconce and waited while the soldier lit it. The oil-soaked torch crackled to life and spilled an oily looking smoke from the bright flames. She handed the torch to Brianna and motioned for her to go first down the stairs.

"Thank you," Wilamet said to the soldier. Then she followed Brianna into the darkness, closing and locking the door behind them.

"That went better than I expected," Brianna said.

"They would never expect you to try to get back into the castle," Wilamet said. "Now come along, this passage isn't short. It may still take us a while to get to the castle."

* * *

Mansel had been restrained and Branock was now waiting for Zollin. He had decided that the best place to meet the boy was in the courtyard. He stood with his cloak swirling in the wind as the guards returned for Zollin. They entered the guardhouse and went immediately to his cell.

"Where's Mansel?" Zollin asked.

"We'll ask the questions, thank you," said the soldier. "Now stand up and approach the cell doors."

They waited until he complied, then the soldier unlocked the door. Guards took hold of each of his arms, and another walked behind Zollin with a drawn sword pointed as his back. Zollin's magic was swirling like mad. He was angry and scared, it was volatile combination.

They led him outside, and the sun was beginning to set. It was shining in his eyes and blinding him from the person who waited for him. Branock had planned every detail, even the time of day he wanted to make the confrontation. The soldiers released Zollin and moved away. He didn't bother to look at them, they were just the messengers. He wanted to end the threat to himself and to his family.

"Zollin," Branock said. "It's so nice to see you again. I'm sorry for your treatment. It seems that you killed an innocent man today."

"I was defending myself."

"Yes, but your power got away from you. I felt it. Doesn't it bother you that you have so much trouble with self control? I was like that once. But I learned to control my magic. I would be glad to show you, if you'd let me."

"I don't need you to show me anything," Zollin said. "I'm not planning on abandoning my friends or kidnapping women."

"Please don't patronize me, Zollin. I warned you about the men from the Torr. You haven't faced all of them. And they won't stop until they have your complete obedience or you are dead."

"Sounds a bit like you."

"No, they are nothing like me. I only want your help Zollin. Yelsia needs us. You can join me here and help protect the realm. I can show you how to take control of your magic. You can assist me in creating a more harmonious kingdom. There are threats coming, Zollin. The dragon isn't the only threat to Yelsia."

"Right now, I'm only concerned about one threat, and that's you."

"I'm no threat," he said, chuckling. "Your power is much too great for me. Although it seems you've misplaced your staff. That is truly a shame, but I assure you, we will bring every resource to bear to find it."

"I don't care about the staff; I only want my friends back."

"And you shall have them. I sent for you, but they brought Mansel by mistake, he's just inside the castle there," he said, waving one arm at the massive castle doors, which swung open so that Zollin could see Mansel.

His friend was still chained and escorted by three guards. Zollin concentrated on his friend, reaching out with his magic to find the lock on the shackles around Mansel's wrist.

"Where's Brianna?" Zollin asked, as if he didn't know that she had escaped.

"She's well," Branock said. "She's also inside the castle. If you'll agree to join me, I'll take you to her."

"I don't think so," Zollin said.

"Why not? Think of all the good we could do together."

"You're a liar, Branock, and my father taught me to know the difference between an honest man and a liar."

"I am deeply wounded that you would slander my reputation like that. I am no liar."

"Then produce Brianna. You took her, against her will, from Brighton's Gate. Now she has escaped, and you stand there promising to reunite us."

"My promise was sound. I have half the King's army out looking for her now. I only want to keep her safe. There was a dragon in Brighton's Gate, and I only wanted to protect her. You can ask her yourself when we find her; I've treated her with all due respect. Not a hair of her head has been harmed."

"And I will take her to be my Queen!" shouted a voice from the top of the castle.

"What?" Zollin said.

"Ignore him," Branock said angrily.

"She shall have every luxury," Simmeron shouted. "I swear it on my father's throne."

"You promised her to the Prince?" Zollin said, aghast.

"We're wasting time here, Zollin. Come inside with me. We can help each other. There is no reason not to."

"Except that you lie and cheat at every turn. I can't trust you and I won't join you. Release my friends, and we will leave the city peacefully."

"That sounds oddly like a threat," Branock said. "This is not the frontier, Zollin. Here the rule of law reigns, the King's law, and you have broken it. I cannot let you just leave."

"I have done what I had to do, and I will do what I have to do now."

He sent an impulse toward Mansel, just enough to click the tumblers in his shackle. The lock popped open and Mansel nodded ever so slightly.

"This is not what I want," Branock said, but he was smiling. He assumed that Zollin had sent a spell against him, and that the young wizard was powerless without his staff.

"Then let us go."

"I can't do that. Can't you see there is simply too much at stake here?"

"Then I have no choice," Zollin said.

He unlocked his own chains and they fell away. Immediately, he raised a shield around himself, but nothing happened. No attack from the rear, no shocking blast from the older wizard. Zollin waited but still nothing happened.

"Please, Zollin" Branock said. "I need your help. It would not please me to destroy. Join me instead."

"No."

"Yelsia needs you."

"No."

"You don't know what you're saying," Branock pleaded. He was no longer afraid of fighting Zollin, but he knew that wouldn't accomplish anything. He needed the boy to join him.

"I know enough not to trust you," Zollin replied.

There was a long moment of tense inaction, and then Branock nodded. The guard standing behind Mansel drew his sword. Mansel jumped forward, twisting in midair and swinging the shackles that Zollin had unlocked. The guard followed Mansel and the chain hit him in the face. The guard cried out in pain and dropped his sword. Then Branock attacked.

He sent fire from both hands that joined into a massive column of flame that slammed into Zollin's shield. The force of the blast made Zollin backpedal several steps. Then the crossbow bolts came speeding from the tower closest to Zollin. He felt his shield shrinking from the repeated impacts, the transferred energy taking more and more of his power to control.

"It doesn't have to be this way!" shouted Branock, surprised that Zollin could block the flames and the crossbow bolts without his staff.

"You know no other way," Zollin shouted back.

He reached out with is power, which was boiling like mad now. He formed an invisible tube around the column of flame and then sucked the oxygen out. The strength it took was like holding a heavy, timber beam while his hands shook and his muscles felt like they would shred to ribbons unless he dropped it. But once the oxygen was gone, the flames were suffocated, and then Zollin opened his shield and sent a bolt of sizzling energy speeding toward his foe. He immediately raised his shield again, but one crossbow bolt made it past his defense. Zollin deflected the projectile, but it was moving too much and he was doing too many things at once. The bolt was knocked off course and skewered his calf muscle.

Branock raised his own defenses before Zollin sent the blast, but the force of the blow sent him sprawling. Zollin turned his attention to the tower where the crossbows were firing at him. His instinct was to tear the build down, but he held that impulse in check. Instead, he sent a shove of magic at the men firing at him. It wasn't strong enough to break through the stone wall, but it did penetrate the firing slots, damaging most of the crossbows and knocking the Royal Guardsmen back.

The pain in his leg was burning like fire. He could feel blood running down his leg and into his boot. It nagged at his mind as he turned his attention back to Branock, who was struggling back to his feet. The wizard's features were a mask of fury and hate. He sent a levitating spell at Zollin that sent him flying into the air. Zollin was caught totally off guard by the tactic and was barely able to soften his landing and avoid being seriously injured on the cobblestone courtyard.

Branock then sent objects flying at Zollin from all directions. Most went zipping harmlessly past him. It was more of a distraction than a true attack, but it did cause Zollin to use his defenses rather than attacking Branock. He was trying to stand, but his injured leg didn't want to support his weight.

Mansel had fended off the other two guards long enough to pick up the fallen man's sword. The guard had several broken facial bones and his face was mass of blood. He lay moaning on the steps of the castle. Mansel ignored him and focused on the other two guards. They had shields and short swords, Mansel had a short sword and the shackle chain. He was out numbered and stuck with inferior weapons. But he was fighting for his life and those of his friends; the guards were members of the King's army and fighting for a pay. They had training, but Mansel was born to wield the sword. He moved slowly down the stairs, twirling the shackle around and around as he went. The guards advanced, but their attention was divided between their adversary and the magic battle going on behind Mansel.

He feinted to the left then thrust the sword to the right. The soldier caught the blow on his shield as Mansel expected, so when the chain came arcing at the soldier's head, he raised his sword to defend himself. The chain wrapped around the sword and Mansel tugged with all his strength. The guard stumbled forward, right into the path of the other soldier, who was now moving to flank Mansel. The soldier struggled to keep his footing, and Mansel dropped the shackle and rained down several blows on the soldier's shield. His blows weakened his opponent a little further, and when Mansel dropped his shoulder as if to attack the man's legs, he dropped his shield in defense. But Mansel was expecting such a move and instead thrust his sword straight at the man, whose fear and fatigue made him slow. He tried to raise the shield, but he wasn't fast enough to avoid the sword. It punched into his left shoulder, breaking several links in the guard's chain mail and puncturing the skin. The wound was minor, but the force of the blow knocked the man's shoulder out of socket. He screamed and fell back, dropping his weapons and calling for mercy. The other guard, who had been pulled down the castle steps by Mansel's chain, was limping from his fall, but back on his feet. He attacked and forced Mansel to move back and avoid the sword play, rather than try to block the strikes with his sword.

The man was strong and, when he was in range, deadly, but moving forward on a wrenched knee was a weakness that Mansel intended to exploit. He kept moving backwards, first to the side, then back up the stairs. The man continued to attack, but he struggled with his footwork. Mansel waited until he was near the top of the stairs, then he kicked straight out at the man, who raised his shield but couldn't stop the momentum from staggering him back. Only, his legs couldn't keep up with the steps, and he fell backwards, dropping his sword and crying out as his body crashed onto the stone steps. Mansel heard what he thought were bones breaking, but he didn't wait to find out. He had glanced up and saw that Zollin seemed to be in trouble. He threw his sword with all his strength at Branock. The sword arced up, flipping through the air, end over end, but flying true to the mark. At the last second, Branock sensed it and halted his attack on Zollin to deflect the blade.

The slight pause gave Zollin the time he needed to get back on his feet. He had already shut down the pain receptors that were screaming in his brain over the pain in his leg. He channeled his magic down into the ground and sent the cobblestones rippling like a wave toward his adversary. Branock's eyes widened as he saw the ground flowing up like a breaker preparing to crash onto the seashore. He focused his power into a concussion spell that shattered the cobblestones that would have hit him, and the wave parted around him.

Zollin was already hard at work: black smoke had been pouring from the palms of his hands, and he was now hidden in a dark cloud. He was slowly moving back and toward the corner of the castle. He had to stop producing smoke when a crossbow bolt came shooting down toward him. He deflected it just as a tongue of fire lanced through the cloud to his left. He hurried then, as fast as his injured leg would allow, keeping a magical shield above his head and watching as the flames snaked back and forth.

Mansel had seen what was happening and snatched up a sword and shield before running into the castle. He ran into the great hall and turned to his right in hopes of being able to somehow help Zollin.

* * *

Brianna and Wilamet were hurrying through the underground passage. Brianna had been surprised how long the tunnel was, and by the fact that it didn't run straight. Instead it zigged and zagged, often switching back to run the same way it had just come. She realized that if the tunnel, which Wilamet had told her was an escape route, had gone straight to the river, the attacking army would have been able to quickly move through the city and catch the fleeing royals. This way, the destination was unknown, and the constant direction changes would give anyone fleeing the best chance to avoid projectiles fired at them from behind. Still, while it made sense for the defense of the castle, it was maddening to Brianna, who was desperate to find Zollin.

When they finally came to steps leading up, she was breathless and her stomach was like a fish out of water. Wilamet threw open the door, which was locked from the inside. They had no need for keys. They found themselves in a long, narrow stairwell that wound its way up. They hurried up the steps and came out in a small room that was dark and quiet. There were several people gathered around a large bed with ornate columns at all four corners. It was King Felix's private chambers. Wilamet went and joined Edina and the other servants who were huddled around their king. Brianna went to the window and looked outside. The room had an excellent view of the river and the countryside beyond. She could also see the castle and guessed correctly that they were on the back side of the massive building.

She looked to her left and saw where she had descended in the inky black night. She was glad she hadn't been able to see just how high she really was. She turned to go search for Zollin when she heard crashes to her right. She looked back out and saw stones flying through the air and crashing into the castle's surrounding palisade.

* * *

Zollin had been successful in moving out of range of the men with crossbows, but Branock had not been held back long by the smoke. He sent a spell that blew like wind and whipped the smoke away. He saw that his quarry was gone and moved forward to find him. Zollin, meanwhile, was still moving back toward the rear of the castle. He needed an edge, but his leg was hurting so badly he felt that perhaps his best option was to deal with the wound, at least in a cursory way, so that he could move and focus on the battle at hand. He dropped to his good knee, with the injured leg in front of him. He took hold of the crossbow bolt and sent his mind deep into the wood, rearranging the composition of the wood until it was nothing more than pure oxygen. He didn't have time to knit the severed muscle fibers back together, but he was able to speed the blood clotting so that the bleeding stopped.

Then, while he was still occupied with his leg, the ground around him began to shimmer and then dissolve. He fell back, rolling away from the ground that Branock was manipulating. The cobblestones became a mass of molten rock so hot the air around it shimmered. Zollin sent a blast of sizzling energy at Branock, who dropped to the ground so that the blast flew harmlessly over his head. There were loose stones behind Branock, and he sent them speeding toward the young wizard. Zollin created a small, magic bubble around himself so that only the rocks that might have struck him were deflected. The rest went flying back and shattered against the rear castle wall.

Zollin moved backwards, still limping, but without the mind-numbing pain of having a foreign object in his leg. There were guards on the wall above and Royal Guardsmen moving into the rear tower to take up firing positions. Zollin wanted to fall back, but he was afraid of coming into range of the archers there. Instead, he fled into one of the buildings that were built onto the wall of the castle. It just happened to be the armory. He moved to the rear of the building and dumped over a barrel that was full of longbow arrows. He was ready, if anyone tried to come through the door, to send the arrows flying toward them. Then let his magic build up, the flames of power inside him seemed to be growing hotter and hotter. He didn't waste time trying to dissolve the stone wall. Instead he unleashed a blast of power that exploded the wall out into the street beyond.

The sound was like thunder, and the people of the town were screaming and running for cover. Zollin hurried through the hole but was soon targeted with arrows by the sentries along the top of the wall. He raised his shields and moved quickly between the buildings. He knew he needed to do something, but he simply wasn't sure what to do. He didn't want to hurt the soldiers and guards who were just doing what they had been ordered to do, but he couldn't fight an army and Branock at the same time.

Mansel had been forced to hide when a large group of Royal Guardsmen came hurrying toward him. He ducked into a small closet that was used for storing cleaning equipment. It was hard to sit back and wait, not knowing what was happening. Once he came out of the closet, he was unsure of what to do or where to go. He was afraid that if he kept trying to get to Zollin from inside the castle that he might run into a group of guards so large that he wouldn't be able to fight them all off. Instead, he hurried the opposite way from where Zollin was, hoping to use the stairs on the far end of the castle to gain access to the roof so that he could see what was happening and form a plan.

He ran as fast as he could and found the corner tower where stairs led upward. He sprinted up the steps. At the top of the tower was a small wooden ladder and a trapdoor in the ceiling. He climbed up, wishing more than ever that he had a good bow and a quiver full of arrows. The rooftop arched, but there was a flat track that ran all the way around the outside edge. He hurried toward where he heard people shouting. There were a group of Royal Guards surrounding Prince Simmeron, all watching the battle play out below. The Prince was shouting for his guardsmen to follow Zollin.

"Go!" he shouted in a hoarse voice. "Find him. Don't let him escape."

There was no way for Mansel to help anyone from the roof, so he turned and headed back down into the castle. He had just come down the ladder when he was surprised by someone in the hallway.

"Mansel?"

He spun around, raising his shield out of habit, but he couldn't believe his eyes. Brianna was standing in front of him, panting and red faced.

"What are you doing here?" he asked. "I thought you escaped."

"I did, but then I heard you were captured so I came back to help."

"We've got to get out of here."

"I can get us out of the castle, but what about Zollin?"

"I can't get to him. There are Royal Guardsmen shooting at him from the towers and Branock is fighting him, too. The last I saw, he was headed for the rear of the castle, but then I just heard someone shouting for the guards to go after him."

"Didn't you hear the explosion?" she asked.

"No, where?"

"On the far side of the castle."

"What should we do?"

"We have to get out of here and help him. Quick, follow me."

Mansel did as he was told. When they burst into the King's bedchamber, Edina looked up in alarm.

"Is this the wizard?" she asked.

"No, we've got to go to him," Brianna said.

"But you said he could defeat Branock."

"He can," Mansel interjected. "But not the Royal Guard and the King's army, too. Besides, we don't want to kill people just doing their jobs defending the castle."

"He must come and heal the King," Edina pleaded.

"I promise we will be back," Brianna said. "One way or another. But for now, we've got to get out of the castle and find Zollin."

Chapter 39

Zollin sent a wagon rolling toward the gaping hole in the wall. It picked up speed and crashed into the wall, sending debris flying through the hole and piling up on the street side. There was a lean-to shed not far away, Zollin used his power to pull it free from the wall and sent it hurling toward the hole. He could hear shouts from the other side of the wall as soldiers tried to follow him through the armory. He needed time and food. His stomach was burning and his throat was parched. He hurried from the scene, joining the crowds and trying to blend in, but his limp and dusty clothes weren't helping.

He found an abandoned vendors kiosk with sausages still sizzling over the coals where they were being cooked. He snatched up several, juggling them back and forth between his hands to keep from burning his fingers. As soon as he judged that they were cool enough he popped one into his mouth. The meat was juicy and hot, full of flavor that made his mouth water. He gave each bite a few cursory chews then swallowed. He felt better, although he was still very thirsty. What he needed was a way to face Branock without interference from the soldiers, but he wasn't sure how to do it.

As he moved deeper into the city, the panic from the area where he had broken through the walls was considerably lessened. People were looking around, asking questions, and wondering what had happened. Zollin needed to draw Branock out of the castle and hopefully get Brianna's attention as well. He raised his hands and sent red bolts of sizzling energy high into the sky. The people who saw it were at first awestruck and then terrified. They ran for the city gates and once again Zollin followed them.

* * *

Branock was furious. He had ordered men to follow Zollin, as well, but he knew that it was a futile gesture. He turned his attention instead to the castle, where Mansel was probably hiding from the guards. He hurried through the grand entrance and into the great audience chamber. People were moving but not Mansel. He searched every room, winding his way up as he went until finally he reached the King's bed chamber.

"How dare you enter here?" Edina said boldly. "This is a sickroom, get out."

"Move aside," he said, his curiosity piqued by the woman's bold accusations.

He looked around the room, which was decorated with rich furnishings. Just then Prince Simmeron came in.

"Oh, there you are," he said to Branock. "It was an amazing display, truly magnificent. Don't worry, my soldiers will catch him again."

"You fool, he let them catch him the first time. Where does that doorway lead to?" he asked, pointing at the door to the hidden passageway.

"That's the secret escape passage, but it hasn't been used in years," Simmeron said. "I don't even know where the key is to get it open."

Branock walked over and pushed on the door and it swung open. Brianna had neglected to lock it when she and Mansel had gone down the passage.

"It seems it has been used, and quite recently," Branock said with a sneer. Then he turned back to Edina. "Who went down this passage?"

"No one. The King must have forgotten to lock it."

"Don't lie to me," Branock said, enhancing his voice so the servants around the King's bed shrank away. "Tell me who they were."

"It was the girl, Brianna, and some man with a sword and shield," said one of the other servants.

Branock didn't wait; he simply whirled around and started after them. Prince Simmeron followed along with four of his guards. As they went down into the dark passageway, Branock kindled two flames that danced above his shoulders. In the darkness he looked like a demon, but Simmeron was more afraid of being left in the dark than staying close to the wizard, so he hurried to keep up.

The physical exertion was taxing on Branock. The battle had been exhausting, but searching the castle, and now chasing the girl through the secret tunnel, was almost more than he could stand. He pushed himself, hurrying down the spiral stairs and running through the tunnel. Only Prince Simmeron seemed to be in worse shape than Branock. He had two of his guards helping him along. It was his fear of the dark that kept him moving.

"Can't we...stop?" he panted.

"No," Branock shouted. "We have to catch up to them."

* * *

Mansel and Brianna had come through the long tunnel without problems, but they found themselves surrounded by soldiers when they came up into the dockside garrison.

"Who are you?" demanded one of the guards.

"Just servants," Brianna said quickly.

"Servants don't carry swords," the man said, eyeing Mansel suspiciously.

"I've been ordered to protect her," Mansel replied.

"That's interesting, I've never heard of a servant ordered to protect another servant. Why would she need it? And why are the two of you using the royal passageway?"

"He's not a servant, he's a knight," Brianna said. "The castle is under attack by a wizard. We were ordered to flee and I had been cleaning the tunnel so I went this way."

The soldiers all looked at each other. It was apparent that none of them were buying the story. Mansel realized they weren't wearing armor, some didn't even have their weapons close to hand. He decided that now was the best time to attack them, before they had a chance to prepare.

He rushed forward, ignoring Brianna's protest. He lowered his shield and slammed into the first two men. There were five soldiers in all, and the first two went down hard under Mansel's charge. He swung the pommel of his sword at another and caught the man on the jaw, knocking him out cold. The two on the ground were scrambling to get back to their feet, and the other two were trying to get to their weapons.

Mansel grabbed Brianna's hand and ran for the door, but then two fully armed and armored soldiers blocked it. Mansel pushed Brianna into the corner and took up a position in front of her. He had enough room to swing his sword, but perhaps the soldiers wouldn't. The two from the doorway came toward Mansel, their shields held at the ready. Behind them the other soldiers were forming up.

"I don't want to kill you," Mansel said. "We are on the same side. We are Yelsians. Let us go and no one has to get hurt."

"Keller's hurt already," said one of the soldiers he had knocked down. "You broke his jaw."

"I'm sorry, please believe me. I'm only trying to protect the girl and get out of the city."

"You're the wizard's girl," said one of the two soldiers facing Mansel. "You've been hiding in the royal passage this whole time?"

"No," Brianna said. "I'm just a servant."

The first soldier to Mansel's right lunged, bringing his sword up to try and get under Mansel's shield, but the warrior simply stepped aside and swung his own sword at the attacker's arm. He was forced to raise his shield at the same time to ward off the other soldier's attack, and his own strike had little power behind it. The blade hit the man's forearm, just above the wrist, cutting down to the bone and causing the man to drop his sword. The other soldier used his shield to push Mansel back, but the warrior was ready for that. He planted his feet, and although the rough, wooden shield bruised his ribs, he pushed back, losing no ground. Instead, he swung his sword in a high arc that caused the soldier to duck.

Just then Branock burst through the door behind the soldiers.

"Stop!" he roared. "Do not harm them."

"Oh...my...angel..." Simeron panted. He was red faced and wheezing. "I've found...you...at last."

"Lower your weapons, Mansel, you're coming with us."

"Never," he said grimly.

The thought went through his head that this was where he would die. He had never really thought much about death. Even when the soldiers were beating him in Felson, he hadn't considered that he might die. Now, without Zollin to fight the wizard, he knew he didn't stand a chance.

Branock waved a hand and the sword Mansel was holding grew hot in his hand. He flung the weapon, but it stopped in midair and dropped harmlessly to the ground.

"This is foolish, boy," Branock said angrily. "I grow tired of your resistance. I only need the girl, so if you persist, I will kill you where you stand."

Mansel still had his shield, and he was about to raise it and charge the wizard, but Brianna put her hand on his shoulder.

"Live to fight another day," she whispered.

He dropped the shield.

"Take them," he ordered the soldiers, who were only too happy to help.

They were rough with Mansel, but he had expected that. They pushed him into the wall and checked for more weapons. He had none and didn't resist. One brought out a set of manacles, much like the ones that Mansel had used on the guards that were holding him before.

"No," Branock said. "No chains. Tie their hands. Make sure the knots are tight."

The soldiers bound Mansel's hands behind his back with a rough cord, tying it so tightly he could feel his hands going numb almost immediately.

"Don't touch her," Simmeron shouted when one of the soldiers started toward Brianna. "That is..." he was still trying to catch his breath, "your future...Queen."

"She still needs to be bound," Branock snapped. "Tie her hands gently," he ordered.

One of the soldiers went forward, and Brianna held out her hands. He wrapped the cord three times around her wrists and then tied it. Simmeron came forward and wrapped his arm around her shoulders.

"It's only a display, my love. Soon we will be together, and no one will ever come between us again."

Brianna did not respond. It took all of her self control not to spit in the Prince's face. They were led outside and brought immediately to the riverside gate to the city.

"My lord," one of the soldiers shouted down from the palisade. "There are strange occurrences in the city."

"Red lightening and green smoke," shouted another soldier, the fear evident in his tone.

"And strange sounds," said the first.

"It is nothing, a distraction," Branock said. "Lock the gate behind us and see that none enter or leave until you have word from us."

"Aye, my lord," the soldier responded.

Branock marched his hostages through the city streets and back to the castle. Zollin saw them. He had taken refuge in a tall house, climbing up to the roof and concealing himself as he cast spells around the city that sent the populace fleeing, and the soldiers from the castle, thinking they were in pursuit of him, went running past his hiding spot. He had found wine and bread. He was eating and regaining his strength when he saw Branock leading a small party back into the castle. He saw Brianna and Mansel, both bound and held against their will. He ground his teeth in frustration and hurried back down to ground level.

He knew this time that there could be no retreat. He raised a shield around him as he walked. There were still a few guards left on the castle walls. They had come down to open the gates and were only just retaking their positions as Zollin neared the gate. They signaled to someone inside the castle walls, but didn't try to harm him, even though they held their crossbows at the ready, bolts nocked and strings set.

Zollin walked through and found that once again Mansel was on the castle steps, only this time Brianna was with him. Two of the Royal Guards held Brianna's arms, and two more had knives at Mansel's throat.

"Zollin, this is your last chance," Branock said.

But Zollin ignored him. He reached out with his power and felt Branock reinforcing his defenses, but Zollin wasn't trying to attack the other wizard. Instead he thrust back the soldiers holding Mansel. The two guardsmen, caught completely off guard, stumbled back and Zollin lifted his friend high into the air. The flames of Zollin's power were raging now. The only safe place for his friend was under the gate, and that is where Zollin sat him, even as Branock blasted Zollin with a river of flame.

The blow felt like being kicked by a horse. Zollin's defense held, but he was sent stumbling, and Mansel dropped the last few feet all at once. Then Zollin turned and sent his own blast of sizzling energy straight into Branock's flame. The sight was dazzling. The flames billowed as Zollin's energy snapped and popped, shaking the ground and castle walls with the thunder they created. Zollin felt the magic inside of him growing hotter and hotter, but his strength did not falter. He was steadily pushing the older wizard back now. The heat from the exchange was blistering, and the cobblestones beneath it were blackened from the exchange.

"Shoot," Branock shouted to the archers, but his voice did not carry above the crackle of Zollin's attack. He felt his heart fluttering and knew he couldn't keep up the attack much longer.

He had only one trick left. He used the last of his energy to create a strong cocoon around himself and then broke off his attack. Zollin's energy slammed into the older wizard and sent him flying across the courtyard.

Zollin knew that the older wizard wasn't dead, but he also knew that there was no more fight left in Branock. His own magic was welling up, threatening to engulf him like an erupting volcano that tears the mountain apart.

He tamped it all down and looked up at Brianna. Her eyes were bright with pride and excitement. Zollin wanted to run to her, but the Royal Guards still held her and Simmeron was coming down the steps toward him.

"You shall be my new wizard," he proclaimed.

"I belong to no man," Zollin said, his voice tight as he controlled the urge to hurl the silly Prince into the wall, crushing every bone in his body.

"I am your King," he said.

"No," Brianna shouted. "Felix is still King. Zollin you can save him. You can heal him."

"No, that's impossible," Simmeron said, suddenly nervous.

Zollin addressed the Royal Guards; all four were around Brianna now. "Release my friends, and I will do all I can for the King."

"No, I forbid it. It's a trick," Simmeron shouted. "He'll kill the King. Don't listen to him."

"He's telling the truth," Brianna said. "I swear it. He won't hurt anyone, I promise."

"Come with us," said one of the guards. "If you do no harm, I'll release the girl."

Zollin nodded and started across the courtyard, but Simmeron came running at him. He was screaming incoherently. Zollin lifted the prince high into the air, causing him to squeal in a high pitched warble that reminded Zollin of a pig. He set the prince on the castle wall and then went inside the castle.

The guards surrounded Zollin, weapons raised menacingly, but he did not resist. One guard led Brianna and the others followed Zollin, who was still limping from the unhealed wound in his leg. They went up to the King's chamber, where the servants were still huddled around the sickbed.

"Is this your friend?" Edina asked Brianna.

"Yes, this is Zollin," she replied.

"Can you help him?" the petite servant asked.

"I am going to try, but I need food and drink."

Edina and two other women hurried from the room. Brianna brought over a padded stool and Zollin slumped down on it. He hadn't realized just how tired he was or how much his leg was hurting. He reached out with is mind, probing the King's body for an indication of what was making him sick. There were foreign particles in his blood. They were attacking his major organs and there was internal bleeding. The liver was overwhelmed, trying to filter the blood and falling further and further behind in the effort.

"He's very sick," Zollin said at last. "He's been poisoned."

"That's impossible," said a tall, skeletal looking man. "I'm his physician, and I oversee every part of his treatment. Who do you think you are, some sort of witch doctor?"

"He's a wizard," Brianna said proudly.

"You're his doctor?" Zollin asked. "What are you treating him with?"

The man's eyes shifted nervously. "It's a mixture of healing herbs and medicines. It's all very technical."

"I'm sure," Zollin said. He turned to the guards. "This is going to take a while, but you'll see immediate results once I'm through. I wouldn't let that man leave," Zollin added, indicating the physician.

"What are you waiting for?" asked one of the guards.

"I need to eat first. Once I start, I won't be able to do anything else until I'm finished."

It was several more minutes before Edina returned. She had bread, cheese, roasted beef that was still quite rare, and some stewed vegetables. The other women had a large bottle of wine, and the third had cups. Zollin ate quickly, oblivious to the half-cooked nature of the food. He drank one cup of wine and then, as he felt his strength returning, he turned his attention to the King.

His first goal was to invigorate the liver; it needed oxygen and help sifting the King's blood. Then he began attacking the poison itself. He couldn't remove it as he had the poison from his own body at Brighton's Gate. He needed to transmute it, which wasn't difficult, just tedious. There were thousands of tiny bits of the poison spread through the King's body. Hours passed as Zollin worked. He could feel the liver functioning as it should again, but the damage to the other organs still needed to be repaired. He sent healing energy into the organs, prompting them to heal and speeding the process.

By the time he finished, it was late into the night. Once he pulled his magic back and opened his eyes, his head was swimming. Brianna pushed another cup of wine into his hand. He had been hunched over the King's bed for hours, and his back popped loudly in the quiet room as he stretched.

"Is he healed?" Edina asked.

"Yes," Zollin said. "There may still be some traces of the poison in his blood, but his liver will clean it.

"You mean he's going to live?" she asked one more time, not quite willing to believe what she was hearing.

"Yes," Zollin said.

He reached out and shook the King's leg. The Royal Guardsmen moved to stop him, but the King's eyes fluttered open.

"Hungry," he said, though his voice was barely a rasp.

The castle servants went to work immediately. They propped the King up in bed. He was still very weak. They brought broth and wine. He ate and his color returned. Zollin moved across the room and tested the physician's medicines. They were all laced with poison, and the Royal Guards took the man to the dungeons.

It was the first time that Zollin had been able to focus on Brianna. She looked radiant, he thought. Her dark hair was tied back into a complicated braid that accentuated her facial features and long neck. Her brown eyes stared deeply into his.

"Are you okay?" she asked.

"Yes, if you are."

"I'm fine," she said, "now that you're here."

Chapter 40

Zollin fell asleep almost as soon as he was done healing his own leg. Brianna stayed with him in the King's chamber, as did most of the servants and members of the Royal Guard. The city had been assured that all was safe and had come back into their homes. Orders had been sent to the King's army and to the Royal Guards who had been sent to find Zollin during the battle. They had all returned to the castle. Prince Simmeron had locked himself in his suite of rooms, and Mansel had chosen to remain at the inn nearby, where a certain serving girl made sure that he was comfortable.

When Zollin woke up it was early, the sun was just beginning to rise. He felt better, hungry, but well rested. Brianna was curled on the large fainting couch beside him. He lay there, luxuriating in just being near her.

"She wouldn't leave your side," said a strong voice that Zollin didn't recognize.

He turned his head and saw King Felix, sitting up in bed and reading from several scrolls.

"We all tried to get her to take some rest, but she wouldn't hear of it. She's quite smitten with you," the King said.

"I'm a lucky man," Zollin said, not sure how to address a King. "Your highness," he added hastily.

"Any man who fights his way into my castle and rescues me from months of poisoning can call me Felix," he said. "I heard all about it."

"Shouldn't you be resting?"

"I've been sleeping for weeks. What I need is information. Who are you and how did you get to Orrock?"

"My name is Zollin Quinnson. I'm from Tranaugh Shire, and I'm a wizard."

Zollin told the King his story, how the wizards of the Torr had come for him and how they had fled into the Northern Highlands to escape. He shared about the dragon and about the Skellmarians, and how he and Mansel had come south to rescue Brianna."

"That's quite a tale," the King said. "So, now that you've rescued your fair lady, what will you do?"

"That's a good question," Zollin said. "I haven't given much thought to anything beyond finding Brianna."

"Well, there will be time for you to decide all of that. For now, I've assigned you rooms here in the castle. I would prefer for you to stick around while I find a way to thank you properly. If you don't want to join the Torr, you will always have a place here."

"Thank you," Zollin said, surprised. "But isn't the Torr evil?"

"I don't know. I've only met Offendorl once, and that one time was enough. I can't say whether he is good or evil, only that since magic has been consolidated there have been less hostilities between the Five Kingdoms."

Zollin nodded, wondering what the King really wanted of him. But then Brianna woke up, and he smiled at her.

"You're awake," she said in surprise.

"It's morning," he said, smiling.

"Yes, but you've been asleep for two days."

Zollin was surprised, but not sure what to say.

"I'm sorry," he said.

"No, don't be. You've been through so much. You saved the King," she said, smiling and looking over at Felix.

"Why don't you show our young hero his rooms?" the King suggested.

They nodded and got up. Zollin's stomach growled as they left the King's bedchamber. They walked hand in hand down the hallway, which was busy with servants hard at work. Brianna was amazed at the difference in the castle since Zollin had healed the king. The servants seemed excited and went about their work with enthusiasm and joy. They had prepared the suite of rooms Branock had used for Zollin and Brianna. There were spring flowers in brightly colored vases on the tables. The windows of the bedchambers were open, and the only things that remained from Branock's stay were the shelves of books.

"Wow," Zollin said when he saw the room. "Kelvich would love this place."

"Where is Kelvich?" Brianna asked. "Is he okay?"

"Yes, I healed him and left him in the valley. My father, too," Zollin said sadly. "I couldn't wait to come after you. I'm sorry it took me so long."

Brianna had not heard the story, although the city had learned of the wizard battle and the rejuvenation of the king. Mansel's part in that story had been told as well, and the young warrior was being feasted and celebrated in the inn where he was staying. He was begged nightly to recount the story of the battle, as men from all over the city bought him drinks. Reena was charged with keeping him happy, which she did gladly, day and night.

Zollin told her of his adventures, how he had driven away the dragon and been captured by the army. He told her about Jute the dwarf and about the troll and the dryads in the forest. He told her of Jax and Miriam in Felson and even about the brigands on the road.

She, in turn, told him about the family of fishermen who had been kind to her, and how Branock had taken them down river and then down the coast. She had much less to tell, most of her time had been spent locked in a cabin on board a ship that she was terrified of. She warmed to her story when she talked about her escape and then how she had fended off Prince Simmeron only to climb down the castle wall and escape again.

They laughed and servants brought them apples and pears, freshly baked bread, and oatmeal with cinnamon and sweetened with honey. That afternoon they took a walk and found Mansel, deep in his cups and entertaining a group of men with his tale. Now that the danger was passed, they explored the city with wonder, amazed at the variety of things that could be purchased. Zollin had been given a new shirt, but he wanted Brianna to patch the one she had made for him. They spent that evening in the castle, and the King asked them to join him for dinner. Mansel was there when they arrived; he was wearing new leather pants lined with wool, a finely made linen shirt, and he had the sword that Zollin had fashioned for him, but now it hung in a fine, leather scabbard with designs worked into the side.

"I believe you all know each other," King Felix said. "We are waiting on one final guest to arrive and then we shall eat."

They were in the King's private audience chamber, the same room on the third floor just down from where Zollin had been given rooms. The wooden doors with horses carved in them were propped open, and a cheerful fire was burning in the hearth.

Brianna was telling Mansel and the King of what they had found in the city when a lone figure entered the room. He was freshly bathed and his beard was trimmed neatly. He had on clean clothes that were plain and simple, just the way he liked them. His face showed a bit of apprehension as Zollin turned to see who it was.

"Dad!" he cried out, hurrying to embrace his father.

Zollin threw his arms around Quinn, who hugged him back fiercely. He had been afraid that Zollin wouldn't want to see him. He had ridden hard to reach the city, but had only arrived that afternoon. It didn't take him long to hear the news and realize that Zollin, Brianna, and Mansel were okay. They had survived without him and been reunited. He was both proud and afraid that his son wouldn't want him there.

"I came as quickly as I could," he said as tears stung his eyes. "I'm sorry I was late."

"No," Zollin said. "I'm sorry. I was wrong when I said I didn't need you. I should never have said that. I'm so sorry."

"Forget it," Quinn said, pulling back to look at his son. "You're a man now, and I'm proud of you. You did what you had to do to protect the people you care about. That's all a father ever wants for his son."

Brianna stepped forward and gave Quinn a long embrace of her own. Then Mansel took his turn; he had tears in his eyes as he hugged his mentor.

"Good to see you, Quinn," he said.

"And you, son," he told Mansel, causing the big warrior to smile.

Zollin clapped him on the back and they all laughed.

"I'm sorry to interrupt such a sweet reunion," King Felix said. "But I'm afraid we must talk. Please have a seat. Quinn, it's been a long time. You have a lot to be proud of."

"You know my father?" Zollin asked.

"Of course, he served me in the Royal Guard, until your mother wooed him away. She was a beautiful woman, and I am sorry for your loss."

"Thank you, sire," Quinn said.

"Now, on to business, I'm afraid," he said as he waved to the servants, who began filling wine cups and serving food. "I wish that things were different, but they are not. Much has happened in the last few months. Reports are that a dragon is terrifying the countryside. Do any of you know more about that than what happened in the Great Valley?"

Zollin and Mansel shook their heads, but Quinn spoke up.

"I do, sire. I was nearby when the legion from Felson was attacked. It was the same creature that attacked Brighton's Gate, I'm certain of that."

"Has Felson been destroyed?"

"No, sire, they were in the field hunting the beast. It attacked them at night. Messengers are coming to bring you a full report."

"That is dire news, indeed," said the King. "Dealing with dragons is outside my experience, but it must be done. The Torr has called a Council of Kings. My son Wilam is serving as my proxy, but I'm afraid his life is in mortal danger. Simmeron has confessed his crimes. He claims that he was bewitched by this wizard Branock, but I doubt that is the case. Apparently, Branock has hired the Mezzlyn to assassinate my son, and I was hoping you might be able to help us."

"We will gladly do all we can," Quinn said.

"Good, I have sent word to my son, but it may all be too late. The Council of Kings is never welcome, and I'm certain the

Torr are behind it. My gut tells me that you are their target Zollin. From what you've told me, and what Simmeron has overheard, Branock was certain that his master would come for him and bring the armies of the other four kingdoms with him. If that is the case, I'm not sure how to proceed."

"We will leave Yelsia, my lord," Zollin volunteered.

"I wish that it were that simple. Unfortunately, it may be better for you to stay and stand with us if the other kingdoms unite behind the Torr."

"What should we do?" Quinn asked.

"I would like to send Mansel south, to help Wilam get home, while Zollin helps with the dragon. Then, when we know more, we will know what to do about the threats facing us from the Torr and the other kingdoms."

They all looked at each other, realizing that their hopes for a peaceful future were still a long way from coming true. Quinn spoke next, his voice a little shaky.

"My first duty is to my family," he said. "We should talk about things, but we will help all we can."

The King stared at Quinn intently, as if some secret knowledge was passing between them. Then the King stood up. He was still weak, and a servant came over to help him away from the table.

"You're right. Take the room, enjoy your supper. Make your decisions and meet me again in the morning."

They all assured the King that they would do as he suggested. Once he was gone, and most of the servants with him, Quinn looked at the others.

"Well, you all know how I feel about helping others," he said. "But this isn't a decision I can make for any of you. This is life and death, which you all know more about than you have any right to know at your age. Still, we've been asked to help, and I would like to know your thoughts."

"We should help," Mansel said. "I don't mind riding south to help the Prince."

"I hate to see you go," said Zollin, "but I can't turn my back on the fact that a dragon I may have woken up is hurting people. I would go to face the dragon, even if the King hadn't asked for my help."

"And I'm going with him," Brianna said. "We won't be separated anymore."

"Alright, Kelvich is in Felson with Miriam. He might know what to do to help you with the dragon."

"How do you know Miriam?" Zollin asked.

"We met on the road," Quinn said. "I think I might be of more use to Mansel than to you, Zollin, but I want you to decide where you would like me. I want you to know that there is nothing more important to me than you. I'm sorry that I haven't always shown you that."

"I..." Zollin began, but he paused as his emotions welled up. "I think you should go," he finally said. "Mansel needs all the help he can get and, to be honest, I don't want you anywhere near that dragon. I know you love me, Dad; I know you love us all."

"That's settled then," he said. "Let's eat, I want to hear all about your adventure, and I may have a story or two of my own."

Epilogue

Branock was tired. He had been knocked unconscious by Zollin's blast, but when he came to, he managed to make his escape. He had gone straight to the docks and taken a ship to the sea. Now he was headed north, but he could trust no one. The sailors would slice his throat just to get the gold in his purse, he knew that just by looking at them. But he had nowhere else to go. His master at the Torr wanted him dead, there was no doubting that. He had no family, no friends, only himself and a spark of hope that, as the events of the future played out, he might find a weakness to exploit or an opportunity to take advantage of.

He was weak, but he would regain his strength. He had one desire left in life and that was to make Zollin hurt, the way he himself was hurting. He wanted to see the young wizard who had destroyed his life lose everyone and everything he cared about. That was the thought that drove him back up into the cold mountains. It was the smoldering ember that gave him purpose and focused his rage. He would have revenge, he thought to himself. One way or another, he would have revenge.

We hope you have enjoyed Magic Awakening. Look for these other great books from Toby Neighbors.

Hidden Fire
The Five Kingdoms Book III

Crying Havoc
The Five Kingdoms Book IV

Fierce Loyalty
The Five Kingdoms Book V

Evil Tide
The Five Kingdoms Book VI

Wizard Falling
The Five Kingdoms Book VII

Also set in the world of the Five Kingdoms,
The Lorik Trilogy

Lorik (Book One)
Chapter 1

Blood dripped from his knuckle. It wasn't his blood, but he didn't bother to wipe it away. It was hard to miss, and the patrons in the busy tavern took notice. He wore dark woolen pants with tall, rugged boots that were covered with mud. His shirt was sweat-stained, but that was not uncommon in the marshlands. He had close-cropped hair, and his face was covered with stubble that wasn't quite a beard. Around his waist was a leather belt that was slung low, and on each hip hung a knife with knuckle guards that arched up and down over his fingers. The weapons were made to be held backward, so that the blade pointed down, and the stranger obviously used them frequently.

Lorik was alone in a corner of the tavern and watched silently as the stranger made his way toward the bar. He wasn't surprised to see a man like the stranger in Hassell Point, which was full of pirates and outlaws. The only thing that made the man different was the state of his clothes, which Lorik recognized immediately as riding gear. From the mud on the stranger's clothes, Lorik determined that he had passed through the marshes, no mean feat for an outsider.

The stranger ordered a drink at the bar. There was wine and mead available at the tavern, but most of the patrons ordered the strong rice liquor that was a speciality in the Marshlands. The pirates who frequented Hassell Point sometimes traded their rum for the spirit the locals called saka, but it was an acquired taste that most visitors to the area didn't care for. The locals all watched to see what the stranger would order and how he would drink it.

Lorik watched Marsdyn as much as the stranger. Marsdyn was the leader of the the local gang known to the Marshland inhabitants as the Riders. Most of the tradesmen in Hassell Point paid the Riders protection money, which made Marsdyn the closest thing to law in the Marshlands. Of course the Earl was the official lord, but the difficulty of crossing the Marshlands made the area a haven for lawless types like Marsdyn's Riders.

Marsdyn took special notice of the stranger. He was young, mid-twenties Lorik guessed, but he had a lot of experience. The knives he wore were custom-made. Lorik had seen a lot of weapons, but never any with knuckle guards like the ones on the stranger's knives. He wore them lower than most weapons as well.

The stranger ordered saka and was given a very small terra-cotta cup. He picked up the drink and sniffed it. Saka had a very strong aroma that would burn a man's sinuses if it was inhaled too sharply. The stranger didn't seem fazed by the saka. He tipped the small cup back, drank it all down, and ordered another.

Marsdyn looked over at his companions and smiled. They didn't seem pleased.

"Go ahead and find out what we're dealing with here," he told them.

"You ever seen blades like that, Mars?"

"Nope," Marsdyn said. "He wears 'em low, too. It's got me curious. I got your back, go ahead and see what he's made of."

Lorik double-checked his path to the door. He wasn't afraid of a fight, but he didn't see the need to get involved in the business of strangers. He wanted to finish his drink, and maybe have another. He also wanted to see Vera. She was a wench, but they had the only thing close to a relationship Lorik had time for. He'd been back in Hassell Point only a few hours and would most likely be heading out again soon. If a fight broke out in the tavern he would have to find another place to drink.

The two men with Marsdyn stood up. The were both big men. Most of the local rice farmers were short and slight of build. The two men with Marsdyn both carried heavy daggers that were shaped like cutlasses but only as long as a man's forearm. The blades were called Hax knives and were common in the Marshlands. As much a tool as a weapon, the knife was easy to make and sturdy, resisting the oxidation that was so common in the wet conditions of the Marshlands. The men wore leather vests and padded riding pants, which were a badge of honor among the locals. Horses were rare in the Marshlands. Marsdyn's crew were the only riders in Hassell Point other than Lorik, who was a teamster delivering the rice crops north through the Marshlands to the Earl in Yorick Shire.

The two Riders approached the bar on either side of the stranger, who acted as if they weren't there. When the tavern host refilled the stranger's little cup, Pazel, who was standing on the stranger's right side, snatched the drink away and drank it down in one scorching swallow. The stranger looked up at Pazel, who was several inches taller, and smirked. The smile made Pazel nervous. He wasn't accustomed to people being at ease around him. He was an imposing figure and he liked intimidating people.

"Drinks for my friends here," the stranger said to the tavern proprietor, "they're thirsty."

Two cups were set on the bar, which was a sturdy structure, made from stone with a long, polished wooden top. More saka was poured and once again Pazel started to take the stranger's drink, but his hand never reached the small cup. The stranger's arm shot out, his fingers bent at the middle knuckle so that his hand was flat and rigid. The blow struck Pazel in the throat, and, even though it wasn't a powerful punch, the big man reeled backwards, clutching at his throat and gagging for breath.

The man on the stranger's left was called Oky. He hesitated for just a second, as shocked as the rest of the locals at how quickly Pazel had been taken out of the fight. Then his hand dropped to his Hax, but the stranger's boot smashed into his knee before he could draw the blade. The leg flexed backward, the bones grinding and the tendons popping. Oky screamed in pain and fell to the floor, clutching his leg.

The stranger seemed undisturbed. He had barely moved from his spot at the bar. He picked up his small cup of saka and drank it down in one quick gulp that was meant to keep the scorching alcohol from burning his throat.

"You gonna drink this?" the stranger said to Oky, who was writhing on the floor. "Do you mind if I...?" he gestured at the drink.

When Oky didn't reply the stranger picked up the drink and sipped it. Then he turned around to face the locals, leaning back against the bar. There were several wenches in the tavern, some serving drinks, others flirting with the locals. The stranger let his gaze move slowly across the room, taking in the scowls of the locals and the few pirates who were busy drinking in the mid-afternoon.

Marsdyn stood up. He was every bit as big as Pazel, but older. He had a scar that ran from his hairline down to his jaw. His hair was salted with gray, and pulled back into a long ponytail that was tied with a leather cord. He had a thick sash around his waist instead of a belt, and a delicate-looking dagger was tucked into the sash at an angle. It was the only visible weapon he carried. He walked up to the stranger and smiled.

"I'm Mars," he said. "I'm what you might call the local overseer. I make sure that the people here understand what's expected of them."

"Is that right?" the stranger said.

Marsdyn nodded. He looked at the stranger's knives.

"Those are some interesting weapons," he said.

The stranger moved his hand slowly down to the knife on his right hip. His fingers slid under the knuckle guard and wrapped around the hilt. His movements were slow and unthreatening. He drew the knife and held it up. The blade was pointed toward his elbow, thick at the spine which angled close to his forearm. There was a fuller groove that ran parallel to the spine to make the blade lighter.

"They're useful in a pinch," the stranger said.

"I can see that," Marsdyn said. "Why don't you put them on the bar and come have a drink?"

"I've got a drink," the stranger said, lifting up the little cup that was in his left hand. "And I don't leave my weapons lying around unattended. That's dangerous."

"Marsdyn smiled. "I like you. You say just what's on your mind, in a fashion, of course."

The stranger raised his cup in salute. "I find that people don't make stupid mistakes about me if I speak my mind."

"You aren't from around here," Marsdyn said. "Although you drink saka like a local."

"I grew up in a coastal dive like this one," he said. "I've drunk much worse."

"You planning on sticking around a while?"

"Maybe."

"You kill anyone I know?" Marsdyn said, pointing to the blood on the stranger's knuckles.

"Didn't kill 'em, just bloodied their noses a little."

"Locals or sailors?"

"Sailors," the stranger said.

"You ride in?"

"I did."

"We've got a stable. Let me offer you a place to keep your horse, and maybe something a little better to drink."

"That's kind of you."

"You have a name?" Marsdyn asked.

"I'm called Stone."

Chapter 2

"So, what'd you think?" Vera said as she circled around behind Lorik and refilled his drink.

"He's efficient," Lorik said.

Vera smirked, "Efficient, that's all you thought, not dangerous or frightening?"

She poured him more mead. The Marshlands didn't allow for the growth of many crops, but there were abundant wildflowers, and many of the local farmers kept bees, making mead much more prevalent than ale.

"Dangerous, yes, frightening, no," Lorik said.

"How can you not be afraid of a man like that?"

"He's just a man. When you work with large animals who can kill you with one kick, a man doesn't seem as frightening."

"Even one who took out two of Marsdyn's thugs without breaking a sweat? Men like that make me nervous."

"So why don't you quit?" Lorik suggested. "There's plenty of other things you could do."

"Like what?" she teased. "You looking for someone to ride on your wagon through the bogs?"

"Come on, Vera, you've got skills. You can sew as good as the tailor. You know how to cook, how to brew mead and saka. You're the best healer in the Point. You could make a living helping people, if you put your mind to it."

"But the problem with all those things is that I'm not a man," she said, trying to hide the disdain in her voice, but failing. She sat down on Lorik's lap, with one arm draped over his shoulder. "There's still one thing I can do that no man can," she said with a smile.

She traced the outline of his jaw with a finger. His beard was thick and unkept, giving him a scruffy appearance, but Vera knew Lorik well. He had never mistreated her, as some of her other customers had. In her younger days she could have worked at one of the waterside bordellos, but she was a local girl. The men in Hassell Point knew her, knew that her parents had died of the wasting sickness when she was young. She had no one to arrange a marriage or pay a dowry for her; she couldn't even get an apprenticeship since there were so few trades in the Marshlands. So she had turned to the one occupation that she could do. It was a viable option for a young woman, and many of the locals had begun their adult lives in just the same way. A woman could earn enough money to get out of Hassell Point if she wanted to, but Vera had stayed and kept working long after most wenches had given up the life.

"Well, you are very good at that," he said, returning her smile.

"You should know," she flirted.

"You could marry," he said.

"Are you offering?"

Lorik grew uncomfortable. He loved Vera in a fashion, but so did half of the men in Hassell Point. Still, the thought of marrying her seemed wrong. He couldn't say why. He didn't think less of her because of her profession, but he couldn't see her waiting for him at home either. He knew it wasn't something she wanted, and he was too set in his ways. He liked living on his own. He liked taking his team through the Marshlands and north through the forests and farmlands. There was a wild sense of freedom in his life, and marriage, he feared, might put too many restrictions on him.

"You don't want an old man like me," he said.

"We're the same age, Lorik," she said playfully.

"In years, yes, but not in experience."

"You think traveling through the marsh is more difficult than pleasing a man? Not all my companions are as easy going as you, Lorik."

"I didn't mean it that way," he said. "I just meant I'm set in my ways. I'm only good in small doses. There are plenty of young men in this town who would marry you."

"I don't want to be a farmer's wife," she said, sipping from his cup. "You aren't the only one who likes a little freedom. I make my own rules here. Quaid doesn't steal my money and lets me do as I please."

"Yes, Quaid is a good man, and I'm glad you're here."

"I'm beginning to notice how glad you are," she said flirtatiously.

"Don't be silly."

"I'm not, I'm just good at what I do. I can tell how many drinks a man needs to get up the courage to pay my price."

"Is that so?"

"Yes, it is. And you only need one more drink," she said, getting back to her feet. "Once you see that Marsdyn's men are carried out, you'll want to take me to my room."

"It's more comfortable," he said.

"Of course it is, and the company is better, too."

She went to refill her pitcher of mead. Lorik watched as she moved among the other patrons. She refilled a mug here and there, never coming too close to the men the other wenches were flirting with. Pazel had recovered on his own, although he still coughed as he helped Oky up and supported the injured man as they hobbled out of the tavern. Lorik watched them go and wondered how long it would take before the stranger joined Marsdyn's gang. Lorik didn't care for the Riders and didn't pay them for protection. He didn't keep goods, just equipment, and he could take care of himself. His horses were Shire horses, used for pulling heavy wagons. They were too slow for outlaws and too heavy to make it through the Marshlands unless you knew the firm paths. He knew how to stay out of trouble in Hassell Point and how to defend himself if he couldn't. His preferred weapon was a traditional longbow, but he carried a small axe on his belt which he could easily use in a close fight.

Lorik was larger than most of the inhabitants of Hassell Point. He was used to loading and unloading his wagons, which was simply a necessary part of moving materials through the Marshlands. Depending on the rainfall, certain paths could grow soft, and he would be forced to remove some of his cargo, sometimes all of the cargo, so that his wagon wouldn't bog down. He wasn't a hulking specimen like Pazel or Oky, but he was stronger than he looked. His father had been a teamster, but once Lorik had gotten old enough he turned the business over to his son. Lorik's mother had passed away several years ago and his father soon after that. Since then, Lorik had been on his own. He was a solitary person and didn't mind being alone. He made a comfortable living hauling cargo, mostly large sacks of rice, through the Marshlands and returning with trade goods.

His team wasn't as fast as sailing around to Quelton Bay, but it was safer. The pirates who frequented Hassell Point had no qualms about raiding the ships that sailed between the Point and other cities. He also charged much less than the trade ships and would take his payment from the money earned when he sold the rice at market. It was an occupation that kept him busy, and he enjoyed his life, although there were times when he wondered if there was something missing. He tried not to dwell on such thoughts, but long periods of being alone gave him plenty of time for introspection.

"I'm done drinking," he said to Vera when she came back around.

"Ooo, does that mean what I think it means?" she teased.

He smiled. It wasn't a broad grin, and his face certainly showed no cheerfulness, but she recognized it for what it was. He stood up and followed her through a small door that led to a set of rooms. In the back was a large room with plush furnishings. When Vera opened the door, she jumped back in surprise.

"Damn it, Grayson!" she shouted. "What are you doing here?"

The man in the chair had silver hair, but his face was smooth and wrinkle free. He was clean-shaven, and although he wore riding pants and the leather vest that marked him as a Rider, he also wore a silk shirt with flowing sleeves that tied at the wrists. He had no visible weapons, but he had a long, narrow dagger inside his vest and another in the leg of his right boot.

"What's he doing here?" Grayson said.

"That's none of your business," Vera said. "You can't just come into my rooms whenever you want to."

"Who's to stop me?" he said, his slate-colored eyes never leaving Lorik's face.

Lorik didn't speak. Seeing another man with Vera was hard, but he wasn't naïve: he knew she got paid to spend time with men. That didn't bother him over much; it was the possessive way Grayson spoke to her that really got under Lorik's skin. He didn't like the Riders, but he saw them as a necessary evil. They were outlaws, but they were familiar outlaws who occasionally helped the people of Hassell Point. Of course, that didn't mean Lorik was happy about realizing they spent time with Vera.

"Grayson, leave," she told him. "Now is not a good time."

"And why is that? You like being with a filthy mud walker?"

Lorik's anger ticked up a notch. He was not generally bothered by insults, but being called a mud walker, a derogatory term to describe people who lived or worked in the marshes, by a man who lived like a parasite off the hard work of those same people, was more than he could stomach.

"She said leave," Lorik said. "I'd listen to her."

Grayson stood up, his hand resting lightly on his stomach. In most people it would have been an innocent gesture, but Lorik knew the man was armed. He guessed correctly that the weapon was in the man's vest.

"Vera," Grayson said angrily. "Send him away."

"Why don't we both leave?" said Lorik, trying to calm the outlaw down.

"No," said Vera angrily.

Lorik wasn't sure if she wanted him to stay, or if she simply resented the loss of revenue if they both left.

"I'm not going anywhere," Grayson said.

"Go have a drink, Grayson," Vera urged. "You'll still have time to visit me."

Both men stared at each other, Grayson's hand inching toward his vest.

"You better make that first strike count," said Lorik, drawing the small axe that hung from his belt. "If you don't, I'll carve you up and feed you to the eels."

"You really think you can threaten me?" Grayson said.

"It's not a threat, just a statement of fact."

"You're a dead man, teamster."

"Not by you," Lorik smirked. "I don't think you're man enough without a gang behind you."

"I'll cut out your heart!" Grayson screamed.

Lorik didn't answer. He simply pushed Vera against the wall of the narrow hallway with a gentle nudge. She didn't resist.

"You're nothing but a clumsy, old wagon driver. You sleep in the mud like a pig."

"We talking or killing?" Lorik said in an icy tone that wasn't wasted on Grayson.

The Rider was angry, but he was also afraid. He wasn't used to direct conflict and preferred to stab his enemies in the back.

"I'm going to kill you," Grayson said, trying to keep his voice from trembling and failing. "Vera, I'll leave, but you better make sure this fool has a good time. It'll be his last."

Grayson stalked between them, his face blushing with shame. Lorik watched until the outlaw left the narrow hallway. Then he turned to Vera, who looked worried.

"I'm sorry if I'm getting you in trouble," he said. "I could leave."

"No, I don't want you to leave," she said. "Besides, he's probably waiting in the tavern for you. Let him have a few drinks and cool down. He'll forget he's angry soon enough, although I don't see why you have to goad them so."

"I didn't goad him," Lorik said. "He's a bully. I called his bluff. It's no different from when we were kids. You remember that farmer's boy who started picking on you in essentials school after your folks died?"

"His name was Rufus," Vera said, leading Lorik into the room.

She pulled him into a padded chair and began massaging his shoulders.

"Yes, Rufus. I had forgotten that. He was a bully, and there's only one way to deal with people like that."

"I remember he was several years older than you, and you broke his nose," she said.

"He shouldn't have been picking on you."

"My point is you push back too hard. You should try using words instead of fighting. You're a better person than that, Lorik."

"I used words," he said.

"No, you used threats."

"I used what was necessary."

"I could have talked him out of the room, and you wouldn't have to worry about getting a knife in your back."

He pulled her around the chair and onto his lap, his arms holding her close and feeling the slight tremble in her body through the thin fabric of her dress.

"I'm not the one who's worried," he told her gently.

She kissed him. It wasn't passionate as much as familiar. She knew she didn't have to pretend with Lorik; she had known him too long. They were good friends and he was a good customer. In a different time or different place, that might have seemed almost perverse, but in Hassell Point it was a comfort.

"Thank you," she said in a sad voice. "There's not many men who would fight for my honor, not anymore."

"Don't sell yourself short," Lorik said, smiling up at her.

"I think maybe it's time I leave the Point," she said. "When I'm ready, will you take me?"

"Of course I will."

"I'll be leaving this life behind me," she said, her voice a little nervous. "You understand?"

"I understand and I approve," he said.

"You're a mystery, Lorik."

"Not really, I'm just a simple man."

"There's nothing simple about you."

It was his turn to smile. "Still, I don't have any secrets from you, Vera. You know that."

"Yes, I know that," she said, and kissed him again.

21766894R00311

Made in the USA
San Bernardino, CA
06 June 2015